WISHBONE

ANNA GARCIA SCHAPER

PIÑATA BOOKS
ARTE PÚBLICO PRESS
HOUSTON, TEXAS

Wishbone is funded in part by a grant from the National Endowment for the Arts. We are grateful for their support.

The author cites excerpts from the following pages in Thornton, Wilder, *Our Town,* September 23, 2003: 87-88, 54-55, 65-66, 99-100, 46, 31, 6-7, 9, and 107-108.

Piñata Books are full of surprises!

Piñata Books
An imprint of
Arte Público Press
University of Houston
4902 Gulf Fwy, Bldg 19, Rm 100
Houston, Texas 77204-2004

Cover design by Mora Des¡gn

Names: Schaper, Anna Garcia, author.
Title: Wishbone / by Anna Garcia Schaper.
Description: Houston, Texas : Piñata Books, an imprint of Arte Público Press, [2020] | Audience: Ages 15-18. | Audience: Grades 10-12. | Summary: Told in alternating timelines, fifteen-year-old overweight Pilar ignores her persistent bullies and pursues her dream of acting in the school production of "Our Town," while in 1976 her grandmother finally finds the strength to leave her abusive husband.
Identifiers: LCCN 2020011493 (print) | LCCN 2020011494 (ebook) | ISBN 9781558858947 (trade paperback) | ISBN 9781518506024 (epub) | ISBN 9781518506031 (kindle edition) | ISBN 9781518506048 (adobe pdf)
Subjects: CYAC: Overweight persons—Fiction. | Bullying—Fiction. | Theater—Fiction. | Mexican Americans—Fiction. | Family life—Texas—Fiction. | Texas—Fiction.
Classification: LCC PZ7.1.S336125 Wi 2020 (print) | LCC PZ7.1.S336125 (ebook) | DDC [Fic]—dc23
LC record available at https://lccn.loc.gov/2020011493
LC ebook record available at https://lccn.loc.gov/2020011494

The paper used in this publication meets the requirements of the American National Standard for Information Sciences—Permanence of Paper for Printed Library Materials, ANSI Z39.48-1984.

Printed in the United States of America
Versa Press, Inc., East Peoria, IL
April 2020–May 2020
5 4 3 2 1

For Bones, who pleaded, pushed and prodded.
And who always believed.

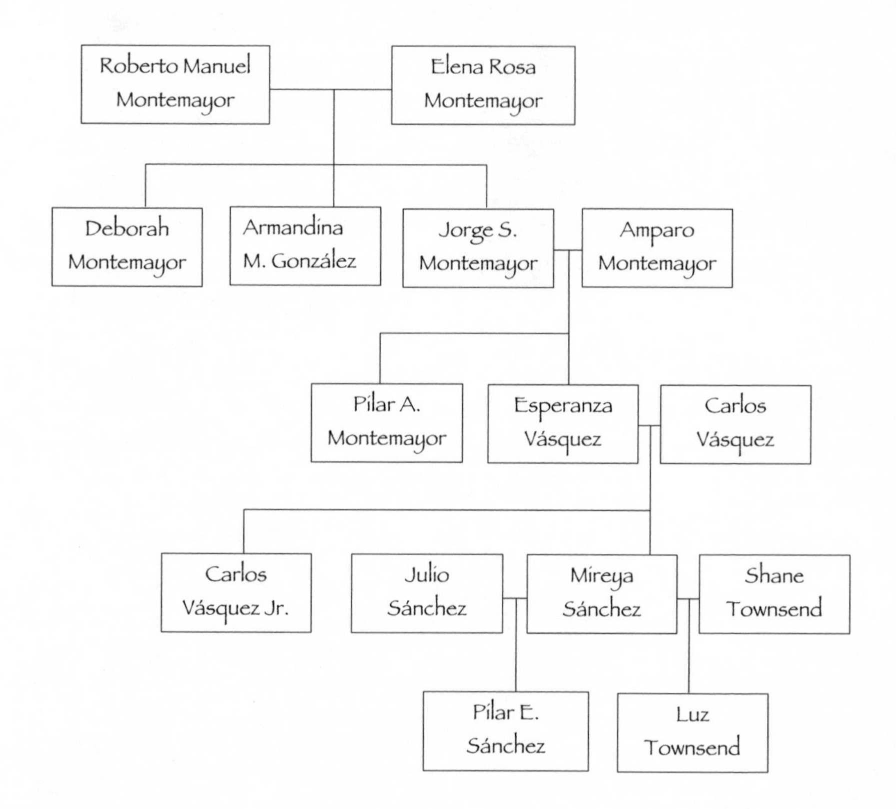
Montemayor Family Tree
Roberto Manuel Montemayor
Elena Rosa Montemayor
Deborah Montemayor
Armandina M. González
Jorge S. Montemayor
Amparo Montemayor
Pilar A. Montemayor
Esperanza Vásquez
Carlos Vásquez
Carlos Vásquez Jr.
Julio Sánchez
Mireya Sánchez
Shane Townsend
Pilar E. Sánchez
Luz Townsend

"Now there are some things we all know, but we don't take'm out and look at'm very often. We all know that something is eternal. And it ain't houses and it ain't names, and it ain't earth, and it ain't even the stars . . . everybody knows in their bones that something is eternal, and that something has to do with human beings. All the greatest people ever lived have been telling us that for five thousand years and yet you'd be surprised how people are always losing hold of it. There's something way down deep that's eternal about every human being."

—Thornton Wilder, *Our Town*

Pili

LAREDO, 1976

Pera had fed her hunger hope, and the more she did, the sharper it grew, an unrelenting jab in her side, rebuking her for her inadequacy.

Getting pregnant that first time six years ago was not easy for her. Pera'd been trying for years and felt she was failing as a woman, letting her husband down. Of course, he didn't help matters any, but was always reminding her of how important it was for a man to have a son to pass down his family name, his legacy, and he wouldn't shut up about his brother's two boys. Checho was only ten and had already shot his first nine-pointer. And the older one, Rodi, had made all-county in football. Pera'd seen the small army of trophies stretched across the mantel, each brassy boy with one knee lifted as if running from the menacing deer head above.

She was desperate. So she went to see Xochi, the woman with the answers. People had been flocking to her tiny house with its corrugated metal roof for close to a hundred years. She'd sit in the patchy dirt yard under the shade of a guajillo tree, the smell of honey emanating from the buttery blossoms dotting the ground around her, and dole out antidotes for various ailments of mind, body and spirit. A person could obtain the cure for a broken heart, for bankruptcy and for arthritis all in one stop. A mystical convenience store.

Xochi had an answer for Pera too. She was afflicted with a *vientre frío*. A cold uterus. She said it could happen if a woman had suffered a deep loss in life. Her body had suffered a harrowing blow and was now rebelling against itself, reluctant to create another life and subject it to the same heartache. She instructed Pera to drink a tea of garlic and tree bark every night for three weeks. But with the pungent odor she was emitting, Carlos wouldn't go near her. For that reason alone I considered the remedy a resounding success, but of course, my sister did not.

She decided to turn to another woman for help, one whom she believed had the very ear of God. She snatched the small wooden figure of San Antonio from beneath her pillow, buried it in the folds of a knitted shawl in her leather bag and set off on a long pilgrimage to the sinking basilica in Mexico City. Sinking, she said, because it had grown heavy with the many burdens people had been bringing to the mother of God for more than four centuries. It didn't help that the entire city had been built atop a lake. But Pera always had her own ideas about things.

I drove her across the river to catch the bus to Mexico City early one morning. On our way to the international bridge, I circled around San Agustín Plaza, Pera's favorite spot in Laredo. Our grandparents used to walk around the square arm-in-arm during their courtship's first bloom, their shadows merging into one elongated veil on the reddish bricks of the street. Pera tilted her head back and peered up at the large, round face of the clock tower high above the trees. I smiled at her and circled once more before heading to Nuevo Laredo.

We inched our way across the congested bridge, backed up with cars waiting to show their ID to border control, the smell of diesel exhaust and fried tortillas filling our nostrils. Barefoot children with grimy faces weaved between the cars selling packets of gum and polyester roses, their petals dotted with dew drops of glue. A girl, aged eight or nine, her hair as shiny as the patent leather shoes on her small feet, scurried up to the passenger side and held out a pink rose. Pera took it from her outstretched hand and pressed two coins into her palm. We finally made it across the murky water of the Rio Grande and through Mexican customs to arrive at the bus depot. I set the car in park, reached behind me for Pera's bag on the back seat and placed it on her lap. She stepped out of the Impala and onto the crowded, dusty bus, a Saint Christopher medal swinging from the wide rearview mirror. The bus driver wiped his bloodshot eyes with the heel of his palm and waved her up the aisle.

Passengers propped their feet on cages crammed between the seats while chickens pecked at the soles of their shoes through the wire mesh, and a large rooster watched her from its hutch against the rear door. She squeezed past an old man in a torn coat, his weathered skin like the ripe, fleshy fruit of a tamarind tree, and took a seat near the window. She drew her rosary from the pouch in her pocket and fingered each bead on the loop three times, praying that the seven-hundred-mile journey would not be in vain.

It was well past midnight when the bus reached the city, too late to catch a shuttle to the shrine of Our Lady of Guadalupe. Pera would have to wait until morning. She lay down on a wooden bench outside the bus station and tucked her feet under her shawl and her leather bag beneath her head. She woke the next morning to a blazing sun and the hubbub of the busy station. Too eager to wait for the next shuttle, she gathered her things and took a short cab ride to the basilica. She was tired and hungry by the time she reached the massive shrine, the sunlight glimmering off its gilded dome, but she got down on her knees in supplication and crawled across the vast stone floor through the large metal doors and down the long aisle to where the *tilma* of Juan Diego hung behind the altar. She laid the rose, now wet with real tears, on the floor before it and gazed up at the miraculous image of the woman from heaven imprinted on the fabric of cactus fibers, never once taking her eyes from it. La Virgen looked down at her with pity from under her veil of stars, and Pera knew that her prayer would be answered.

When she finally stood up, her knees were marked with a grid of crosses from the uneven tiles. She walked back out into the bright sunlight, bought a corn cob dripping with butter and chili powder from a street vendor and hailed a taxi to take her back to the bus station for her journey home.

A month later, she was pregnant.

I don't know what did it; whether it was the garlicky tea, all those rosaries or the trip to the basilica—if La Virgen had heard her and interceded on her behalf. If it was all or none of it.

Pera believed it all, and that's what mattered.

Pilar

HOUSTON, 2020

Many a clean getaway has been ruined by a squeaky wooden floorboard. I try to think light, airy thoughts as I teeter down the hallway on the balls of my bare feet, my fingertips grazing the small bumps of the textured walls for support. I imagine myself a misty cloud floating soundlessly through the sleeping house. I should've put socks on. Then I could glide across the glossy slats without lifting a foot.

Shane had pulled up the carpeting and re-stained the floors before we moved in. He did it for Mom. She's always hated that pressed-down, matted look that carpets always get after only a few months, dust particles and grime buried stubbornly in the fibers.

I inch my way past Luz's open door. She's lying on her bed facing the wall, the glow from her Abby Cadabby night light gleaming off the soft curls of her blonde hair and a menagerie of my old stuffed animals piled up at her back. She is a perfect doll in a sea of misfit toys. Most are in bad condition, but ever since Shane read her *The Velveteen Rabbit*, she refuses to get rid of any.

I keep moving. I'm not the stealthiest person to begin with, but the sound of my flannel pajama-covered thighs rubbing together could wake the dead. I have to be extra cautious: Mom's a light sleeper. And she's been ultra-vigilant about my diet since I came home from school in tears two weeks ago. It wasn't the first time, but she doesn't know that. Since then, she's kicked this health thing into overdrive. It's annoying, but she's only trying to help me. She doesn't want to see me hurt anymore.

It's true what my grandmother says: seeing someone you love in pain is a million times worse than being in pain yourself. It's even worse for women because God gave us more empathy than men. Buela says that's what also makes us stronger. The power to create comes at a price. *El que lleva al niño, lleva el dolor.* That's why she has so much devotion to La Virgen. Buela says, women know what it means to suffer.

Whenever Mom lectures me about my diet, Buela tells her to leave me alone, to let me eat what I want, that I'm only fifteen and have a lot more growing up to do. She says I'm perfect the way I am. They argue about it a lot. They argue about a lot of things.

I miss Buela. We don't see her nearly as often as we used to. She hasn't come to visit since Mom had Luz and we moved in with Shane. It's Mom's fault, though. We used to go to Laredo all the time, every Thanksgiving and New Year's and for a couple of weeks in the summer. Mom says she's too busy with work and school now, and that it's easier for Buela to come to us. After all, she doesn't work, so what's to stop her? She could come and stay as long as she wants.

Luz and I begged her to take us for a visit last August, told her it wasn't fair to keep us from our own grandmother. She shook her head, her lips locked up like a vault. But the following Saturday, she drove us to the Greyhound station downtown, handed me a letter for Buela and a turkey sub for Luz and me to share. When the bus driver pulled the door open at the Laredo terminal six hours later, Buela was standing there holding a heart-shaped *churro* in each hand.

I must've inherited my love of food from her. According to Buela, you feed a cold and a fever and anything else that ails you. She says food is a gift from God: something to enjoy, not to spurn or fear. Says she doesn't understand the way people demonize food nowadays.

"How come everyone's stopped eating bread? What's wrong with bread? *Dígame*. The host is made from bread. What? Am I supposed to stop taking Communion? Tell Diosito, thanks but no thanks? *No, están locos*."

By the time I get to Mom and Shane's door, my feet are barely touching the floor. My arms carry most of my weight. I lay my palms flat against the walls like I'm keeping them from closing in on me. Then I get to the trickiest part. I hold my breath and take another step, careful to avoid that treacherous floorboard, which lies just past the door.

I should've waited longer, stuck to my normal routine. Usually I poke my head out of my room and listen. When Shane switches off the TV after the late news, I look at the digital clock on my nightstand and start the countdown. Wait a full twenty minutes to make sure, not a second before. Only then do I dare leave my room, the "Mission Impossible" theme song on a loop in my head, and make my way down the hallway, which seems to get longer and longer each time.

That's what I do. Usually. But not this time. This time I jumped the gun. Waited until the clock said 12:17 instead of 12:20.

I couldn't help it. Shane went shopping today, and I spotted them as soon as I got home from school. Peeking out from the top of a green grocery bag on the kitchen counter, the afternoon sun reflecting on the deep blue sea of rippling plastic packaging: Double-stuffed Oreo cookies.

Dinner was hours ago: baked tilapia with broccoli and roasted potatoes. A nutritious, sensible meal. A meal to be proud of. A gold star in my food journal. I was lying in bed feeling proud of myself, determined that this would be a new, healthy beginning, when those cookies popped into my head. I pictured them sitting there on the top shelf of the pantry, lording over all the other substandard food: dented cans of kidney beans, bags of boring muesli and boxes of hard, uninviting pasta. The sirens of the snack world, their dark cookie covers snapping open to reveal creamy white tongues-they sang out to me. I pulled my pillow over my ears to shut them out, but their soothing voices penetrated the billowy cloud of downy feathers. *Pi-laaar. We're waiting for you. Come to us.*

I tried to distract myself, turned over onto my side and started counting sheep like you're supposed to. But their fluffy white fleece started looking more and more like puffs of cream, and their black little legs, like bits of cookie. Before I knew it, I was out of bed, tossing the ombré shawl Buela made for me around my shoulders and making my way down the hallway like a ninja hippo.

The living room is easier to navigate. The shaggy rug muffles any sound. I'm so anxious to get to it, I get careless and stub my toe on a leg of the coffee table. Rookie mistake. Curse you, Ikea and your pointy edges, your sharp, clean lines. My teeth sink into the fleshy part of my hand. Well, the fleshier part.

Inhale. Exhale. Keep going.

The truth is I wouldn't mind losing a little weight. Sometimes I try to eat the right things and even do a bit of exercise. I can do fifteen jumping jacks in a row now before stopping. I make it a few days eating healthily, but then something happens, like a Girl Scout will come knocking on the door with her sad, blank cookie form or the swim team will have a bake sale, and I finally give in to temptation and later feel so bad about it that I eat more. One slice of cake or pizza is not enough. I want the whole thing. The words *portion control* are not in my vocabulary. Once I've had one piece, I figure I've already failed, so I might as well eat it all and try to do better the next day.

"You should finish what you start," Mom says all the time.

Besides, Mexican women are naturally curvy anyway, so it's not only about will power; it's also genetics. Some of us have one big curve, that's all. We're round. Not Mom, though. My father always said her curves were in all the right places, like a vintage Coke bottle. He used to call her Boti, short for *botella*, the Spanish word for bottle. Mom hated it. "It's Mireya!" she'd yell at him. "My name is Mireya!"

When you think about it, it's also a matter of bad timing and geography. I was born in the wrong place at the wrong time. If I'd been born in seventeenth-century Italy, I'd be considered the ideal of beauty. Famous artists would be painting my portraits and hanging them in fine houses all over Europe—the equivalent of today's *Vogue* cover. Anna Wintour would be knocking on my door in her corset and oversized sunglasses, begging me to grace her pages.

Unfortunately, I'm here and now . . . in this kitchen. The terra cotta tiles feel warm beneath my feet as I creep over to the pantry, where I spy the unopened bag of cookies stashed behind a box of shredded wheat. A ceramic rooster eyes me dubiously from its perch on the countertop as I slide out the package and slowly pull the sides apart, careful to apply the right amount of pressure, not so much that the plastic rips and sends cookies flying like clay discs in a skeet shooting competition. The bag sighs open in my expert hands.

Then, light from above. The searchlight of a helicopter hovering over an escaped convict jumping from an outer wall. Mom's thunderous voice fills the room: "*¡Pilar Elvira! ¿Qué estás haciendo?* What do you think you're doing?"

My thoughts bounce against the sides of my skull like pinballs.

I was sleepwalking. I watched an episode of Hoarders *before bed and felt compelled to organize the pantry. I'm collecting cans for the Amnesty International Club food drive.*

Not a single plausible explanation presents itself. Not one Mom would believe, anyway. So I lower the cookies and slowly turn to face her. Shame and defeat cling to me like cheese to the top of a pizza box.

My eyes slink from her face to my feet. The nail polish has started to chip off the nail of my big toe, and I make a mental note to fix it. I take ridiculous pride in my feet. Fat people have nice feet. They're soft and fleshy like cherub feet, not knobby or bony like skinny people's feet. And my toes are all nicely shaped and even.

I lift the fuzzy shawl off my shoulders and pull it down over my face, the minty green hem shading into a vibrant teal from my chin to my forehead. Buela used to make all kinds of things—blankets, socks, hats, even Christmas ornaments shaped like Baby Jesuses—but she stopped for a long time. Said it was too hard with the arthritis stiffening up her fingers. She finally picked it up again after I was born.

I sneak a look at Mom through a wide stitch in the middle. Her hands are on her hips, and she's staring at me with a look on her face she wore often when she was still married to my father: her eyebrows, black chevrons against her olive skin. I haven't seen that look since before she got fed up and left him, it reminds me of moving to Houston. We'd been on the road that day for barely an hour and I already had to pee, but

I didn't want to tell Mom. She'd be annoyed. I averted my eyes from the long yellow line dividing the road in front of us. When I thought I couldn't hold it in a second longer, I spotted them—the McDonald's golden arches lit up against the darkening sky like a beacon in the night to guide us through the storm.

I lower the shawl again and wrap it tightly around my shoulders. "I was hungry?" I'm so lame.

She folds her arms in front of her and shakes her head from side to side. "*Ay*, Pilar, what am I going to do with you?" Her hands fly up in frustration. "Those cookies are for your sister."

I should've gone with the Amnesty Club excuse and implanted the word in her head. "I was just going to have one," I say to the floor.

"Yeah, and your father was just going out for one beer. And he was just 'good friends' with all those women." She makes the quotation sign with her fingers when she says good friends. "You sound just like him!" She shakes her head again. "Don't you start lying to me too, Pilar Elvira. I bled for you."

Shane stands in the doorway rubbing his eyes, his light brown hair sticking up like the soft peaks on a lemon meringue pie.

Mom brings the fingertips of both hands to her forehead and throws them out in front of her. "Am I going to have to put a lock on this door? I thought you wanted to be a movie star like Meryl Strip. Well, who's going to put you in a movie as big as you are?" She pauses for a moment as if expecting an answer and folds her arms across her chest again, but I keep my mouth shut. "*¡Dígame!* All the girls in those movies you watch are all *flacas*." She puts particular emphasis on the last word. "Skinny."

Shane takes a step toward her. "Take it easy, Rey."

Mom stops him with a wave of her hand before he can continue. "No, Shane. She has to learn. It's a cruel world out there, full of nasty, hateful people." She turns back to me. "When was the last time a Latina girl won Oscar's award?"

Rita Moreno. 1962. But I don't say it out loud. I get Mom's point. There should be more.

I know her anger isn't really about me. It's about the world I live in. One that can be unfair, especially if you don't fit into its mold of beauty. Her anger is born of this and of other things she can't even begin to articulate. Of her helplessness, her frustration and, most of all, her fear of not being able to protect me. I understand this, but it still stings.

I look up at her then down at my feet again. "I'm sorry. I couldn't help it."

Her face softens, and she studies mine for a long time, a sad look in her eyes, a look worse than anger. Finally, she takes a cookie from the package and breaks it apart, hands me the half with the most filling and pops the other half into her own mouth. She finishes chewing and puts an arm around my shoulder.

"You have to try, *m'ija*. I want you to be happy, but happiness is going to take some work."

"I promise, Mom. I'll try."

Even though I don't really want it anymore, I bring the cookie to my lips and scrape off the smooth white cream with my teeth, let it sit on my tongue, savoring the sweetness before finally swallowing it. I imagine it sliding down my throat and blanketing my insides like snow covering a junkyard. For a moment, at least, it stifles the voice that always echoes inside me, the one that says, "You are not enough."

Pili

LAREDO, 1976

I can't stand the way she gets up to fetch him a beer, how she sets her knitting aside and eases her way off the flattened chair cushion, one hand at her lower back for support, the soft grunt she makes as she hoists herself up, the scratchy sound of her rubber-soled slippers on the linoleum floor.

It about sends me over the edge. I want to pull my hair out and yell, shout at him to get his own damned beer. Tell him he should be fetching things for her, rubbing her feet and massaging her shoulders. It's never been that way with them, and it never will be.

I've never understood it. The way Pera waits on him hand and foot, anticipating his every need. As though her whole reason for being were to serve him. It's even more unbearable to watch now that she's so far along.

Mamá was like that with Papá too, but it was different. With them, it was a two-way street. They did things for each other, both giving and taking in equal measure, the way a marriage should be. There's no balance where Pera and Carlos are concerned. She gives and gives, and he takes and takes.

If he'd show her some small inkling of appreciation, it might not be so bad. He doesn't. He sits back with his hands clasped behind his head, a scattering of dust falling from his scruffy boots as he props them up on Mamá's oval coffee table, the sturdiest piece in this house of flimsy, particle-board furniture. He doesn't even ask her for it, just holds up his empty bottle and gives her a look.

I sit up straight at the opposite end of the couch like someone's shoved an ironing board up the back of my T-shirt, rub my hands on the rough denim on my thighs until they're warm from the friction and stare at the wall in front of me with my lips sealed tight. I try not to be around them if I can help it. It's hard to be. It gets my stomach all in knots and makes my blood pressure shoot way up. But I promised Pera I'd help her paint the baby's room, and she's due in less than a month.

She calls out from the kitchen. *"¿Te ofrezco algo, Pili?"* "Can I get you something?"

"No, thanks. I'm good," I say and shut my mouth again quickly. I don't trust myself to say any more. If I let out any more words, there's no telling what I might unleash—a tidal wave, a flood, a whole ocean of words. I tell myself to do it for Pera's sake, that she doesn't need any more stress, but dammit, it's hard to stay quiet. I've never been good at it, especially when my temper is flared up. As a matter of fact, that's what everyone used to call me in school. *La lengua*. My tongue's gotten me into plenty of trouble over the years. It's beyond my control.

Mamá used to tell me to count to ten before speaking whenever I was angry. I never even made it to three before the words pried their way out of my mouth. I've gotten better, though. Speaking English helps. It slows the words down a bit. They don't shoot out of me the way Spanish does. I've had to bite my tongue plenty over the last seven years. Unfortunately, the day Pera got a wedding band, I got a muzzle.

Carlos walks over to the Zenith, too big for its wobbly chrome stand, and flips through the channels before stopping at an old black and white movie. John Wayne wears a Civil War uniform and sits on a horse. It rears up, but he tugs sharply on the reins, and it settles down again.

"Oh, this is a good one. It's the one where they're fighting the Apaches. You seen it, Pili?" Carlos backs up to the couch again, his eyes never leaving the screen.

I bend an elbow and study the cuticles of my right hand. "Mm-hm."

Pera waddles in from the kitchen and hands him his beer wrapped in a paper towel. He tilts his head to look around her, balls up the paper and tosses it on the table in front of him. I have to sit on my hands, resist the urge to grab her arm and drag her out the front door.

"Baby, I can't see with your stomach in the way." He waves his hand as though dismissing a servant.

I'm dying to tell him what he can do with that television, where he can shove that beer bottle. The waters are rising behind the floodgates. Instead, I take a deep breath and look at my sister, the dark circles under her eyes, the skin taut over her swollen ankles, the strained buttons of her housecoat on the verge of popping off. I wish they would pop off and hit Carlos square on the forehead, knock some sense into him, but I'm afraid that would take more than a few buttons. Mamá's old sewing machine with the cast iron legs, maybe. That would be a good start. But it's not really sense he's lacking, it's more than that. It's empathy. Decency. Love.

It's hard to believe he and I were friends once. We'd run around town getting into trouble when we were kids, swiping cigarettes and liquor bottles from Señor Garza, the old man with the bad eye who ran the corner store. I'd order a pineapple snow cone, and when he turned his back to scoop the ice, Carlos would stash the items inside his waistband. We'd spend the rest of the afternoon drinking and smoking and looking at the girly magazines he'd snatched from beneath his older brother's mattress. He'd tease me about my underdeveloped chest, and I'd tell him he wouldn't know what to do with boobs anyway.

Pera sits down between us and picks up her knitting, a blue blanket for the baby. I grab a small, round pillow and tuck it behind her lower back.

"Oh, man," Carlos says, holding a fist up to his mouth and biting his knuckle. "Would you look at that? Now *that* is a woman." He shakes his head and lets out a long whistle.

Pera glances at the television screen, then focuses on her knitting again, her fingers deftly working the needles.

"That's what's-her-name. That actress from Ireland. Look at that creamy white skin. It's like soft serve. And you can't tell 'cause it's black and white, but she has this flaming red hair. Like a fire. Shoot, I wouldn't mind getting scorched on that." He slaps his thigh and takes a swig of beer. "They don't make 'em like that down here. Nothing but dark meat 'round these here parts," he says, imitating John Wayne's accent.

His eyes slink over to Pera. "Baby, maybe you should dye your hair like that."

Pera instinctively touches her long, dark braid, and an image of her sitting on our bed when we were young pops into my head. She'd sit there each night in her favorite nightgown with the pink piping around the collar, brushing her thick, silky hair, the moonlight pouring through the window shining off it brighter than any flame.

"But, nah, it wouldn't look right. Your skin's too dark. You'd look like Pancho Villa in a clown wig. Besides, you'd have to dye those little hairs on your upper lip to match too." He laughs and nudges her leg with his knee. "I'm only messing with you. Don't be so sensitive."

He winks at me and takes another swig of beer. "Touchy, touchy. Must be all those baby hormones."

Pera drops the needles into her lap and works a finger through one of the stitches in the blanket. I can see her shrinking before my eyes, getting smaller and smaller, closing in on herself, and something wells up from deep within me, forcing me to my feet.

I stand up, blocking Carlos' view of the television. He looks at me with a smirk. I want to knock that smug look clean off his face. It wouldn't be the first time. I'd always warned him to stay away from Pera, that I'd remove his *huevos* with a spoon if he got near her. When I found out he had her in his sights, I tried to deter him, threw a few punches, even knocked out a tooth or two. Didn't work. Carlos has always been like a spoiled child; the more you tell him he can't have something, the more determined he is to get it. And Pera was the gleaming train set in the window, the expensive candy on the top shelf. She was already far gone by then, too. I could tell by the way she'd blush like an overripe mango every time he walked into a room. I knew it was too late.

You can't control other people. Especially not a woman in love. I learned that lesson a long time ago. You have to let people make their own mistakes, no matter how deep a hole they dig for themselves. The best you can do is be there to lend a hand when they're ready to climb out. But it doesn't mean you have to stand by silently while they dig either.

Pera scoots forward to the edge of the couch, her toes peeking out from her thin slippers, and looks up at me with pleading eyes, but I can't stop myself. The words want out. I think of counting, but my lips part, and the floodgates open, water rises up my throat like a geyser and bursts from inside me, soaking the shaggy rug and the couch cushions, toppling over lamps and chairs. The album covers stacked against the stereo in the corner float up. The members of Los Tigres del Norte drift down the hallway in their slick blue suits. The water rises steadily but swiftly up the walls, making everything weightless and filling the room. It bursts through the windows, saturating the parched, cracked earth outside.

"Pera is perfect the way she is," I say. "Better than any Hollywood floozy with hair from a bottle." A powerful wave lifts the set of wicker shelves beside the stereo and sends them floating out the door.

Pera pushes herself up from the couch and grabs my arm.

I glare at Carlos over my shoulder. "Who do you think you are? Paul Newman? Well, let me tell you, you're no leading man yourself."

John Wayne lifts his mouth toward the top of the screen as it fills with water, trying to catch one last breath of air.

"The only role you'd be good for is Mr. Ed's butt double!"

Pera drags me toward the hallway. "*Vente*, Pili. Help me spread the drop cloth over the carpet."

And just like that, the floodgates shut again.

Pilar

Anyone who makes it through high school with their psyche intact should get a diploma. Regardless of what their grades are, they've earned it.

Mom is always talking about how hard the real world is, the world after high school where you have to fend for yourself, but it can't possibly be worse than these four years. Anyone who survives them is battle-ready in my book. It's not the school work that's hard. That part's always been easy. It's all the other stuff that's the problem. Being a teenager is an achy, treacherous thing. And it's a hundred times harder when you're fat. Kids learn this lesson early: anything that makes you different from the rest of the pack makes you a target. The hardest difference to hide is fat.

I'm not the fattest person in my school. There are a few who're even bigger than me. Most have found ways to fit in or at least not stand out quite so much. Everyone knows a lone animal is easier prey for predators. There's safety in numbers.

Take this one girl I've known since elementary school: Whitney Hall. She's got at least twenty pounds on me, but she was smart. She came up with a strategy. In fourth grade this one mean kid with buck teeth sat behind her in math class. I don't remember his name, but I remember his pencil. He must've gotten it from his dentist's office. It had a picture of a smiling tooth on it and the words, "Ace Dental—Dentistry With A Gentle Touch," written on it. He jabbed it in her side over and over, watching her stomach jiggle while he sang the song, "Poker Face," by Lady Gaga under his breath. Except he changed the words. Instead of poker face, he said, "Poke her fat." He thought it was the cleverest, funniest thing in the world. I sat next to him in the back of the room, so I witnessed this daily torment. I wanted to tell him that Lady Gaga hates bullies and would not appreciate him changing the words to her song, but I didn't say anything.

One day Whitney finally had enough and raised her hand to tell the teacher. Of course, Bucktooth denied doing anything. So Mrs. Conley looked over at me and asked if I'd seen him do it. That's when I did something I'll regret for the rest of my days. It doesn't matter how many novenas Buela prays for me. I've definitely got a few years in purgatory coming to me for that one.

I looked from him to her, then down at my math book, slowly shaking my head from side to side. That's not even the worst part. The worst part was Whitney's reaction after I did it. She didn't get mad, accuse me of lying and demand I be punished. She wasn't indignant at the injustice of it. She didn't fight back at all. It was almost as if she expected it. She turned around, picked up her pencil and continued doing her work.

Some events in life are so significant, full of such magnitude, that you can feel them reverberating out in the universe somewhere, happening over and over again through different times and planes of existence. You carry them inside of you forever. They never leave you. They change who you are.

People teased Whitney all through middle school and well into freshmen year until she put her plan into action. She came back from Christmas break with her ashy blonde hair dyed jet black, her earth-toned Gap clothes replaced by studded black ones, and started hanging out with the emo kids. Marilyn Manson with a thyroid problem. She even wore black lipstick and pierced her bottom lip. It was a drastic measure, but who could blame her? Camouflage is camouflage. It's all about survival and what gets you through the day. It beats eating lunch by yourself in the restroom, anyway. Something I do on a regular basis.

I hate eating in the cafeteria. I hate eating in front of other people, period. You should see the way people look at fat people eat. They look at you like you've committed a crime, set fire to a puppy. It doesn't matter what you're eating, either. I could be chomping on a celery stick, and people will still look at me like I've gone up for thirds at a fried chicken buffet. I know what they're thinking. They're thinking, "How dare that fat girl put anything more into that body. She already has enough food for a lifetime stored in there."

Despite this, I'm having a rare moment of fortitude and decide to attempt lunch in the cafeteria. Maybe all that high fructose corn syrup has finally affected my brain the way Mom warned it would. Or maybe I'm feeling that certain sense of optimism that Fridays bring. Whatever the reason, I decide to go for it.

Most of the tables are still empty. I scan the large room and make my way through the maze of them to one in the corner that's partially hidden by some vending machines. I squeeze into a seat at the end of the long table and remove the turkey sandwich from the brown paper bag Mom packed me this morning.

My eyes are glued to the round clock on the far wall. I've set a goal for myself. I have to sit here for ten minutes. One sixth of an hour. One twelfth the length of an average movie. Ten minutes is a reasonable time for eating lunch.

If I play *The Godfather Part II* in my head from the beginning I have to make it to the part where a young Vito Corleone stands on the deck of the ship as it draws near Ellis Island and looks up from under his newsboy cap to see the Statue of Liberty looming over him. Give me your tired, your poor, your flabby, ostracized masses. Then I'll be free to walk out of here to the library, where I can watch episodes of "Inside the Actors Studio" until the bell rings.

No one should have to think this hard about lunch time, but I do. In a way, it's true that fat people do obsess about lunch, but not in the way most people think.

I take a bite of my sandwich with my eyes still locked on the clock. My heart is pounding in my ears so loudly, I'm sure even the lunch ladies working way back in the kitchen can hear it.

They say the longest minutes are the ones spent during labor or on a treadmill. Not true. Time crawls by the slowest when you're sitting by yourself in a high school cafeteria. The clock hands tick by at an agonizing pace, as slow as a toddler putting on her shoes on a Monday morning. It's torture. I try to divide the time into smaller segments and take a bite every thirty seconds. Finally, there's one minute left to go, and I think I'm actually going to make it.

Then she walks in, sandwiched between her friends, Lynn and Hailey—bad things always come in threes. Becca Barlowe. Usually, she's not here. Most days, she sneaks off campus with her meathead boyfriend, Connor Sims, who's a senior.

I feel like the lead runner in a marathon who trips just before the finish line. I imagine myself laying there helplessly as the other runners leap over me. There's a crushing sensation in my chest, like someone's dropped an anvil on me. My palms start to sweat, and my heart is beating so fast, I'm sure I'm going to have a heart attack and die right there on the macaroni encrusted floor.

I've wished for death before when it got to be too much. The idea of offing myself has entered my thoughts. But just as quickly it slips away like a dream you forget the instant you wake up. I could never do that anyway. I'd miss Mom, Luz, Shane and Buela too much. And I could never put them through that kind of pain.

Becca is the reason there are carrot sticks in my lunch bag. She is the reason I came home in tears two weeks ago and why Mom is now on a mission to help me lose weight. She looks down at her cellphone with a smile on her face, which by the way, looks like the smile on the face of one of Luz's Barbie dolls after you push it in with your thumb. Becca whips her long hair to one side of her head and types something into the keypad. Lynn and Hailey read over her shoulder, and all three start laughing hysterically. They are loud and obnoxious. They don't care if they make spectacles of themselves. They don't care if people look at them. They prefer it.

Becca holds her phone out at arm's length, and they squeeze their faces together to take a selfie. Hailey sticks out her ample chest (rumor has it she got a boob job last summer) and makes a peace sign with her fingers. Lynn tilts her head and puckers her lips into a duckbill.

I close my eyes and picture myself surrounded by the large votive candles Buela keeps lit in front of the statue of La Virgen in her bedroom. I say a silent prayer to her, her Son, the angels and saints, then to Vishnu, Buddha, Brahma, Allah and anyone else who will listen. *Please don't let her see me. Please don't let her see me.* I say it over and over in my head like a mantra and crouch down in my seat as low as I can, trying to make myself as small as possible, but it's like trying to shrink down an elephant in a neon jumpsuit. I'm completely exposed.

I make like a statue and await my fate. Like most things, this is beyond my control.

For a moment, it seems as if the gods have heard my pleas. Becca turns away and heads to the other side of the cafeteria with her two minions at her heels. I breathe a sigh of relief. Suddenly, Duckface Lynn turns back around and yells over her shoulder. "Save me a seat, Bec. I'm gonna get a Diet Coke."

As soon as the words Diet Coke are out of her mouth, I know I'm doomed. Sitting near the vending machines was a mistake. My snack food fortress has turned against me. Once again, food proves to be my downfall.

She slips a dollar bill into the slot, but the machine spits it back out. Apparently, it doesn't want anything to do with her either. I wait with bated breath, motionless as a pool man in a housewife's closet. She rolls her eyes and tries again. Again, the machine spits the dollar back out. She gives it a swift kick, looks around and starts to say, "Does anyone have change for . . . ," when her eyes zero in on me. Her face contorts like she's sipped orange juice after brushing her teeth. She snorts and spins on her heel, sashays to a table full of people on the other side of the cafeteria, where Becca is sitting on some guy's lap, chewing on a straw stuck in her bottled water.

The romanticism of it fills me with longing. Will I ever get to sit on a boy's lap? Probably not. Not unless he's been in a terrible accident, lost both his legs and has to wear prosthetic ones made of titanium.

Lynn whispers something in her ear, and they look over at me. Then Becca says something, and everyone at the table laughs. To my horror, she rises from the boy's lap. Hailey, Lynn and a few others follow as she moves toward me. I look down at what's left of my lunch and brace myself. It's like being on a beach buried up to your neck in sand, watching a tsunami roll in.

She half-sits, half-leans on the edge of the table in front of me and crosses her ankles. At first she doesn't say anything, just looks down at me with a saccharine smile plastered on her face.

To look at her, you wouldn't think she was capable of so much evil. She's an average-looking girl with a slight frame and the right clothes. I don't have the right clothes, the right shoes, the right friends, the right body, the right anything. I'm helpless, powerless before her. I'm completely at her mercy, and she knows it.

I wish I could stand up to her, tell her to get the hell away from me, hit her even, like George McFly when he finally stands up to Biff at the end of *Back to the Future*. I could definitely take her. I'm twice her size, so I've got the advantage there. But she doesn't throw punches, she throws insults. And she's good at it.

A part of me wishes she would punch me and be done with it. She doesn't. Her weapons are more powerful, they're words, and she has the temerity to use them. People are always willing to listen. Even me.

I wish I could be brave. I'm not. I'm weak and scared and alone. I hate myself for it. I resign myself to what's happening and look up at her, see my reflection in her eyes and all the fear mirrored there. Sweat trickles from the base of my bra down over the fleshy waves of my stomach.

A small group has gathered around us. A few people shake their heads and keep walking by, but several stay to watch the show.

Becca grabs my lunch bag and turns it upside down, dumping the remaining contents out on the table in front of me: a few grapes in a plastic bag, a granola bar and a neatly folded napkin.

"Oops." She gives her cheek a light slap and opens her mouth wide, an expression of mock shock on her face.

There's a scattering of howls and laughter. A boy in a Texas Longhorns football jersey with a scrawny mustache across his upper lip gives the boy next to him a fist bump.

The folded napkin makes me think of Mom. I picture her standing at the kitchen counter dressed for work, her long hair swept up into a neat bun, carefully placing each item into my lunch bag and taking the time to fold the napkin, not just balling it up and shoving it in.

I'm old enough to pack my own lunch, but she insists that she likes doing it. Really, she's afraid I'll stuff it with Gansitos and candy bars if I do it myself. The thought of how heartbroken she'd be if she could see me now sends a sharp pang to my heart. She doesn't know about Becca or any of it. When she caught me crying two weeks ago, I told her some random kid who doesn't even go to my school called me fat while I was walking home. For two weeks afterward, she hid behind a bush at the end of our street trying to catch a glimpse of him. If she knew the truth, she'd be at school every morning demanding someone's head on a platter.

They say there's nothing more lethal than a mother whose child is in distress. Well, that goes double for Mexican mothers.

Becca's had it in for me for a while now. I'm not sure why. I mean, I know I'm overweight and that makes me an easy target, but so are other people. Why me? I've laid awake at night pondering why she is how she is, why she does what she does, studying her cruelty like a puzzle I could solve if only I could get the pieces to fit right and see the bigger picture. But there is no rhyme or reason to it, no logical explanation. The truth is, for some people, cruelty is its own reward. She derives pleasure from my suffering, delights in my pain. It's that simple.

Her eyes search the table, and she lifts her palms parallel to the ceiling. "Well? Where's the rest of your lunch? I know this can't be all of it. And you're obviously spending all your money on food 'cause you're definitely not spending it on clothes. Seriously, are all fat people clothes this ugly?"

I sit there, dumb with humiliation, waiting for it to end and praying that sweat doesn't start seeping through my shirt, giving her even more ammunition.

This unprovoked cruelty always stuns me. It's like an alien ship has landed and little green men have disembarked in front of me. My body goes into a state of shock and bewilderment, and I can't find the words to defend myself. My brain shuts off all communication with my mouth. Inside, I'm pleading.

Hailey arches her back and chimes in. "Actually, it probably *does* cost a lot for all of that fabric." Another peal of laughter.

"True." Becca laughs and flicks a grape at me. "And it looks like she'll be needing even more. Her fat ass has already devoured most of her lunch. Truly tragic. God, you are so disgusting." She shakes her head from side to side. "They shouldn't even let you eat in here. There should be a separate room for people like you. With a trough in the corner. That way nobody has to look at you and lose their appetite."

A Brillo-pad voice scrapes my back. "Hey, I'll buy you a Twinkie if you blow me. I've got your cream filling right here."

"That joke is so lame, Jake," Becca says, her nose wrinkled up in disgust. "And even you can't be that desperate."

She puts her foot up on the edge of the table and tucks a shoestring into the inside of her sneaker. "This is stale. I'm over this. Let's go," she says to Lynn and Hailey.

She lowers her foot and looks me in the eye. "You are such a waste of space. You should do your bit for humanity and kill yourself already."

The words land on me like stones, leaving me feeling even heavier than before. Every time she says them, every single time she says those words or others like them, a part of me believes her.

Everyone disperses, and I'm left mercifully alone. I gather what's left of my lunch and toss it into the nearest trash bin. The napkin hits the edge of the opening and floats to the floor. I leave it there and make a beeline for the nearest restroom, my denim-covered thighs shooting off sparks. Tears sting my eyes, but I will myself not to cry with every step. When I finally reach the restroom, I rush into the first stall. The lock is missing from the door, so I hurry over to the next one, slide the metal rectangle into place and sink onto the toilet, my thighs hanging over the sides like dough over the edges of a pie plate. I let the tears fall, their weight boring trenches as they roll down my cheeks.

Pili

Pera sits by the open window, with the sun streaming in at her back like a malfunctioning sunflower. She strokes a toy truck in the shadow of her belly while a portable fan oscillates on the dresser next to her, its movement choppy and sluggish, its whirring, a series of snorts, as if the fan itself were mocking our attempts to stay cool, as if it understood the futility of its effort.

People are saying it's the hottest April in fifty years. The kind of heat that melts eight-track cassettes left on dashboards down to gooey puddles and makes shade obsolete, the kind that turns rolled-up car windows deadly.

You'd think I'd be used to it by now, having lived here all my life, but some things you never get used to, some things stay with you. In the desert, the heat is always a palpable presence weighing everything down. Blocks of it fill the room, but there's another weight here too.

Mamá made the curtains. I took her to the big Woolworth's downtown to buy the fabric—vintage planes on a cloudy, blue background. They billow up around Pera, the planes rising briefly, then falling limply as the fan turns away again. I finally convinced her to take them down and wash them because it wouldn't be good for the baby to breathe in all that dust. I told her she could hang them back up afterwards, which she did.

She gazes at the truck and spins the wheels against her palm. I can tell by the distant look in her eyes that she's no longer here, but in another time with another baby. "This one was his favorite," she says.

I sit cross-legged on the floor, wipe the sweat from my brow with the back of my hand and run my fingers over the rough texture of the pale blue wall. There are smudges here and there, crayon markings, even a small handprint. I steal a look at Pera, wondering if she's seen it too. She must've. With as much time as she's spent in this room, she must have every inch of it memorized.

"I know," I say gently. "Hey, you sure you don't want me to paint the whole room? We could do it yellow this time. Something bright and cheerful." As if paint could seep into the cracks of a broken heart and make it whole again.

She came home from the hospital a week after it happened. That day changed everything. She forgot how to be in the world, holed herself up here for weeks and refused to come out. Carlos was nowhere to be found. It was Mamá and I who stayed with her, who sat here in silence because there were no words. Mamá prayed, and I rubbed Pera's back as she lay curled up on the small bed between us, the unfathomable weight of it crushing us like a pestle. She lay there in a puddle as though all the bones had disappeared from her body. After a while, she rolled onto her back and stared at the ceiling for hours, getting up now and then to wander about the room in a daze.

Other times, she'd jump up and pace the floor like a caged animal desperate for a way out, frantically touching everything within reach, as though the objects could moor her, could keep her from tumbling into the dark abyss that had sprawled open before her.

She'd go as far as the doorway but no further. At first, I tried to coax her out, but Mamá said to let her be. She said you couldn't shove grief out the door like some unwanted house guest. It was her new constant companion whom she needed to get acquainted with in order to go on living. Her world had changed, and she had to relearn how to live in it in order to survive.

Mamá sat on the bed with Pera's head in her lap, fingering the beads of her rosary as she stroked her hair, finally lulling her into an unsettled sleep.

When she woke a few minutes later, we helped her sit up. I gathered her hair from around her shoulders, where it hung in oily clumps, and tied it back, while Mamá fed her broth from the big pot of *caldo de pollo* warming on the stove. Pera stared ahead vacantly as Mamá dipped the spoon into the warm soup and brought it to her dry lips. She took a few mouthfuls, then stood up to patrol the room again, lightly touching each object as if it were a bubble threatening to burst.

She drifted over to the bedside table and ran her fingers along the rigid spines of a neat stack of books, tracing the creamy sphere on the cover of *Good Night Moon*, then to a shelf beside the bed where she brushed the edges of a model train, the shabby fur of a teddy bear and the frayed edges of a hole left by a missing button eye. And on to a holster holding a cap gun and the dusty surface of a dresser where she stroked the leather pocket of a baseball glove and the seam of a red canvas lamp shade, down the curve of the ceramic base, rubbing her thumb across a small chip, her fingers like feathers.

She moved about the room like fog until something on the wall between the dresser and the doorway caught her eye, and she leaned in to get a closer look.

It was a Batman sticker that had started to peel off at one corner.

A wail issued from her cracked lips as she slumped to the floor, tears streaming down her face and strands of hair sticking to her wet cheeks. "I'm falling, Pili." She sat back on her heels and vigorously rubbed the furled corner with her thumb, trying to smooth it out and adhere it to the wall again.

I rushed to her side and wrapped my arms around her as she leaned against the doorframe and hugged her knees to her chest, rocking back and forth. Faint pencil lines marked the wood above her head, a date next to each. November 7, 1971. November 7, 1972. November 7, 1973. And the last date, November 7, 1974.

I tucked the loose strands behind her ears and rocked with her, afraid to be still, to feel the earth jar beneath us. I closed my eyes and held her tight, felt her tears fall onto my rigid arms like drops of rain, wished and prayed to absorb her pain into my body, to take it on as my own, through my skin, my blood, my bones, to the very heart of me, to spread it backward and forward onto those who came before and those who'd come after so that we could all help carry it.

Mamá stood up from the bed and slipped her rosary into the front pocket of her dress.

"Where are you going?" I whispered over Pera's head.

"It's time," she said, bending down to kiss Pera's forehead. "I'm going to see Xochi."

Pilar

It's my favorite sound. The solid thud of the front door closing behind me. A rush of cool air conditioning hits my face as I drag my battle-weary self into the living room, where Shane and Luz are sitting on the rug, an array of brightly colored drawings scattered on the coffee table in front of them.

Luz drops the crayon in her hand and runs over to me. "Pipi!" she yells, throwing her arms around me. "I missed you so much." She says it like I've been gone for years, not only since this morning, each word thick with emotion.

I drop my backpack and hug her. "I missed you too."

It used to grate on my nerves when she pronounced my name as "pee pee." It always brought to mind the smell of a backed up urinal. But Mom pointed out that nicknames are good things, signs that you've made a connection with someone, an intimate bond. She says they represent the best version of you, how the ones who love you most in the world see you. Now. I don't mind it so much anymore.

Luz grabs a sheet of paper from the table and holds it close to my face. "Look what I made you."

It's a drawing of the two of us in a field. I'm sitting on a giraffe with purple spots and flourishing a wand shooting off bright yellow sparks, and Luz is standing in the grass holding a bouquet of colorful flowers bigger than her head. Above us is a blue sky full of fluffy white clouds and a smiling yellow sun wearing a top hat. Looking at her drawing fills me with gratitude. I'm grateful that this is how she sees the world, and I pray she always will, although I know it isn't likely.

At the bottom of the picture, she signed her name in big letters. It's funny how little kids love to write their names over and over, taking their time on each letter. It's an accomplishment to be proud of. Later, it becomes a chore. The older you get, the smaller and faster you sign it until it's nothing but an illegible scribble.

"Do you like it?"

I open my eyes wide and answer in a voice more animated than I feel. "Do I like it? Are you kidding? I love it! It's a work of art. It should be hanging in a museum."

She shakes her head emphatically. "Nuh-uh. This is for you to keep."

"Thanks, Luz." I kneel down next to her and unzip my backpack. "I'm going to put it in my bag so I'll always have it with me."

"Okay." She smiles proudly. "And you can show it to your teacher and your friends if you want."

I collapse onto the couch, and Luz grabs a purple crown from the table and climbs onto my lap. It's made of construction paper and sticky with glue and glitter that sheds all over me.

To look at us, you'd never guess we're related. Luz is little and cute with golden curls and Shane's cornflower blue eyes. She looks like she should be on the cover of a greeting card wearing ruffled socks and licking an ice cream cone. My hair's curly too, but that's where the similarity ends. She's the sun. I'm a cloud.

She flings her arm around my neck. "Did you have fun at school?"

I brush a curl away from her face. "Yeah, it was okay."

Glitter falls onto my cheeks as she places the crown on my head. "Did you color and read stories? That's what I'm gonna do when I go to school. I already know all my colors and my numbers. And my letters."

"That's because you're so smart." I give her a weak smile.

"Daddy says you have to work hard and do good in school so you don't have to race the rats and you can be whatever you want, even a famous painter."

Shane squats down next to Luz, and she hops onto his back for a piggyback ride. A long, angry scar peaks out from beneath his cargo shorts and runs down over his knee in a neat stack of crosses.

"Come on, princess. Let's go make your sister a snack," he says, shooting me a sympathetic smile.

"Daddy, I told you, I'm not a princess. I'm an artist. Like Michelle Angelo."

They head toward the kitchen. "Can I paint the ceiling?"

It might sound pathetic, but I admire my little sister's self-assurance and fearlessness. She'll shout out her dreams from the rooftops. Most kids will. They're not afraid to dream. The older you get, the harder it is to do that. My dream sounds ridiculous even to me. Every time I say I want to be an actor, I feel stupid. It sounds trite and self-absorbed, like a beauty pageant contestant wishing for world peace or someone saying they're going to spend the summer working on their music. So I try not to say those words, not even to myself. I'm afraid to say them, afraid they'll make me want it more, and I'm afraid to want it. Acting is the Mount Everest of dreams, right below supermodel. Why can't I dream of being an accountant or a real estate agent, or a nurse, like Mom's studying to be? Or a dental hygienist? There's no cliché about out-of-work dental hygienists having to moonlight as waiters.

Kate Winslet said she used to practice her Oscar acceptance speech with a shampoo bottle in front of the bathroom mirror. Well, I'd be too scared to even do that. I'd feel so stupid. It takes courage to dream. Courage, which I am sorely lacking.

It would be easier to let it go. Lots of people do that. Every day, someone shoves their dream into a briefcase and snaps the locks shut, stuffs it under their desk in some dismal office cubicle with beige walls and florescent lights that hurt to look at. That's how a dream dies.

I don't want to let go of my dream, but thousands of people want to be actors. Hundreds of thousands. Talented, beautiful people willing to bare their souls. People who run five miles every morning and who have the discipline and willpower to avoid the doughnuts and guacamole dip at craft services. And there are only a finite number of roles. Why in the world would a casting director choose me, a fat Mexican girl from Texas, over them?

Thinking about it makes me want to dive into a bag of Cheetos and bury myself in that bright orange powder.

Shane and Luz come back from the kitchen with a plate of apple slices and pretzels. I'd rather have an ice cream sandwich. Or two. Or five. Or at least some cream cheese frosting to dip the pretzels into, but I promised Mom I'd try, and I'm going to. I grab a handful of pretzels and toss a few into my mouth. Their buttery crunchiness starts to take the edge off immediately. I bite down on Becca's concave Barbie face, grind Duckface and her wrinkly dollar to a mushy paste, crunch away at slow-moving clock hands and outstretched arms taking selfies, chew up teenaged boys with healthy limbs and doors missing locks. I snatch a few more and chomp away at mouths sealed shut and shampoo bottles that will never become trophies. I swallow them down deep inside me, where I shove all the scary and damaging things, and lean back into the sofa cushions, imagining I'm falling into one of the fluffy clouds in Luz's picture, grateful for a soft place to land.

Pili

Mamá was right. When Pera was ready, she rejoined the world. It was slow going at first. She wouldn't leave the house for weeks. Mamá stayed by her side, armed with her rosary and the herbal bouquet Xochi had given her.

The morning sun would filter through the lace curtains, splintering the coverlet on Pera's bed into jagged shapes as Mamá slipped through the door with a bowl of water tucked in the crook of her arm. Sprigs of lavender floated at the top like broken bits of coral dislodged from the bottom of the sea. Pera would turn away as Mamá gently drew the covers back and dipped a washcloth into the bowl. Ringing out the excess water, she'd wipe her daughter's thin body, the body she had carried inside her own, the one she'd nestled in her arms, suckled at her breast and soothed to sleep with the steady rhythm of her own heartbeat.

She'd run the damp cloth along Pera's heart-shaped hairline, down the slope of her nose and across the vales of her sunken cheeks, caressing her face like Veronica on the Via Dolorosa. Moving steadily and resolutely, she'd work her way down to the soles of her feet, grazing the bends and hollows of her body. Down the ridge line of her neck and around the bluffs of her shoulders, across her frail chest, tracing the rip-ple lines of her ribcage and the knolls of her hips, over each arm and leg, hand and foot.

After she'd covered every inch, she'd unwrap the fragrant bouquet from its cellophane wrapper and brushed it across Pera's skin, making the same journey from head to foot. Pausing at Pera's chest, she'd lower her head and pray a Hail Mary asking for La Virgen's intercession, imploring her to heal her daughter's broken spirit, to wash her body clean and empty it of its heavy burden.

By the time she finished, Pera's skin flushed a deep pink, the blood rising to the surface as it responded to Mamá's touch and the spray of rosemary, sage, hawthorn and mimosa.

Mamá would set the bowl aside and pull back the curtains to open the windows. The sweet smell of mesquite would drift into the room and mingle with that of the herbs as Pera sat up and lowered her legs over the side of the bed. She'd wipe her eyes and blink at the wall in front of her, weighing something in her mind and tentatively lowering one foot onto the floor. Then the other. Mamá would hold her hand as she got up from the bed and teetered across the room and through the doorway like a newborn calf. When she'd falter, Mamá would grab her round the waist and hold her fast.

They'd spend the day in the kitchen. Pera would sit at the table with Tía Debi's patchwork quilt draped across her lap while Mamá busied herself at the stove, cooking all day and into the night, determined to fill Pera's purged body with good things. She'd cook and pray, pray and cook, both at the same time, her prayers entwined with the litany of ingredients she'd recite before adding each to the large, simmering pot.

Remember, Oh most gracious Virgin Mary
that never was it known that anyone
cloves of garlic
a few pinches of salt who fled to thy
protection, onion slices
implored thy help, three tomatoes
four ears of corn
or sought thy intercession,
was left unaided
carrots, head of cabbage inspired by
this confidence, handful
of cilantro
I fly unto thee, Oh Virgin of virgins,
chunks of meat
bones to add flavor

Those weeks Pera was ill, Mamá prepared all the dishes she knew, her hands peeling, slicing and stirring incessantly as the setting sun threw shadows across the floor at her feet. *Arroz con pollo, chorizo, arroz con leche, pozole, empanadas, enchiladas, flautas, flan, menudo, caldo de res, chalupas, chilaquiles, mole*—meals she'd learned from her mother, who'd learned them from her mother, and her from hers, each dish, a link connecting one generation to the next. The aroma of the food would waft through the house, filling the empty spaces like incense and swaddling Pera. At first, she refused to eat, but Mamá persisted, and every day she managed to swallow a little more until her body regained its former fullness, its sharp edges receding into fleshy folds.

Pilar

"What play are they doing this year?" Shane hands me a stack of plates.

I orbit the table, setting one on each woven place mat. "Nothing good. Just boring *Our Town*."

"Sweet. We did that one in high school, too."

I stare at him wide-eyed and set down the last plate. "Shut up! You were in plays? I didn't know that. That's so cool. Why didn't you tell me that before?"

He tugs on his collar and cocks an eyebrow. "And jeopardize my status as a neighborhood man of mystery? I think not. Anyway, I wasn't really in them. I was more of a behind-the-scenes guy. Handled the props. You know, made sure Mary Poppins had her umbrella, the wicked witch had her broom. That sort of thing."

"Well, that's still super cool. Shane 'Hooah' Townsend, a drama geek. Who knew?" I line up the corners of a napkin, fold it in half and lay it beside Luz's plate.

"More like, Shane Townsend, lovesick fool. I liked this girl who was into it, so I signed up, too."

"So what happened? Did y'all hook up?"

"Nah, she broke my heart. Got together with Rich Elben, who played Howie Newsome. She literally ran off with the milk man. Brutal." He shakes his head and chuckles. "What do you have against *Our Town*, anyway? A small-town girl comes back from the grave to relive a moment of her life. Kind of like a zombie or a ghost. Sounds legit to me."

"I was hoping it'd be something different this year. Something a little more interesting . . . with a role I could really sink my teeth into."

"Well, I guess they decided to *play* it safe this year. Badum-dum." He beats an invisible drum, looks down and clears his throat. "Sorry," he mutters.

I smile and grab a few glasses from a cabinet.

He's referring to what happened last year when the drama teacher decided to put on a play he'd written himself called *Birth of a Tire Salesman*, a twist on the Arthur Miller play. It was about a middle-aged man who quits his job and moves to Alaska to open a gym with the personal trainer his wife hired for his fiftieth birthday. It wasn't overtly gay, but some parents complained it was homosexually suggestive. There was a line of them waiting outside the principal's office one morning, and nobody was surprised when the drama teacher didn't return the following semester.

This year, we have a drama teacher with more traditional views. Surprise: *Our Town* it is.

"I don't see what the big deal was with Mr. Day's play. It was different, but so what? *Our Town* is some boring play about boring people doing boring things. Eating breakfast, doing homework, using the toilet, then . . . they die."

He laughs. "Hmm, I don't remember any bathroom scene, but I get what you mean. It's a play about everyday life."

"Exactly. Everyday. Ordinary. Bor-*ing*."

"What? Life's anything but that. I mean, it can be. It's up to us to do something with it, to make it mean something, to make it extraordinary. And the way to do that is to open our eyes and see it for what it already is. That's the whole point of the play."

"I guess. But it's good to shake things up every now and then. Why are people so close-minded? I mean, you can't always play it safe where art is concerned. You have to dare to put it all out there." I sweep my arm across my forehead dramatically. "Take risks. Only actors who do that become truly great. Do you think Meryl Streep plays it safe? Or Cate Blanchett? Damon? DiCaprio? Hoffman or Hanks?"

"I get it. I'm a firm believer in taking risks too." He glances down at his knee. "Always have been. But I think you've got *Our Town* all wrong. You should give it a shot. Thornton Wilder was a risk-taker and a rule-breaker. Dude totally changed my perception."

"He was?" My eyebrows shoot up. "How so?"

"Well, for one thing, he didn't bother with props . . . although I was almost out of a job because of it. And he blended everyone together, sat cast members out in the audience, brought people who'd usually remain behind the scenes out on stage and made them a part of the action. Like the stage manager, for instance. He gave him lines and made him part of the cast. He wasn't afraid to break with convention. He had a vision, and he did it his way."

"Like Frank Sinatra? Or Burger King?"

"Very funny. But yeah, he got down to the bare bones. The actors saying their lines. Just the people and the words. That's really what it comes down to when you think about it. That's what made it so good. Anyway, I'm glad to hear you've decided to audition this year. More power to you."

"Well . . . not exactly." I grab the salad dressing from the refrigerator door. "I'm kind of still on the fence about it."

Shane takes the bowl of salad from the counter, his brows furrowing. "Why? What's stopping you? You're the biggest movie buff I've ever met. You love acting. And you're a natural. You'd be great at it." I go quiet at that. Shane doesn't prod me as he moves around the kitchen getting dinner together.

He's right, I do love it. But it's more than that. It's a need deep down in my soul, a hunger like no other.

Mom says when I was Luz's age, I watched *Braveheart* for the first time and ran around the house with a plaid Christmas tree skirt wrapped around my waist and blue eye shadow smeared all over my face yelling, "I am William Wallace!" in a Scottish accent.

Mom and I watched tons and tons of movies together. My father would go out with his friends, and she'd grab a bag of popcorn from the kitchen and turn on The Movie Channel. She always fell asleep, even when she picked the movie, but I never did.

I watched *Braveheart* over and over until I practically had the whole thing memorized. I even dressed up like William Wallace for Halloween that year. Mom still has a picture of me trick or treating with some of the neighborhood kids, my face a blue island in a sea of Disney princesses.

You'd think that movie would be too gory for a five-year-old, but the gore wasn't what stuck in my head anyway, it was the passion of the actors. When Mel Gibson sat on his horse trying to convince his countrymen to stay and fight the English, I felt like I was right there with him. When he lay dying at the end with his insides all pulled out and opened his mouth to yell, "Freedom!" I yelled it with him. I felt all of it.

I love everything about movies, especially watching them in a darkened theater. The lights go down, and you become invisible. A hush falls over the audience, and the air is filled with the smell of popcorn and charged with a certain energy, a sense of anticipation. A feeling that anything is possible, that magic is real. For the next two hours you're taken to another place, another time. You lose yourself in what's happening on the screen, experiencing things you'd never get to experience in real life . . . like escaping from a mental institution, visiting Mars, falling in love with a vampire, dancing on point as the Black Swan and having a nice guy hold up a stereo outside your bedroom window.

You feel connected to the people around you, united in the experience. You cry at the same things and laugh at the same things. And when the credits roll and the lights come back on, you experience a sense of fulfillment, like you've shared something worthwhile with your fellow man. That's what movies do. They take the limp, tattered curtain of mundane life and push it aside to reveal how extraordinary life can be. That's something I often forget.

Actors are at the heart of that. The best thing about acting, though, is you get to be someone else . . . Shane drops a metal spoon, startling me out of my daydream. I realize he's looking at me pensively.

"I don't know," I shrug, "I'm not so sure I can do it. I mean, I'll have to stand on stage in front of the whole school. Everyone'll be looking at me. What if I trip on something and fall on my face? What if I have a major brain fart and forget all my lines? What if I totally suck? Like to the zillionth degree? Uber suck."

Shane rests his hands on my shoulders. "Pilar, do I need to get the hose? Relax."

I take a deep breath and let it out slowly, loosen up my shoulders and roll my neck. "I'm good."

"Besides, I already told you, *Our Town* is done with minimal props." He grabs an olive from the salad bowl and pops it into his mouth. "There won't be anything to trip over." He finishes chewing and swallows. "But seriously, what's the worst thing that could happen?"

"Let's see . . . I could forget my lines, trip on my own feet, fall off the stage, land on a small child, get charged with manslaughter, plead insanity and live out my remaining days in a psych ward with make-up caked on my face like Baby Jane, incoherently rambling lines from *Our Town* to my roommate, a woman who thinks her pimento cheese sandwich is Elvis' baby."

"That could happen. Better not risk it." He laughs. "But you're wrong. There's something worse than that. It's living in the land of What If. That's worse than failing. Worse than dying even. 'Cause, if you spend your life there, you're dead already." He walks over to the oven and peeks inside. "You should never be afraid of something you love, of something you feel passionate about. That passion is there for a reason. It must mean something. You just have to take it from that dark place of doubt inside of you and let it out into the light. Study it. Explore it. Then grab it with both hands and run like hell. That's the stuff dreams are made of." He grabs a dish towel, pulls the door open and slides out a metal tray. "I know, I know. Easier said than done. But in my experience, when it comes to life, if you're not scared shitless half the time, then you're probably not doing it right."

I take an empty basket from the counter and hold it out as he tilts the tray over it. Hot rolls tumble in like doughy chunks of gold. I cover them quickly with a napkin to capture their warmth, to preserve it until I'm ready to sink my teeth in.

At the table, Shane passes me a bowl of peas. "My sister called today. Apparently, things aren't so great with Gabe."

Mom sips her iced tea and leans forward on her elbows. "Uh-oh, is it drugs? I heard all about it. They were talking about it on 20/20 last week. Did you know kids are pouring vodka into their eyes and sniffing computer cleaner to get high now?" She waves her hand in front of her face like she's shooing a gnat. "*Dios mío*, these kids today . . . *Están locos*."

"Last year, a boy got caught drinking hand sanitizer at school," I say. "So ridiculous."

"Wow, hand sanitizer? Computer cleaner? That's messed up." Shane shakes his head. "No, it's nothing like that. Some kids have been messing with him at school, and Megan's worried."

"What do you mean 'messing with him?'" Mom says.

"At first it was taunting and name calling, but now it's getting more serious. He's been coming home with cuts and bruises. Even a bloody lip."

"*Pobrecito*. That's terrible. Your sister should go talk to his teachers. Or the principal maybe."

"She's tried that, but it hasn't done much good."

"Yeah, Mom. Most teachers are too busy teaching to deal with that stuff," I say.

"*Pues*, forget the teacher. She should go to the school district and talk to the superintendent. Go straight to the top. That's what I would do."

"I'm sure she's tried everything," Shane says.

"*Ay*, kids can be so cruel. I blame the parents. They should teach their children the right way to treat people. It makes me so mad." Her hands are like fireworks bursting.

"Agreed. But kids get into fights. It happens. I did when I was his age. Only, Megan says it's happening more and more." He drizzles dressing on Luz's salad. "I feel bad for him. He's always been a sensitive kid, and I'm sure it's hard not having his dad around. You really need that when you're sixteen."

Luz's eyes widen. "I know! Why don't you go beat them up, Daddy? You could put on your uniform and go to his school."

"I wish I could, sweetheart. But it's important for people to learn how to fight for themselves."

"Then you could teach him how. You could train him like Mr. Miyagi teaches Danielsan."

Luz and I hold our palms out in front of us and sweep our arms inward and outward.

"That's not a bad idea," Mom says. "Not the wax on, wax off part. Maybe he should come and stay with us. Let him get away from all of that for a while."

Shane crosses his thick arms and scratches his chin. "I don't know. You think?"

Mom reaches over and cups his face with her hand. "He's family. Of course, he should come."

Shane kisses her palm. "Okay. I'll call Megan tonight and run it by her. If she's onboard, I can go to Pilar's school this week and see about getting Gabe enrolled."

The phone rings, and Mom gets up to answer it. I can tell right away who it is even before I hear her sigh, "*Hola*, Mamá."

Whenever Buela calls, Mom gets this look on her face like she's about to do something unpleasant, like clean the cheese grater or change clothes for gym class.

She walks into the living room for privacy, but she shouldn't bother. We'll still hear her. Mom and Buela only speak to each other in one volume. Loud. You should see them talking to each other in person: hands flying everywhere.

It hurt Mom when Buela didn't come to visit after Luz was born. Buela had vowed never to set foot in this house and she was true to her word. They didn't talk to each other for a long time after that.

Buela says Mom's soul's in danger because she and Shane aren't married. She says the flames of hell burn hottest for child molesters and adulterers. When Mom left my father, Buela wasn't exactly thrilled, but she got over it. She said, "What is done is done." But this is different. This sin keeps on going. Every day that Mom and Shane spend unmarried in this house is a fresh offense against God.

Buela prays that Mom will see the error of her ways. She keeps a large candle with a picture of Mary Magdalene on it lit on Mom's behalf. Every night, she asks La Virgen to help her convince Mom to go to Confession. It hasn't worked so far, but Buela's not giving up. She says La Virgen gets things done in her own good time.

Mom is getting increasingly louder, and I can hear the frustration in her voice when she says, "*Ay*, Mamá, why do we have to do this over and over again? No, I haven't gone, and I don't plan on going."

Shane and I exchange looks and chew our food in silence.

There's a long pause, then Mom says, "Because, Mamá, I haven't done anything wrong. I love Shane, and I don't need a piece of paper to tell me that. . . . Well, God was there when I married Julio, and you saw how that turned out."

Luz pretends to feed peas to her favorite toy, a mangy kangaroo with missing eyes. My dad sent it to me a month after my ninth birthday when I'd already long outgrown stuffed animals.

Mom stomps in from the living room, slams the phone on the counter and crosses her arms.

"Everything all right, Rey?" Shane asks, scraping pieces of cut-up chicken onto Luz's plate.

Mom rubs her temples. "That woman is *tan terca*." So stubborn. "She thinks she can control everyone. *¡Me vuelve* *loca!* Her way is the only way." She sits down and mumbles to herself in Spanish, punctuating her words with her fists.

Shane butters a roll and offers it to her. "She'll come around. She just needs more time."

"*Pues*, how much more time does she need? It's been almost five years." She stabs a cherry tomato with her fork.

"She has traditional views, that's all. She's old school. Nothing wrong with that. To be honest, I admire her for sticking to her principles. Besides, she happens to be right. . . . We should get married."

I know it's none of my business, but I'm Team Buela on this one too. Mom should marry Shane already. He's good for her. He's got this calming effect on her, like smoke to a beehive, and, more importantly, he makes her happy. They're different, but they complement each other. Like cookie dough and ice cream.

"We've already been over this before, and now is not the time to talk about it, anyway."

Mom cocks an eyebrow and nods toward Luz, who's stuffing a pea inside the kangaroo's pouch.

Luz sits up straight. "Is Buela finally coming to visit?"

Mom helps herself to another serving of salad. "I don't know when she's coming. She's a busy lady. There're a lot of souls that need to be saved and people who need to be judged. Now, leave that kangaroo alone, Luz, and eat your dinner."

"Esperanza's a hard nut to crack, but her heart's in the right place," Shane says.

"I wish she could be more like Tía Pili was. Easy-going and level-headed, full of life. Sometimes crazy, but in a good way. How does the saying go? Full of oil and vinegar?" Mom says.

Shane smiles. "I think you mean 'piss and vinegar.'"

"That doesn't sound so nice, but yes, like that." She gazes out the window at the backyard. "I wish you all could've known her."

"I wish we could've too. But you talk about her so much I feel like I did."

Luz smiles at me. "She's Buela's big sister, right? Like Pipi is to me?"

"Yes, she was."

"But not anymore?"

Mom puts her fork down and reaches across the table to wipe Luz's chin. "She died a long time ago. When your sister was a baby."

"Is she the one who Pipi's named after?"

"Yes."

"How did she die?"

"She got sick."

"Why didn't you take her to the doctor like you take me when I get sick?"

"We did, *m'ija*, but she was too sick. There was nothing he could do."

"Oh." Luz's bottom lip quivers, and her eyes well up. "Poor Buela. I'd be sad if Pipi died."

I pat her arm. "Don't worry. I'm not going anywhere."

She smiles and wipes her eye with the back of her hand. She's quiet for a moment, then her forehead wrinkles up. "When you die, do you stop being sisters?"

"Of course not. I'll always be your sister."

"Forever and ever?"

"Forever and ever. You're stuck with me."

"Everyone dies. There's no getting around it," Mom says.

I take a sip of iced tea. "Geez, Mom. Tell it like it is, why don't you? Don't sugarcoat it or anything."

"I don't believe in sugarcoating. I think kids should know the way life is. And it's better if they learn while they're young so it's not such a shock when bad things happen."

Shane turns to face Luz. "If people didn't die, how would they get to heaven?"

"Why can't the angels come down and pick them up in a spaceship?"

Shane smiles. "I'm afraid it doesn't work that way, sweetie. You see, when you die, your soul leaves your body, and that's the part that goes to heaven."

"What's your soul?"

"It's your spirit, the part of you that makes you who you are. The part that keeps on going even after you die. Like a piece of God in your own body."

"Do I have one?"

"Yup."

"Do you? And Mommy?"

"Yes. Everyone does."

"It's kind of like the dragonflies we saw on TV, remember?" I say. "Remember how they shed their skin? Leave it behind and fly away?"

"I remember." She wrinkles up her nose. "It was all brown and crinkly."

"Right. Well, it's kind of like that."

"So dying is just shedding your skin?"

I shrug. "Yeah."

"And we'll still be sisters even if God wants his pieces back?"

"Always."

Pili

"The trunk . . . *del árbol* . . . should be in the middle of the wall so it's right beside the crib. *Quiero que tenga* lots of branches full of leaves of all colors and sizes. And make sure you paint it nice and thick."

"I will," I assure her from my spot on the floor. "And why don't you take that empty box I brought and put a few things in it? Just a few to make some room."

I dip the brush into the metal tray and scrape it along the edge to remove the excess drips. The rich, brown paint runs down the sides like melted chocolate. I paint a broad stroke down the wall and steal a look at Pera through the corner of my eye as she gets up from the rocking chair and walks slowly to the cardboard box in the middle of the room. She studies it for a moment before finally picking it up warily and holding it out in front of her as though it were a bomb.

I know what I'm asking of her. I know what it means. Our eyes meet and, even though we're only a few feet apart, it feels like there's an ocean between us.

She carries the box over to the dresser and sets it down between her feet, picks up a baseball glove, barely used, and traces her fingers along its leathery seams as though along the lines of someone's face, searing them into memory.

I nod and give her an encouraging smile. Inside I'm pleading, urging her on. *You can do it. It's time.* I focus all my energy on her, willing her to proceed. She nods, and a look of determination settles on her face as she brings the glove to her chest.

Outside, the cicadas cease their lazy drone, and the crinkled petal of a crepe myrtle pauses midair as it falls to the earth.

Pera opens her eyes again and gently lays the glove inside the box.

Carlos appears from around the corner and leans against the door frame, blocking the penciled measurements with his leg. "That color looks like shit. Literally. Looks like you've taken a big turd and rubbed it right down the wall," he laughs. "I'm hungry. When's dinner?"

Pera gingerly folds the flaps of the box closed and heads for the doorway. I reach up and grab her hand as she passes by. This time I will not be silenced.

I lower the brush. "Carlos, you're so blind. You don't see," I say dejectedly.

He gives me a puzzled look. "What the hell are you jabbering about now? I can see just fine."

I sigh. "Well, you see those two things beneath you?"

He looks down. "What two things?"

"Those two things you walk around on. Your legs. They work don't they? You're not crippled. Why don't you use them? Let them carry you back down the hall the way you came. Through the living room to that large white box in the corner of the kitchen. The one filled with food. You like to hunt. Go hunt in there."

That smirk I can't stand is back on his face. His eyes hold my gaze for a few seconds before his attention shifts to Pera. "You gonna let her talk to me like that?"

Pera sighs at the ceiling. She must be tired of being the rope in our tug of war. That's why I vowed to ease up on the slack, not to engage Carlos, if I can help it, but there's only so much a person can take. It feels good to tug back and release the words I've been holding back.

"Leave her out of this. And what do you mean, 'let her?'" I challenge. "I'm a grown woman. I don't need anyone's permission to do or say anything."

"Well grown, maybe. Not so sure about woman, though. Jury's still out on that one."

Pera lets go of my hand. "*Está bien*, Pili. I can make him a sandwich real quick."

Carlos jams a thumb into the belt loop of his jeans and points a finger at me. "You need to mind your own damn business. You're here to paint, so stick to that. What happens between a man and his wife doesn't concern you." He juts his chin at Pera. "Besides, she likes doing things for me. Don't you? It gives her a sense of purpose. The devil makes use of idle hands and all that. Maybe if you'd learn to keep your mouth shut a little more, you could find a man."

"Why should I? It hasn't worked for my sister."

Pera lets out another sigh of exasperation.

I understand the struggle she's been through today, the battle she's fought and won, the bravery she's shown. Even if her husband does not. I swallow hard and stop tugging. For Pera's sake.

I press my lips together and rise from the floor, walk over to Carlos and drape an arm around him. "Let's not argue. It's not good for Pera or the baby. I'll cook you something. What would you like?"

He looks from me to Pera and shakes his head. "Never mind. I'm going out for a beer."

He swaggers down the hallway like the king of his castle, the chief of his tribe, the alpha male, dominant and strong, tough and virile—rugged, confident, manly. With a brown smudge down the back seam of his jeans.

I wave the paintbrush in front of me like a wand. Yes, sir. I'm here to paint.

Pilar

Eleanor Roosevelt keeps talking to me. What she said about looking fear in the face keeps running through my head. It's on a poster hanging in the main office at school. Well, fear is an eight-and-a-half-by-fourteen-inch piece of notebook paper stapled to a bulletin board in the drama hallway: the sign-up sheet to audition for *Our Town*. The moment I saw it posted, my palms got all clammy, and I felt the urge to run home and lock myself in my room with a cheesecake sampler and Netflix. But no, Eleanor says we must do the thing we think we cannot do. Ha, easy for her to say. I'm sure she wasn't standing in the hallway of her high school's drama department when she said it.

School let out almost an hour ago, but I've been standing here gripping this pen and chewing a hole through my bottom lip for the past twenty minutes.

Being in a play would be amazing. It would mean standing on a stage and doing what I'm meant to do. But it would also mean standing on a stage in front of everyone. It's crazy how you can want something so badly and be terrified of it at the same time.

Scalloped strips of cardboard surround the board like an oversized picture frame. My hand drifts up to the yellow sheet of legal pad paper at its center. This is the moment of truth. The pivotal moment in my thus far uneventful life. My stomach flips, and I taste the chicken salad Mom packed me for lunch. The rows of lockers dissolve, and the blue and gray speckled carpet disappears beneath my feet, replaced by a long, red one leading to the doors of the Dolby Theatre where the Academy Awards are about to take place. Skinny blonde reporters wearing tight dresses and even tighter smiles stick microphones in my face and fire meaningless questions at me. What designer am I wearing? What brand of toothpaste do I prefer? Do I own a cat and if so, what does it eat for breakfast?

Hollywood can be absurd, and the idea of fame freaks me out a little; people rifling through my trash can and following me around the grocery store snapping photos of my tortilla chips and feminine products. It would all be worth it if I could act. No matter how successful I became, I'd stay grounded, do my own dishes and scrub my own toilet.

My fans shout my name and wish me luck, the beat of my heart syncing with the beat of their chants. *Pi-lar! Pi-lar! Pi-lar!* They admire me. They respect me. They love me. I stop to shake hands with a group of girls a few years older than Luz. One of them hands me a pen for an autograph. I'm reaching out to take it when a custodian wheels a large, gray trash can around the corner at the end of the hallway, and I'm back at school again, a pen poised in my hand.

I'm about to write my name but stop and lower my arm again. I scroll down the list of names. It's only the first day, and thirty-two people have already signed up. Thirty-two people who don't approach doorways with a niggling sense of doom before stepping through them sideways, who don't wear T-shirts in the swimming pool feigning sensitive skin or lower themselves into chairs the tentative way most people step onto escalators. I turn my face away from the paper and shut my eyes tight. Just looking at it is nerve-racking, like watching someone walk a tightrope. My eyelids flutter, and I take a peek through a veil of lashes and raise the pen again, touch the nib to the paper and move it straight down. Back up and around to the right in a half circle. A letter P. That wasn't so hard. It's only a letter. A name. A word. I'm about to write another letter, when Sissy Spacek materializes next to me covered in pig's blood. It drips down her face and spatters onto the sign-up sheet. "They're all going to laugh at you," she warns. The folds of her pale pink prom dress expand and fill like a deployed life raft, and her long, strawberry tresses crinkle up into my dark curls, and I'm the one covered in pig blood.

What was I thinking? I can't do it. I can't. I can't stand up on stage in front of the entire school, including Becca and her friends. I'm too fat. Too ugly. Too everything. I'd be like a slice of contraband pizza smuggled into an Overeaters Anonymous meeting. I'd be devoured.

I scratch out the P I've written and recap my pen. It clicks like the lid of a coffin. I pretend not to hear it, and jam it inside my backpack and trudge down the hallway of deserted classrooms. It feels wrong, like I'm refusing a gift, turning my back on a sunset. My legs keep moving out through the heavy metal doors into the blinding sunlight. My hand rises to my forehead like a visor, casting a long shadow before me.

That overwhelming, anxious feeling comes over me as my eyes zigzag down the refrigerator shelves. Like the only food left on earth is in this stainless steel box and if I don't grab it fast, it'll disappear like a desert mirage.

This is exactly what I'm not supposed to do. The nutritionist with the protruding clavicle Mom took me to see last month told me I'm not. I'm supposed to decide, then open. She said someone with a food addiction should treat a refrigerator like a minefield. Before I even open the door, I should know what I'm going in for. Carrot sticks, for instance. Or a container of yogurt. "I like to throw in a few blueberries and almond slices. That's the perfect snack," she said, smiling at me with lipstick smudged teeth, her belt so tight around her tiny waist, the overlap reached the loop at the back of her skirt. She said to tell myself that that single item is the only one that will not detonate if I touch it. If I grab anything else, it will explode in my hand.

The problem with that is, I wouldn't go through a minefield for carrots or yogurt. I would go in, however, for the leftover lasagna in the Tupperware container on the second shelf. Or the tub of Cool Whip and the casserole dish full of green Jell-O on the shelf above it. No question about it. I'd definitely go in for what's hidden in the narrow space beneath the meat drawer, behind a few cartons of Chinese take-out. Leftover cake Mom's coworkers surprised her with for acing her first round of exams: chocolate with buttercream icing, my favorite. Icing for Acing. Now, that's an academic motivator.

I ease the refrigerator door closed again and take a quick peek down the hall. Shane took Luz to a birthday party, but Mom's where she usually is after work: in her room studying. Her door is slightly open, which makes it even riskier. I'll have to level up my ninja skills now. Her ear is already trained to hear that breaking-suction sound of the refrigerator door opening. If she hears it, she'll come running, calorie counter app in hand.

I nudge off my sneakers and skate back to the kitchen in my socks. Keeping one eye on the hallway, I slide out the rectangular box from the shelf and set it on the counter before it can explode. Most of the cake has already been eaten, but there's still a sizable chunk with what's left of the words, "Congratulations Mireya," scrawled in red icing. What's left says, "rat mire."

My seventh-grade math teacher, Mr. Burris, sits on the counter with his pasty arms crossed over his chest and a mechanical pencil tucked behind his ear. He always said math would be useful in everyday life. "Told you so," he says, the glow from the refrigerator bulb reflecting on the shiny bald spot on the crown of his head.

How many of the 8 or so inches left of a 12" x 16" sheet cake can a fat girl eat without her mother noticing?

This is going to take some strategy, and luckily there are a number to choose from. There's the Slim 'n Skim, which consists of skimming a narrow sliver from around the entire piece. Or, the Safety in Numbers, a modified version of the Divide and Conquer, which is usually done with a larger piece. It consists of cutting the cake into an odd number of equally sized pieces, spreading them out tactically on the tray and eating one, maybe two. The irony of this strategy is not lost on me; kids usually spread food around a plate to make it look emptier not fuller, like they've eaten most of their brussels sprouts.

I can't push my luck with Mom at home. It's better to err on the side of caution. So I decide to go with the Border Patrol, stay away from the cake altogether and eat the ribbon of leftover icing along the edges of the plastic base. I run my index finger along the periphery and lick the thick curls that cling to it until it's wiped clean. The sugary frosting gives me an immediate rush.

I'm still not satisfied.

So I move on to my go-to strategy: the Cleaner, that is, eat it all and hide the evidence. My hands scoop up chunks of cake and shovel them into my mouth one after the other like tandem bulldozers. I don't even bother with a fork. That would mean messing with the noisy utensil drawer, which rattles like a fire alarm every time it's opened.

I suck the last bits of icing from my fingers, tug my sneakers back on and carry the evidence outside through the side door of the garage. I shove the empty box, along with any sliver of self-esteem I might have left, under a pile of newspapers in the recycling bin and slam the lid shut.

The narrow strip of windows along the top of the wide garage door rattles as I lean back on the aluminum panels to catch my breath. Pretty soon, this is the only door my body will be able to fit through to enter the house.

I've done it again. I'm pathetic, a hopeless loser with zero self-control. Mom should give up on me already and let me eat whatever the hell I want until I'm too heavy to lift myself from the bed. I'll stay in my room for the rest of my life with my fat splayed around me like water balloons ready to burst, watch movies and stuff my face with takeout until I've entombed myself in a Styrofoam sepulcher. I'll be a mysterious recluse all the neighborhood kids tell each other stories about.

The boy who lives across the street waves to me from the end of his driveway. I babysit him and his younger sister sometimes. It's awesome. Not only are they quiet and well-behaved, but Mrs. Gossett is the last mother on earth who still buys snack food. I'm not talking goldfish crackers and string cheese. I mean the good stuff, like Little Debbies, Drumstick ice cream cones and Fruit Roll-Ups. I usually sneak a few while they play on their iPads.

It must be Sadie's purple bike Jude's holding upright by the handlebars. Their front door opens, and she skips over to him, swinging a helmet in her hand. He tightens the strap under her chin and holds the bike steady as she hoists herself onto the narrow seat.

"What if I fall?"

He gives the bike a push. "Keep peddling. If you don't stop, you won't fall," he calls after her.

I watch her peddle to the end of the street, then heave myself off the garage door, drag my hulking flesh to the side of the house and reach for the doorknob. My hands are stained red with icing. I hurry over to the kitchen sink, squeeze generous dollops of bright green dishwashing liquid on each of my palms and rub them under the hot water like Lady Macbeth: "Out, damned spot."

When my palms are a normal pink color again, I creep down the hallway to my room, careful to step over that noisy floorboard. Not this time, Squeaky.

"Pilar? Is that you? Come here. I need to talk to you."

The screeching violins from *Psycho* fill my head.

Busted. But how could she know? I was so careful. Did she have Shane install a hidden camera in the kitchen? I bet it's in that shifty-looking rooster with the beady eyes.

I take a deep breath and steel myself before walking in to face the music.

Mom sits on the floor surrounded by books. One is opened to a diagram of the human body, each sinewy, red muscle labeled in perfect block letters. She motions to the bed and caps the highlighter in her hand.

"Sit down."

I slump down on the edge of her bed, ready to throw myself at her mercy and beg for forgiveness, but when I open my mouth to speak, she beats me to it.

"I got you something today."

"You got me something?"

"Yes." She grins like the Cheshire Cat.

My eyes narrow to slits. "What?"

"Guess."

"Mo-om," I groan. "Not another Richard Simmons DVD. I'm done sweating to the oldies."

"Nope. Guess again."

"It's not another set of Spanx, is it? 'Cause Luz uses the other pair you got me as a trampoline for her dolls."

She shakes her head from side to side emphatically. "Better."

"Tell me already!"

She smiles at me with her lips pressed together.

So annoying. "Give me a clue at least."

"It's a gift that keeps on giving."

"Oh, no. Did you get me a membership in the Fruit of the Month Club again?"

Her face brightens. "No, but you're getting closer," she says in a singsong voice.

"Vegetable of the Month?"

She shakes her head again and blurts it out. "It's a gym membership!"

"I'd rather have the fruit." I frown and fling myself back onto the mattress.

"Oh, Pilar. Don't be like that. You're going to love it. And look," she says, jumping up from the floor and grabbing a sheet of paper from the dresser. She sits down next to me on the bed and reads the list. "They have all these classes you can do. Ab Unflab, Belly De-jelly, Bunburn, Bodypump, Core Cross, Plates2Pilates, Turbo Kick, Yoga-naluvit. Oh, and Zumba. That's supposed to be really fun."

I stare at the ceiling. "Yeah. Really. Fun."

"You should be excited. You're going to feel so much better once you lose a few pounds. It's not only about eating right, you know. Exercise is important too."

Yadda yadda yadda. "I know, I know." I roll my eyes.

"You can go in the morning before school. That way you'll be energized for the rest of the day."

"Can't I just snort coke like normal people?"

"That's not funny, Pilar Elvira. Drugs are no laughing matter. But as far as I'm concerned, you are addicted. Food is your drug. But don't worry, *m'ija*." She pats my leg. "I'm going to help you."

Mom's right. I need to be proactive. The pounds aren't going to magically melt away because I want them to. Maybe if I manage to lose a few, Becca and her friends will leave me alone. I'll find the courage to stand on stage in front of everyone. I'll do great, and some talent scout will be sitting in the audience. Or a movie director. And he'll offer me a part in his next film. Actors get discovered in all kinds of places. Shelley Duvall from *The Shining* got discovered while spraying people with perfume in a department store here in Houston. It happens. And everyone at school will realize that I'm not some useless blob, that I'm talented.

"Come on, Pilar. You can do it. Try it out for a few weeks. If you don't like it, we'll cancel it. I promise." She holds her hands out to me. "Deal?"

"Deal." I grab onto them, and she pulls me up to a sitting position, then lifts me to my feet.

Pili

I always leave the top down. Even when the car's sitting in the driveway or in a parking lot. Pera worries. She shakes her head and warns me of all the possible repercussions.

What if a thief happens by?

He'll inherit a stack of coffee-stained maps and a pair of fluffy dice.

What if an animal builds its nest in the crook of the dashboard?

He'd better buckle up,'cause I've got a heavy foot.

What if it starts to rain?

Then everything'll get wet.

I leave the top down anyway. It feels wrong to have it up, like I'm keeping something from its purpose, from being what it's meant to be, its destiny. It's my own small act of defiance against the irrepressible heat, a fist held high in the face of the blazing sun. Blaze on, worthy opponent.

I veer left onto San Bernardo past the Piggly Wiggly and the cinderblock walls of the Safari Motel, easing my foot off the gas pedal as I drive by El Rincón, a squat concrete building painted a gaudy pink color. The brassy chords of a saxophone blend with the reedy notes of an accordion and spill from the open windows onto the sweltering sidewalk.

Sure enough, Carlos' rusty pickup is parked outside, like I knew it would be. I consider turning the car around and pulling into the unpaved parking lot, barging through the imitation wood saloon doors and giving him a piece of my mind; telling him all the things I've been holding in all these years, like how worthless he is, how he doesn't deserve my sister and how lucky he is to have her; how I'm going to storm into the bar in a fuzzy bathrobe and slippers with curlers in my hair, wave a rolling pin like some deranged housewife and embarrass him in front of all of his friends if he doesn't start treating her better. After all, everyone knows there's no greater affront to misogynistic pride than a man who can't control his woman.

I don't mind making a spectacle of myself for a good cause, and Pera's as good a cause as there'll ever be.

I swerve into the right-hand lane and switch on my blinker but think better of it and switch it back off, drive past the large marquee sign with the flashing arrow and the buckling plastic letters at the entrance to the parking lot.

My words would be wasted. He won't listen, won't hear me. Even if he did, it wouldn't do a bit of good. It would be asking too much of him. He isn't capable of that level of self-evaluation and reflection. It'd be like asking a jellyfish to undergo an examination of conscience.

No, if anyone is going to change, it'll have to be Pera and, unfortunately, that's not happening anytime soon.

I wish she would stand up for herself and put Carlos in his place once and for all. I wish I could do it for her, but I know the words will be meaningless unless they come from her. I wish I could give them to her, pour them down her throat like a mother bird feeding its young. Well, even if I can't, there are other ways to help her.

The tires screech as I swing the car around in the middle of the busy intersection and head back toward the bar. People honk their horns and shoot me the finger, but I pay them no mind. I'm on a mission.

I jerk into the parking lot, kicking up a cloud of dust and gravel. The blinking bulbs of the arrow on the sign urge me on as I screech to a halt behind Carlos's truck and jump out of my car, leaving the door wide open behind me. The curvy female forms outlined on the splattered mud flaps send a shudder of disgust through my shoulders, and my eyes dart away quickly to the truck bed where a tire iron beckons from beneath a stained canvas tarp.

I'd be lying if I said I wasn't tempted to grab it and exact sweet revenge. I imagine the satisfying crunch of glass breaking as I smash the headlights, and the fissures spread across the windshield as I bring the long metal bar hurtling down. I see myself pounding large dents into the fenders, like crushed beer cans. It's all right here in front of me. I could do it.

I don't. It might make me feel better, but it wouldn't do anything to improve Pera's situation. I leave the tire iron where it is and walk to the front of the truck to release the latch above the bumper.

A woman chewing a large wad of gum eyes me from the next row of cars. She sits in the passenger seat of a green Chevelle and fans herself with a magazine. I stare back at her as she tosses the glossy pages onto the dashboard and blows a huge pink bubble.

What if she knows Carlos? What if she's a regular here, like he is? What if she tells him she saw me messing with his truck? There's no mistaking my car, the only gold convertible in Laredo. Pera would never hear the end of it. She'd be the one to pay for it in the end, not me.

The sun lingers above the horizon, ready for a good rest after a long day of scorching. It casts long shadows across the rectangular patch of cars and gleams off the white racing stripes running down the hood of the Chevelle, throwing their reflection onto the windshield, where they extend upward across the woman's face.

My legs stretch in the dirt before me like spindly redwoods. We squint at each other, two gunslingers in a western showdown. My eyes remain locked on hers as I reach down to pop the hood. Beads of sweat glisten on her upper lip, and the corners of her mouth twitch. She blows another massive bubble that covers her entire face, then sucks it back into her mouth.

It occurs to me that if she is a regular here, why isn't she inside drinking beer and tapping her foot to the polka rhythm of the band along with everybody else? Why is she waiting in a stuffy car in a deserted parking lot? The answer comes to me as quickly as the question.

Of course, she's not a regular here. She's a woman, and women aren't welcome. It's been the unwritten law of a distorted patriarchy in this town for centuries, one that I've never bought into, nor Papá either—thank God, one proudly handed down from generation to generation, forged by grandfathers and fathers alike who forbade the shedding of masculine tears or any other perceived displays of weakness, who taught their sons that a woman's place was behind them, unaware or indifferent to their daughters listening in from kitchen doorways, impressionable girls who believed their words and grew up to become unwitting accomplices as they swaddled their own sons and held them close, whispering into their malleable ears those detrimental words which would shape an entire culture—*mi rey.* My king.

Only a certain kind of woman is allowed inside, the kind who knows her place, who understands what she's good for: the pleasure and service of men.

I study the woman peering back at me, the rounded collar of her buttoned shirt, the black, feathered hair framing her smooth delicate face, like one of Charlie's angels, trying to be something it's not, unadorned save for the blue smudges of shadow brushed ineptly across her eyelids. She's young, younger than Pera, closer to girl than woman, really. And she's not the kind they let in here. She's been left outside to wait for someone like an abandoned dog, until the band finishes its last set or the beer money runs out.

Anger ripples inside me.

She gives me an almost imperceptible nod as the latch gives way and releases the hood. I survey the filthy bowels of the truck, lean in toward the engine to remove the distributor cap, and slam the hood shut again, wiping my hands on my jeans.

That should do it.

If only it were as easy to disable Carlos' mouth. At least now, he won't be able to drive home and drag Pera out of bed to cook him scrambled eggs. After last call, he'll stumble into his truck, and when it doesn't start, throw himself into the truck bed and pass out until morning. Pera will finally have a night off. Maybe she can relax a little and take care of her own needs for a change.

The girl leans back and props her knees up against the dashboard. A smile plays on her lips as she reaches for the magazine again. I tip an invisible hat to her and turn to go home, where nobody waits for me to walk through the door, to my house full of memories, full of ghosts who glide through the rooms and wander the hallways together, side by side.

Pilar

I'd rather sweep mud than go to the gym first thing in the morning. Or go to the gym any time of day, really. First thing in the morning is definitely the worst time to go. That's when they're there: all those self-disciplined, Fitbit-wearing, kale-eating people who make exercise the number one priority of their lives, the ones who make sure they do it before anything else. So if the four horsemen of the Apocalypse come charging through or aliens attack later in the day, at least they'll be comforted by the fact that they got their workouts in.

The whole world seems to be on a health kick nowadays, but health is not why most people exercise. The real reason is vanity. So they'll fit into their size four jeans or look hot for Spring Break. So they won't look like me.

A girl with pock-marked skin and a name tag that says, Treasure, stands behind the reception desk. She looks as happy to be here as I am. Her long, bubble gum pink nails make a clicking sound as she grabs the plastic card from my hand without looking at me and swipes it into the computer. The rhinestone stud in her left nostril sparkles as she hands it back. Her eyes are quick, but I catch it anyway. That look. The one full of judgment and pity that says, I am so glad I am not you. She gives me a smile faker than her nails and in an artificial-sweetener voice too perky for six o'clock in the morning says, "Enjoy your workout."

I step away from the desk and scan the large room. It's filled with all sorts of shiny metal contraptions with pulleys, levers and footpads. It's like being in a medieval torture chamber choosing the method of my demise. Which of these will hurt the least? There are three main areas—cardio, strength training and free weights—and two large rooms in the back for fitness classes. Floor to ceiling mirrors cover the walls on every side, so there's no escaping your reflection.

The majority of people lift weights, but a few jog on treadmills and elliptical machines. Everyone looks slim and fit. Everyone but me. I don't belong here. If only there were an intermediate gym where fat people could go before going to the regular gym. Where we could get in shape before getting in shape. A place in between. Like purgatory.

I take a peek in a room where a yoga class is in session. People sit on rubber mats with their arms and legs bent this way and that, contorted like pretzels. Not for me. I'll take my pretzels with salt, butter and melted cheese, thank you.

I head back to the cardio room and carefully step onto a treadmill. A woman in a neon coral tank top and black yoga pants is hauling butt on the one next to me. I might run that fast if a serial killer with a butcher knife were chasing me. Maybe.

Her sneakers match her top, which also matches the thin elastic band around her head, and her hair is gathered in a messy bun. She looks so sporty in her coordinated, form-fitting outfit that I feel even dumpier in my oversized Balboa vs. Lang T-shirt and Shane's old maroon and gray Texas A&M ROTC sweatpants.

She steals a look at me and runs even faster.

I am the enemy. Worse than a knife-wielding serial killer. I'm the embodiment of all of her fears, the image in the mirror she never wants to see looking back at her. I'm what's waiting the minute she hits the snooze button and skips that morning cycling class or forgets to order her salad with the dressing on the side. The *before* photo to her *after*.

I look down at the start up screen, but I might as well be firing up the Millennium Falcon. There are a bunch of numbers and buttons and what looks like a bar graph. I hit the one that says, Start, and a prompt pops up asking for my weight. I glance around and almost lose my balance and fall off the machine as I enter the numbers quickly while trying to shield them with my hand at the same time. When I hit Mode, twenty other options appear on the screen. Why can't there be one button that says, Start Running? My pulse is racing, and I haven't even started walking yet. I feel stupid and look around to ask someone for help, but there's no one nearby except Neon Lady, who's really moving it now, her arms in full swing. She's wearing earbuds and wouldn't hear me anyway.

I'm about to go try my luck on a rowing machine instead, when a guy with thick, black hair and beefy arms steps out in front of me. He's wearing a red polo shirt with the gym's logo stitched on it. "Need some help?"

"Yes, please," I say gratefully. "I'm not really sure how this thing works, and I've got to destroy the Death Star."

He comes around to my side and presses buttons on the machine. "No worries. The interface can be a bit tricky. I'm Mando, by the way. This your first time here?"

"What gave it away? My killer coordination or my athletic physique?"

He laughs. There's a large gap between his two front teeth. Seeing it makes me feel less intimidated. "Hey, we all have to start somewhere, right?"

I smile back.

He explains the different buttons on the machine, how to switch modes, how to increase and decrease the incline, how to set it to interval training and even how to check my heart rate. I must look overwhelmed because he says, "Let's keep it simple for now. I'm going to set it to Manual, and you can use these arrows here to increase or decrease your speed."

"I'll only be using the one for decreasing."

He laughs again. "You may surprise yourself. Don't worry about the incline, just start out at a moderate pace for fifteen minutes, then jog for two minutes."

Two minutes? I'm no track star, but that sounds easy to me. I really am eager to lose weight, and since I dragged myself here before even God's woken up, I figure I might as well push myself at least a little.

"Are you sure we shouldn't set it to Fatburn? I mean, let's be honest, I've got a lot of burning to do. Is there a Bonfire setting, maybe? Incinerator?"

"Don't be so hard on yourself. You showed up. You could be home in your bed or eating fresh donuts at Shipley's, but you're not. You're here. So give yourself some credit. Focus on building up your stamina for now. Fitness is a marathon, not a sprint."

He pushes a final button and steps away from the machine. The conveyor belt starts moving beneath my feet. It's a bit disorienting, but I put one foot in front of the other at a steady pace, trying to convince myself that I'm finally headed somewhere, to believe there's something good waiting around the bend.

Pili

Papá was born in this house. Its single story sits squarely on the corner of Rosario Street and Palmas Drive with entrances on both sides, cemented walkways flanked by Mamá's miniature yellow roses leading to the ornate iron railings of identical porches.

We could always guess who the visitor might be by which door he or she used. Traveling salesmen peddling Bibles and cleaning supplies and perky, pink-clad women clutching cosmetic cases buzzed the bell on the busier Palmas side, while the milkman and mailman rapped on the inlay of beveled glass on the Rosario door. Friends and family always used the back entrance on the east side of the house.

The thick foundation sits two feet above its plot of land as though the house were hovering, suspended between heaven and earth, the middle space surrounded by bricks and a small stretch of lattice beneath the kitchen door. Pera and I once stole behind the bursts of bougainvillea bushes, their magenta bracts forming a canopy above our heads, and pulled back the glossy, whitewashed trellis. We crawled on our hands and knees in search of the bones Abuelito assured us were buried somewhere beneath the house, remnants of an old Indian graveyard.

Pera was afraid to go looking. I promised not to leave her, and crawled in first, waving a flashlight in front of me to remove any spiderwebs from our path. Pera followed close behind, gripping Mamá's small gardening spade, Tío Ricardo's old garrison cap askew on her head. We dug into the packed dirt for hours but never found any skeletons. We did find a clump of feathers partially buried in the southwest corner. Pera was convinced we'd discovered the resting place of some greatly revered Comanche warrior. She was so excited, I didn't have the heart to tell her a dead bird had probably been dragged there by a stray cat.

I pour myself a generous drink and carry it out to the back porch, the largest of three separate ones attached to the north, west and east sides of the house like aprons. A thin streak of vibrant red-orange fades into the darkening sky. Even the brightest blaze is eventually consumed.

Papá loved to sit out here too. Every night, he'd trot down the few steps into the yard to stroll amid the grapefruit trees, their branches heavy with golden orbs. I'd lean my elbows on the balustrade with my chin resting in my hands and watch the fireflies blink on and off around him, convinced if there were any magic to be found in this world, it was right there in front of me.

I rock back and forth in one of the metal rockers, the steel slats cool even through the thick fabric of my jeans. The strong smell of citrus drifts up from a few feet below as I bring the tumbler to my lips, savoring the smoky leathery taste. I remember the first time I snuck a swig from Papá's bottle all those years ago. It felt as if I'd swallowed the sun. It doesn't burn anymore. I got used to it maybe. Or maybe my throat's gone numb from all the words it's had to swallow.

Papá always ate the worm. He knew it wasn't supposed to be there, that it was a sign of an inferior bottle and something the Mexican producers put in to impress the gringos. But he ate it anyway. For Pera, who'd get a huge kick out of it. He'd hold up the bottle so that it caught the light of the sinking sun and made the worm look as though it were swimming in a pool of fire. Pera's eyes would widen to saucers as he tipped back the bottle and the worm floated down through the amber liquid to the narrow opening. He'd make a show of chewing it up slowly, nodding his head and swallowing it with an exaggerated gulp, then open his mouth wide and stick his tongue out to show her it was gone. Pera would roll onto her back and kick her legs in the air laughing while Mamá rocked back and forth next to Papá, the corners of her lips tugging upward in an amused smile as her floury fingers left cloudy traces on the glass of iced tea in her hand.

Papá told Pera that *el gusano* was imbued with magical powers and that whoever ate it would have the strength of a hundred men and the skill to charm even the most unattainable women.

Pera would stop laughing and sit up with a troubled look on her face. "You don't need that magic, Papá," she'd tell him. "You already have Mamá."

He'd pull her up onto his lap. "You're right, *gordita*. I already have Mamá, *la reina de mi corazón*. And you and your sister, *mis princesas*. No more worms for me."

Pera would frown at the thought of no more worms until Papá relented and promised to eat one again soon.

Those were happy times. But life is the trickiest of swindlers, dangling a coin in front of you with one hand and snatching your purse with the other. I was ten and Pera six when it stole our greatest treasure from us.

It was only Papá and I at the store that day. My cousin, Beto, was out making deliveries, and Mamá was at home with Pera, who was sick with a stomach bug. I sat behind the counter, half-heartedly restocking the small shelf beside the register with packets of Wrigley's chewing gum, wishing I were playing ball in the lot behind the school with my friends. To this day, even the slightest whiff of spearmint fills me with a paralyzing anxiety.

Papá stood on a ladder behind me whistling the new Everly Brothers song and gathering items to be delivered to Señora Lara that afternoon. He grew silent, and a burlap sack landed with a thud on the counter next to me. It fell open, spilling rice onto the white enamel scale. A strange gasping sound issued from Papá's lips. I jumped up from the stool and tried to hold him as he crumpled to the floor clutching his chest. He opened his mouth to speak, but nothing came out. His eyes stared into mine as he lay still. I shook him hard and screamed his name, but he was gone. Rice rained down on us from the counter above as I cradled his head in my lap, my tears dripping onto his forehead.

An eternity passed before the small bell above the door chimed again, signaling a customer.

We found out later. He'd had an undetected condition that caused his heart muscles to thicken. His heart had been growing and growing until it finally grew so big, it killed him.

When Papá died, a part of Mamá died with him. That night, Pera and I slept in the bed they shared, nestled on each side of her. She'd wake with a start from dreams of floating untethered into dark space, where a multitude of stars jabbed at her raw skin. We traced our fingernails up and down her arms soothingly and joined hands across her waist, enfolding her between us.

I always knew I'd never find a man who could measure up to Papá, so I never bothered looking for one. And that has suited me fine. But I worry about Pera.

I knew from the start that Carlos was no good for her, but my sister is cursed with the same flaw as countless other misguided women: a stubborn heart that won't let go of something gone bad. She calls it being loyal, but loyalty to the point of self sacrifice is plain stupid. A person has to be loyal to herself first, I tell her.

The older we get, the less she listens to me. God needs to have a word with her Himself. He's the only one she'll listen to.

It's not that Carlos hits her. He's never laid a hand on her, to my knowledge. It might sound strange, but in a way I'd prefer that. I could handle it. Somehow, that problem would be more clear-cut, easily labeled and dealt with. It would call for drastic measures, but there would be no mistaking that line in the sand.

I don't think Pera would stay if he put a hand to her. At least, I like to think she wouldn't, but who knows really? A woman in love can endure a multitude of sins.

No, Carlos doesn't beat her. It's worse than that. He knocks her down with words, makes her question her worth, her womanhood. And doubt has a voracious appetite. It's never full.

If only Papá were still here. If only he hadn't left us so soon. Maybe things would be different now. Maybe she wouldn't have been so desperate to fill the void he left. Maybe she would've steered clear of Carlos.

If only.

Maybe.

Three of the most futile and forlorn words ever spoken.

A full moon hangs above the tree line, keeping vigil like a matriarch, and bathes everything in its glow. It gleams off the smooth, round skin of the fruit. I breathe in the powerful aroma and reach into my shirt pocket for a cigarette, take another sip from my glass and blow smoke rings into the night. They start out strong and well-defined but quickly spread and dissipate like memories, the echoes of things gone by, leaving no trace that they ever existed at all.

Pilar

The best stall is the last one in a second floor restroom in the southwest corner of the school. It's tucked away at the end of a short hallway behind a row of lockers. This restroom has two advantages. One: it's next to the art classroom, and most people like art, so they don't ask for permission to use the restroom as often—unlike the restroom near the Health classroom, which is never empty. And two: it faces a small park. The stall door bisects the window, but there's still a decent view of the seesaw. You can watch little kids go up and down, imagine the sounds of their laughter. It's better than staring at a wall all lunch period, anyway.

A narrow ledge surrounds the building, and you could climb out onto it and shimmy down a drainpipe, if you had to. I'm not one to shimmy down anything, but it's nice to know the possibility of escape is there. It makes me feel better.

As usual, the restroom's empty. I scramble into the last stall beside the window and hang my backpack on the hook behind the door. Somebody's scratched some words into the ocher paint, and I lean in to get a closer look. It says, "Don't Look Down." So I don't. Instead, my eyes wander upward to rest on my backpack. I stare at the red canvas fabric and bite my lip. It's in there. I took it from the box hidden under my bed this morning and shoved it in the outer pocket. I can feel it pulsing like a heartbeat, its rectangular shape bulging through the thick cloth. I cross my arms in front of me and chew on my thumbnail.

I'm at a crossroads. The same one I've been at countless times, and I already know, as I did each time before, which path I will take. As if there were even a decision to be made, as if it hadn't already been made for me fifteen years ago when my parents created me, gave me the genes for my curly hair and brown eyes, but also the fat gene, the one that makes me a slave to chocolate. I stand there fooling myself for a few seconds more before finally surrendering, exhaling loudly as I slowly unzip the pocket. One bite. A small one. Not even a bite. A morsel. A nibble.

The king size candy bar rests pleasantly in my palm like Chinese medicine balls. I close my eyes and feel it's perfect weight in my hand. Inner peace. Inner peace. My stress level is already lessening. I tear off one end of the wrapper and sink my teeth into it. A celestial choir sings, "Hallelujah!" in my head. I'm not kidding. I take a bigger bite and feelings of relief and comfort wash over me. It's like putting balm on a burn. At this moment, my weight doesn't matter. School doesn't matter. Becca Barlowe doesn't matter. All that matters is the exquisite taste of chocolate.

This particular combination was a gift of mercy from God. He knew humanity would have to endure poverty, war, famine, disease, natural disasters, jeggings and reality television, so he created this chocolate-covered caramel to get us through life. God created this and saw that it was good. And He was pleased. Amen.

This is what drug addicts must feel like after they shoot up. I picture myself roaming the streets all shaky and wild-eyed, strung out for a fix and staggering into my version of a crack house: an old dilapidated building that was once a bakery, its split wooden sign hanging from a single hinge above the doorway. The Get Baked Bakery.

Scatterings of people lie around the grimy kitchen in various states of consciousness. A portly man leans against a counter beside a large oven. His eyes are closed, and his bald head hangs down as powdered sugar falls from his beard onto his grease-stained T-shirt. I step over him to a smudged metal counter, where I take a needle filled with Nutella from a bent up cookie sheet and slowly push it into my arm. My eyes roll to the back of my head, and I'm taken away, blissfully floating down a warm and creamy hazelnut river.

Before I know it, the entire candy bar is gone. I'm savoring the last bite, my eyes still shut tight, when I'm startled by a loud knock on the window next to me. I'm confused and don't know where I am. The walls close in on me, and I remember I'm in a toilet stall at school. Who in the world would be outside a second-story restroom? Nobody. It must be my guilty conscience playing tricks on me. I must really be losing it.

Then I hear it again. Someone is definitely knocking.

Pili

The next morning I pull up to Pera's house and smile to myself when I see the empty driveway. My plan worked. Pera opens the front door and looks bright eyed and more like her former self, BCV—Before Carlos Vásquez. I follow her into the kitchen, where she's been sorting through piles of clothes.

I pour myself a cup of coffee from the pot and open the box of *pan dulce* on the counter. "He home?" I say, nodding toward the hallway.

Pera lines up an impossibly small pair of socks and rolls them into a tiny ball. "He never came home last night. *No sé* where he slept, *pero* it wasn't here."

I open my mouth to speak, but she holds up a hand to stop me.

"I know what you're going to say, Pili. *Por favor,* I don't want to go through all of that right now."

I choose an ear-shaped pastry from the box and push it toward her on a napkin. "I wasn't going to say anything about it. I swear."

I hold my hands up next to my face, feigning innocence, then grab a *concha*. "Besides, I already knew he wasn't home. His truck's not in the driveway."

Sugary lines fan out on the round pastry like ridges on a seashell. I take a large bite, savoring the sweetness. I could eat this all day, every day. Man does not live on bread alone? I sure could.

"But really, I knew before that."

"How did you know?" She narrows her eyes at me and lowers the tiny shirt in her hand.

"Pili, what did you do?"

"Me? I did nothing. And nobody can prove anything. They can't convict me without a body."

Pera's eyebrows arch toward the ceiling and her eyes follow me as I get up to rinse my hands at the sink.

"Oh, relax. He's fine. He's sleeping it off in the parking lot of the bar. I drove by, and his truck's still there."

She stares at me in disbelief.

"Come on, Pera. Don't be mad. I wanted you to get a good night's sleep for once. And you did, didn't you?"

"*Sí,* but that's beside the point."

"No, Pera. That IS the point."

Her face softens, and I can tell she's not really angry. She picks up the shirt again and lines up the sleeves. "Spark plugs?"

I shake my head no. "Distributor cap."

She lifts her chin. "*Ah . . .* "

A grumbling engine pulls up outside, and Pera stiffens. Her hands fly to her belly instinctively, and a look of panic crosses her face. It's only there for a split second, but I catch it.

Carlos stumbles through the front door and falls forward onto the couch, his disheveled hair falling across his ruddy face. "I need a beer and some aspirin," he mumbles into the coarse plaid upholstery.

I grab the box with sweet bread from the counter and carry it into the living room. The sour smell of alcohol permeates the air, and I wave a hand in front of my nose. "Wow. Nobody light a match next to this man. We'll all go up in flames. You must've really tied one on last night."

He sits up and scratches the dark stubble on his cheek. There's a long stain down the front of his red western shirt. "Yeah. So?" He calls out to Pera, "Warm me up some of that *menudo* you made . . . add lots of lime."

"Geez, you don't have to be so grumpy. Here, have something to soak up the liquor. It'll help you feel better." I offer him a flaky pastry from the box.

When he reaches for it, I open my fingers and let it fall to the floor. "Shoot. Butter fingers. I've done it again. Made more mess for Pera to clean up."

With my hands on my hips, I look down at the small sprinkle of flakes and shake my head from side to side, putting everything into my performance. "Don't worry. I'll take care of it," I call over my shoulder as I head for the hallway closet.

Pera brings him the beer along with a few aspirin. He swallows them down with a swig from the bottle and leans back into the couch groaning, his arm flung across his forehead. I plug the vacuum into the wall and run it across the shaggy carpet. Back and forth, back and forth. Pushing and pulling, spinning a web of lines and swinging it around like Fred leading Ginger. I orbit the coffee table, paying particular attention to the area beside the couch, making sure to pick up every last crumb.

Carlos yells for me to stop, but I curve a hand around my ear and shrug my shoulders. He rolls his eyes, pushes himself up from the couch and staggers into the kitchen, where Pera is still folding clothes at the table. I shut off the vacuum and follow him.

"I thought I told you to give me some *menudo*."

"It was in the freezer. *Está congelado*. It's thawing out," Pera says quietly.

"What the hell is all this mess? It's a pigsty in here. What are you, a pig?"

"It's the baby's clothes. I'm getting them ready."

"The baby's clothes? What about my goddamn clothes? Baby's not even here yet. I am! What the hell am I supposed to wear to work tomorrow? Not even a single undershirt left in my drawer."

He pulls apart the faux pearl snaps running down the front of his shirt in one fluid motion, flings it off his shoulders and onto the pile of neatly folded clothes. "Wash this. Some idiot bumped into me last night and spilled beer all down the front."

I'm not sure how he can act like that stain is Pera's fault, but I'm not surprised. He blames her for everything. He even blamed her when he got a flat on the interstate, and she wasn't even with him. Since then, I've been extra careful that my tactics don't leave a trail.

I stand between them and snatch up the dirty shirt. "Don't yell at her, Carlos. It's not her fault. It's mine. I told her I'd help with the laundry."

I hold it out next to me like a matador enticing a bull and step through the kitchen doorway into the adjoining laundry room, where I throw it onto a basket full of colored clothes. My teeth dig into my bottom lip so hard, I taste blood. I pluck white clothes from a plastic hamper and toss them into the washing machine: ribbed undershirts with circular stains around the armpit holes, stiff, smelly tube socks and thinned yellowed briefs.

Carlos is still yelling on the other side of the wall. "Dammit, Pera! You're worthless. Can't you do one goddamn thing right?"

A Cool Whip container full of clothespins sits on top of the dryer. I think about grabbing one, puckering my lips and fastening it on. My head feels like a corked volcano. Any second the pressure is going to build up and blow it off. My hands are shaking. They shake as I grab the box of powdered detergent from the small shelf above the washer and pour it into the machine and onto the soiled clothes. I pretend it's dirt I'm throwing onto Carlos' grave. My hands shake as they reach for the bottle of bleach, then one trembling hand pauses midair in front of me. My eyes veer to the bright red shirt at the top of the pile. I leave the bleach where it is, and my hands have a will of their own. They speak the words my lips cannot. I watch as they lift the shirt from the basket and drop it in as well. My fingers drift to the selector knob and close around it, slowly turn the dial and set it to hot. Steam rises to the top of my head as scalding water rushes into the large drum and soaks the clothes.

My hands are still shaking. They have more to say. They ache to lead me back into the kitchen, to grip Pera by the shoulders and shake her loose from this life. To set her free.

Instead, I stretch my arms out in front of me and lay my palms flat against the wall as though I'm holding up a house of cards, trying to keep it from tumbling down on my sister.

Pilar

The knocking is growing more and more insistent. Whoever it is, is desperate to be let in. I stuff the empty wrapper into the front pocket of my jeans, open the stall door and hurry over to the window. There's a girl crouched down on the ledge outside, her knuckles white against the glass and her gnawed nails painted a sparkly blue. She cups her hands around the corners of her eyes to block out the sunlight as she peers in. When she sees me standing there, she breathes a sigh of relief and motions for me to unlock the window. I flip the lock and tug on the frame. It's heavy, but we manage to pull it open together.

A Union Jack backpack falls through the opening and lands at my feet. The words, "Girl Power," are scrawled in glittery letters across the outer pocket, and two large metal buttons are pinned to the flap. One says, "Save Ferris," and the other: "Mrs. Timberlake." Next, a leg in purple leggings and a cheetah print sneaker comes through, followed by another leg, a torso and the rest of a body until there's a whole person standing there.

She shakes out her short, dark hair, which is oddly wet, considering there's not a cloud in the sky. She lays a hand on her chest and says, "Thank God you were here. I thought I was going to have to crawl around to the other side. I'd have to pass Ms. Taylor's room, and her desk is right next to the window."

"Uh, no problem." I stare at her. It's rude, but I can't help it.

She mumbles something under her breath, hits the large silver button of a hand dryer mounted on the wall, bends over, and maneuvers her head under the blast of hot air.

"That window's usually not locked," she shouts over the noise. "See that park across the street? They're some townhouses on the other side with a decent-sized pool, and there's never anybody there at this time of day, so I have it all to myself. Sometimes you just have to get away, ya know?" She makes a strange gurgling sound in her throat.

I nod my head slightly, but the rest of my body won't move. I'm mesmerized. Like the good girl Sarah Jessica Parker plays in that '80s movie my mom likes from when she was a kid, *Girls Just Want to Have Fun*, when she meets the rule-breaker Helen Hunt, who helps her sneak out of choir practice.

When the dryer stops, she straightens up and takes a good look at me. "Holy shiitake," she says.

I brace myself.

"That shirt is spooky sick. Where'd you get it?"

I'm wearing one of Mom's old T-shirts that reads: "REALITY BITES." Mom used to wear clothes that were two sizes too big just to bug my father. This shirt fit her like a tent, so it fits me a tad snug.

"Thanks. It's my Mom's?" It comes out like a question.

"Man, you're so lucky you can borrow her stuff." A shadow crosses her face but disappears again quickly. "Most moms wear nothing but pastel polo shirts from L.L. Bean and pleated jeans. Not having it." She sticks her finger in her mouth like she's gagging herself. "My mom had a few dime things, but we got rid of most of her stuff a long time ago. At least I managed to keep her old backpack." She rummages inside it and pulls out a bottle of purple body splash. "Chlorine," she says, sniffing her forearm and dousing herself with the spray.

I stand there transfixed, not sure what to say next.

"I'm Sonny, by the way." She holds her hand out in front of her as if she's pushing something away. "And before you ask . . . yes, unfortunately, that is my real name. It's not a nickname." She clears her throat. "It's from *The Catcher in the Rye*."

"I know. I love that book. We're reading it in Mr. Novo's class now."

Her eyes roll up toward the ceiling like she's annoyed, and she whispers under her breath, but I manage to make out her words: "I love that book. I love that book. I love that book."

I'm not sure if she's talking to me or to herself, but I respond anyway. "Oh. Um. Cool."

Her shoulders sink, and a look of frustration clouds her face. "No, it's just that . . . I mean, yes, I do like it too, but . . . never mind."

"Okay."

"Anywho, you know Sonny? The girl who shows up in Holden Caulfield's hotel room? Yup, that's right. My mother named me after a prostitute."

I shrug. "I don't know. I think it's kind of neat being named after a literary character."

"Yeah, well, she said she chose Sonny because she's innocent or something." She rolls her eyes and pulls a hairbrush out of her backpack.

"Hmm. Interesting choice. I'm surprised she didn't go with Phoebe, though. She's really the innocent one. I mean, she's a little kid."

"I know, right? Me too. But she said Sonny was the more endearing character because she represents innocence lost or whatnot. Whatever." She turns around to face the mirror and runs the brush through her hair. "I wish she would've named me something normal, like Elizabeth or Jenny or even plain old Jane and called it a day. It's too bad she wasn't a bigger Austen fan. My older brother has it even worse. His name's Humbert, but we call him Bertie."

"Humbert? Isn't that the creepy guy from *Lolita?*"

She rolls her eyes again and nods her head.

I smile and wrinkle up my nose. "Yikes!"

"I know, but my mom preferred the flawed characters. She said they were way more interesting. And more honest."

"Is your mom a teacher?"

"No, she just liked to read. She was a hairdresser. She died when I was nine. The big C."

I think of Buela's sister, Tía Pili. I don't know what to say. Any words that come out of my mouth will be wrong, but I have to say something to fill the dead space. "That sucks." The words are meager and scrawny, but they're all I have to offer.

She clears her throat again and whispers to herself. "That sucks. That sucks. That sucks."

Is she mimicking me? Making fun of me? Or is she offended? I'm confused.

"Yeah, it happened a long time ago. And it's funny, but I feel like she's still with me sometimes. Like I'll be lying in bed listening to music or something, and I'll catch a whiff of her perfume. Or I'll try to remember her laugh, and her favorite song'll come on the radio. I know it sounds dumb, but I don't know . . . I can't explain it. She used to love dragonflies, and one year on my birthday, one landed right on my shoulder. That's happened a couple of times, actually." She turns away from the mirror and looks at me. "I'm not weirding you out, am I? Despite what everyone in this school seems to think, I'm not some crazy person who communes with the dead and wears necklaces made of chicken feet and hats with stuffed birds glued to them, I promise."

I laugh, and the sound is strange to my ears. I'm not used to hearing it in school. I realize that I haven't looked at my phone once in the last ten minutes. I'm enjoying this. It's nice having someone to talk to for a change, even if we are surrounded by toilets and rusty tampon machines. It makes me think of *Our Town*. Maybe Shane was right. Maybe Thornton Wilder was on to something: the dialogue IS more important than the setting. I picture Sonny and me sitting atop ladders on a bare stage, a spotlight trained on each of us.

I'm about to tell her that I don't think she's crazy, when she starts to say something else: "They also think that because of this other thing. See, I have this thing I do. I've had it since I was little, but it got worse after my mom died." She inhales deeply. "Sometimes I repeat things that other people say. I can't help it. It's called echolalia, and usually I can control it, but it gets worse when I'm stressed out or nervous. That's why I kind of keep to myself. I can't believe I'm telling you this."

Again, I'm not sure what to say, so I don't say anything. I listen.

"Nobody knows what causes it, but some things can aggravate it—certain foods and stuff. My dad used to keep a food journal so we could figure out what my triggers were. He would literally write down everything I ate until he detected a pattern. It's really bizarre having someone so focused on every single thing you put into your mouth."

Amen.

"It's like this one time when my cousin Riley and I were eating at T.G.I. Friday's in Austin, and the drummer from some band she loved sat down at the table next to us. Riley asked the waiter what he'd ordered so she could order the same thing. I mean, whatever, Riley's always been a bit of a cheese-ball, but seriously, who gives a crap what he eats? I was hoping he'd ordered something crazy like nachos with marshmallows and marinara sauce but all he got was a boring cheeseburger."

I laugh. "So what are your triggers? I mean, if you don't mind me asking."

"Oh no, that's okay. I'm not supposed to eat aspartame or high fructose corn syrup. But it's hard. That crap is in everything. That's not even the worst trigger, though. The thing I'm supposed to avoid like the plague is red food dye. And usually I do, but sometimes I can't resist and give in to temptation." Her eyebrows stretch up toward her hairline as she pulls a wad of Jolly Rancher wrappers from her pocket. "I love cherry candy. It's my absolute favorite, but it's also my kryptonite. And, of course, that would be the one I want. Not green apple or banana or grape. You always want what you can't have, I guess."

"Yeah, I totally get that, but for me most food is kryptonite," I say. "That reminds me of the movie, *The Village*, with Joaquin Phoenix. Have you seen it?"

"Yes! The one where the people are supposed to avoid anything red 'cause it's the bad color." She makes quotation signs in the air with her fingers when she says, the bad color. "I love Shyamalan. My favorite is *Signs*."

"Yeah, I like that one too. 'Swing away, Merril.'"

She laughs. "Those space aliens were intense but not too smart. Seriously, if you were an alien and water was your weakness, would you invade a planet whose surface is, like, seventy percent water? Whichever alien's job it was to research potential planets to harvest should have been fired!"

"I know! I thought the same exact thing."

She stops laughing. “Hey, thanks for not freaking out on me about my repeating things. It’s really decent of you. I think this stuff’s too crazy for most people to deal with.”

“It’s no big deal. Everyone probably has something different like that. People are good at hiding things.”

“Yeah. Anyway, it’s like I said. It’s usually not so bad.”

“Well, I don’t think you’re crazy at all. And what you were saying about your mom . . . about sensing her presence? I believe that too. I mean, there’s got to be more to life than this.” I sweep my arm outward.

“God, I sure hope so. If high school is the apex of my existence, life is going to really bite.” She bends down to shove her brush back into her backpack. “I just realized something. I’ve already talked your ear off, and I haven’t even asked your name. I’m usually not this obnoxious, I swear. You’re just easy to talk to.”

“You are too. I’m Pilar.”

“Thanks for helping me out. I really do appreciate it.”

“It was nothing. And thank you for . . . ” I hesitate because even though I’m positive she has given me something, I don’t know how to put it into words. “Thanks.”

Sonny smiles at me. “Thanks. Thanks. Thanks.” She says it unabashedly, in a loud, clear voice, the perfect cadence of her words echoing off the glossy white tiles around us, beating like iridescent wings.

Pili

"You win again!" shouts the man in the red and white striped vest standing at the carnival booth as he offers me a shabby teddy bear with a missing eye. He tips his straw hat and gestures toward a row of empty beer bottles lined up in front of me. "Now, let's see if you can win the pig."

I choose a bottle and let it fly, following its trajectory to the back of the tent, where Carlos' head pokes out from a hole in the center of a bright yellow curtain. It makes a loud thud as it hits him between the eyes.

"Ouch," he says, shaking his head. "I want a sandwich."

I pick up another bottle and hurl it with all of my might. This one also smacks him in the forehead with another satisfying thump. I'm enjoying this.

I grab another one, but this time look down at it before releasing it. There's a word written on it in bold white letters. "PLEASE." I launch it and choose another. This one says two words. "THANK YOU." I study the other bottles. There's something written on each of them. They start moving to the left, and I realize they're stretched across a long conveyor belt. My eyes dart from side to side like the eyes of the Kit Kat clock hanging in the kitchen, trying to read each bottle as it sails past me.

"Hurry, or you'll run out," the man warns as the belt picks up speed and sends bottles crashing to the ground at the end of the rubber track. I gather up as many as I can and fling them at Carlos, one after the other in quick succession, relishing the knocking sound each one makes as it connects with his head.

The digital clock on the bedside table reads 2:17 a.m. I'm wide awake now, but I still hear the knocking. I sit up and switch on the lamp next to me, rubbing the sleep from my eyes.

Someone is banging on the back door.

Pera.

I grab my robe from the foot of the bed, throw it around my shoulders and hurry down the hallway to unlock the door.

She waits on the narrow doorstep clutching her stomach with one hand and Papá's leather bag with the other. She drops it at my feet and leans on the doorframe, breathing heavily as the wind kicks up around her and sends her hair flying around her face.

"What's wrong? Is it the baby?" I scoop up her bag and help her inside.

"*Ay*, he's . . . coming . . . now," she says in between breaths.

"Now? But you're not due for a few weeks yet."

"Well, tell that . . . to him."

"Where's Carlos?"

"*¿Quién sabe?* Probably passed out somewhere." She winces in pain. "I couldn't wait any longer."

"How'd you get here?" I look around her for a car, but my Impala sits alone under the carport. "You walked all the way?"

"Five blocks isn't so far, Pili."

Soft pellets of rain tap the windowpane as Pera leans back into the couch cushions.

"It's a lot farther than that. You should've called. I would've come to get you."

She exhales loudly and squeezes her stomach.

"I have to get you to the hospital. Let me go throw something on." I turn toward the bedroom, but Pera grabs my arm and shuts her eyes tight.

"No, Pili. I don't want to go to the hospital," she says, opening her eyes again.

"What do you mean you don't want to go to the hospital? Why the hell not? You have to go."

"No, I want it to be different this time. I want to do things right. I need something more than a doctor with medical training." She wraps her arms around her belly. "I want Xochi."

I shake my head emphatically. "No damned way, Pera. Absolutely not. You need a real doctor."

"*Por favor*, Pili. I don't want to have my baby in some cold hospital room surrounded by strangers and sickness. I want to have him here in this house. It's safe here. This is our home. It's where we belong. Please."

I look at my sister and hear the resolve in her voice. She's finally asserting herself, fighting for what she wants—what I've always wanted her to do. I know I have to give in to her wishes, to listen to her words. I can't stifle her voice. Otherwise, I'm no better than Carlos.

"I don't know, Pera. Xochi? She must be a hundred years old by now. Are you sure?"

"*Sí*. I'm positive. I've thought about it for a long time. I didn't tell you before *porque* I knew you'd only try to talk me out of it. Besides . . . " She moans softly, then continues. "I won't make it to the hospital, and Xochi's a lot closer."

I cross my arms in front of me, contemplating the crossroads I'm at, but there's really nothing to consider. It's Pera's decision, and I have to let her make it.

"Trust me, Pili. I know this is the right thing to do. I can feel it. Call her, *por favor*."

Pilar

I know she's there even before I set eyes on her. The smell of onions, lime and red chili pepper hits me full force as soon as I walk through the door. *Menudo*. And something sweet, too. *Café con leche* and *pan dulce*. The aroma engulfs me like a warm blanket.

It's funny what a smell can do. I feel recharged and something like hopeful, like I've stepped outside of myself, and I can see things from a distance, that I'm part of a long line of something bigger, and I feel fortified by it.

A memory comes to me. It feels like mine, but it could be one Mom told me about. I'm in someone's arms being rocked on a porch somewhere. The sun is setting, and the porch must be on the east side of the house because it's entirely in shadow. The air is warm but there's a breeze, and a wind chime tinkles somewhere close by. I'm safe.

Sure enough, there on the living room rug next to a pair of beige square-heeled sandals is Buela's worn white leather bowling bag. Buela doesn't bowl, but she's had it forever. It belonged to my great-grandfather. She says it's sturdy and roomy enough to carry all of her things. Whenever she comes to visit, this is the bag to look for. It's the ultimate goodie bag, always full of fun and delicious treats, like playing cards, Mexican candy, notepads, crayons, old wigs, sour cherry lollipops and *lotería* game cards. It's partially unzipped. When I bend down to take a peek inside, I get a whiff of Canel's gum.

I resist the urge to dive into the bag and hurry to the kitchen, where Buela is standing at the counter, a housecoat over her polyester pants and pink, terry cloth slippers on her stocking feet, emptying a spoonful of vanilla into a bowl of something creamy. I barely have time to drop my backpack before she's at my side wrapping her arms around me. I close my eyes and let her softness envelop me. I breathe in her smell, a mixture of chamomile, Aqua Net and honey. She finally pulls back and cups my face in her dry, calloused hands.

"Pilar, let me look at you, *gordita*. Look how big you are. *¡Eres tan hermosa!* Here, sit down." She pulls out a chair from the table. "You must be tired after a long day of school. I'm making you some flan."

Buela's called me *gordita* ever since I can remember. It literally means 'little fat girl' in Spanish, but it's a term of endearment, like cutie. It's said with affection. You can be skinny and be called *gordita*. It doesn't hurt when Buela calls me that. I guess it's not only the words but who's saying them. Besides, she isn't calling me fat. It's not about my body at all. It's about how she feels about me. Her affection for me is fat. Her love for me is fat. Full, unconditional and all-encompassing.

I sink into the chair and kick off my shoes. "Where is everyone?"

"*Tu mamá* is still at work, and Shame took Luz to the park for a play's date, *o algo así*."

I stifle a laugh. "Play date, Buela. And his name is Shane. Not Shame."

"*Ay, sí*. Shame. Chain. *Es* the same thing," she says, cracking an egg into the bowl and holding up her index finger.

"Why is he at the park in the middle of the day, anyway? He should be the one at work, not your mother."

"Buela, Mom likes to work. She's happy to be out of the house. And Shane did work, but he got hurt. He gets a pension from the Army. Besides, he does a lot around here."

"Well, I still don't think it's right." She shakes her head and cracks another egg into the bowl. "The man should be the one to cook the bacon, *como dicen*."

I suppress another laugh and tell her how happy I am that she finally came to visit.

"I had to come. I had no choice." She cradles the bowl in one arm and stirs with the other. "La Virgen came to me in a dream and told me I should. Also, I know how pig-headed your mother is. I knew I would have to be the bendy one."

I'm not buying it, though. I know my grandmother, and she's as 'bendy' as a crowbar, but I let it slide and ask her how she got here instead.

"You remember *mi amiga*, Horti? Her son, Memo, gave me a ride. He's a nice boy, but not too smart," she says, dropping the spoon and pointing to her temple. "Six hours in the car listening to that crazy music. And the whole thing reeked of *mota*. I was half *pedo* by the time he dropped me off."

She pours the custard into a round baking pan, then covers it with a sheet of foil and sticks it in the oven. "It'll be ready in an hour. Here, have a *conchita* while you wait. They're from the best *panadería* in Laredo."

She chooses a round pastry from a blue, square box at the center of the table and places it on a napkin in front of me.

"No thanks, Buela."

"Go ahead and eat a little bit. I know you must be hungry."

She pushes it closer to me and sits down. But she's up again a few seconds later, opening and closing cabinets.

"Who organized this kitchen? I can't find anything. And who's been doing the shopping? No *tomatillos* or cilantro or a single *aguacate* in this house. We're going to have to go to the store later."

She fills a mug with milk, adds a splash of coffee from the pot on the counter and three heaping spoonfuls of sugar. The sweeter, the better. That's Buela's motto. She stirs it and sets it down in front of me before finally sitting down for good.

"Now tell me, *chiquita,*" she says, resting her chin in the palm of her hand. *"¿Comó has estado?* I want to know everything. How's school? You like your teachers?"

Sitting there with my grandmother, surrounded by the smells and tastes of family, I realize how hungry I've been.

Pili

Xochi steps over the threshold, gripping a knitted shawl under her chin and a bulky woven bag at her waist, just as the gentle tapping on the roof becomes a pounding. No one knows her actual age, but she's looked the same for as long as I can remember. It's hard to believe she was ever young, to imagine the cracked clay of her face smooth and guileless. Word is she's been delivering babies since she was thirteen. She delivered Papá and his sisters as well as me and Pera, all of us in this very house.

She lowers the shawl from her head onto her shoulders. Small beads of water glimmer like jewels in the edges of her snowy hair, which is pulled back in a bun at the nape of her neck. She looks so frail, I'm convinced this is a mistake. For the hundredth time, I'm tempted to call an ambulance or throw Pera into the backseat of my car, kicking and screaming if I have to, and race to the hospital.

Instead, I lead Xochi down the hallway to Papá and Mamá's bedroom, where Pera lies clutching the chenille bedspread and rolling from side to side like a boat adrift.

Xochi's thick nylon stockings make a shushing sound as she walks to Pera's side and rests a hand on her swollen belly.

"Oh yes, this little one is ready to come out. She wants to meet her mother," she says, her voice like honey over a grindstone.

The rain beats on the window like someone begging for admittance, and I pull the curtain aside to make sure there's no one there. A gash of lightning rips the dark sky, illuminating the heavily laden trees. Their branches sway in the wind, dropping some of their fruit.

"She?" Pera gasps, leaning up onto her elbows. *"Pero* it's supposed to be a boy."

"Well, supposed to be or not, this one's a girl."

Xochi drops her bulging bag on top of Mamá's cedar chest at the foot of the bed and stretches it wide open. Her arms delve inside shoulder-deep and withdraw items one by one.

"I've been bringing babies into this world a long time now, and I've never been wrong. Not once."

She pulls out two plaster statues from her bag and places one on each of the spindle-legged bedside tables. Niño Jesús de Praga stands erect at his post, despite the cumbersome crown on his small head, while San Antonio guards the opposite side with a book in his hand, his sandaled feet barely visible beneath his long, brown cassock.

Xochi lays a hand on Pera's forehead and orders me to fetch a teapot of boiling water from the kitchen. I'm not sure if it's something she needs or a ruse to get me out of the way. I step into the hall and watch from the doorway as she continues extracting items from her bag and arranging them around the room, moving with such purpose that my doubts begin to wane.

She grins at me as she dips a eucalyptus branch into a Tropicana juice bottle filled with a clear liquid, her pruney lips folding into the toothless crevice of her mouth. Pera squirms and flops onto her right side, and Xochi shakes the wet branch above her, turning the world inside out as water rains down onto the bedcover. She cuts a path around the room, rattling the fragrant branch in front of her like a spirit stick before depositing it on the windowsill.

When I return with the teapot, she's wiping down La Virgen de Guadalupe with the hem of her shawl. The statue is more than half her height and looks to be as old as she is. The paint is worn off on some of the folds of La Virgen's rose-colored dress, and there's a small gouge at the back of the base. Her mantle is lined in gold and dotted with stars, and sun rays flame out from her back, while an angel floats in a cloud beneath her feet, holding up her garments. Xochi positions the statue in the center of the thin lace cloth running the length of the dresser top opposite the bed, beside a framed photograph of Mamá and Papá taken the day they opened the store. They stand squinting into the sunlight with their arms around each other and the words, "Dolores Goods," painted on the stuccoed wall above them.

Xochi lights small votive candles on each side of the statue and slides her weathered hand down the blue veil. *"Mi virgencita."*

Pera's breathing has grown more labored, and her body coils up like a spring every few seconds. I stand beside the bed feeling useless and let her squeeze my hand. Her fingernails dig neat crescents into my palm, but I'm glad to share even a small portion of her pain. If only I could take on more of it. It comes in waves, building up steadily and crashing down on her with shortening intervals of reprieve.

It was the same with Mamá those excruciating last days. The cancer had eaten away at her once full figure, leaving little more than skin and bones. That's the way with life; it takes twice what it gives. She laid on this very bed, betrayed by her own body. It hurt her even to be touched. So Pera and I sat on each side of her with our quivering hands clasped behind our backs to keep them from doing the one thing they longed to do: cling tightly to her and never let go. My eyes met Pera's, and I knew she felt the weight of it too, that all the moments of our lives flowed into and out from that one.

The doctors tried to convince her that she'd be more comfortable in the hospital. We did too, but she insisted Papá would come for her here in the home they'd shared, and she wanted to be ready. And that's the way she went.

Xochi removes the lid from the teapot and sprinkles in herbs from a cluster of leather pouches: chamomile, spearmint and a few others I don't recognize. She pats my arm with her dried apple face full of sympathy.

"Don't worry. This is the usual way of things," she says, adding a few raisins and pouring the mixture into a cup.

The aroma of tea fills the room as Xochi brings it to Pera's lips. "Drink. It will help."

Pera takes a sip and buries her face in my side. When she looks up at me a moment later, her face is shiny with perspiration, and her fingers bore into my arm like she's holding on for dear life.

"*¡Ay*, help me, Pili!" she begs, and her plea is about more than the pain of childbirth.

Thunder cracks, and the room goes dark, the only light coming from the sporadic flashes outside the window and the flickering flames on the dresser. I ease Pera onto a stack of pillows and step into the darkened hallway. My fingertips brush the walls on each side as I feel my way toward the dining room in search of more candles. It's pitch black. Not even light from the streetlamps filters in. The storm must've knocked out the electricity on the entire block. I stumble around the long mahogany table with my hands stretched out in front of me, groping blindly to open the credenza. My hands rummage inside the cabinet until they land on a set of small metal rings, the handles of Mamá's brass candleholders. I light the melted-down stubs inside them and hurry back to Pera.

Pilar

I'm out of time. It's the last day to sign up for auditions, and I've made a decision. I'm going to do it. I'm going to write my name on this paper, even if it kills me. If I'm going down, I'm going down swinging.

I've been thinking about what Shane said about your passions being there for a reason, and he's right. What's the point of living if you're not doing what you love? You might as well throw in the towel and call it a day.

That's the thing about bullies. They're the curtain closers. They make you lose sight of what's real. Not only do they say cruel things, they make you believe them. Their words stick to your insides like napalm. They become a part of you, permeating your cells and binding themselves to your muscle fibers. Well, they can't have this, not my dream. I've given them too much already. I think of *Braveheart*: "They may take my life, but they will never take my freedom!"

The pen hovers near the sign-up sheet, and my mind wanders. I can see it clearly. Mom and Buela sit in the front row, their faces aglow with pride and their hands clasped together as they watch me give a brilliant performance. Everyone is in awe of my talent, and afterwards when I step forward to take a final bow, they jump to their feet unable to contain their excitement. Shane hands Mom a handkerchief from his pocket as her eyes well up with tears of joy. He claps and whistles and carries Luz to the foot of the stage, where she hands me a bouquet of flowers, like the colorful one in her picture.

It would make them so happy to see me on that stage. They'd be so proud. It would all be worth it to see them like that, to make them feel that. It's in my power to do it. I can create that moment. I can give it to them.

I slowly write my name on the paper, like a surgeon with a scalpel. It's like I'm cutting into my own skin, leaving bloody traces with each letter, like Harry Potter writing with that cursed pen, and whatever he scrawls on the paper gets etched into his skin.

I take a step back. It's done. My name in black ink. Pilar Sánchez.

Number sixty-four on the list. I stare at it trying to take it in, to fully realize what I've done. Then I scan the rest of the list to make sure her name's not there. It's not, thank God. Not that I thought it would be. Becca's not the school play type. She already has enough drama in her life as it is.

I cram the pen into the side pocket of my backpack and scurry away quickly before I can change my mind, making my way down the hallway to the auditorium. I take a peek in the rectangular window of the door at the back. It's empty, so I swing it open and step inside the cavernous room.

It's the exact opposite of a cubicle. Three long aisles lead up to the stage—on the right, the left and down the center. I follow the center aisle to the wide sweeping arc of the stage apron and gaze up into the dark rafters. I climb the side steps, drop my backpack in the corner near the curtain and walk slowly to the center of the gleaming floor. I lift my chin toward the row of lights above with my arms open wide and my palms facing upward like I'm offering myself as a vessel.

Jolts of electricity shoot down my spine into my arms and legs, fingers and toes, and my shoulders shudder as I scan the sea of empty seats. I'm limitless here, not confined by time or space, or my situation in life. I can be anything. Anywhere. At any time.

This is where I belong. The absolute certainty of it penetrates from deep within my core like a potent seed sprouting roots. They burst forth from me and pour out over the stage into the house, flowing down the aisles and between the rows of auditorium chairs. They become thick, strong and unyielding. I'm filled with gratitude for the gift of this knowledge. I slip off my flats and plant my feet firmly on the floor, run my toe along the small scratches and grooves in the wooden slats, imagine a story embedded in each furrow. They remind me of the scar on Shane's leg and the lines on Buela's face. So many stories, some tragic and some joyful, others simple and predictable. More likely, patchworks of all, but each one beautiful and worthy of the telling. I want to tell them all.

Buela is waiting for me at the front door when I get home from school.

She hands me the keys to Shane's truck. "I need to get some things from the store. *Vamos al* HEB."

"Buela, I only have my learner's permit. I can only drive if there's a licensed driver in the car with me."

"*Pues, ¿qué crees?* I am a licensed driver."

"You are? But I thought you didn't drive."

"I don't. But I have my license. Pili made me get it a long time ago. She said she wasn't always going to be around to take me everywhere and that I had to learn to do things for myself."

"Oh. Well, good for her. And good for you too." I swing open the driver's side door. "I guess it's okay, then."

"She made me learn in that big boat of a car of hers. I could barely see over the steering wheel. Took me forever just to back out of the driveway." Buela reaches back for her seatbelt and sets her handbag squarely on her lap. "Now, I'd give anything to sit in it with her one more time."

I adjust the side mirrors and turn to look at her. "Mom felt awful selling it. We really needed the money, though."

Buela waves her hand dismissively. *"No importa*. Pili wouldn't have minded. She was practical that way. It was only a car. It did its job."

❧❧❧

When I come to the grocery store with Mom, I want to grab everything within reach off the shelves. It's all I can do not to shove a bag of powdered donuts under my shirt and go scarf them down in the restroom. But with Buela, it's different. I don't feel that urge, for some reason. With Mom, I know better than to ask for cookies, chips or other junk food, but Buela lets me put whatever I want into the cart. It's like I said, I don't feel tempted when I'm with her. Not even when we pass the candy bins.

Buela slowly pushes the cart down the pasta aisle, her head swinging from side to side as she scans the shelves. "I need noodles to make *fideo*, but I don't see the kind I use. I don't think they have it." She grabs a box from the nearest shelf, lifts her chin and reads through her glasses.

"¿Qué es esto? Glutton free. *¿Qué quiere decir eso?"*

"Gluten free, Buela. Not glutton. A glutton is someone who eats a lot." Like me. "Gluten is a protein that's found in certain foods like bread and pasta. Some people can't eat it."

"*Ah sí,* Marta, the lady who lives in the apartment two doors down from me, the one with the breath like a dragon, *pobrecita*—her daughter, Beatriz, is like that. *No quiere comer nada.*" She sweeps her arms outward. "Marta says all she'll eat is diet soda and half an apple."

"I think that's something different. It's not that these people don't want to eat the food. They do. But they can't, or it'll make them sick."

She clutches the small, gold cross on her necklace. "*Pobrecitos. Pues,* it's no wonder they're not gluttons. They can't eat anything good."

"It's probably not so bad. I think there's a gluten-free version of most foods now. Even pizza."

A look of relief crosses Buela's face, and she kisses the cross, then lets it hang again. "*Gracias a Dios.*"

We head for the shortest checkout line, and Buela grabs a *National Enquirer* from a rack while we wait our turn. "*Mira,* someone saw *Diosito* in their French toast. See? There's a picture *y todo.*"

"Jesus? On French toast? Let me see that, Buela." I study the magazine over her shoulder. "Yeah, right. That picture's probably photoshopped. I mean, don't you think God has better things to do than hang out on someone's sticky breakfast plate? You can't believe everything you read, and definitely not what's in the tabloids."

"*Ay,* Pilar. You sound exactly like your mother. So quick to doubt everything. Why can't God show up on somebody's breakfast? He's God. He can do whatever he wants, appear wherever he wants. If I were Him, I'd use food to communicate with my people, too. The Ten Commandments would be singed onto tortillas. What better way? *Dígame.*" She slips the magazine back in the rack. "That's the trouble with people today. Nobody believes anything. First they say, 'I'll believe it when I see it,' but then when they do, they still don't believe it. They always want a scientific explanation for everything. Well, sometimes there is no explanation. Sometimes you have to believe."

I start placing items on the conveyor belt in order of food group while Buela goes to stand in front of the cashier and pulls her wallet out of her purse.

"Divine. I never heard that name before. I like it," she says.

I look up to see whom she's talking to.

The cashier goes to my school. His name is Devin Gillespie, and he's a junior.

The scanner beeps as he slides a jug of milk across it. "Thanks, but it's Devin."

He's on the baseball team, and he's quasi-popular. Not exactly in the inner circle of the most popular guys, but hanging around the periphery like a remora, one of those suckerfish that cling to whales and sharks and eat the dead skin and discarded food from their hosts.

Buela slides her debit card into the electronic reader and squints at the small screen. "This is too dark. *No puedo ver*. I can't see what it says."

I walk over to help her and push the buttons quickly, hoping he won't recognize me, but when I steal a look at him, our eyes meet.

"Hey, you go to Welch, don't you?"

"Yeah."

"Thought so. I go there too. I'm a junior."

"I know. You're on the baseball team, right?"

"Yeah, you play any sports?"

"No, I have this self-imposed rule to avoid anything that involves excessive sweating or playing with balls."

The words are out of my mouth before I can stop them. Playing with balls? My brain finally decides to communicate with my mouth and that's what comes out?!! I can feel the blood rushing to my face. It must be a brighter shade of red than the tomatoes he's bagging, but he just laughs. I study the tiers of gum to the left of the conveyor belt. I want to grab every single stick inside each and every pack, chew them all up and blow one massive bubble big enough for me to climb inside and float away.

I sneak another look at Devin.

He's still looking at me. "We have a game tomorrow at one. You should come."

"I don't know. I might have to babysit my little sister."

"Bring her too. Come on, where's your school spirit?"

Shoved at the bottom of a restroom stall at school with the ashy dregs of my self-esteem. "Okay. Maybe."

"Cool. See you then." He hands Buela her receipt.

I push the wobbly cart through the sliding doors and across the scorching pavement.

Buela rushes up beside me. "What's the hurry, *gordita*? Are we late for something?"

"No, no hurry. I don't want the ice cream to melt."

"He's cute," she says, suppressing a smile. "He likes you. I can tell."

I avoid her gaze and load the bags into the car. "I don't think so, Buela."

"I do. Why else would he ask you to go watch his game?"

I rack my brain but can't come up with a logical answer. There's no explanation, scientific or otherwise. It's a mystery. A miracle. The smell of cinnamon fills the air, and maple syrup drips from the tree branches. I smile in spite of myself as it gloops onto my chest, igniting a delicate yet dangerous ember of hope. And try as I might, there's no stifling it.

Pili

The flame reflects on the blue orb resting securely in Niño Jesús' left hand as I set a candle next to him on the nightstand. Xochi's fingertips probe Pera's belly, gently applying pressure, and her deep-set eyes shoot up at me from under furrowed brows.

I place the other candle beside San Antonio and mouth out the words to her so as not to alert Pera. "What's wrong?"

Pera sits up and tugs my arm. "Don't let her take him. Please, Pili. It's all my fault. I'll be better. I promise."

I wipe her face with a damp cloth and rub her back in a circular motion with the heel of my palm. "It's okay, Pera. Everything's going to be okay." The words are for my sake as much as for hers.

Xochi guides me away from the bed and toward the wall. Family members peer down at us from picture frames of various shapes and sizes, filling the space from the wainscoting to the crown molding like spectators in box seats. Most of the photographs are black and white, but a few are in color. The candles cast light onto some while leaving others in shadow.

"The baby is facing the wrong way. We have to get her to turn around," Xochi whispers.

My eyes dart from frame to frame as though there were a solution to be found in the maze of faces. They rest on a gilded one in the center of the others. It's a picture of Mamá and her four siblings taken when she was fourteen years old. She sits between her two older sisters and gazes directly at the camera while her brothers stand at her shoulders.

Mamá would be disappointed in me now. The thought makes my heart heavy. I've failed Pera again, and I've failed Mamá by failing her. I should've insisted that she go to the hospital. What was I thinking, letting her give birth here? How could I let this happen? I'll never forgive myself if anything happens to her or the baby. I can't let it. I won't.

I stride determinedly toward Xochi to tell her I'm calling an ambulance, but the words slide to the back of my throat when I see her pull something round and plastic from her bag. I rush to Pera's side, determined to shield her from this senile woman.

Pera lets out a deep groan and arches her back with her arms splayed out at her sides, like something out of *The Exorcist.* It's too late to take her to the hospital. Whatever's going to happen is going to play out here in this room. My only hope is Xochi.

I scramble back to her side at the foot of the bed, and my words come out shakily, "What the hell are you going to do with that?"

Xochi ignores me and walks around to the side of the bed, where she slides her arm behind Pera's back. "Help me get her on her hands and knees."

I scrutinize the faces of my relatives again, most of them long gone from this world, hoping they'll whisper down to me, tell me what to do, but they remain silent. I grab Pera by the arms and pull her up to a sitting position. She clings to my shoulders and pivots to face the rolling curves of the headboard. Her calloused feet push down on the firm mattress, and her dark hair falls around her face like a shroud. I tie it back.

Xochi pulls up the hem of Pera's dress and knots it above her waist. "Now, get down and lean forward on your elbows. That's it," she says, her voice now a taut rope. "Tuck your chin to your chest and stick your butt in the air."

As soon as Pera's in the proper position with her bare backside facing the dresser, Xochi hits the flashlight twice against the heel of her palm and switches it on. With more agility than she looks capable of, she hikes up her thick cambric skirt, climbs onto Mamá's wooden chest and stretches her arm between Pera's legs to prod around her belly.

I tug on the loose skin of Xochi's bicep. "What are you doing? How will this help?"

She reaches up between Pera's legs and presses the end of the flashlight against the top of Pera's stomach then slides it down slowly to rest on her pubic bone. "The baby will move toward the light," she says evenly.

I lean in closer to search her face for signs of madness. "But what if she doesn't? Then what?"

"She will."

"But how do you know she will?" I hear the squeaky note of panic in my voice.

"Because," she says, the flashlight, a beacon reflecting in her eyes like pinpricks at the bottom of two deep wells, "that's how we all start out."

Pilar

There are two things Buela will not miss, come hell or high water: Sunday Mass or her *telenovela, Ciudad de Amor y Cenizas. Town of Love and Ashes*. It's this cheesy soap opera about a small-town waitress who's ostracized after she has an affair with the mayor and gets pregnant with his baby. The entire show is about her exacting revenge on all the townspeople who've treated her badly. Actually, it's not so terrible.

Every day at five o'clock, Buela sits on a stool at the kitchen island with a cup of coffee in front of her, her eyes glued to the small television on the counter, and we all understand that she is not to be disturbed, that she is unavailable until the closing credits.

Mom came home from work early, so she and Buela are in the kitchen now watching it together while they make *empanadas*. Luz and I work on a puzzle at the table and listen as Buela fills Mom in on the backstory. Buela's been here a few weeks already and things have been going better than expected. They've kept the peace by treading lightly, avoiding certain topics, or rather Mom avoids them. Every time Buela brings up marriage or Confession, Mom changes the subject, and Buela frowns but lets her do it. They're both trying. And so far, so good, but I can't help thinking there's lava bubbling under the surface, waiting to erupt.

Buela rolls out small circles of dough and nods toward the screen. "See that lady with the big butt in the purple dress? It's all her fault. She's the one who told everyone about the affair. That's when all the *problemas* started."

Mom adds salt to the meat simmering on the stove. "*Espérate,* Mamá. Just whose side are you on? Because it sounds like you're siding with the woman who had the affair with the married man?"

"She didn't know he was married." Buela spoons beef into the circles of dough. "And even if she did, that other one shouldn't be telling her business to everybody. *Mugrosa nalgona*. You shouldn't fold other people's dirty laundry."

Mom rolls her eyes. "*Ay, por favor,* Mamá. Give me a break. Was she living under a rock? She didn't know the mayor was married? Let me guess . . . " She smacks her forehead with the palm of her hand. "She hit her head and got amnesia."

"No, that happened in the third season, and she only had it a little while. She didn't know he was married because she'd just moved to town. *Además,* he lied to her." She folds the dough over the meat and pinches the edges closed with her thumb and index finger. "*Cabrón*."

"I don't know, Mamá. It sounds like you're trying to justify her actions, making excuses for a sinful woman."

"We're all sinful. Every single one of us. Nobody's perfect. The only perfect people are Jesús *y su madre*." Buela makes the sign of the cross and kisses her thumb before dipping an *empanada* into the pot of hot oil. "And anyway, people in houses shouldn't throw glass, *como dicen*."

Mom hands her another *empanada*. "Not glass. Stones. How does it go? Let he who is without sin cast the first stone?"

Buela stares at her with eyes like an anime character and waves her hand in exasperation. "*Bueno*. Stones too. Nobody should throw anything, okay?" She removes the *empanada* from the pot and lays it on a brown paper bag to soak up the grease. "Anyway, she was in love. People do stupid things for love. But we're not supposed to judge." She brings the fingertips of her right hand together. "We're supposed to have *compasión*. *Empatía*."

I can practically hear Mom biting her tongue.

Shane's truck pulls up outside, and we all exchange looks. Luz and I push away from the table, our chairs scraping loudly against the floor, and race to the living room while Mom and Buela arrange the *empanadas* on a plate. Luz plops down on the edge of the ottoman and fans her rainbow-colored tutu out around her. I drape myself into a chair, crossing one leg over the other, and rest my elbow casually over the armrest, then think better of it and scramble to the window to look out at the backyard. The moment they walk into the room, I'll sweep around dramatically with one eyebrow arched way up, like a 1940s starlet. I picture myself in a flowing chiffon robe, a rhinestone clip in the smooth waves of my hair and a long cigarette holder resting languidly between my fingers. I catch a glimpse of my darkened reflection in the blank flat screen and shock myself out of my reverie. My blobby silhouette is crowned with a mass of unruly curls, and I hear Becca's voice calling me twat-head. I remove the elastic band from my wrist, twist it around my gathered hair and go stand next to Luz with my hands clasped behind my back.

I still can't believe we're going to have a boy living with us. Maybe he'll be the one I've been waiting for: Smart. Sensitive. Funny. Kind. With a penchant for full-figured women. We'll split bagels in the morning before school and become close friends. Fall deeply, madly in love. John Cusack holding up a stereo in

Say Anything . . . , Sylvester Stallone teaching Talia Shire to sing "do do do do" in *Rocky, The Notebook's* "If you're a bird, I'm a bird," kind of love. I'll teach him how to salsa, and we'll spend weekends cuddled up on the couch watching movies and holding hands under a blanket. And years from now, he'll escort me down the red carpet and chat with my publicist while I field questions about my pre-awards show rituals.

The front door opens, and Shane walks in with a large black duffel bag slung over his shoulder. A few steps behind him, walking slowly and looking around like a freshman caught in the senior hallway, is a wiry boy in gray jeans, checkered Vans and a sleeveless Austin City Limits Music Festival T-shirt. He has a backpack flung over his shoulder with paintbrushes sticking out of the side pocket, and his nose is big for his delicate face á la Adrien Brody, but his eyes, shaded by lashes so thick it looks as though he's wearing mascara, are the color of a jar of honey backlit by the sun.

This is not my love story. He is way too beautiful for me. Too cool. Too . . . everything.

Shane sets down the duffel bag as Mom and Buela come in from the kitchen carrying a pitcher of iced tea with at least a dozen limes floating at the top and a plate piled with enough *empanadas* to feed the whole neighborhood.

Shane lightly places a hand on the boy's shoulder. "Gabe, I'd like you to meet Mireya and her mother, Esperanza."

Mom sets the plate on the coffee table and gives him a hug. "It's so nice to meet you. Call me Miri. Or Rey, like your uncle, if you want." She leans in and kisses him on the cheek, then steps back. "Please make yourself at home. This is your house."

Gabe swings his sandy bangs away from his eyes, but they fall back into place when he looks down at his shoes and mutters, "Hi," with the hint of a smile on his face.

Shane introduces him to me and Luz, and Buela grabs the plate from the table and offers him an *empanada*. He refuses it at first, but she insists, so he takes one from the edge and nibbles on it. We stand around awkwardly while Shane chitchats about the drive from Dallas and how they made good time getting here. Gabe nods his head in agreement every so often. Finally, Mom and Buela go back to the kitchen to clean up. Shane hoists Gabe's bag over his shoulder again and heads down the hall toward Luz's room.

Gabe drops his backpack between his feet and lowers himself onto the couch, still holding the *empanada*. His movements are hypnotically graceful. It's like watching a swan glide through water.

"You don't have to eat that if you don't want to. My grandmother likes to give people food. It's kind of her thing."

He smiles at me and shakes his bangs off his forehead again. "That's okay. I don't mind."

Luz twirls around the coffee table then sits down next to him. "You get to sleep in my room. You can turn on my night-light if you get scared. It's okay if you do. It doesn't mean you're a baby."

"Thanks." He smiles and clears his throat.

Luz points to a strap of braided leather around his ankle. "I like your bracelet. Where'd you get it? I'm getting my ears pierced on my birthday."

"Thanks." He rubs a turquoise bead near the silver clasp. "It's supposed to be for healing and wisdom. Not so sure it works, though," he says with a shy chuckle. "I got it in California when I went to visit my dad."

"Oh, I know all about Calfornia," she says, pushing her hair out of her face in the exaggerated way kids do. "That's where they make movies. Pipi's gonna live there when she gets big."

My face feels like a rotisserie chicken under a heat lamp, but Gabe nods politely. "I've been on a couple of movie sets. My dad's a gaffer, so I go every summer."

"What's that?" Luz says, scratching her nose.

"The guy who's in charge of the lighting on set." His honey-glob eyes land on me, warming my skin. "You wanna be an actor?"

I shrug my shoulders and look to the side. "I don't know. Maybe."

"That's cool. Some of them are real douches, but I've met a few nice ones."

I'm dying to know what it's like being on a movie set, which ones he's been on and whom he's met, but I feel stupid asking.

Shane returns from Luz's room and rests his hands on his hips. "You're all set, Gabe. I hope you won't mind sleeping in a Dora the Explorer bed. I'm afraid Esperanza beat you to the guest room."

Gabe laughs, and a dimple appears on his left cheek and sends me right over the edge. "I don't mind. Thanks, Uncle Shane. For everything."

~~~

When I get back to my room after brushing my teeth, Buela is tucking Luz into bed. A row of shabby animals stretches across the mattress to my side. I climb in next to them, and Buela pulls the comforter up to my chin and kisses me on the forehead.

"Buela, me and Pipi are having a sleepover. You want to sleep here too? You can. You're invited."

"Thank you, *chiquita*, but that's okay. I won't fit. Besides, you and your sister can stay up late telling stories and sharing secrets about boys and things."
~~~

Luz covers her mouth with both hands and giggles. "Did you used to do that with your sister?"

Buela sits down at the foot of the bed. "*Sí*, Pili used to love to tell stories. Especially scary ones, like the one about La Llorona. She was good at it. I had a hard time falling asleep sometimes."

"Will you tell it to us?" Luz says.

"It's a story about a lady who cries a lot. I'll tell you the rest of it when you're older." Buela cups a hand around her mouth and pretends to whisper to Luz. "We don't want to scare your sister," she says, winking at me.

"Was Tía Pili scared of My Sharona too?"

Buela smiles. "La Llo-ro-na," she enunciates. "No, never. Pili was always a lot braver than me."

I pull my arms out from under the blanket and lace my fingers over my stomach. "You must really miss her, Buela."

"Every day. Some days more than others. But it's not like before. It's not a stabbing pain anymore." She lays a hand on her chest. "It's more of an ache, but with a promise in it."

"What kind of promise?" Luz says.

"A promise of more to come."

"Like a cliffhanger?" I say.

"*¿Qué es eso?*"

"It's a movie ending that leaves the audience in suspense and eager for the sequel. Like the end of a *Star Wars* movie."

Buela snaps her fingers. "*¡Eso!* Exactly. I'm waiting for the sequel."

"What do you miss about her the most?" Luz says.

"I miss her laugh and the way she would tug her lip when she was deep in thought, how she could never do anything halfway, and how nothing scared her." Buela sighs. "That was Pili."

"Don't be sad, Buela. She's in heaven now. She took her skin off, and it isn't dry and wrinkly anymore. It's new. And she gets to paint every day for as long as she wants. She doesn't have to stop to eat dinner or take a bath. And there are lots of colors and no spills. And God never runs out of pink or purple."

Buela smiles. "That's beautiful. Who taught you so much about heaven?"

"You did."

"I did?"

"Yes, you say it all the time. And the man in the dress at church said it, too."

"What man in a dress?"

"I think she means the priest," I say.

"Oh, Father Keeley?"

Luz shrugs. "He wasn't the only one. Everyone said it: 'Our Father who does art in heaven.'"

Buela stands up. "Oh, right. Of course. *Pues*, I'm sure Pili is having a wonderful time up there. She was always good at painting. *Buenas noches, mis princesas*." She blows us each a final kiss from the doorway and closes the door behind her.

We lay there in the dark listening to the muffled voices of Mom, Shane and Buela coming from the living room. I pick up the scruffy animal next to me and run my fingers over its tatty fur and its smooth, plastic eyes.

"Pipi?" Luz whispers.

"Yeah?"

"Don't tell anybody, but I'm going to marry Gabe."

Pili

The rain falls in heavy sheets, and the wind wails like La Llorona crying for her drowned children. I pull back the curtain to catch her gliding beneath the trees, her white gown shimmering in the moonlight, but there're only the branches swaying fiercely, bending toward the earth and back up toward the stars, like arms entreating heaven.

Pera lays on her back with her knees bent up to her shoulders, moaning. I wait as Xochi presses around her bulging belly for what seems like an eternity. Finally, she looks up at me, nods her head and smiles. I rest my forehead against the wall and let out the breath I hadn't realized I was holding.

Suddenly, Pera sits up and makes a sound the likes of which I've never heard before, a grunt with power behind it, not only loud, but opaque and elemental, like tectonic plates coming together.

I want to run away, fling open the window and let the wind carry me off to some remote island where nothing can touch me—no pain or loss, birth or death, save my own. But I can't run. Pera needs me. The piercing, dark eyes of a middle-aged woman bore into me from a plain square frame on the wall. I gaze back at my great-great-grandmother, willing her courage and strength into my own body, then I turn and face the bed again.

My sister lies like an open wound before La Virgen, who looks on from her cloudy perch atop the dresser. The waves of pain have finally broken free, and water gushes everywhere, soaking the blanket and bedsheets, and dripping over the sides of the bed. I'm afraid it will float Pera over the edge. I clutch her arm to hold her fast.

"I'm here." The words drop like anchors around the bed. I say them over and over because it's the only thing in the whole tenuous world that I'm sure of.

Xochi sits back on her heels at Pera's feet, candlelight radiating from behind her head like the beacon of a lighthouse. For once, I'm comforted by the furrows of her face and the history they embody, for her steadfastness and wisdom.

She pushes her sleeves above her elbows and looks up from between Pera's legs. "Okay, *niña*, now push."

My great-great-grandmother's eyes, along with those of the rest of our family, feel hot against my back. The room grows loud with their voices as they shout words of encouragement, urging Pera on, exhorting her to bring forth the new life within her and add another link to our ancestral chain.

Outside, the storm has subsided. A beam of light from the rising sun steals beneath the curtain and runs across the bed onto the wainscoting, where it stretches up to the array of pictures.

Deep lines fan out from Xochi's twinkling eyes. "That's it. Good. Her head is out. *Dios mío*, look at all of that hair."

Pera lifts forward, her face flushed from the strain of pushing. I climb onto the bed behind her and mold my body around hers. She falls back into my arms and murmurs breathlessly. "I can't, Pili. I'm tired."

"Yes, you can. Come on, Pera. You can do this."

"*Ya mero*. One more good push, and she'll be out," Xochi says.

La Virgen gazes at us dreamily from over Xochi's shoulder, the candles forming long shadows around her, up the walls and across the ceiling. I keep my eyes trained on her folded hands as the same three words stack up in my head like monolithic stones, one on top of the other. *Please help us*.

I thrust my chest into Pera's back and push her forward. She shuts her eyes and grits her teeth, bracing for impact. A final, drawn out groan issues from her very pores as though she were emptying herself completely, and she sinks back into my arms again, overcome with exhaustion.

Silence. Like a hesitation, an intake of breath or backdraft, the potent sliver of time when the first wisp of light grazes the darkness. The candle's flames stand motionless over their glistening pools of wax. Then, the rich, trembling notes of a cry, the frames quaking on the wall with each reverberation. *I'm here*.

Pilar

On Monday morning, Gabe and I walk to school together. He's a year ahead of me, so we won't be in any of the same classes. It's comforting knowing he'll be in the same building. It helps me not feel so alone.

We join the swarm of bodies bustling through the double doors. It's a lot easier walking into school with someone by your side. It's good to have a battle buddy, especially one who looks like Gabe, who has a casual coolness about him. The funny thing is, he doesn't even realize how gorgeous he is. Everyone else will, and maybe when people see us together, they'll think I'm not such a loser, after all. Maybe they'll think: There must be more to this girl than fat. We should probably hang out with her and get to know her. The best part is we have the same lunch period, so my restroom days are behind me.

Gabe and I make our way to the cafeteria, where everybody waits for the bell to ring before homeroom. My stomach is doing somersaults, and the potato and egg tacos Buela made us for breakfast are threatening to come back up. It's been great having her here, but she's not making it any easier to lose weight. The woman loves to cook. It makes her happy to feed us, and who am I to deny happiness to an old woman?

Starting a new school always sucks, especially if the year's more than halfway over, and all the cliques have already jelled. I'm nervous for Gabe. He had a rough time at his school in Dallas. He said it was one of those Athletes Are Gods type of schools, where everybody worships you if you wear a jockstrap and can throw a ball, even the faculty. I'm hoping things will be better for him here.

We stand, surveying the room, and something occurs to me that hadn't before, something that drags me down. Being seen with Gabe might help me, but it won't help him. If he's seen with me, he'll be guilty by association. I should stand aside and let him make his own way. I don't want to ruin his opportunity to make friends. I don't want my weight to drag him down to the land of the social pariah, too. It's not fair to him.

I'm Leonardo DiCaprio in *Titanic,* freezing in the water after the ship has sunk. And Gabe is Kate Winslet floating on the door. If I climb onto it with him, we'll both sink. I don't want to take him down with me. I should suck it up and stay in the water. Let him float away.

I wish I had a circle of friends to introduce him to, to make him feel welcome and included. I imagine us walking up to a table full of people and announcing, "Hey, everybody, this is Gabe," and everyone reaching out to shake his hand or pat him on the back as they make room for us to sit down. Unless I introduce him to the cafeteria ladies or the librarian, I've got *nada*. I'm failing him already, and it's even worse than standing by myself.

"Where do you usually sit?" he asks, scanning the room with his thumbs hooked to the straps of his backpack.

I'm too embarrassed to tell him that I usually wait outside the building until it's time for the bell to ring. "Oh, usually I flit about. You know, work the room. But if you want, you can sit over there." I point to the other side of the cafeteria. "That's where most of the juniors sit."

Gabe shrugs. "Nah, it's cool. I'll hang here with you, if that's okay."

I smile gratefully at him until I feel a hand grip my shoulder. I'm afraid to turn around to whatever fresh hell is waiting behind me. I turn slowly. It's Sonny. She's wearing a plaid skirt and a shirt that reads: "Frankie says Relax." The tips of her hair are dyed bright blue.

"Hey there," she says, nudging me with her elbow.

I've never been happier to see anyone in my life. I mentally breathe a sigh of relief and introduce her to Gabe.

"Welcome to the jungle," she says, then asks to see his schedule.

It turns out they have a few classes together, and Sonny gives him the lowdown on his teachers—which ones are nice, easy or hard. Out the corner of my eye, I spot Becca and Hailey walking toward us, like the shark in *Jaws* approaching the swimmers. Hailey's shirt is so tight, it looks like she's got corks stuffed inside her bra, and Becca's wearing a T-shirt with her initials monogrammed in a scrolling chevron pattern on the pocket: B.I.B. Wonder what the I stands for. Ingrid? Imelda? Irene? I know. Imogen. Her sweet, round-faced grandmother whom she's named after. How ironic.

"O.M.G.," Becca squeals, "This is too much. The fat-ass and the freak are friends? Fabulous."

"Wow, those are a lot of F-words. I am a little freakish, but it usually takes people a lot longer to figure that out," Gabe says, smiling.

Becca looks at him. "No, I was talking to . . . wait, what? You're not with them, are you?" She swings her long hair to one side of her head. "You're new here, huh?"

Gabe nods twice as he answers, "Yes and yes."

She leans in and touches his arm. "Let me give you a bit of advice. You do not want to hang out with these losers. Trust me. You'll be committing social suicide. Come and sit with us," she says, cocking her head to the side.

"Sit with us. Sit with us," Sonny mumbles to herself.

Becca hears this and thinks Sonny's challenging her. Her mouth drops open in shock. "Yeah, right. Who'd want to sit with you? It's super pathetic you have to beg someone to hang out with you."

Gabe's eyes veer from me to the other side of the cafeteria, the honey color of his eyes darkens to molasses and his brows furrow. Finally, he drops his backpack like he's staking a claim. "Thanks, but I'm good here."

Becca looks stunned but recovers quickly. "Suit yourself. If you'd rather sit with Chubbychanga, that's your business. But don't say I didn't warn you."

Sonny swallows hard and takes a step forward. "Look, it's been two minutes; time to update your Facebook status, and those comments about Justin Bieber's new haircut aren't going to tweet themselves."

"Whatever, Fucknut. I can't even . . . ," Becca says as she rolls her eyes and walks off with Hailey trailing after her.

Gabe gives his head a shake. "Wow. Did that really just happen, or am I on the set of some cheesy Disney movie? Is she for real?"

"Unfortunately, she is. That," Sonny says, "was Becca Barlowe. She's her own biggest fan. She thinks she's amazeballs just because her boyfriend's a senior, but he's totally using her. I wouldn't spit on her if she were on fire."

"Nice alliteration, though," Gabe says, picking up his backpack. "Double B's."

"Yeah, well there's another B word I'd like to add to the mix," Sonny says.

"And who's her friend?"

"That's Hailey Carson. She's not much better," I say.

The bell rings and the three of us leave the cafeteria together, Gabe on my right and Sonny on my left. Another thought occurs to me: Maybe you don't have to be brave all the time. Maybe sometimes all you need is the right armor.

But then, that scene from *Titanic* pops into my head again, still starring me and Gabe. Only he's not floating on the door, now he's climbing down to join me in the icy water.

Pili

I haven't felt like this since before Papá died. This new life is reviving something that has long been dormant inside of me, something like hope. I stare in absolute astonishment, completely captivated, as Xochi holds up the baby in her wrinkled hands and lays her on Pera's chest, the umbilical cord still connecting mother to child. The baby's chin-quivering cries simmer down as soon as her skin touches her mother's. She stretches and kicks her legs, while Pera's hands hover over her tiny back as though reluctant to make contact, afraid she'll disappear from beneath her fingertips like a desert mirage.

Xochi says it's important not to cut the cord too soon in order to ensure a strong bond between mother and child, that once cut, they won't ever be tangibly connected in the same way again. "There'll be enough letting go down the road. I always like to wait a little longer, especially when it's a mother and daughter. That relationship is fraught with push and pull. It's what happens when you pass so much of yourself onto someone else."

She wipes the baby with a clean towel and gently tugs on the twisted, gristly rope. "This is a good one. Nice and thick. See how long it is? It means a long and healthy life. I'll wrap it in a cloth, and you can bury it under one of the trees in the yard. That way she'll always be connected to her roots. Should she ever lose her way in life, she will always find her way back."

I untie Pera's nightgown from around her waist and undo the top buttons so that it's open at her chest. I dislodge myself from behind her back, and she leans back on the pillows with her hands now firmly on the baby, who extends and bends her limbs, adjusting to the vastly roomier world around her. I watch closely in a state of amazement as though my eyes cannot fully take her in, cannot fathom what they're seeing. It's like observing a beautiful alien life form. The edges of everything around me grow fuzzy and recede into the background. Nothing exists but her. She moves her head from side to side and whimpers softly, breathing heavily from her nose while her open mouth searches. She finally finds Pera's nipple and latches on, taking long drafts, her small jaw working.

Xochi ties two pieces of string a few inches apart on the cord and cuts the space between them. She holds the scissors away from the baby, but their glinting, metal jaw juxtaposed to the soft, delicate skin gives me an unsettled feeling at the pit of my stomach, and my own skin prickles with alertness. The room comes into full focus again, but more vividly. Everything appears clear and well-defined, outlined by halos of light, like in a drug-induced euphoria.

Pera's fingers trail after the baby as Xochi scoops her up to swaddle her in a fresh blanket, then hands her to me.

The moment she's in my arms, I feel a profound fullness, as though I've been an empty shell unknowingly walking around in a haze. The poignancy of the moment hits me full force, and a keen awareness blooms within me, a realization that seeks out and fills the hollow spaces: I'll always be holding this baby, through countless lifetimes in infinite somewheres.

Xochi tends to Pera, who's fallen asleep with her mouth hanging open, an arm draped across her stomach. I cradle the baby in my arms and take careful steps around the bed to the wall of pictures, where the eyes of our family peer down at us. I pause in front of a photo of Papá as a young boy standing in the yard beside his two older sisters. Tía Debi crosses her arms and scowls, her scabby knees visible beneath the hem of her dress and a bow hanging from her dark wavy hair like a drooping rose. Tía Monina hangs on to her older sister's arm smiling contentedly. Above it is the one of my great-great-grandmother, Elvira Rosa. She sits with her hands in her lap and stares into the camera with a look of defiance on her face. Her black hair is pinned on top of her head, but some curls hang over her high, lacy collar down to her pudgy jawline. By all accounts, she was one tough cookie and someone you wanted to have on your side. She saved her whole family once on a stagecoach voyage. Pera and I have been regaled by stories about Elvira Rosa all our lives.

I walk slowly from one end of the wall to the other, then over to the dresser to stand before the picture of Mamá and Papá. If only they were here now. I yearn for it so strongly, I feel as if the sheer intensity of my longing will make them materialize before me.

The room fills with morning light as Xochi draws the curtains back and blows out the candles on the bedside tables. She squeezes my shoulder as she passes.

I focus on the picture of my parents again, blinking back tears. "Here's your granddaughter. She has your thick hair, Papá, and your full lips, Mamá. I wish you could hold her."

Xochi holds the blanket down under the baby's chin to get a better look at her face. The sharp contrast between Xochi's dark, shriveled hand and my niece's smooth olive skin is like witnessing a convergence of the past with the present.

"You see it too, don't you?" Xochi says. "This one is marked. It's in her eyes. The strength of lions."

She chuckles and totters from one side of the bed to the other, removing the statues from each nightstand and wrapping them in towels before placing them into her bag. "When she wakes, give her a bit of chocolate to drink," she says, nodding toward Pera. "It will help her recover quicker." She pats my arm. "And maybe you should have some, too."

"All this must be old hat to you by now, but I could use something a bit stronger than chocolate."

Her pink tongue protrudes from her cavernous mouth like an unfurled rug as she laughs again. "Some parts, yes. But others you never get used to. It's always a brand new baby, a new life. So each time is the first. Each time is a miracle. You never get used to miracles. At least, I hope I never do."

She's right about that. It was a miracle. I'd witnessed it myself. One moment there were three of us in the room, and then suddenly four. A whole other person, a warm, solid weight in my arms.

The wheels of a delivery truck rattle down Palmas Drive, reminding me of what exists outside this room. All around us people are going through the motions of everyday life, waking up and getting dressed for work. Children gather schoolbooks and scarf down bowls of oatmeal in time to catch the bus while the landscape of the world has changed. It feels different, is different with this new life in it.

I sit down on Mamá's cedar chest and trace my finger along the perfect softness of the baby's even hairline. "Pera's daughter." I say the words out loud to let them sink in.

Xochi pulls the drawstrings of her herbal pouches taut before dropping them into her bag and turns to dip her fingers into the bowl of water on the dresser. "So what name will we be giving this new angel?"

"I don't know." I walk to Pera's side and nudge her leg. "Pera? What do you want to call her?"

Pera's eyelids open slightly, then droop back down as she mumbles sleepily. "*Mi rey*." My king.

"Mireya. *Perfecto*." Xochi makes the sign of the cross on the baby's forehead, then lifts her from my arms and lays her down next to Pera. "Now this little one needs some rest. I bet you could use some, too. I'll be by later to check on them," she says, wrapping her shawl around her shoulders.

I clutch her hand in both of mine. "Thank you, Xochi. Thank you. I don't know what I would've . . . " The words catch in my throat, and her face grows blurry.

She squeezes my hands and her eyes search mine, the rutted lines encircling them like tree rings. "Blessed are they who know they're blessed."

She lets go of my hand and plods to the doorway, where she turns back and takes a last look at Pera fast asleep on the bed. "She's going to be okay, you know. Everything balances out in the end, comes full circle."

The statue on the dresser catches my eye as she turns to go. "Xochi, wait. You're forgetting La Virgen."

"I didn't forget her. She's staying with Pera now."

Pilar

It's been great having Gabe here. He's not so shy anymore, and I get him talking about art or music, and he really opens up. He's an amazing artist too. His paintings are hauntingly beautiful, full of lonely figures and rich, dark colors. Sometimes it takes a moment to figure out what the subject is. It's like he zooms in on some small detail he wants to draw your attention to, to make you see what's right in front of you but in a different way. There's one he did that's the corner of someone's eye. You can just make out part of the iris and a couple of eyelashes. At first, I guessed it was an olive on a toothpick. It took me forever to figure that one out, but when I did, his whole face lit up. His waters definitely run deep.

"I'm Emily Webb, and you're George Gibbs, the boy next door. The one I end up marrying. This is the part where we're walking home from school together."

Luz jumps up and down. "Who can I be? I want to be somebody too."

"You can be the audience."

She grabs a cucumber slice from the plate on the table and drags a chair around to face us. "Should I clap when you're done?"

"Sure. If you think we did a good job."

Gabe tosses his script in the air. "I can't work like this. I need direction. What's my motivation?" He paces the floor with one hand on his hip and the other rubbing his temples. "These working conditions are inhumane. I thought I specified, the walls of my trailer should be lined with chinchilla fur, and I only drink water infused with the tears of a newborn unicorn." He throws his hands in the air. "That's it. I'm calling my agent. It's no wonder I had to spend the last four months in St. Bart's recovering from exhaustion."

I laugh. "You done?"

"Thought I'd show you the dark side of the business. Where fortune and fame can lead."

"Fortune. Fame. Chinchilla fur. Got it." My eyes fall to my script, and I clear my throat and read. "'I don't like the whole change that's come over you in the last year. I'm sorry if that hurts your feelings, but I've got to tell the truth and shame the devil.'"

"'A change? What do you mean?'" Gabe says, playing the part of George.

"'Well, up to a year ago I used to like you a lot. And I used to watch you as you did everything, because we'd been friends for so long, and then you began spending all your time at baseball and you never stopped to speak to anybody anymore. Not even to your own family you didn't and, George, it's a fact, you've got awful conceited and stuck-up, and all the girls say so. They may not say so to your face, but that's what they say about you behind your back, and it hurts me to hear them say it, but I've got to agree with them a little. I'm sorry if it hurts your feelings, but I can't be sorry I said it.'"

"'I'm glad you said it, Emily. I never thought that such a thing was happening to me. I guess it's hard for a fella not to have faults creep into his character.'"

"'I always expect a man to be perfect, and I think he should be.'"

"'Oh, I don't think it's possible to be perfect, Emily.'"

I flip through the script. "I think I've got this part down pat. Let's go back to page fifty-three. I'll start with Mrs. Gibb's line." I hold an invisible coffee cup in my hand and pretend to take a sip. "'Yes . . . people are meant to go through life two by two. T'aint natural to be lonesome.'"

"Hold up. I'm lost. Where're you reading from now?" Gabe says, scanning his script.

I lean over and point to the bottom of the page. "Here. You're Dr. Gibbs now, George's dad."

He gives me a thumbs up. "'Julia, do you know one of the things I was scared of when I married you?'"

Luz folds her arms over her chest and blows a curl away from her face.

I wave my hand in front of me. "'Oh, go along with you!'"

"'I was afraid we wouldn't have material for conversation more'n'd last us a few weeks.' Oh wait, it says we're supposed to laugh now."

We laugh, but it sounds forced. "That sucked. It sounds bogus. How do you fake a laugh?" I say.

Gabe lays the script face down on the table, grabs a slice of cucumber sprinkled with chili powder and dunks it into the lime juice pooled at the edge of the plate. "It's hard to fake euphoria. Try to think of something funny when you're up there auditioning."

Buela walks into the kitchen wearing the maroon dress she usually reserves for church. She studies her reflection in the stainless steel door of the refrigerator and lays a black, lacy veil over her teased out hair.

"'Let's skip to Act Three, page ninety. It's the part where Emily's in the graveyard, and all the other dead townspeople are warning her about going back to relive a moment of her life. I'll be her, and you read everyone else's lines. Start at Mrs. Soames."

Gabe flips through the booklet and nods his head when he finds the right page. "'Oh, Emily. It isn't wise. Really, it isn't,'" he says in a high-pitched voice. He's not trying to be funny. He's serious, and I love him for it.

"'But it's a thing I must know for myself. I'll choose a happy day, anyway.'"

"'No! At least, choose an unimportant day. Choose the least important day in your life. It will be important enough.'"

"'Then it can't be since I was married; or since the baby was born. I can choose a birthday at least, can't I? I choose my twelfth birthday.'"

Buela circles the island like a horse in a corral searching for an opening.

Gabe continues reading the part of the stage manager. "'All right. February 11th, 1899. A Tuesday—Do you want any special time of day?'"

"'Oh, I want the whole day,'" I say.

Buela paces from the counter to the table and back to the counter, her thick heels clacking on the tiled floor.

"'We'll begin at dawn. You remember it had been snowing for several days; but it had stopped the night before, and they had begun clearing the roads. The sun's coming up.'"

I gaze to my right. "'There's Main Street . . . Why, that's Mr. Morgan's drugstore before he changed it! . . . And there's the livery stable.'"

"'Yes, it's 1899. This is fourteen years ago.'"

"'Oh, that's the town I knew as a little girl.'" I point toward the stove. "'And, look, there's the old white fence that used to be around our house. Oh, I'd forgotten that! Oh, I love it so! Are they inside?'"

Buela circles back to the table and pulls a small, round compact from her purse.

I lower my script to my lap. "You need something, Buela?"

"No, no," she says distractedly, aiming the mirror toward the living room, where Mom is sitting on the couch leafing through a magazine and munching on an apple. She snaps the compact shut and slips it back into her bag. "I'm getting ready to go to church," she announces to no one in particular. "I'm going to Confession. Now, if anyone wants to join me . . . "

Luz turns her chair away from us and watches Buela click-clack into the living room, where she removes the veil from her head and pulls invisible lint from the lace, stealing side-long glances at Mom, whose eyes stay focused on her maga-zine.

Buela coughs, and Mom finally looks up. "Did you say some-thing, Mamá? Oh, look at you! All dolled up. You have a date or something?"

"*Ay, sí,* I have a date. Me and Mr. Phong from the dry cleaners are running away to the Riviera. I already packed my thong in my bag." She lays her veil on her head again and waves a hand above her head. "*Un* date. *Estás loca*, Mireya."

Mom shrugs and goes back to reading her magazine.

Gabe and I scoot our chairs to each side of Luz, and I grab the plate of cucumbers from the table and place them on her lap.

Buela hits her forehead with the palm of her hand. "I just thought of something. *Ya van a ser las cuatro*. It's getting late. The bus is going to be so crowded, and the last time the air conditioner wasn't working right. I almost got the heatstroke and passed out right there in the aisle."

Mom languidly turns a page and takes a bite of her apple.

"That's if I even make it to the bus stop. The cracks on the sidewalk hurt my bunions so bad, *es un milagro* I can even walk."

Buela frowns and sneaks another look at Mom. "Mireya, do you think you could drop me . . . "

"*No empieces*, Mamá," Mom says, shaking her head. "Don't start. I am not going to Confession. Read my lips. Not. Go. Ing."

Buela slouches onto the ottoman and slips off her shoe, massaging the balls of her feet with a grimace. "I'm not asking you to go. I was only asking for a ride. *Pero está bien*," she says, shoving it back on and straightening the straps of her purse. "Don't worry. I'll jus' walk. Maybe some gang members *que les gustan las viejas* will stop and give me a ride."

Mom props her feet on the coffee table and crosses her ankles. "Great. Hey, maybe you can convince them to go to Confession, too." She holds up her index finger. "Remember. It's not our place to judge."

Buela keeps fidgeting with her purse straps and points a finger at Mom. "*Bueno*, but don't feel bad when they force me to join their gang and make me work as their drug mule. They do that now, you know. *Vas a ver*. They've been snatching old ladies all up and down the border."

Mom rolls her eyes and lowers her magazine again. "Mamá, Houston is hundreds of miles from the border, and there aren't any gangs in this neighborhood."

Buela marches to the front door shaking her head. "No, no, I don't want you to feel bad if something happens to me. Remember all the good times. Like when I walked the five miles in the pouring rain to give birth to you. It hurt like crazy, and I almost got struck by lightning twice, but I was happy to do it because I love you," she says, closing the door behind her.

Mom half-heartedly flips through the pages of her magazine before finally tossing it aside. We swivel our chairs and scramble back toward the table as she stomps into the kitchen to grab her car keys from the small dish on the counter.

"*Ay, esa mujer*. She is going to drive me crazy. I mean it! I'm going to end up in the mental hospital trying to eat my own face!"

She shoots a look at me and shoves her purse under her armpit. "Pilar Elvira, consider yourself lucky you have a mother who is understanding and reasonable." She heads for the back door, muttering to herself. "And if she thinks I'm going in, she better think again. I'm going to wait for her in the car, and that's it," she says, slamming the door so hard, the dishes rattle inside the cabinets.

Pili

A baby changes things. Not only the obvious things, like the piles of diapers stacked across the dresser, the bottles drying on the kitchen counter or the smell of baby powder ground into the rug. It's more than that. The house feels transformed, like it's come alive again. As though some benevolent hand has placed defibrillating paddles on the curved clay tiles of the roof and hit the charge button. A renewed energy radiates from the walls.

I found our old crib tucked in a corner of the attic under a dusty sheet. It hadn't been used since Pera was a baby, but I wiped it down and set it up in Mamá and Papá's room, where Pera's been staying. She says she's not ready to go back to her house yet, where she'll have to divide her attention between Carlos and the baby.

I think she's scared to be on her own with Mireya, but I keep my thoughts to myself and let her be. I'm happy to have them here for as long as I can.

A hurricane is churning off the coast of California, and unprecedented flooding ravages Colorado. On the other side of the world, an earthquake in Uzbekistan buried people under landslides, many are still missing. Then an even more devastating earthquake happened in the Philippines. Over five thousand people perished then.

A woman's smooth, even voice delivers the news in a clear British accent, detached and unaffected. I imagine the words traveling from an unadorned desk in some stuffy windowless broadcasting studio thousands of miles across the ocean, down through the wires of the portable radio on the porch rail to my ears.

It seems there's been a rise in natural disasters lately. They don't graze off my skin the way they used to, but burrow down and set up camp, resurfacing in the quiet of night when I'm alone with my thoughts or drifting off to sleep. It's become a nightly ritual. My eyes pop open at odd hours, and I disentangle myself from the muddle of sheets to sit on the porch, where the tranquil sound of the rustling leaves are a sign of something true and unwavering that calms and reassures me.

The newswoman is good at her job—neutral and pragmatic—but her objectivity is unnerving. Some stories deserve the imbalance of a flustered tongue, words rising and falling like seesaws. The ahem of a throat clearing or a sniffle perhaps, some seemingly insignificant gesture revealing humanity.

I switch off the radio and stamp out my cigarette, stand up and stretch my legs. I've been thinking more and more about quitting, stubbing out my last butt like the man in the commercial who realizes his young son is mirroring his every move. I can't blame Carlos for everything, but he was the one who dared me to take that first drag years ago. It was all downhill from there.

I ease the door closed behind me and tiptoe down the hallway, grateful for the thick runner beneath my feet, which muffles my leaden footfalls. Pera's always teased me about my heavy step, says I walk like I've got chains looped around my ankles. When I pause to listen at her door, my ears catch the faint coos of the baby stirring between the soft shushing of Pera's snores. I slip through the door and over to the crib. Mireya looks up at me wide-eyed, pumping her fists in the air and jerking her little legs. I wrap the blanket around her and pick her up, brushing my lips on her silky tufts of hair.

We stroll from room to room, listening to the tick-tock of the cat-tail pendulum swinging in the kitchen and the creak of the floorboards as the house strains and shifts on its foundation.

I carry her into what used to be Pera's and my bedroom and tug the chain of the green banker's lamp on the mahogany desk. It's become a catch-all room, the odds and ends of various lifetimes stacked up against the walls. A house adapts. There's a box for every member of the family who's ever lived here. Boxes filled with Mamá's dresses and hats, Papá's books and his menagerie of whittled wooden figurines, Abuelita's quilts and haircombs, Abuelito's bowties and pocket watches, Tía Debi's baseball cards and stoles, and Tía Monina's prayer books and costume jewelry as well as a set of her false teeth.

Pera's and my things are boxed up now, too. The only displayed remnant of our childhood is a faded Beatles poster hanging behind the door. The heads of George, Ringo, John and Paul float against a black background beneath the words, "Do You Want to Know a Secret?"

I had let Pera choose the wallpaper. Pera's always had her head in the clouds, but I prefer to remain on firm ground. She wanted something bolder than the muted paper Debi and Monina had grown up with. So we covered it, their pale pink rosebuds blooming into large, psychedelic daisies bigger than Mireya's head.

I slide the curtain over to look out the window. Aside from a lone gray cat jumping onto the metal lid of a trash can on the curb, Rosario Street is deserted. I wonder if it's the same hoarding cat who hid the feathers Pera and I found beneath the house when we were kids. It couldn't be. He must be long gone by now, must have used up every one of his nine lives.

I sit in the swivel chair behind Papá's desk with Mireya tucked cozily in my arms and peel back the layers of memories, contemplating all the things a house must see. These four walls in particular witnessed two sets of sisters shed the supple skins of childhood to take on the tougher, fibrous ones of adulthood, growing together side by side, like parallel rivers coursing through life at the same steady pace, overlapping like the strands of a braid or drifting apart to rush and rage separately for a while, only to merge again into the same wide mouth.

Was there a symmetry in our stories and those of our aunts, events in our lives which echoed theirs? Did these battle-tested walls stand more securely upon their studs the second time around, the whispered sorrows and fears, hopes and dreams of two generations penetrating the sheets of paper to seep through the plaster into the bones of the house?

Did that first set of sisters play contentedly on opposite sides of the bed before meeting in the middle, the cowboys of the elder dismounting from their horses to join the youngers' raggedy dolls for a tea party?

Did they lie here on a lazy summer day with the smell of their mother's *pozole* wafting in from down the hall and mingling with that of the ripened grapefruit outside the window, their bare feet resting on the headboard as they counted each flower climbing the walls around them?

Did they huddle together in the corner beneath the window wrapped in their father's coat after a day amid the headstones, clutching the broken pieces of their lives?

Did a teenaged Monina run in from school with a blushing face, toss her books on the bed and clasp her older sister's hands in the exquisite throes of first love? Two years later, did Debi put out the light and turn away from what had been her sister's side of the bed to water those flowering walls with her silent tears?

Mireya stretches in my arms, and I fold the blanket around her legs again. I wish this room could be a witness for her as well. That she could grow up within its walls with someone by her side to navigate the obstacles of life, like her great-aunts, like her mother and I had.

She should.

Pilar

"Here, *gordita*. Have another pancake." Buela carries a platter full of them and flits around the table like a fairy godmother with a spatula wand. Mom shoots her a look as she drops two more onto my plate, but Buela ignores it and moves on to Gabe's plate. He tries to cover it with his hand, but she's too fast. Two more for him as well.

"Whoa, Esperanza! Pancake ninja! Those are some quick reflexes." He waves his hands in the air like blades. "Hwah! You ever play Xbox? You'd be an excellent gamer."

Buela smiles at Gabe and leans over to whisper into Mom's ear. "*¿Qué?*" She straightens up and looks at Gabe again, who's taking the butter dish from Luz. "You can call me Pera. Or Buela, *si quieres*."

She's about to toss a pancake onto Mom's plate, but Mom sweeps it out of the way. "*No, gracias*, Mamá. Just toast for me."

Buela shakes her head. "*Ay*, Mireya. You don't eat enough. *Te vas a desaparecer.* You're going to waste away to nothing. One stiff breeze blows, and you'll be up and away. We'll have to go pick you up in Canada. At least let me put some *cajeta* on that toast," she says, grabbing the jar of caramelized goat's milk from the counter.

"I'm fine, Mamá." Mom rolls her eyes and takes a sip of coffee.

"I want to go to Canada. Can I come too?" Luz says.

Gabe pushes his spiral notebook toward Shane. "You mind taking a look at this, Uncle Shane? We're supposed to find the roots, but I'm not sure I did it right."

"Quadratic equations, huh? *Oy vey*. Let's take a look . . . Yup . . . M-hm . . . x equals negative four and two. Looks right to me. Good job."

"Thanks. We have a unit test in a few weeks that'll count for a big chunk of our grade," Gabe says, spearing a bite of pancake and soaking it in a puddle of syrup.

Buela steps around Shane's chair and flings a pancake loaded with chocolate chips onto Luz's plate. Luz grabs the syrup bottle and squeezes a steady stream before Mom snatches it from her hand. "That's enough, *m'ijita*."

"I'll take a couple more too, please," Shane says, holding up a finger like a weathervane.

Buela rolls her eyes, then backs up and lobs a small thin one onto his lifted plate.

"Thank you. These are really good, Esperanza. What's your secret?"

"No secret. Some things take a woman's touch."

"Well, they're delicious. Much better than mine."

Shane's right. Buela's pancakes are the best. She says the secret is to leave the batter in the fridge overnight. That makes it extra thick, and the pancakes come out fluffier. Also, she adds lots of melted butter and an extra tablespoon of vanilla. I usually polish off a stack of them in no time, but today I can barely finish one. That's saying something, because most of the time, I have no problem eating when I'm feeling anxious. But this is a new level of emotion. This really matters.

Shane spreads butter in between the layers of his short stack and glances at me. "So, you ready to kick some butt today?"

Mom looks up from her anatomy book and smacks her forehead. "That's right! Your audition is today. You're going to do great, so don't be nervous," she says, biting her thumb. "But even if you don't get a part, you're still good. So don't be disappointed."

Buela brings a plate of bacon to the table and doles out three strips each to everyone. "*Qué* nervous *ni que nada*. What's there to be nervous about? Acting is in her blood. Your second cousin, María, is an actress, remember?"

"She is not an actress, Mamá. She works on a cruise ship."

"I know she works on a cruise ship, Miss High Almighty. She's on the stage every night. Your tía Lupita sent me a picture."

"It's not the same thing. She doesn't act. She dances around waving big feathers. She doesn't even have to say anything."

"It is too the same thing. You think she goes to the Walmart in a sparkly bra and satin gloves? No. It's an act. She's acting!"

"It is not. Is it, *amor*?" Mom says, batting her eyes at Shane.

He holds his palms up. "No way. I'm Switzerland. Leave me out of this."

"Okay, fine, Mamá. She's an actor. Whatever you say. There's no use arguing with you. I don't know why I bother. You're always right, no matter what."

Buela nods her head and folds her arms.

Mom turns her attention back to me. "If you get nervous, just do what I do whenever I have to give a presentation in front of the class. Take a deep breath and picture everyone in their underwear."

Buela shakes her head. "I don't know why people say that. That's terrible advice. I tried that once, and it was horrible." She sets the platter down on the table and sits down. "I was in school at Holy Cross, and I had to give a speech on Santa Mónica, my Confirmation saint. I was so nervous, I didn't even want to get up that day. I pulled the covers over my head and told Pili to tell Mamá I was sick, but she wouldn't. Instead, she threw the covers off and dragged me out of bed." She pours herself a small glass of orange juice and takes a sip. "We met up with our cousin, Beto, on the way to school, and he gave me that same advice. When it was my turn to speak, my hands were shaking so bad, I couldn't make out the words on the paper. They looked like a bunch of squiggly lines. So I followed Beto's advice, and it did help at first, but then I made the mistake of looking over at Padre Francisco sitting at his desk. I got so distracted picturing his big stomach hanging over his white *calzones*, I froze. I opened my mouth, but no words came out. I had to say a quick prayer to San Antonio to help me find my voice."

"That's why you're not supposed to have food in the classroom," Luz says.

Buela wrinkles her forehead. "What food? I didn't have any food."

"Not you, Buela. Father San Francisco. You said his belly was hanging over his *calzones*."

Buela laughs. "Not Italian calzones. Spanish *calzones*. Underwear."

"Oh," Luz says.

Buela puts her arm around my shoulder. "But you're not scared are you, *gordita*?"

"Maybe a little."

Mom squeezes my hand. "Listen, *m'ija*. It's okay to be scared. I was scared when we left Laredo to come to Houston.

I'd never been on my own before, and I had you to take care of, too. I wanted something better for us. I knew you deserved that. I did too. So as scary as that step was, I took it. And I learned there's a good kind of scared. It means the universe is beckoning, letting you know you're on the verge of something."

Mom was scared when we left. I could tell. She may be willing to admit it now but back then, she tried to hide it. I closed my eyes and tried to ignore the jittery feeling at the pit of my stomach as she slowly pulled away from the curb of our old house.

I remember I slid down in my seat and propped my knees on the glove compartment. The beefy smell of Buela's *empanadas* wafted up from the basket between us on the old convertible's big front bench.

"Don't look so worried," Mom said that day, glancing at me from the corner of her eye. "Everything's going to be okay. Better than okay. Think of this as an adventure. Like that movie. What's it called?" She snapped her fingers. "You know, the one with the two women on the run?"

"*Thelma and Louise*," I said, laying my head on the basket.

"*Ah sí, ésa es*. Think of this like that. Pretend we're them. Two friends on a road trip. It'll be great. You'll see."

I lifted my head and looked at her. "You know they die at the end, right?"

I pictured us meeting the same fate, the Impala shooting over a cliff, shrunk down to Matchbox size against the backdrop of sweeping canyon walls, and Buela's basket flying over the windshield, *empanadas* falling through the air. That hadn't happened to us, thank God. But I'd felt like it might. I have the same uneasy feeling now.

"Yeah. Be scared. You can do it, Pipi," Luz says. "I'm crossing my fingers. And my toes."

"Me too," Gabe says, dropping his fork and crossing his fingers as well.

Mom and Shane do the same. "Us too," says Shane. "We're all rooting for you."

Luz tugs on Buela's elbow. "Buela, cross yours too. That way Pipi will have extra, extra gooder luck."

"Me too," Buela says, touching the fingertips of her right hand to her forehead before bringing them down to her chest, then to her left and right shoulders. "But it's got nothing to do with luck."

Pili

"Get your things, Pera. It's time to come home. It's been almost three months already. Vacation time is over."

Carlos snatches Papá's leather bag from the top of the closet and lobs it onto the bed. He pulls clothes out of the dresser drawers and stuffs them inside. Pera watches from the doorway with Mireya in her arms as he shakes the pillowcase loose from a bed pillow and takes it over to the dresser, where the baby's things are neatly arranged next to La Virgen. In one sweeping motion, his arm sends stacks of diapers and bottles of powder and lotion falling into the makeshift sack. A container of disposable wipes falls to the floor and pops open. Pera hands me the baby and kneels to scoop the damp cloths back into the rectangular box.

I gently sway Mireya in my arms. "What's the rush? Don't you even want to hold your daughter?"

He grabs the bag from the bed and nudges past me. "Let Pera hold her. She's the one who needs the practice. And what's with the blue blanket? Blue is for boys, and pink is for girls. Jesus, everybody knows that. You keep putting her in blue like that, she's gonna end up all mixed up and confused, like one of those girls with the buzzed haircuts who hang around the pool hall. You want that?"

Pera takes Mireya from my arms and follows Carlos down the hallway. I lift the statue of La Virgen, wipe the dust from her veil with my sleeve and follow them to the door. "Blue's a color like any other. I suppose if we dressed her in black and white, she'd grow up thinking she's a zebra?"

He drops Pera's bag by the back door. "Go ahead and make jokes. I bet you wore your fair share of blue when you were a kid."

"I wore lots of colors, and I'm not confused at all. No, I can see things very clearly."

I stare him down.

He turns to Pera and points a finger at her. "And don't you go getting ideas like some women. They think once there's a baby in the picture, they can forget all about the husband. Well, I'm the one who puts food on the table and a roof over your head, and don't you forget it." He nods toward the baby. "Besides, you want to set a good example for her, don't you?" Pera turns away and pulls the blanket higher over the back of Mireya's head, shielding her.

Seeing my sister with a baby in her arms feels right, like equilibrium has been restored. I wasn't sure she'd ever recover from the loss of Carlitos, but over the past few weeks I've watched her open up again. Like a shriveled plant sprouting new leaves. I should've known better, had more faith in the resilience and generosity of her heart, in its capacity to find its way back.

Carlos crosses his arms in front of his chest and snorts. "You don't know how good you have it, Esperanza. You're lucky I'm such a tolerant man. No one else would've let you stay gone so long. You should be grateful."

"Yeah, I'm sure you drenched your pillow every night with tears of loneliness," I say.

"Stay out of it, Pili," he says.

"I will not. This is my house, and no one shuts me up in my own house. Anyway, you're the one who should be grateful. These past months should've made you realize all the things my sister does for you. I'm surprised you survived so long without her."

"Of course, she does things for me. That's what she's supposed to do. She's my wife, isn't she?"

"Unfortunately."

"The problem is I've been too easy on her, given her too much leeway. She's gotten downright spoiled. But things are going to change."

Pera looks down at Mireya nestled in her arms and sighs deeply.

I want to throw myself across the threshold and bar the door, do something to stop them from leaving, dig a moat around the house and push Carlos into it, then pull up the drawbridge and keep them safe inside.

But I can't. It's different now. Now, there're two people to protect instead of one. The only thing I can do is try to make it easier for them by kneeling at the inflated altar of the machismo gods and appeasing Carlos.

I sit at the table with La Virgen in my lap and look up at him. "It's not Pera's fault she stayed so long. She was ready to go weeks ago, but I convinced her to stay. Besides, newborns are up at all hours crying to be fed. She didn't want all that fussing to bother you. As usual, she was only thinking of you. She knows how important your sleep is." The words coat my tongue like bile.

"Well, I'm sure you've been filling her head with all kinds of crazy notions, but I'm her husband. She belongs with me."

He bends over to pick up the bag, and his underwear, tinted pink from my stint with the laundry, peeks out from above the waistband of his jeans. "Come on, Pera. Let's go."

I follow them outside to the driveway, hugging La Virgen to my chest. “Carlos?” He tosses the bag into the bed of the truck and flings open the driver’s side door. “Yeah? What?”

A breeze rushes through the trees, shaking grapefruits loose from their branches and sending them rolling across the yard. The wind chimes softly jingle outside the kitchen window, and I picture the morning sun filtering through the shards of stained glass, the array of colors splayed across the tiled floor.

I elbow past him to place the statue on the lowered armrest at the center of the torn vinyl seat, then straighten up to look him in the eye. “This was the first place on earth she ever belonged. She still does. In ways you’ll never understand. This was her home long before you came along.”

I turn to face Pera. She gazes at me from the other side of the truck, Mireya asleep in her arms. My eyes lock onto hers. “And it always will be.”

Carlos snorts again and hops into the driver’s seat. Pera stands there a moment longer before opening the passenger door and sliding in. The truck rumbles to life and peels away from the curb. I watch them through the rear window as they drive to the end of the street, La Virgen’s blue veil rising up between them like an impenetrable mountain.

Pilar

The last bell of the day rings like a death knell at two-thirty sharp, the minute hand shooting straight down like an arrow directing me to hell. I shut my math book and squeeze out of my chair, sling my backpack over my shoulders and head for the auditorium. I'm Sean Penn shuffling down the prison corridor on my way to be lethally injected in *Dead Man Walking*, cotton slippers on my shackled feet.

The vending machine catches my eye as I pass the cafeteria, and my body draws in on itself. My arms and legs retract into my shrunken torso until I'm small enough to climb through the narrow slot at the bottom. I jump onto a shiny metal coil and make my way across a row of candy bars, swinging from spiral to spiral like a hypoglycemic Tarzan. I eat my way through columns of Kit Kats, Reese's Peanut Butter Cups, Butterfingers, Baby Ruths, Hershey bars, M&Ms, Milky Ways, Snickers and Twix bars, then climb up to the next few rows, where I devour bags of Doritos, Ruffles Potato Chips, Funions and Fritos. Then, on to the next and the next. I polish off corn nuts, snack cakes, cream-filled cookies and moon pies, growing bigger and bigger as I make my way up. By the time I reach the last row at the top, I'm back to my normal size, the crown of my head pushing against the hard steel plate above. I swallow the last bite of Oatmeal Creme Pie and realize I'm stuck. My neck bends awkwardly toward my right shoulder, and my feet are buried in discarded wrappers, the toes of each foot facing opposite sides of the machine. My cheeks and stomach press against the glass, and the empty metal rings dig into my spine and the backs of my legs.

I shake my head like I'm erasing an image from Luz's Etch-A-Sketch and continue down the hall. I've got to focus. Maybe if I get there before everyone else, I won't be so nervous. As if arriving first will make a difference. The first person in line to jump from a burning building probably doesn't feel any better because he's first, but I quicken my pace anyway.

The audition will be a cold reading, so I won't know which part Mr. Leal will ask me to read beforehand. It doesn't matter, anyway. I've been using every waking moment of the last few weeks to study the script. Every line is seared into my brain like ranch symbols branded onto cattle.

A door at the end of the drama hallway opens to the right wing of the stage. Jessica Holley and Tara Simonton, seniors who've been in every single production since their freshman year, are already there running lines together. They're so focused on what they're doing, they barely look my way, which is fine by me.

I plop myself down on the floor beside the wall and remove the furled copy of *Our Town* from my backpack. The red letters of an exit sign glare at me from above a doorway. I ignore their emphatic suggestion and skim the pages for the millionth time. By the time I get to Act Two, the wings of the stage are filled with people waiting to audition. Some practice lines together, others read silently to themselves and a few don't look at scripts at all, but lean on their backpacks texting or listening to their phones.

The door opens promptly at three o'clock, and Mr. Leal strides in wearing jeans, a lime green Oxford shirt and a red tie. He takes a clipboard from under his arm and scans the sea of faces. "Okay, people, gather 'round. Come closer. Don't be shy. This is how we'll proceed. There are eighty-five names on this list and twenty-two parts. So do the math. Not everyone will get a part, and I don't do understudies. It might seem harsh, but if you want to act, rejection is part of the game. So you better get used to it. If you do earn a part, you need to commit to it. That means being here every day after school for rehearsals from three to six. No excuses. It means performing all three shows with a concussion, a broken leg or a 105 degree fever, if need be. If any of that is going to be an issue for anyone, you might as well leave now."

He peers at us over his thick-rimmed glasses. The dark and light browns mingled on the tortoise frames remind me of my favorite candy combo, chocolate and caramel. I take it as a good omen. "Anyone? Okay, good. Let's get started then. When I call your name, you will stand center stage with your script in hand. I'll tell you where to begin, and you will read until I say, stop. Brynn here, will read with you." He gestures toward a tall girl with a severe black bob and an even row of bangs across her forehead like Cleopatra. "Any questions? Let's get started then," he calls over his shoulder as he trots down the side steps.

Mr. Leal takes a seat in the fifth row and lowers the clipboard to his lap. "Tara Simonton."

Tara gives Jessica a high-five and strides confidently to the center of the stage. She reads the part of Rebecca, George's younger sister, in a loud, clear voice. "'I never told you about that letter Jane Crofut got from her minister, when she was sick.'"

My eyes rest evenly on my script as her voice rises and dips like a roller coaster cart.

"'He wrote Jane a letter and on the envelope the address was like this: It said: Jane Crofut; The Crofut Farm; Grover's Corners; Sutton County; New Hampshire; United States of America.'"

"'What's funny about that?'" Brynn says flatly, her lips and brows like hyphens across her face.

"'But listen, it's not finished: the United States of America; Continent of North America; Western Hemisphere; the Earth; the Solar System; the Universe; the Mind of God—that's what it said on the envelope.'"

"'What do you know,'" Brynn says, disregarding the exclamation mark at the end of the line.

Tara presses on more enthusiastically, as if making up for the deflated tire that is Brynn's voice. "'And the postman brought it just the same!'" she says, ad-libbing Brynn's unused exclamation mark.

Mr. Leal stops her and summons the next person. Then the next and the next, one after the other, directing them to various parts and pages with no discernible pattern. Some read well, others not-so-well. Some overact. Some underact. But they all must want it badly, too. The sound of their sneakers squeaking across the varnished floor makes my heart hurt a little. I picture them as little kids and someone, their mothers probably, teaching them to tie their shoes, how to bring the loose ends curving toward each other and entwine them securely. Like magic.

"Mikayla Reynolds," Mr. Leal calls out.

I know that name. Number sixty-three on the sign-up sheet. The one immediately before mine. I push myself up from my place against the wall and peek out from behind the blue velour curtain into the audience. People are seated here and there. I spot Gabe and Sonny halfway down the left aisle. Gabe leans forward, drumming his fingers on the upholstery of the chair in front of him, and Sonny crosses her arms and chews on her thumbnail.

Even though I know it's coming, I still jump when Mr. Leal calls my name. It couldn't sound scarier if I were Marie Antoinette being called up to the guillotine during the French Revolution.

I'm having an out-of-body experience, watching myself from a distance through a gauzy curtain. My legs have softened to noodles, but somehow they carry me to the center of the stage, where an X is taped to the floor in thick, black strips. The moment my eyes look out into the audience, I jolt back into my body, fully conscious of the weight and span of it. My chest constricts, and it's hard to breathe. I'm Scarlet O'Hara, and Mammy is behind me tightening my corset before the picnic at Twelve Oaks.

"Page thirty. Emily. Brynn, you read Mrs. Webb. Start at: 'Emily, come and help me.'"

I know exactly which part this is. It's the one where Emily wants reassurance from her mother. She asks her if she thinks she's pretty, and her mother says those dreaded words well-meaning people always say to fat girls: You have a pretty face. Mom's said the same thing to me plenty of times. It sounds like a compliment, but it's not because it begs another question. What about the rest of me? Unfortunately, my face is not a floating entity. It's attached to my body.

Brynn reads in her deadpan way, her words drifting to the floor like dried cornhusks. "'I've already told you yes, now that's enough of that. You have a nice young pretty face I never heard of such foolishness.'" She delivers the lines in a seamless stream, ignoring any punctuation.

The blood is pounding in my ears so loudly, the words sound muffled, like she's saying them under water.

She blinks at me expectantly. It's my turn to say something, but I can't. My tongue has swollen. My eyes cling to the script in my hands, but the words fail me. They start swimming on the page as if bobbing on choppy water, like a broken string of pearls after a shipwreck.

The enormous room grows completely quiet. Even the hushed murmurs of the people running lines backstage have stopped. I stand there frozen, wishing someone would do something to break the cacophonous silence.

And then someone does.

Someone laughs at the back of the room. My first thought: Now, that sounds genuine. My second thought: I know the nasal tone of that cackle.

Sure enough, my eyes scan the expansive room and land on Becca, who's sitting in a row toward the back with her knees bent up to her chest. Hailey leans in and says something in her ear, but she might as well shout it because this auditorium is completely devoid of noise, and the acoustics are excellent. Her words bounce from the walls around me as if they popped into existence of their own volition, bereft of any speaker, and ricochet to the stage where they make contact, smacking me in the face. I actually stumble back.

"She is such a joke. She's going to fall right through that stage."

I gasp for breath as my face heats up and my eyes fill.

Mr. Leal calmly rises from his seat and turns toward the back of the room. "Girls, you are being disruptive. Not to mention, extremely rude. Leave. Now."

They slink from their seats and stumble through the rear set of double doors, clinging to each other and doing a terrible job of stifling their laughter.

When the doors clang shut behind them, Mr. Leal turns back to the stage and asks me to continue. I blink back tears, but the words still won't come, so I just stand there. The seconds stretch and the longer they do, the heavier I become as if the words trapped inside me are expanding within me like foam on the waves, weighing me down even more. The floorboards creak from the strain, threatening to break apart at any moment.

And then they do.

Gabe and Sonny watch in horror as the wooden planks split apart, and I go tumbling into a pool of dark, swirling water that's opened up beneath my feet, still clutching the script in my hands. Only now, it's blank. The words have fallen loose from the pages and float around me in the rough water. I thrash about, grasping at them with both hands, but they slip through my fingers. I finally manage to grab one and open my hands to see what I've caught, open my mouth to say it.

"CAN'T."

The word fills my head, and I'm not sure whether or not I've said it out loud. I can feel everyone's eyes on me as I drop the script and run off the stage, through the side door and down the hallway.

Gabe is behind me calling my name, but I keep running, my thighs jiggling like vats of boiling jelly. He catches up to me where the drama hallway intersects the main one and grabs my arm. I finally stop running and surrender. I let the tears flow freely.

He wipes them from my cheeks and puts his arms around me. "It's okay, Pi. Everything's going to be okay."

I step away from him. "No, it's not. Why do people always say it?"

"Because it is," he says.

"No, not that. That other thing everyone always says. From the time you're a little kid, they say it. Over and over. They make you believe it. Why do they do that? Don't they know how cruel it is?"

"What, Pi? What do they say? Who says it?"

"Everyone. Teachers, parents, librarians, troop leaders, Abraham Lincoln, Walt Disney, Patrick Dempsey in *Can't Buy Me Love.* Everyone!'" I stammer and try to catch my breath, but I'm sobbing hard now, tears dripping from both of my chins.

"They say, you can do whatever you want to do. Whatever you put your heart and mind into, you can achieve. It's always on some stupid poster in some stupid hallway. There'll be a cute little kitten hanging from a tree limb, trying to climb back on, and those words written underneath. Like if he falls off, those words will bounce him back up onto the branch like a trampoline. But they won't. They'll just disappear, and he'll fall flat on his face, break all his bones. It's not true. Why do they lie?"

Gabe looks at me with a deflated expression on his face. We stand there in silence, heat radiating down from the thick, plastic dome in the ceiling above us.

Finally he says, "Maybe you're right. Maybe it is a lie. Maybe you can't be whatever you want to be. I mean, it would be epic if I could be the heavyweight champion of the world. But I know that's not happening. Would you look at these scrawny arms?"

I manage a feeble smile. I know he's trying to cheer me up, but there's no use.

"Or a rock star. I'd love to be a rock star. That would kick ass, but I can't sing for shit or play any instrument besides the recorder, so that's out the window. And as much as I dig surfing, I'll never be like Kelly Slater. Not even close. So you're right. You can't be whatever you want to be," he says, shrugging his shoulders. "But you can be what you were meant to be. And that's what matters."

"But aren't they the same thing?"

"Nope, not always."

I wipe my face with the cuff of my sleeve. "Then how do you tell the difference?"

"That's easy. If you give up, it's not what you were meant to be. Just something you thought you wanted." He holds up his palms in surrender. "It's okay. Maybe you weren't meant to be an actor. I mean, I've been around actors, and you're smarter and more talented than a lot of them. Some of them have to have every word fed to them 'cause they can't be bothered to memorize their lines. But hey, it's cool. Maybe you could be a movie critic or something, I don't know. Write your own blog, maybe. You could call it, 'Pilar's Picks.'"

His attempt at reverse psychology is obvious, but his words sink in anyway and hit their mark. That feeling of conviction I experienced the day I signed up to audition and stood on the empty stage rushes back to me. If I truly love acting, if it is my passion, if it really is what I'm meant to do, I can't let anything stop me. Not Becca. Not anyone. Ever. Least of all, myself.

"Look, forty years from now, the sun'll rise, and you'll climb out of bed, pour yourself a cup of coffee and read the paper. That's gonna happen no matter what you do. Life will go on whether you walk back out on that stage or not."

I shift my weight from one foot to the other, crossing my arms in front of me. "I don't even drink coffee."

Gabe frowns. "Well, maybe you'll start. Anyway, you get the idea. Sadly, Hailey will have grown even more shallow than she is now. She'll spend all her time ignoring her grandchildren and obsessing over how many 'likes' she gets on her selfies. Becca will be on her fourth marriage and working at the make-up counter at CVS. She won't be the one looking back at you in the mirror. She'll be a fuzzy image in some remote corner of your brain. I doubt you'll even remember her name. And this day will be a distant memory. Maybe you'll remember it, or maybe you won't. But if you do remember, what will it feel like? You can't control everything, but you can control that. Right here. Right now."

He pulls my script out of his back pocket and holds it out to me. "So, what's it gonna be? Are you going back into that auditorium to do what you were meant to do, or should we go home and set you up a webpage?"

I look down at the cover of the thin booklet in his hand. A wooden ladder reaches up to a full moon, and the title *Our Town* floats above it. I don't know where it comes from: the force that stirs within me and compels me to move my hand toward the script. I trace the moon's outline with my finger, then take a deep breath and take the curved pages from him.

"I'm going back in."

Gabe's face breaks into a grin, and he punches the air with his fist. "Yes! You got this, Pi."

I try not to smile, but the corners of my lips jerk up. "And 'Pilar's Picks?' Nice touch."

He laughs. "Well, it worked, didn't it?"

We head back to the auditorium. Gabe walks behind me with his hands on my shoulders, guiding me back to the stage like Apollo Creed guiding Rocky to the ring.

I glance at him over my shoulder. "Gabe?"

"Yeah, Pi?"

"Who's Kelly Slater?"

Pili

I wrapped the presents myself. In the nicest paper I could find. It's covered with pictures of a little prairie girl wearing a patchwork dress, pantaloons and a large bonnet. Pera's much better at it than I am. She's got more patience for that sort of thing. She's downright meticulous, carefully creasing each side in neat, even folds, creating a perfect symmetry. The corners of the paper crinkle up over trapped pockets of air as I stack them up on the porch step, and an unwelcome thought comes unbidden. This is where she was sitting. This is where she watched it happen. I shake the thought from my mind and jog back to my car to grab a rope from the trunk, lasso it over a lower branch of the sturdiest tree in the yard and tie the other end through the loop at the top of the clown's bowler hat.

Pera peeks out from beneath the frilly valance in the kitchen window and says, "*M'ija*'s too little for a piñata. She won't even be able to reach it."

"That's no problem." I loosen the slack, and the clown drops closer to the ground, its red paper shoes brushing the dry grass. "See? Trust me. She's going to love it."

Pera shakes her head and lowers the curtain again. I raise the clown higher and tie the end of the rope loosely around the tree trunk, load up my arms with packages and nudge the screen door open with my foot.

Pera's at the kitchen sink rinsing off a baking pan. She glances at me over her shoulder as I set the boxes on the table next to the cake. A clown's red crescent mouth smiles up at me from its surface.

"And how's she supposed to chew candy? She's only got two teeth. *Qué loca.* You really shouldn't have gone through all that trouble."

"It was no trouble at all. This is her very first birthday party. It should be special. Besides, it's mostly empty. I only threw in a few *obleas de cajeta*. They're soft enough for her to gnaw on. I figure she'll have fun swinging away at it. Cake looks great, by the way." I swipe a ruffle of red icing from the bottom edge and lick my finger clean. "Where is the birthday girl anyway? Still napping?" Pera ignores me and grabs a bag of tomatoes from the fridge. "You better wake her up and get her dressed. Everybody'll be arriving soon." I glance down at my wristwatch, the worn leather bands bleached from the sun. "And speaking of empty-headed clowns, where's Carlos? His truck's not outside. By the way, is Tía Irma coming? I hope she doesn't drink too much and start telling dirty jokes. And Checho and Rodi better not bring their *cholo* friends, either. I know they were all toking up in the bathroom the last time they were here. The towels still smell like pot."

Pera doesn't say anything but chops up a tomato into tiny squares. Juice drips from the wooden cutting board onto the counter as she tilts it over a glass bowl and slides the pieces in, but she doesn't seem to notice.

I take a step closer to her. "Pera?"

She grabs two more tomatoes and dices them up deftly, splattering seeds and juice onto the front of her white dress. She doesn't seem to notice that either.

"Tía Irma won't be here. Neither will Checho or Rodi. Or anyone else. *No viene nadie*," she says flatly.

"What do you mean, no one's coming? Why not?"

"Because I told everybody the party's cancelled."

"Cancelled? Why?"

She wipes her brow with the back of her hand and continues chopping.

"Pera?"

Finally, she sets the knife down and turns to look at me. Dark circles ring her eyes, and the top two buttons of her dress are fastened into the wrong holes. A crimson splotch dots the center of her lips, the lipstick not quite reaching the upper or lower curves, making her mouth appear smaller than it is.

"I told them the baby has an earache. I didn't want to have to explain."

"Explain what?"

She studies her feet. "Why her father isn't here."

My heart sinks, and my stomach feels as though I've been sucker-punched. "No, Pera. Not today of all days. Where the hell is he?"

She picks up the knife again and cuts up another tomato. "Don't know. He's been gone since the night before last."

She's trying to keep her voice free of emotion, but I can hear the hurt singeing the edges of her words. It's hard to hear, and my hands fly over my ears. "Don't tell me anymore. I don't want to hear it." I lower them again after a few seconds. "Well? Did he say where he was going?"

"For a few beers."

She walks over to the sink and stands staring at her reflection in the window above. I'm counting to ten in my head.

When I reach number four, Pera breaks the silence. "You ever feel like you took a wrong turn somewhere and now your skin doesn't sit right on your bones? Like you're a guest in your own body?"

"It's not your skin that doesn't fit. It's this house, this marriage, this life."

"It's funny." She rips off a paper towel from the dispenser fastened to the bottom of a cabinet and wipes the lipstick from her mouth. "I don't even remember choosing things. *Es como* one moment I was a girl going through the motions, taking steps on a path already set in front of me. And suddenly I'm here and now. In this kitchen. I don't even recognize my own face when I look in the mirror sometimes."

I walk over to her side and study her profile. "Well, I recognize your face. You're Pera. Jorge and Amparo's daughter. My sister. And Mireya's mother."

The shadow of a smile tugs on her lips briefly, then disappears as she reaches up to open the cabinet door. "I wasn't going to show you this, *pero* I might as well." She takes a ceramic sugar bowl from the bottom shelf and removes the mushroom cap lid. "I found it in his truck last week," she says, turning the bowl upside down over her hand. "Under the seat."

I lean in to get a closer look, and my mouth gapes open in disbelief. A cheap, brassy gold hoop the circumference of a quarter rests in her palm. Anger pulses through me, but a small seed of hope sprouts in my chest at the same time. This could be it, the thing that forces Pera to open her eyes and see clearly, the push she needs to leave Carlos once and for all and start over. But something about the way the earring rattles when she drops it back into the empty sugar bowl makes the seed shrivel up and die.

I pace the floor, trying to contain the rage rising in me like a fanned flame. "I'll kill him. I swear to God, I will. I'll choke him with my bare hands."

She returns the bowl to the cabinet and closes the door. Her movements are irritatingly calm, but she's not fooling me. I know my sister. She's stifling her feelings, bottling them up, suffocating on the words she's too afraid to say, as if expressing them will make what's happening more real. But I won't let her off the hook so easily. I'll make her say them, let them come tumbling out in front of her like tangible things she can no longer ignore.

"Well? What did he say when you confronted him with it?"

"*Nada*."

"Nothing? He didn't say anything?"

She gathers the last bits of tomato and drops them into the mixing bowl. "He doesn't know I found it. I haven't told him yet."

"Why the hell not? What in the world are you waiting for?"

"I didn't want to stir things up right before Mireya's party. It's like you said . . . It's a special day, a day for family."

As if on cue, Miri starts to whimper down the hall.

I stare at Pera, wide-eyed. "Are you kidding me? You didn't say anything? How could you not say anything?"

"*No comiences* . . . don't start, Pili. It's not that simple. Not everything is black and white. I don't want to talk about it. It's none of your business, anyway."

"You listen to me, Esperanza," I say, spitting out the words like hot coals. "Anything that involves you or my niece is my business."

"*Pues,* we're just going to have to disagree to agree," she says.

I take a deep breath and try again. "When will enough be enough? He's never going to change. You want to be miserable for the rest of your life?"

"*Ay, no sé*, but it's my decision to make. And it's not only about me. I have Mireya to think about, too. He's her father."

"You'd never guess it the way he acts. I'll bet I spend more time with her than he does. Open your eyes, Pera. He's barely ever at home. He's always God-knows-where doing God-knows-what. For all you know, he's got another family somewhere." I take a deep breath. "He doesn't love you."

The words slice through the air like daggers. It hurts to say them, but she needs to hear them. She winces and turns away from me, the ensuing silence spreading like a chasm between us. The only sounds are Miri's muffled cries.

Pera's head droops to her chest and her fist slams down on the countertop. She sweeps her arm across it and sends the bowl of tomatoes sailing to the floor. It shatters, and she slumps to the floor sobbing, tomato juice soaking into her dress like blood into a dying soldier's uniform. I grab a dish towel and squat down to wipe her face and neck. Miri wails louder, and I'm torn between staying with Pera and going to get her. Finally, I stand up and walk toward the doorway. Pera says something to me, and I stop in my tracks. When I turn back to listen, I realize she isn't talking to me at all. She's talking to herself, saying the words over and over.

"Why am I not enough?"

Pilar

X marks the spot under my bed. I push aside the dusty set of five-pound hand weights Mom got me last Christmas and pull out the treasure chest. It's covered in pink and purple paper and has plastic jewels glued all around the sides and my name in glitter across the top. I made it out of an old shoe box in Brownies when I was in second grade. We were supposed to bring a small mirror to glue to the bottom so we'd see our own reflections when we looked inside, but I'd forgotten mine, so the troop leader gave me a wrinkly strip of foil she found in a cabinet of the classroom where we held our meetings. It made my face all wavy like I was looking into a swimming pool. I figured I'd replace it with the mirror when I got home, but I never did.

We were supposed to fill the box with cherished mementos, like pictures of loved ones, seashells we collected on vacation or friendship bracelets from summer camp. It's filled with my secret stash now.

Mom would freak out if she found it. She'd set it behind the rear tire of her car, back out over it and drive me straight to the gym.

Sweating out my embarrassment and humiliation did enter my mind, but it flew right out again. I've gone to the gym three times already, and it's sucked each time. I loathe the *dreadmill* and I'd rather walk the plank over shark-infested water than do a plank. I'm definitely not feeling it today. All that brightly colored spandex and those six-pack abs would send me right over the edge. I'd much rather hide out in my room with my stockpile of goodies.

Today was one of the worst days in the history of days, up there with the invention of the three-way mirror and fluorescent lighting. I'm ready to empty the box of its riches and stuff it all down my throat until there's nothing left but a pile of crumpled wrappers.

I did go back to the auditorium today. As hard as it was, I knew if I didn't, I'd only end up feeling worse. I'd never be able to look at myself in the mirror again, and that's already hard enough as it is. Not to mention, I wouldn't be able to even think about auditioning next year. So I forced myself to get back up on that horse. Besides, I already knew Becca wouldn't be there.

I waited in the stage wing as the crowd there dwindled, until the last person finished his audition. Mr. Leal had already gathered his clipboard and stood up when I walked out onto the stage. He looked surprised to see me standing there, but he sat down again, Brynn's stony lips bowed slightly upward. He flipped a page over the top of his clipboard and took the pencil from behind his ear. "Page twenty-three, Emily's first line."

It was easier the second time around. I'd already screwed up so monumentally that I had nothing to lose. The only way I could've humiliated myself any worse was if I'd lifted my shirt and done The Truffle Shuffle like Chunk in *The Goonies*.

Gabe and Sonny had moved up to seats in the front row. I focused on their faces, pretended they were the only two people in the humungous room. Gabe gave me a nod of encouragement, and Sonny mouthed out a few words from her favorite movie, *Signs,* to me. "Swing away, Meryl."

Before I knew it, I was in the zone, lost in the words, letting them transform me until I wasn't myself anymore. I was Emily Webb, a sixteen-year-old girl from the small town of Grover's Corners, New Hampshire, a girl at the brink of womanhood who marries the boy next door, has a baby and dies young, before her life really begins, before realizing the beauty of it.

I did okay, but there is no way I'll get a part, not after the way I ran out of there like a rhino fleeing poachers. In a way, I'm relieved. Now I definitely won't have to stand on stage in front of everyone. And there's always next year.

There's always next year. What a depressing batch of words. I say them to make myself feel better, but they fall flat.

I'm about to tear into the comfort of a Twix bar when Gabe taps on my door.

"Hey, Pi?"

"Don't come in! I'm naked!" I yell quickly, throwing the candy back into the box and shoving it under my bed. I fish a magazine out of the wastebasket under my desk and open it to a random page.

"Okay, come in."

He peeks his head in. "You good?"

"Peachy keen, jelly bean. Why wouldn't I be after my stellar performance today?"

He opens the door wider and steps inside. "It was stellar. You went back in there like a boss and kicked ass. It took guts to do that. You've got balls of steel."

"Yeah well, if nothing else, at least I made an impression. Hopefully, Mr. Leal will keep me in mind for next year. If he decides to do *The Lion King*, I'm a shoo-in for a charging rhino."

"You never know, Pi. I think you've still got a good shot. Better than good. In fact, he'd be an idiot not to choose you."

I give him a look that says, "You've got to be kidding."

"Anyway, what're you doing tonight? You have plans?"

"Let's see. I was going to fly to LA to choose the spot for my star on the Hollywood Walk of Fame, but the airline ran out of seatbelt extenders, so there goes that. Why? What's up?"

"You wanna go to a party?"

A party? Me? I haven't been to a party with people my age since Robby Miller's skating party in fifth grade, where I spent most of the afternoon clinging to the wall with my ankles bent awkwardly inward. His mom made him invite the whole class, so it doesn't really count.

Before that, it was Marcy Cantú's sixth birthday, where I accidentally spilled red punch down the front of my white dress at Chuck E. Cheese and had to get picked up early.

So a party? Oh, hell, yeah! I thought this day was Peter Panned. In Neverland. Like never going to happen. I am beyond excited, but I play it cool.

"Uh, sure. I guess so. Whose party is it?" I am the epitome of nonchalance.

"A girl in my English class, Jordan Wells. Her parents are out of town for her brother's Little League tournament or something."

"Are you sure it'd be okay if I came? I mean, what if she's only expecting a certain number of people? What if she runs out of food or drinks or whatever? I wouldn't want to impose."

Gabe laughs, and it's the nicest sound. "It's fine. I'm sure there'll be plenty of everything."

"But I'm a sophomore. What if only juniors were invited?"

"Well, I'm a junior, and I'm inviting you, so get ready. Uncle Shane said we could take his truck. Meet me out front in ten minutes."

As soon as the door shuts behind him, I jump to my feet and do a happy dance, twirling my arms from side to side and kicking my feet. My first high school party. Like the transit of Venus across the sun, this opportunity might not come again in my lifetime.

A thought occurs to me that stops me mid-twirl. What if Becca and her friends are there? What if they humiliate me in front of everyone, as usual? Of course, they'll be there. Why wouldn't they be? This could be disastrous. A small voice in my head whispers for me to stay home and watch *Out of Africa* again, work on perfecting Meryl Streep's Danish accent, study the movements of the larger animals.

On the other hand, this party could be a blessing in disguise. Becca might be in a more magnanimous mood outside of school. Maybe she'll be relaxed and having too much fun to even bother with me. And when she sees me with Gabe again, she might start to see me in a new light, she might even change her mind about me. This could be a chance for her to finally get to know me.

I can see it now. Gabe and I walk in together, and everybody starts whispering. Gabe goes to get us some drinks, and the minute he's gone, a gaggle of girls flock to my side. They ask me about him and whether or not we're a thing. I explain how Gabe would like us to be, how we talked about it at length and decided we value our friendship too much to jeopardize it with a romantic entanglement. We are consciously uncoupled. They are impressed by my mature, detached demeanor, and the conversation moves on to other topics. They ask my opinion on other guys in school and for advice on their own love lives. My answers are breezy, funny and wise.

Soon, we're all bonding, laughing and throwing our arms around each other like Bette Midler and Barbara Hershey in *Beaches*. Becca saunters over to join in and takes her cue from the others. She hands me a cup of punch as a peace offering, and we toast our new-found friendship.

Anything's possible.

It could happen.

I fling open my closet door, yank clothes off hangers and toss them on the bed. There are four simple guidelines fat people should follow when dressing for social occasions:

- Button down shirts are the devil. Avoid them like the plague.
- Use patterns with caution, or you could end up looking like a wall in the billiard room at Graceland.
- If you're going to wear stripes, choose vertical. Never ever, under any circumstances, horizontal.
- Solid, dark colors are the safest options. Black is your BFF. Simple, yet sophisticated. Think, funeral chic.

I try on six different outfits before settling on Audrey Hepburn's look from *Funny Face*: a black turtleneck (excellent for hiding double chins), black cropped pants and black flats. I pull the shirt down over my head and channel Fred Astaire, who plays the fashion photographer. "'When I get through with you, you'll look like . . . What do you call beautiful? A tree. You'll look like a tree,'" I say to myself in the mirror.

By the time I'm finished getting dressed, beads of sweat dot my forehead. I wipe my armpits with a tissue and slather on extra deodorant, lift my shirt and squeeze powder all over myself, paying special attention to the folds of my belly and my cleavage. I run my fingers through my curly hair and add a touch of lip gloss before surveying myself in the mirror.

I search and search, sweeping my fingers over my entire body, but there are no signs of bone structure at all. I'm beginning to doubt I even have any bones. No hard lines or angular corners anywhere. Not at my elbows, wrists, shoulders, hips, jawline, ankles, knees or knuckles. Not even in my face when I pucker my lips and suck in my cheeks. Nothing but a sludge of pudge. I turn to study my profile and lift a flabby arm, push the sagging skin up above my bicep, then let it droop again. I don't even bother trying to hold in my bouncy castle stomach. Not even an industrial grade Hoover is capable of that level of suction. It's been years since I felt a hint of my rib cage, traced my finger along its contours. It's like someone stole it. Like I'm the victim in one of those urban legends where someone wakes up in a tub of ice missing a body part.

I move on from the lost cause that is my body and focus on my hair. Maybe I should wear it up like Audrey too. I gather it together and twist it up into a bun, tilt my head to the side.

Air escapes from my lips like a deflating balloon, and my hair falls around my sagging shoulders again. I give myself one last look in the mirror. This is Helen Hunt dating Jack Nicholson—*As Good As It Gets*. I slip my cellphone into my cross-body bag and turn away from the mirror, wishing my reflection weren't so clear, wishing I could replace it with a sheet of crumpled foil.

Pili

As I sweep up the broken glass from Pera's kitchen floor, my mind drifts back to the summer I was twelve, when I fell from a rope swing and broke my arm. I swear I could hear the bone snap. It hurt like hell, but the pain wasn't the worst part. The worst part was having to wear a cast for the rest of that summer, sitting by myself at the lake, shooing the flies away from the picnic baskets while everyone else splashed in the water and had fun.

I remember picking up a twig and shoving it down inside the hardened plaster as far as it would go, trying to reach the clammy, itchy skin beneath with the sun beating down on my bare shoulders.

Pera stood gazing at her rippling reflection, my cousins beckoning her to jump in and join them. She held her foot out over the cool refreshing water and turned to look at me over her shoulder. In a show of solidarity, she lowered it again, spun on her heel and strode over to the blanket, vowing not to set foot in the water until I could go in with her.

I remember we lay on our backs on the warm, fuzzy fabric, squinting up at the satiny sky. It seemed close enough to touch, like we could reach up, pull down a few billowy clouds and throw them behind our heads for pillows.

I rolled over onto my stomach and plucked at the small balls of lint while Pera rummaged inside one of the large picnic baskets. She pulled out a thick Styrofoam plate heaped with something delicious-smelling and set it down between us. I opened a corner of the foil dome and breathed in deeply. Tía Norma's *empanadas*. We spent the afternoon stuffing ourselves with the doughy pockets of beef and daydreaming about our futures, the blanket morphing into a flying carpet and lifting us off the ground. Pera was going to be an Olympic gymnast like María Goro and a famous chef, and I would be a world-renowned heart surgeon.

I remember, warm grease trickled down my fingers and seeped into the plastery edge, soothing the skin beneath. I wadded up the crinkled sheet of aluminum and tossed it aside while Pera removed the woven lid from a basket of tortillas and placed it on my head, the straw flowers, vibrant against my dark hair.

She borrowed a pen from Tía Irma's handbag and stretched my encased arm across her lap. A small blade of grass was stuck to the plaster below the knuckles. Pera blew it off and started writing. On the back of my hand, she wrote Abuelito's and Abuelita's names, Roberto and Elena, then gently turned it over and wrote Antonio and Alicia, Mamá's parents. Beneath theirs, she wrote the names of our parents, Jorge and Amparo, then hers and mine. She added the names of every member of our family—aunts, uncles, cousins—down the length of my arm on every side, retracing each bold, even letter until every bit of white was covered in ink from my wrist to my elbow.

Fragments of glass clatter to the bottom of the wastebasket beneath the sink, waking me from my daydream. That summer, it seemed like forever before that cast came off, but when it finally did, my arm was as good as new. No sign of a break at all. If only the heart were like that, like a fractured bone that could be set right again.

I return the metal dust pan to its place behind the pantry door while Miri watches from her high chair and gnaws on a cookie, saliva dripping down her plump chin. I bend to kiss her soft cheek and place a few more on the tray in front of her. "Extra cookies for you. Happy Birthday, *mi reina*."

She clutches one with both hands and squeals happily. I sit at the table next to her and say the word slowly. "Coo-kie. Can you say that? Coo-kie. Now, you try." Her mouth stops mid chew, and her eyes focus on my lips, her downy brows scrunching together in concentration. "You can do it. Coo-kie."

She offers me her soggy wafer, and I kiss her small fleshy fist. "Puh puh puh ba-ba," she says, slapping her hand on the tray.

"Okay, okay. I'll get it." I grab a bottle from the drying rack on the counter, fill it with milk and hand it to her. "Here's your ba-ba."

She sucks it down in long gulps.

"Don't worry, *gordita*. I get you. Sometimes I feel like you're the only one I do understand."

Pera walks into the kitchen and over to the sink, where she wets a sponge and squeezes it out. She's changed into a clean dress and washed her face, but her eyes are still puffy from crying. They avoid mine as she wipes tomato juice from the countertops.

Miri sucks the remaining bits of cookie from her fingers and babbles to herself.

I wish my words would come as easily as hers. There's so much to say, but I don't know where to begin. I have to tread lightly, choose my words carefully. If I say the wrong thing, it'll only make Pera defensive and then she won't listen to me. I sip my coffee quietly and watch her clean.

She scrubs every inch of the cabinets, even the insides of the doors, and wipes the entire floor, including the baseboards and the area in front of the refrigerator where the tomatoes didn't reach. Finally, she tosses the sponge into the sink and looks at me.

"I'm sorry."

I pull out the chair next to me. She sits down, and I lay my hand on hers. "I'm sorry too. I hate seeing you so unhappy."

"I know. I hate feeling this way. *Pero* I don't know what to do." She leans forward on her elbows and presses the heels of her hands into her eyes.

"You could leave him," I say too quickly. "You and the baby could move back home with me."

"If only it were that simple."

I lean forward in my chair. "It is simple. Just say the word, and I'll have you packed up and out the door. You could start over. A new beginning for you and Mireya. Think of her, Pera. Do you really want her growing up with a father like that? And I use the term loosely."

Pera lowers her hands from her face and gets up to pour herself a cup of coffee. "I am thinking of her. How would I support us? How would we live?"

I get up from the chair and stand next to her at the counter. "You never have to worry about that. You could help out at the store in the mornings and take classes at LCC in the afternoons, earn a degree. You're smart. You've always been good at school. I'll help take care of Miri. You've still got your whole life ahead of you. Anything's possible."

She sets down her coffee cup and gazes out the window above the sink. A brown delivery truck is parked at the curb blocking out the sky. Tree branches scrape the roof of its boxy cargo container.

"You've given up so much already. You could've gone away to medical school, like you wanted. But you didn't. You stayed for me and Mamá. You gave up your dream. *Por nosotras.*"

"I have a new dream now. A better one. Mireya. Being here for her and watching her grow up," I say.

Pera tears off a paper towel and wipes Miri's chin. "It's not only that. Marriage is a sacrament, a vow. You can't break a promise to God because things get tough. When the tough get going, the going gets tough, *como dicen.*"

I'm trying to stay calm, but my jaw clenches and my palms start to sweat. "Don't do that, Pera. If you don't want to leave, then don't. But don't hide behind God. Don't use Him as an excuse."

"I'm not hiding behind anyone. I'm trying to do the right thing. For me and for *m'ija.*" She unlatches the tray and lifts Miri out of her high chair. "You don't understand, Pili. You've never been married. *No sabes.* You don't know what it's like. Sometimes you have to suffer for love, to make sacrifices."

Miri reaches her arms out to me and says my name: "Pee-Pee. Pee-Pee."

I take her from Pera's arms. "And sometimes, you have to learn to let go."

Pilar

When we pull up to Jordan's house, the party is fully on. Parked cars line both sides of the street. Gabe finds a spot a few houses down. I pull down the visor and give myself a final look in the mirror as he slides in beside the curb. Yup, still a fat loser. Glad I checked. At least there's nothing hanging from my nose or stuck between my teeth.

"I'm not a hundred percent positive this is a good idea. Maybe I should wait for you in the car."

"No way. I'm not going to leave you sitting out here by yourself. We're going in together. Come on," Gabe says, tugging my arm. "You're overthinking this, Pi. If it sucks, we'll go home and watch a movie. No big deal."

I flip the visor back up and reach for the door handle. "Fine, but I get to choose which one."

Gabe smiles. "Deal. As long it's nothing too sappy. Or anything that involves supernatural creatures falling in love with humans. I'll even make the popcorn."

I shut the door behind me and join him on the sidewalk. "Okay but remember: you didn't say anything about *Gone With the Wind*."

"I believe that falls under the sappy category."

"It's more of a period piece. Historical drama."

The closer we get to Jordan's house, the more fervently I wish for a crack in the sidewalk to open up and swallow me.

Becca.

Please don't let her be here. Please don't let her be here. I send the words out into the universe, pouring all of my energy into them and praying that it will respond and mold itself to my will. But something gets lost in the translation. The words have the opposite effect.

Jordan's two-story colonial looms before us like the Dark Tower of Mordor from *Lord of the Rings*. We walk up the curved driveway and run smack-dab into the very face I've been dreading to see.

Becca and Hailey strut up to us from the opposite side of the street. A pink and brown camouflage baseball cap sits on Becca's mousy hair, and her flat stomach is visible beneath the hem of a pink tank top. She looks surprised to see me, and not in a good way either. Not the way Mr. Leal looked at me when I walked back out on stage earlier this afternoon.

Her eyes bore into me like lasers aiming at a target, and her mouth draws open.

Before she can say anything, Gabe blocks her words with his own. "Hey. Becca, right?"

Just like that, Gabe has her full attention.

She flips her hair to the side and blinks at him, her hip bones jutting out above her cut-off jeans. "Yes, and you are?"

She's trying hard to act disinterested, but her blatant attempt is having the opposite effect. It's obvious she remembers him, but Gabe plays along.

"I'm Gabe. And this is Pilar." He keeps talking before she can react. "Did anyone ever tell you, you look like the girl from that movie? What's it called . . . *The Duff*? The girl with the reddish hair."

Bella Thorne, I think to myself. She's the actress who usually plays the beautiful, yet snobby prom queen type, the quintessential mean girl, and Becca looks nothing like her.

"Bella Thorne!" Becca and Hailey yell it out at the same time.

"Yeah, her. It's crazy how much you remind me of her."

Becca twirls a strand of hair around her finger and tries not to smile. "Whatever. My hair's not even red."

"I know, but there's something about you. A certain quality. Your facial features are kind of similar. I don't know. . . . " He shrugs and turns to lead me through the set of sentinel lions flanking the front door.

Becca follows him inside with Hailey in her wake. "You really think so? Well, maybe a little, I guess. Our names are almost exactly the same. Only one letter's different."

Music pours out of the house and drowns out the rest of her words. As soon as we cross the threshold, we watch Hailey grab Becca's arm and drag her to the kitchen, where Connor stands at a table playing drinking games with a bunch of guys from the football team.

Gabe and I step into the darkened living room, which is packed with people and pulses like a heartbeat. The furniture is pushed against the walls, and a strobe light blinks from a table in the corner. Colored lights shoot down from strips of tract lighting and bounce off the walls. It's like we've stepped inside *Saturday Night Fever,* not someone's house. Like any minute, Tony Manero is going to come strutting by in his white suit and thick gold chain ready for a dance off.

Exactly like the scenario I played in my head at home, a cluster of girls do flock to us. To him, I should say. They grip Gabe's arm and pull him onto the makeshift dance floor, but he breaks free, glides back over to me and asks if I want to go with him to get a drink. I make some lame joke about getting my groove on. It's best to keep a safe distance from Becca.

"Okay, back in a flash."

My eyes follow him through one of the wide twin archways into the kitchen, and mine aren't the only ones. Becca sits on a stool at the crowded kitchen table and watches him from the corner of her eye. Connor watches her. And Hailey watches him.

A muscular guy with shoulder-length hair that flares out above his shoulders stands at one end and aims a ping pong ball toward a triangular formation of red plastic cups at the other end. He releases it, and it bounces on the table and lands in a cup in the middle, then he holds it out to Becca victoriously.

Becca rolls her eyes and takes the cup from him. She chugs down the contents, wrinkles up her nose and sticks out her tongue. Her lips move like she's saying something, but I can't hear it. She's probably complaining about the taste of the beer. *Why does beer have to taste so disgusting? So not worth the calories.*

Sure enough, through the other archway I can see Connor survey the granite countertop beside the sink, which is covered in liquor bottles of various shapes and sizes. He winks and pours a healthy dose of something clear into her cup, adds a splash of fruit punch and hands it back to her.

When she takes a sip, her face lights up.

The music grows louder, and two girls in strappy dresses and cowboy boots stop dancing and sidle up to me. One of them has blonde hair bleached nearly white, and the other wears fake eyelashes like a 1960s-fashion model. They hang down over her eyes like drawn-down window shades.

Twiggy leans in and yells over the music. "Hey, you came here with Gabe, right?"

I nod.

Her eyes travel up and down my body like she's searching for something to explain why a guy like Gabe would be with me.

Cowgirl Barbie chimes in, her voice dripping with doubt. "Y'all aren't like . . . together, are you?"

I imagine Gabe and me sitting side by side under the shade of a willow tree in a field of golden wheat, our initials carved inside a heart etched on the thick trunk above our heads. I wish I could say yes, and I wish it would be true.

I explain that Gabe and I are friends, and their faces perk up like wilted flowers touched by ET's glowing finger.

Cowgirl Barbie says in a high-pitched voice, "Oh, we were just wondering because we've seen y'all eating lunch together in the cafeteria."

"Yeah, with that weird girl with the butchy haircut," Twiggy says.

"Omigod, yes! She's in my chem class," Barbie says. "I heard she hangs out in cemeteries."

"She sees dead people!" They yell it out at the same time and dissolve into laughter.

"I heard her Mom killed herself."

"Well, wouldn't you kill yourself if you gave birth to that?"

They seem to remember I'm standing there and stop laughing.

Twiggy looks at me with feigned sympathy. "Oh. Sorry. Y'all aren't friends, are you?" One of her eyelashes is coming unglued, and she blinks like mad trying to keep it out of her eye.

Everything slows down, the swirling lights, the rhythm of the music and the movement of the dancing bodies. It's like the gravity has been sucked out of the room. I feel light-headed and dizzy, like the time I wolfed down a Hawaiian snow cone at the rodeo carnival, then got on the Tilt-a-whirl. The floor melts away, and the walls and ceiling quickly follow suit. A paved road appears beneath my feet, stretching out into barren desert as far as the eye can see, nothing but sand for miles. No signs of life anywhere. No cars or houses, sidewalks or mailboxes, lawns or streetlights. A tumbleweed blows across the road, and a bird of prey circles ominously overhead. Something glimmers in the road a few yards in front of me, and I walk over to take a closer look. It's a fork. Literally, a fork. A silver one with a curvy scrolling pattern on the handle. I bend down to pick it up, but another hand snatches it away before I can. When I look up to see whose, I recognize the menacing grin and jagged incisors of Bucktooth, Whitney Hall's fourth grade tormentor. He holds the fork out to me and as soon as my fingers close around it, I'm back at the party but things still feel different; Twiggy and Barbie appear next to him, holding an enormous cake in their outstretched hands. Sonny's face covers its gooey surface. The bluish tips of her hair melt into the chocolate and run down the sides like muddy waterfalls. My eyes bounce from the fork to the cake and back to the fork. I grip it tightly at both ends and snap it in half.

I'm back at the party, and the two girls, empty-handed now as well as empty-headed, stand waiting for an answer to their question. Everyone and everything around me takes on a flimsy, superficial quality, like cardboard backdrops on a set. One solid piece of certainty looms before me, and I understand: Even though Sonny isn't here now and even though she'll probably never hear what I'm about to say, my words will still affect her somehow. They'll still mean something.

Twiggy's eyelash dangles from her eyelid like a caterpillar clinging to a leaf, and she lifts her chin to peer out from beneath it. I'm tempted to reach up and pull it off, but I leave it where it is.

"Yes. We are friends. And she's not weird at all. Actually, she's really interesting and really nice. I was just saying that very thing to Gabe this morning while he was toweling off after his shower." (It's sort of true. I did say something to Gabe after his shower this morning. But it was through the bathroom door and not about Sonny. I yelled at him not to use up all of the hot water.)

My words have the desired effect. Their mouths fall open in shock.

Finally, Barbie shuts hers and runs her fingers through her hair, draping it over her shoulders. "Oh. Well . . . that's what we heard."

We stand there awkwardly, when a hand holding a plastic cup reaches out from behind me. I turn around expecting to see Gabe's lovely dimpled face, but it's not him.

"Remember me?"

Something takes flight in the pit of my stomach and flutters around my chest. It feels light and heavy at the same time. "Sure, I do. Hi, Devin."

"It's Divine, actually." He pretends to fling back his tousled brown hair and laughs. "Hey, ladies. We'll catch you later. We're gonna sit this one out."

He leads me through the maze of bodies to the other side of the room, where we sit down on the stone apron of the fireplace.

"Thanks for that. That conversation was going nowhere fast." I have to yell it into his ear.

"Yeah, Vanessa and Maddie aren't exactly known for their verbal prowess. They're not the brightest bulbs in the box. Actually, they're pretty annoying. I mean, you can only talk about different shades of nail polish for so long."

He takes his phone out of his back pocket and texts something into it. "It's my friend, Sam. He can't find Jordan's house."

I nod and watch Gabe across the horde of gyrating bodies as he carries two drinks to the spot where he left me. His eyes scan the room. When he sees me sitting with Devin, he raises one and smiles.

Devin looks up from his phone again. "So, how come you didn't come to my game? I looked for you."

I take a sip from my cup. It's beer, and I don't want it, but I don't want to be rude either. I figure I'll take a few sips and pour it into a plant or something.

"I was kind of hoping you'd show up," he adds.

I choke on the beer, and it almost shoots out of my nose. Classy. I am a smooth operator.

"You were?"

He laughs again. "Yeah, why do you sound so surprised? I like you. You're chill."

I swallow wrong again and clear my throat. "I am?"

He nods. "You're not like most girls. With them, it's all about clothes and hair and trying to look hot, but it's not like that with you."

"Gee, thanks." I pretend to be offended, but I'm not. I know what he means.

He gets flustered, and it's cute the way his eyes dart to the sides and his mouth gets all wavy like a spaghetti noodle. "Don't get me wrong. You're smart. And funny."

"Like Jack Black."

"Yes! Wait, what? No! What I mean is . . . you're pretty, but there's more to you than that."

I laugh. "I'm messing with you. I know what you mean. Thanks."

He laughs too. "See what I mean? You're funny."

His phone buzzes, and he looks down at it again. "Shit. Sam again. Dude is really bad with directions. I should probably call him. You want to come with me upstairs? He won't be able to hear me with all this noise."

I steal a look at Gabe who's surrounded by a group of girls vying for his attention. They fling their hair, throw their heads back laughing and lean into him, touching his arm or reaching up to ruffle his hair. My eyes jerk from him to Becca, who's still watching him from her perch in the kitchen. Connor glances at her, then motions Hailey to follow him outside to the patio, where people are smoking. As soon as the back door shuts behind them, Becca refills her cup from one of the big, clear liquor bottles and totters into the living room. She dances her way through the crowd, holding her drink high above her head, and when she reaches Gabe she drapes an arm around his waist.

The sight of Becca touching him makes my stomach lurch, and heat rises from my neck up to the sides of my face. It's not that I'm jealous. Not really. Gabe's his own person. He can flirt with whomever he chooses. It's not like I want him for myself or anything. It's just that he's way too good for Becca. There's no way she could ever deserve him. I wish he'd pull away from her and go talk to someone else. Anyone else.

I swallow a mouthful from my cup. It's bitter. But if I'm eating-slash-drinking my feelings, this is definitely the right flavor.

Becca whispers something in his ear and leans her head on his chest. He blushes and looks around uncomfortably. She laughs, and he puts a hand on her waist. It's like I'm watching them from the end of a long tunnel, and Gabe is slipping farther and farther away.

I want to grab something and stuff it into my mouth. If I were home, I'd already have my face buried deep in the pantry or in the treasure chest under my bed. I consider sneaking into the kitchen, grabbing a bag of chips and locking myself in an upstairs bathroom. Instead, I take another sip of beer and think of ocean waves washing ashore, crashing down and silently receding, carrying me with them back into the obliterating darkness.

Devin waves his hand in front of my face. "Hello? Earth to Pilar. Where'd you go?"

"Oh, sorry. Um, yeah."

"Yeah?"

"Yes, I'll go upstairs with you."

Pili

I swing Pera's screen door behind me as hard as I can, but the hollowed wood only makes an unsatisfying poof. The frame is infested with dry rot so it can't be slammed. My hands rest on top of my head as waves of heat roll onto the porch and swallow me up. Warring tornados of anger and frustration whirl inside me, and I close my eyes and watch the splotchy colors of sunlight play on the insides of my eyelids.

There's so much I wanted to say to Pera, but she wouldn't let me. We spent the last few hours opening presents with Miri. I sat with her on the living room rug surrounded by her new toys while Pera folded the discarded Holly Hobby wrapping paper into a neat pile. She prattled on about everything under the sun but the one thing worth talking about, completely ignoring the two-timing elephant in the room. Whenever I brought up Carlos' name, she quickly changed the subject, reverting to an approved script she'd composed in her head.

I dumped out plastic shapes from a yellow cylinder and showed Miri how to deposit them into the corresponding openings on the lid. She grasped a round piece in her chubby hand and banged it repeatedly against the triangular hole trying to make it fit.

"Not there, *mi reina*. Try another one. You can do it."

She slid the red block over to the circular hole and dropped it in, her face beaming with pride.

"Good job, *gordita*! What a smart girl you are."

Pera rolled up a yarn ribbon and babbled on and on, jumping from topic to topic: from the comedian on *Johnny Carson* last night, to President Carter's pardoning of the draft dodgers, to her neighbor Señora Ochoa's gout, to Ghandi . . . a steady stream of safe, unoffending words. I let her jabber on, half-heartedly nodding my head every so often.

When my eyes open again, the papier mâché clown is smiling right at me as it swings from the tree branch. Its bright red nose and green tissue bow tie mock me, and something inside me snaps. A broom leans against the decorative column of cast iron oak leaves and acorns on the corner of the porch. I grab it and stride across the lawn wielding it high above my head. A breeze sends the clown twirling away from me. It spins around again and peers at me with its farcical black eyes encircled in ridiculously thick halos of white. I hit it over and over with all of my might, smashing a hole in its polka dot pants. It swings out of reach again, but I circle around and keep swatting until it breaks apart with a satisfying thwack. The lower half falls to the ground, and its candy innards spill out. I lower the broom handle and stand back, my chest heaving and sweat seeping through my cotton shirt. Small white discs litter the scant patch of grass like spilled Communion wafers. I gather them up and shove them in my pockets as the dismembered clown swivels slowly above my head, shreds of paper hanging from its torso, its stringy red-orange hair shooting out in all directions like a madman's. The sinister curve of the clown's lips so much like Carlos' smug expression.

Pilar

Devin sits on what must be Jordan's little brother's bed, giving his friend directions to the party while I wander about the room. It's weird being in a stranger's bedroom looking at all of his things. It feels wrong, like I'm walking on someone's grave, trespassing on something sacred. I keep my hands clasped behind my back, careful not to disturb anything.

Superhero posters cover the navy-colored walls, and the ceiling is painted to resemble outer space. Luz would love it. A large, homemade model of the solar system hangs above the bed, the Styrofoam planets dangling from varying lengths of fishing line. A bookshelf filled with baseball plaques and trophies is tucked in an alcove beside the closet. Golden, boy-ish figures brandishing baseball bats stand in perpetual batting stances.

Devin pats the spot next to him on the blue and red striped comforter. "Sit with me."

I lower myself slowly onto a corner of the bed. I don't know whether it's the beer or the fact that I'm alone in a room with a boy who is in no way related to me, but I feel painfully self-conscious. I pull my turtleneck away from my body so it doesn't cling to my stomach, then swallow the last sip of beer. I hadn't meant to drink it all.

"Should I get you another one?"

"No, thanks. I'm not really a big drinker." I don't tell him that, unless you count the small sip of wine I take whenever I go to Mass with Buela, this is the first time I've ever had alcohol.

He scoots closer to me. "You sure? I can get you something else if you want. Some killer lemonade?"

"No, thanks. I'm good."

"Yeah, me too. Coach is always hounding us about drinking too much." His phone buzzes, and he looks down to read it. "Finally. Sam found the house, but he says he had to park all the way down at the end of the street." His fingers fly over each tiny letter on the small screen.

"Should we go downstairs and wait for him?"

"Nah, I'll catch up with him later. It's too loud and crowded down there. I'm not really comfortable around lots of people. The only reason I came to this stupid party is because Sam convinced me to. Said he needed a wingman. I think I kind of suck at it, though."

He rolls his eyes and laughs, then looks down at the bedspread and tugs on a loose thread. "You don't mind if we hang up here for a while, do you?"

My fingers and toes are numb, and it feels like I'm floating down a lazy river on a donut-shaped inner tube. "Sure." Why not? It's not like he's going to throw himself at me or anything. There's no danger of that, and I'm not sure if I'm relieved or disappointed. Maybe both. Either way, my chastity is safe. He'd have to consume a whole brewery to develop beer goggles thick enough to pose a threat.

He falls back on the bed and looks up. "Cool ceiling, huh? I would've loved this when I was a kid. Don't laugh, but I used to dream of being an astronaut when I was little. My mom had this clear plastic salad bowl that I'd pretend was my space helmet. Stupid thing didn't even cover my face, but I wore it all the time, even to my piano recital. Ridiculous, huh?"

"No, not at all. That's sweet. And astronauts are awesome. Who wouldn't want to float around in space weightlessly? Sounds ideal."

He sits up and turns to face me. "Anyone ever tell you, you're really easy to talk to?"

I smile and shrug my shoulders.

"Okay, your turn now. Tell me something embarrassing about you. What skeletons have you got rattling around in your closet?"

His phone buzzes again. "Sorry, it's my mom this time. Making sure I don't drink and drive. Lame."

He lays the phone face down, but not before I catch a glimpse of his screensaver. It's a picture of him and a boy around ten years old wearing NASA T-shirts. They're sitting on some porch steps with a shaggy dog between them.

"So you were about to tell me . . . "

I giggle. Yes, I'm embarrassed to admit it, but I actually giggle. "I don't know. I can't think of anything."

He leans over and nudges my shoulder with his. "Come on. Everyone has something."

"Well . . . "

"I won't tell a soul." He holds up three fingers. "Scout's honor."

I think about it for a moment, then shake my head. "No, nevermind. It's too embarrassing."

"It can't be worse than wearing a salad bowl on your head."

I bite my lip and pull the cuffs of my sleeves down over my hands. "Okay, I'll tell you." I pull my hair back from my face and turn to face him. "I have a widow's peak, see?"

He surveys my forehead. "Yeah? Okay?"

"Well, I used to hate it when I was little. I thought it made me look like Dracula. So, one day when I was eight, I decided to get rid of it. I thought if I cut that little triangular section of hair, I could even out my hairline and make it straight instead of heart-shaped, but I didn't really think it through. I grabbed a chunk of hair and cut it as close to my scalp as possible. It didn't work, of course, and I cut way too much. My widow's peak was a short patch of hair. Looked like a tiny baseball diamond with black Astroturf." I smooth my hair over my forehead again. "I had to wear a hat every day until it grew out."

He laughs. "That's not so bad. I bet you looked cute anyway."

I feel myself blush, and it's even more humiliating than my story. I might as well be holding a lacy parasol and batting my eyelashes like some cartoon southern belle. Fiddle dee dee.

The smile disappears from his face, and his eyes take on a serious expression as they search mine.

Something epic is about to happen. I can feel it. I'm not floating any more, now I'm ultra-alert and aware of my body. Every single inch of it.

Devin leans in close, brushes a lock of hair away from my face and tucks it behind my ear. Time slows again for the second time tonight, and my heart starts racing in contrast. I can't believe this is happening. It's like I'm watching it on a screen happen to someone else. He tilts his head to the right and moves in even closer. I'm overcome with elation and disbelief, and also relieved I took the time to use those pore strips on the oily patch on my nose this morning.

Is this really happening or has my imagination run away with itself again? An effect of the beer maybe?

His lips brush mine, and I know it's real. The glow-in-the-dark star decals twinkle, and the planets twirl above us as my eyelids fall. I've imagined this moment countless times, put myself in the female lead's place in hundreds of romantic comedies, but this is better than I ever could've imagined, better than pizza, French fries, cheesecake or chocolate, better than anything that's ever touched my lips before.

Maybe I've been too hard on myself all this time. Maybe I'm not as bad as I thought. If a guy like Devin can like me, I must be okay.

He lays his hands on my waist, and my body stiffens. I am mortified, imagining the rolls of fat seeping between his fingers like Silly Putty.

It's happening too fast.

He plays with the hem of my shirt for a few seconds before his hands fly up to my bra. I want to tell him to stop, but I'm afraid. My lips are paralyzed. I don't want him to think I'm uptight, but I'm not sure I'm ready for this. I barely know him. Words rattle around my head like coins in a dryer, but none make their way to my lips.

He continues to kiss me, but I don't kiss him back. My lips just hang there. I'm frozen. My limbs refuse to move. I picture Jordan's little brother lying here each night, the smell of bubble gum toothpaste wafting from his slightly parted lips and a trickle of saliva seeping into his pillow as he dreams about pitching for the Astros. I don't know why, but it makes me sad.

Mom and Buela. What would they say if they could see me now? They'd be so ashamed of me. Suddenly they're there, standing on either side of the bed. Mom's head swings from side to side, and her arms are crossed in front of her. Buela leans over and shakes a small vial over the bedcover, dousing us with holy water. Something about it feels familiar. Like déjà vu. She makes the sign of the cross and buries her face in her hands.

Then Luz shows up, blinking at me and hugging her stuffed kangaroo to her chest.

I pull away from Devin and stand up. “I'm sorry. I can't.”

He looks up at me, then down at his hand, brings it to his nose and sniffs it. “What is that? Powder?” His face breaks into a grin. “Ah, shit. I can't do this. I thought I could, but I can't. It's too twisted.” He flops back on the mattress, lacing his fingers behind his head, and stares at the ceiling.

“What do you mean? What's too twisted?”

He lowers his arms and props himself up on his elbows. “This. You. Me. I bet the guys I could do it, but I can't. Just forget it.”

The pieces come shooting together like a magnetized puzzle. Realization whacks me in the face. A voice in my head begs me to save myself, to keep my mouth shut, but I don't listen.

“What kind of a bet?”

“A stupid bet that I could . . . ” He rolls his eyes. “You know what FAF is?”

“No. What is it?”

“Never mind. My buzz is wearing off. I'm going downstairs to chug more beer.” He opens the door and walks out.

I'm left alone.

The large, round bodies of the planets above me spin uncontrollably, hurtling toward each other faster and faster. They collide and shatter into a million pieces, then float away to the place where nothing is. Weightless.

Pili

"Who do you think shot him?" I plop a heap of stuffing onto my plate. The TV show *Dallas* is all anyone can talk about, and I'm no exception.

Miri sits next to me in what used to be Mamá's chair, facing what was her favorite piece of furniture in the entire house, Abuelita's burled walnut credenza. She tugs on her father's arm. "Can we light the candles now, Papi? Pili said we could."

"In a minute," Carlos says, shrugging off her hand. "Sue Ellen did it. It's always the wife."

I butter a roll. "That's because the wife usually has the most compelling motive."

"What the hell does she have to complain about? JR gives her everything she could want. A big, fancy house. All those expensive dresses and furs. She's dripping with diamonds. That huge rock on her finger covers her entire knuckle, for chrissake."

Pera reaches across the table to pour gravy on Miri's turkey slices and passes the boat-shaped pitcher to Carlos. "I think it was her lover," she says, wiping her hands on her apron.

"Hell, no. Dusty? That wimp and his sissy thin neckerchiefs no real cowboy would be caught dead wearing? He couldn't fire a BB gun. Besides, he died in the plane crash, so it couldn't be him."

"It could too. They're always killing off people and bringing them back to life in these shows. Cemeteries in soap operas should have revolving doors." I lay Miri's napkin neatly across her lap and pass around the bread basket. "I bet it was Sue Ellen's sister. She hated him more than anybody."

"Maybe it was Jeannie. She was probably pissed at him for sticking her in that bottle all those years," he says, referring to the actor who played JR's TV wife in *I Dream of Jeannie.* He obviously thought the joke was funny, laughing to himself. "Wish I had one of those myself."

"Which? A genie or a bottle? You must mean a genie 'cause you keep yourself in a steady supply of bottles, already," I say.

Pera grabs my hand and Carlos'. "Let's say grace so we can eat."

Miri puts her hand in mine, and Carlos narrows his eyes at me as we all make the sign of the cross and bow our heads.

"*Gracias, Diosito*, for the food before us. And for this time together as a family. Please be with those *que sufren hambre* and those who are alone. Give them strength and nourish them with your abundant blessings," Pera intones solemnly.

We all lift our heads and lower our hands to our plates, except Pera, who continues praying. Our heads drop again. "*Y gracias por cuidar del Papa* John Paul on his trip to Germany last week. Thank you for allowing him to have a successful visit. Please watch over him always." We lift our heads again, but Pera goes on, so we lower them one more time. "*Y por favor*, guide him in all he says and does."

Carlos lets go of Miri's hand. "That's enough, Pera. I'd like to eat this bird before Santa comes down the chimney and eats it for me."

Pera opens her eyes and lifts her head. "*Amén*."

"A-men," we all echo.

I watch Pera's magnified face through one of Abuelita's crystal candlesticks. "Everything looks delicious. And the cranberry sauce came out perfect. Tastes exactly like Tía Norma's."

"You did the turkey. That's the hardest part," she says.

"It is not. I just stuck the thing in the oven. You did all the work."

"I hope you put enough butter in the potatoes this time. Last time they were all lumpy. Not creamy enough," Carlos says.

"Now, Papi?"

Carlos rolls his eyes again and drains his glass. "First, go to the kitchen and get me another beer."

Miri hops off her chair.

"No," Pera says abruptly.

We all look at her.

She smiles self-consciously. "I'll get it, *m'ija*," she says, untying her apron. "You sit and eat."

Miri sits down again and looks at me. "Can we light them now? You said on special occasions, and I want to make rainbows."

"Of course, we can." I pat my pockets, but they're empty. It's been years since I carried any matches or lighters.

Carlos scowls. "Jesus Christ, already. Go get the lighter from my coat. It's on the couch."

Miri lays her napkin neatly on her chair and skips happily to the living room.

"I swear, that girl is getting to be more and more like her mother."

"I hope so," I say instinctively, but I'm not sure it's true.

"I can't find it," Miri calls from the other room.

Carlos exhales impatiently and shouts back. "It's in one of the front pockets. Look in both. Sunny as hell outside, and she wants to light candles," he mumbles under his breath, helping himself to another serving of potatoes.

Pera drifts back from the kitchen and hands him his beer.

He wipes the condensation off the bottle with his finger and wipes it on the lacy tablecloth. "She's getting to be as helpless as you are. Can't do a thing for herself."

I pass the butter dish to Pera. "She's only five years old. And she can do plenty. She's the smartest one in her class. She's already reading books while everyone else is still eating paste and learning to color inside the lines."

Miri runs back from the living room out of breath. "Yeah, Papi. I know all my colors and my shapes. Like this one. I found it in your pocket." She holds up a plastic key chain with the word, Safari Motel, and the number twelve etched across it in chintzy gold. "It's a blue diamond like the ones in my cereal. See?"

Carlos' eyes plummet to his plate, and he runs his fork across the mound of potatoes, leaving deep ruts. My eyes leap to Pera, but her chair is empty. She's become invisible. Vanished into thin air. Nothing left of her but a stained apron draped across the back of her chair.

"What's it open?" Miri says, clutching the diamond in her small, dimpled fist. It dwarfs her entire hand, covers all of her knuckles put together.

Pilar

The key glides in smoothly and turns with a satisfying click. I turn to wave at the Uber driver, but he's already gone. Once again the pitiful irony of my life is revealed. Most kids my age sneak in through a back door because they're late for curfew, not early. Fortunately, it appears everyone's already gone to bed. It's quiet, and all the lights are out, except for the one above the sink. Fresh tears spring to my eyes as I lean against the door and slump to the floor, hug my knees to my chest and rock back and forth. It feels good to let go.

A twinge of guilt nags at me for bailing on Gabe, but it couldn't be helped. There was no way I was staying in that house another millisecond. I had to get out of there pronto. If only I had Sonny's scaling ability, I could've climbed out a window onto a sturdy tree limb and dropped down to the manicured shrubbery below. Instead, I scrambled down the stairs, concentrating on each carpeted rectangle in front of me, out the front door and into the muggy night. A crescent moon hung above the rooftops and gleamed on the shiny mineral flecks embedded in the pavement as I trudged past lamp-lit houses, where families watched movies and played board games together, and kids held sleepovers, building forts out of living room chairs and old bedsheets.

Thank God, Gabe isn't here. It would be even more humiliating if he saw me like this. Besides, he shouldn't have to leave the party because of me. That would be even more pathetic.

He probably hasn't even noticed I'm gone. He's probably too busy having a great time with Becca and his new friends, and I'm glad for him. I am. Really.

I send him a text explaining that I wasn't feeling well and I'm already home. I shove my phone back inside my purse. A light bulb turns on in my head, and I feel the blood drain from my face and my heart slink to my toes. All those texts Devin sent. His navigationally challenged friend and his helicopter-parenting mother. Was he even texting anyone?

I am such an idiot.

I grab my phone from my purse again and stare at the screen saver. It's a picture I took last summer in Port Aransas. Mom and Shane stand barefoot in the sand with Luz between them, the sun shimmering on the water as it sets behind them. I remember that moment so clearly, how happy they were and how happy it made me to see them that way. Luz would laugh and pull her knees up to her chest every time the water washed up on shore, and Mom and Shane would swing her up by her arms. Their faces peer back at me as if shielding me from the words I know I'll find inside the phone.

My finger slides across the screen in one fluid motion, unlocking it. I hit the blue bird icon and find Devin's username. My finger hovers over the word, Follow. The point of no return. It reminds me of one of the motivational posters at school. A line of ducks waddle single file, but the last duck faces the opposite direction and the words, "Lead, Don't Follow," are in a puddle under his webbed feet. There is no "Lead" option here.

I touch my fingertip to the screen. There they are. The words. Out there for anyone and everyone to see.

@DevinGillespie: Operation FAF is a go. Doing some ground work.

@DevinGillespie: Ha! upstairs now. phase 2 complete. #smoothoperator #fluffchaser

@DevinGillespie: This might be harder than I thought. nt lube with more liquor. #thoughtfatchickswereeasy

@DevinGillespie: aborting mission. someone beer me. #faffailure #chubflub

I type FAF into Google and a link to "Urban Dictionary" pops up. I click on it and a list of definitions appears:

"FAF: fancy and free, fine as fuck, fit as fuck, funny as fuck, fuck a fatty . . . "

When I read the last one, I drop the phone in my lap, pull the long neck of my shirt up over my face and wail silently into the ribbed fabric. When I lower it again, my eyes and cheeks feel raw and swollen. Now, there's nothing left. Not a single tear.

The light above the sink reflects on the stainless steel of the refrigerator door, making it glow like a neon motel sign in a blizzard. I heave myself off the floor and stride over to it, determined. FAF. Fridge and Freezer. My eyes scour the shelves like a mother scanning a missing persons database. My hands twitch, eager to clutch something and stuff it into the immense hole that is my mouth, desperate to fill the darker, more cavernous one which lies below it. A bottomless pit. My hunger.

I rummage:

half a cantaloupe
tub of cottage cheese
2 avocados
bowl of something brown and soupy
½ a tuna sub
package of uncooked bacon
bottles of salad dressing, ketchup, horseradish

bag of shredded cheese
carton of eggs
jug of milk
orange juice
jar of jelly
relish
a stack of Whataburger ketchup packets

There it is. Jackpot. A freezer bag holding four slices of pepperoni pizza leftover from dinner and a large bowl of Buela's rice pudding.

I grab a bottle of ranch dressing from the refrigerator door and squeeze huge globs onto each slice, fold them in half lengthwise and shove them into my mouth one after the other. They're good. Amazingly good. So good I wouldn't be surprised if I died, went to heaven and found God sitting on His golden throne eating this very thing.

I toss the empty bag on the counter with my mouth still full of pizza. Next, I tear off the cellophane wrapping from the top of the pudding bowl. Spoon. Need a spoon. I'm not going to mess with that noisy drawer, so I grab a large wooden one from the utensil jar by the stove instead and finish off the pudding in four mouthfuls. I lick the spoon while I continue my search. Aha, a carton of potato salad. I yank off the lid, pitch it behind me and tilt the tub up to my mouth, slapping the bottom to loosen every last bit and wiping the sides clean with my finger. I scan the fridge once more before moving on to the freezer. I slip four frozen waffles into the toaster and finish off what's left of a half-gallon tub of low fat vanilla ice cream while I wait for them to pop up. It's not my first choice of flavor, but it makes a good base.

Vanilla ice cream is the naked mannequin of snack food, waiting to be dressed up and accessorized. I crumble up a package of graham crackers into the round container and squeeze in what's left of a bottle of Hershey's syrup. I shovel in spoonful after spoonful as fast as I can, pressing my tongue against the roof of my mouth to avoid brain freeze, buttering the waffles between bites.

A familiar sense of urgency overtakes me, and I can't get the food into my mouth fast enough. It's like I'm competing in a hedonistic race against myself.

I scoop ice cream onto each waffle and fold it up like a taco. A new culinary creation. If necessity is the mother of invention, then desperation is its father. I barely taste the food. The overloaded nerve endings on my tongue have gone numb. I'm not hungry anymore either, but I can't stop. My hands have taken on a will of their own. They keep reaching for the food and shoving it into my mouth like they're on autopilot. I'm not in my body but floating above it, watching myself from a distance again.

I'm completely out of control.

I'm not done. I want more.

Shane pulled out a box of chocolate chip cookies from one of the grocery bags earlier this afternoon. I search the pantry and all the cabinets, but no dice. Mom must've upped her game and found a better hiding place. I haul a ladder-back chair over to the fridge and step up onto the balls of my feet to search the cabinet above it. The cookies aren't there either, but something else is. The Easy Bake Oven Shane and Mom gave Luz for her birthday.

It's heavy, and I almost lose my balance and fall off the chair trying to pull it down. Packets of powdered cookie and cake mix are crammed inside the small, purple oven. I rip them open and empty them into a clear plastic bowl, add water from the faucet and stir it up into a big, gloopy mass of dough. It's not as good as a log of Nestle Toll House, but it'll do in a pinch. I polish it off so quickly, I barely remember eating it. The last few minutes are a blur. I feel sick and exhausted.

I hate myself.

I hate myself.

I ate myself.

I slump back into the chair and catch my reflection in the refrigerator door. Dressing and syrup drip down my chin onto my shirt, and bits of graham cracker and cookie dough stick to my hair.

This is a new low. Eating my little sister's birthday present. This is it. I've hit it. Rock bottom. Not the bottom of the barrel. Below that. The bottom of a barrel buried in the deepest part of the ocean, where no light filters through from above and nothing exists but microbial life forms.

I need help.

Shane's truck pulls up outside. Gabe's home.

My eyes leap around the room inspecting the crime scene. Evidence of my binge is strewn all over the floor and countertops. The sound of the truck door slamming spurs me into action, and I jump up from the chair like someone's shoved a cactus down my pants. I gather the empty bags and containers and stuff them into the trash can under the sink. My foot catches on the small rug in front of it, and I stumble to the fridge, clutching the bottles of dressing and syrup. I haven't moved this fast since they handed out free sundaes at the new Dairy Queen on Bellaire.

Stray crumbs fall from my hair as I speed walk through the living room and down the hall, squeaky floorboards be damned. The smell of Aqua Net and Palmolive soap lingers in the air, and the door to Buela's room closes. She must've gotten up to use the bathroom.

I ease my bedroom door closed behind me and feel around in the dark for my T-shirt, pull it over my head and slip into my pajama bottoms. Moonlight spills through the window onto Luz's side of the bed. Her curls are splayed across the pillow, and her mouth hangs open in a perfect pouty O, like she's expressing shock at the enormity of my consumption even in her sleep. Her yellow hair actually glimmers like that of a fairytale princess. I wish she were one, and I could lock her up in a tower, far away from boys like Devin.

I climb into bed and bury my nose in her hair. She still has that baby smell, that unearthly one that no words can accurately describe, the human version of new car smell. I slip my arms around her waist and tuck my knees behind the backs of hers, spooning her small frame.

Pili

Miri's hand clasps mine as we stroll amid the fruit-filled branches, patches of peachy sky scarcely visible through the awning of thick, green foliage. I remember walking beneath them when I was her age, the way they towered over me then like benevolent beings. They reminded me of the Christmas trees at midnight Mass, half a dozen of them set up in an elaborate display beside the altar. That night, I sat next to Pera, tugging at the scratchy plaid dress Mamá had bribed me to wear, our cousins nodding off in the pews behind us, and counted each golden ornament, fingering the candy cane in my pocket in an effort to stay awake.

Miri points to a grapefruit hanging from a tree in the center of the yard. Her tree. The one that produces the largest and sweetest fruit. Its branches drape so low they nearly touch the ground. It's always been my favorite, the one I'd run to for refuge whenever the tide of the world carried me from the tolerable shores of listlessness to the rough, open sea. The day Papá died, I sat here for hours with my arms wound tightly around my shins. The soothing voices of my aunts drifted out from the open kitchen window, and soft light formed a path across the grass to my feet. The cloak of branches enfolded me in wide sweeping arcs, shielding me from the encroaching darkness as I cried and cried until there were no tears left. I made certain of that, made sure my face was dry and my jaw set before stepping out from under the canopy of my tree's protective limbs and marching determinedly toward the house where Pera was waiting for me to utter the words I'd say to her countless times in the ensuing years, without ever being certain they were true: "Everything is going to be okay."

It seems like only yesterday that I claimed that same tree for Miri. The memory springs forth from the recesses of my mind. Pera and the baby were asleep inside as I carried the burlap sack across the yard. The morning sun glinted off the skins of the fruit as I sat on my heels at the base of the trunk and dug a crater roughly two feet deep with Mamá's spade, rainwater dripping from the dark glossy leaves onto my back and shoulders. I lowered the bag into the hollow and untied it, revealing the thick, blood-soaked tissue.

The umbilical cord ran up the center of the placenta like a trunk, branching out into a network of smaller, bluish vessels. I dropped it in, swept the piles of dirt into the hole again and patted it smooth with the palms of my hands.

"That one," Miri says. I grab her round the waist and lift her up. She tugs and tugs, but the grapefruit won't budge.

"Pull hard, *gordita*, and twist. Show that fruit who's boss."

I hold her up higher, and she yanks with both hands, finally freeing it and hugging it to her chest. I carry her to the porch steps, where we sit down side by side.

"Why did Mami and Papi have to leave so fast?" she says, handing me the fruit. "They didn't even finish their turkey."

"They have some grown up things to talk about."

"Are they going to come back?"

"Your mami is. We'll go get her after she talks to your father and packs a few things. You two are going to stay here with me for a few days." I dig my nails into the thick rind and peel it off in strips.

"Is Papi coming too?"

"No, not this time."

"Why not?"

Juice drips down my fingers as I dig my thumbs deep into the pulp and break it apart.

"Sometimes people need time away from each other to cool off and think things over."

"You mean like a time-out? We have those in school. The teacher makes Linda Galván sit in the stinky corner next to the hamster cage when she's bad. One time she was really bad. She told Ms. Suárez she looked like Boss Hogg in her white jacket and had to sit there until lunchtime."

I've seen Ms. Suárez, and she does look like the villain from *The Dukes of Hazzard*. Even without the jacket. I try not to laugh as I hand her a wedge of grapefruit. "That is bad."

"Eduardo said the hands of the clock would stop moving if Linda looked at it, since she was in time-out. I told him they wouldn't, but I kept sneaking looks to see if it was true."

I offer her another wedge. Most kids find the bittersweet flavor off-putting, but Miri sucks on the pink flesh with relish. I like to think she'll handle the bitterness of life in the same way.

"Is Papi in time-out for making Mami cry?"

I kiss her forehead. "She wasn't crying. She's upset, but she'll be okay."

"Not today, but she has before." She looks down and bites her bottom lip. "Don't tell her, but sometimes at night, I can hear Papi yelling at her through the wall, telling her it's all her fault."

"Telling her what's her fault?"

"That he's not here. That he's dead. And then Mami starts to cry. Who's not here? Who's dead?"

Pilar

Gabe's acting weird. Not his usual warm and friendly self. As a matter of fact, he was quiet all weekend and kept to himself. He even ate dinner in his room Saturday night, said he was feeling tired. I think he's avoiding me. He must've heard about what happened between me and Devin. After I left, news must've spread through the party like wildfire.

Buela's acting strange, too. Her cooking has changed. From mouthwatering medleys, blended beautifully and rich with cheeses and sauces, to plain meals, each food group distinct and compartmentalized. Last night, she made grilled chicken for dinner. She served it with peas and carrots instead of rice and beans, wheat rolls instead of flour tortillas. Even Mom noticed and asked her about it.

Buela said, "I'm not getting any younger and need to take better care of myself. I'm turning over a blank leaf, *como dicen*."

For the first time in my life, she didn't try to shove second helpings onto my plate.

My alarm clock beeps. When I reach over to slam the snooze button, my hand hits something small and hard on the nightstand. I wipe the sleep from my eyes and squint it into focus. It's a small wooden statue of a man in a brown robe carrying a bunch of lilies and a book. I tuck it under my pillow and pull the comforter over my head. There is no way I'm going to school today. I'd rather spend the day shopping for swimsuits with the models from the Victoria's Secret catalogue.

Luz is already up and dressed. The room brightens as she slides the curtains open and pulls the blanket away from my face. "Pipi, it's time to get up. You don't want to be late for school."

I cover my head again. "I don't?"

She uncovers it. "Nope. You've got to get up and be you. Nobody else will do."

I scoot up higher onto my pillow and wrap the corner of the blanket around my face. "Where'd you hear that? Dr. Seuss?"

Luz jumps up onto the bed next to me. "No, silly. Dr. Phil."

"School is not a possibility today, Luz. Tell Mom I have cramps or something."

She leans her face in close to mine, the sweet smell of Lucky Charms marshmallows on her breath. "But you have to go. Don't you want to know what part you got?" She tugs on my arm and helps me sit up. "Come have breakfast. Buela made you some oatmeal with strawberries on top. You can go to camps in summer." She draws back the sheet and drags my legs over the edge of the bed one at a time.

Gabe is sitting at the kitchen table forking *chorizo con huevo* onto a tortilla. He looks up and smiles when I walk in. "I'll be ready to go in ten minutes. Figured you'd want to get there early to check the list."

I flop down onto a chair. "What's the point?"

Gabe shrugs. "You have to know one way or the other. So you might as well get it over with. Otherwise, it's going to bug you all day."

He seems to be back to his usual self. Maybe he was tired.

I pour myself a glass of orange juice. "Why can't Mr. Leal just post it online?"

Gabe shrugs again. "Beats me. Maybe he wants to prolong the suspense."

"More like prolong the torture."

Buela sets a bowl of oatmeal down in front of me and kisses my cheek. "*Buenos días, gordita*. You sleep good?"

"Yes. Thanks, Buela."

I lift a spoonful of the lumpy, beige cereal to eye level and turn it upside down, let it plop back into the bowl and steal a look at the refried beans and melted cheese oozing out of the rolled up tortilla on Gabe's plate.

"*Avena*'s good for you. It will help settle your stomach," Buela says.

Mom stands at the counter pouring coffee into her thermos. "Don't be sad if your name's not there. There's always next year. Good luck, *m'ija*," she says, planting a kiss on the top of my head.

"You're not supposed to say that, Mommy. It's bad luck. You're supposed to tell her to break her leg," Luz says.

Mom gives her a puzzled look. "Why would I tell her that?"

Luz shrugs and climbs into the chair next to Gabe's.

"Okay then, break your leg, *m'ija*. Break both of them."

~~~

When I spot Sonny leaning against a bike rack, waiting for us in front of the school, a few of the butterflies in my stomach find a place to perch and rest. She's wearing yellow argyle socks pulled up over her knees and a T-shirt that reads: "Vampire Love Stories Bite." Her short hair is divided into sections and twisted into knots all over her head.

"Hey, Sonny," I say.
~~~

"Come with us to the drama hall," Gabe says. "We're gonna go check the cast list."

Sonny runs her toe over a flattened piece of gum stuck to the pavement. It's black and hard and has lost all of its gooey-ness. Too bad. If only I could step on it and get myself stuck. Anything to keep me from having to walk into the building in front of me.

"I already did. Sorry, Pi. You didn't get a part."

The center of my body feels like a gaping hole left by a shotgun blast. Rejection sounds like a rush of wind. It whooshes right through me, and a feeling settles over me like a buzzard on roadkill. A confirmation. YOU ARE NOT.

Gabe laces his fingers on top of his head and looks up at the sky. It's gray but bright as if the sun still might burn its way through the shapeless, wispy clouds scattered across it. "I can't believe it. This sucks. You really were awesome, Pi. I'm not just saying that to make you feel better. Mr. Leal's useless. He wouldn't know talent if it were clipped to his dorky red tie."

"Abso-freaking-lutely. You were the best by far. We're talkin' red candy good," adds Sonny. "You were like . . . you know, when a song comes on the radio and you kind of like it, but you keep on searching the stations to make sure there's not a better one on. Well, you were like a song you get to and stop searching."

"Better than that," Gabe says. "She was like a song that you stay in the car to listen to even after you've reached your destination."

"Thanks guys, but it's probably for the best. I've just been fooling myself."

Gabe grabs my hand and jiggles my arm. "You can't give up that easily."

"I'm not. I'm getting real. It's time to get my head out of the clouds and onto firm ground."

He blows the tuft of hair out of his face. "Firm ground is overrated."

"Well, it's not all bad. At least, you still get to be a part of it. Even if it's not on stage," Sonny says.

"I will? How?"

"Yeah, you get to help out. You got picked to be the stage manager."

My eyes lock onto Gabe's.

"That's kind of a big deal, right? Pi? Gabe?" she says. "Hey, where are y'all going?"

Sonny calls after us as we dash up the concrete steps to the double doors, fling them open and speed walk down the hallway. We almost collide with Ms. Stone, who steps out of the faculty lounge carrying a stack of papers. She yells for us to slow down, and we do until we turn the corner, out of sight. Then we're off again. Running so fast now, a breeze hits my face and blows my hair back. I am a woman in motion.

Sonny catches up to us as we race past the cafeteria. "Why are we running? What's going on?"

"Not sure yet. Maybe nothing," I yell.

We're smiling and laughing, making spectacles of ourselves, but we don't care.

When we get to the drama hallway, there's a small crowd gathered around the bulletin board outside of Mr. Leal's room. My heart has bounced up into my head and thumps in my ears. The three of us squeeze to the front. I clutch my side, trying to catch my breath, and Gabe runs his finger down the list of names. He doesn't have to go far before he comes to mine. It's there in black and white. In Times New Roman. Twelve point font. Out there for the whole world to see: "Stage Manager—Pilar Sánchez."

Gabe throws his arm around me and squeezes my shoulder. "I knew it! I told you, you did awesome."

Sonny waves her hand in front of my face. “Pi? You in there? Hello?”

The corners of my mouth creep upward, but my eyes refuse to blink. They stay glued to my name on the paper. It’s like witnessing a miracle. Like God Himself came down from heaven and seared my name onto the list with a lightning bolt.

Sonny lays her palm on her chest. “I’m so relieved you’re happy. Sorry I scared you. I didn’t think you’d be so psyched to be a part of the crew. I thought you wanted to be out on stage.”

“You don’t get it. She will be on stage,” Gabe says. “In *Our Town*, the stage manager is part of the cast. In the play. It’s hard to explain.”

“You mean a character? With lines and everything?”

“Yes! Tons of lines.”

“What! Shut up!” Sonny hops around in a circle from one foot to the other shaking her hips. “Awesome sauce. Way to go! You did it!”

“Thanks, Sonny,” I say with my eyes still pinned to the wall. It’s like they can’t fully take in what they’re seeing, no matter how hard I stare. “Somebody pull me away from here. I can’t move.”

Gabe grabs my shoulders and turns me away from the bulletin board. “Come on. Your name’ll still be there after you move your eyes away. It’s not going to disappear if you stop looking at it.”

“Are you sure? Because it feels like I’m in a dream.”

“You are in one,” says Sonny. “A dream come true. Yea-uh.”

They steer me down the hall, but I stop in my tracks. “I almost forgot. I’ve got to do something real fast. I’ll meet you guys in the cafeteria.”

"Actually, I have to talk to Mrs. Miles about my chem test. I'll catch y'all later," Gabe says. "And congrats, Pi. You deserve it."

He and Sonny head down the hallway together.

There's only a small scattering of people left around the bulletin board. I knock softly on Mr. Leal's door and poke my head in. "Mr. Leal?"

The room is dark except for the soft glow of a lamp in the corner. "Ms. Sánchez. Come in. What can I do for you?"

I follow the aroma of tea to his desk, where he's writing notes in a copy of the script. Classical music plays from a portable radio on a shelf behind him, and a framed poster of cartoon pictures hangs above it. There's Santa Claus. A mermaid. The Easter Bunny. A triangle with Bermuda written across it. A fairy holding a molar. A unicorn. A tall, furry creature—Bigfoot, maybe. And a playbill with the words, "Small Parts," written on the cover.

"I don't want to bother you. I just wanted to say thank you. For casting me. I really appreciate the opportunity, and I'm going to work really hard."

Mr. Leal takes a sip from a mug that says: "Drama Queen." "I don't doubt it. But you don't have to thank me. You earned it."

I shuffle from one foot to the other, twist my fingers together and look up at the ceiling. "Okay, well . . . thanks."

I give an awkward laugh when I realize I've thanked him a second time and turn to leave. When I reach the doorway, I stop and turn to face him again. "Uh, Mr. Leal?"

He looks up from his script again, lamplight reflecting on the shiny lenses of his glasses.

"Why did you choose me?"

He puts down his pencil and leans back in his chair, brings his fingertips together under his chin. He's quiet for a moment, as if forming the words in his head. "Talent, which by the way you have in spades, isn't really all that rare. It's like buried treasure. People think it exists mainly in the movies. But there are millions of undiscovered shipwrecks all over the ocean floor waiting to be found. It takes time and energy to find them, but they're there. Talent is like that. There is something else, though," he pauses and tilts his head like he's searching for the best way to explain.

I try to help. "Was it because I came back?"

"You surprised me. But it was more than that. You ran out of there upset and crying, but when you came back and started reading, you changed right before my eyes, became someone else. You became Emily. I'm betting the same thing would happen no matter which part you read. You'd become that person, too. You have that gift, that ability to take a part of yourself and connect it with someone else's experience. It allows you to immerse yourself fully into a character, to think what they think, to feel what they feel. It's empathy."

Steam rises from his mug and I imagine I can feel it drifting over to me, permeating the pores of my skin and suffusing me with warmth.

"You believed you were Emily," he says, taking another sip. "You made me believe it, too."

Pili

Carlos' truck is gone when we pull into the driveway of Pera's house. It's finally happened. She's sent him packing. I'm so relieved and grateful, I feel like I'm floating, like a massive weight has been lifted off my shoulders. A one-hundred-ninety-pound weight to be exact. Miri hops out of the car and runs across the sparse lawn into the house ahead of me, calling for her mother. I bound up the porch steps after her and fling the screen door wide open.

Pera slouches on the living room couch with her knees pressed together and her hands in her lap. Her eyes are vacant, and wisps of hair have fallen loose from her hair clip. Miri climbs into her lap and leans against her chest.

"You ready to go?" I say, ignoring the uneasy feeling at the pit of my stomach.

Pera kisses the top of Miri's head. "Go play in your room while I talk to your *tía*," she says.

My heart plunges.

Miri jumps down from her mother's lap and disappears down the hallway. Pera crosses one leg over the other, her ratty slipper dangling precariously from her foot.

"Where are your bags? In the bedroom?" I turn toward the hallway. "I'll go put them in the car."

"We're not coming, Pili."

I stop dead in my tracks. "What do you mean, you're not coming? Did you make him leave instead? Good idea. Why should you be the one to leave?"

Her eyes drift to the carpet. "I told him it would be better if I talked to you alone. *Pero*, he's coming back. He had some things to take care of."

It feels as though she's punched me in the stomach, knocked the wind out of me. I hunch over and clutch my side.

"He said it only happened one time. It didn't mean anything."

"And you believe him!" I scream.

"Don't yell. Miri will hear you."

I cross my arms in front of me and shift my weight from foot to foot.

"He's sorry," she says.

Thoughts flood my brain in a mad rush. Like on one of those highway interchanges, the kind with overpasses stacked one on top of the other, words are zooming like cars in every direction. So I respond to the last thing she said. "Did he *say* he was sorry? Because I don't think he is. I don't think he knows what that word even means."

Pera uncrosses her legs and finally looks up at me. "Not in so many words, *pero* . . . "

"In any words?"

"I knew you were going to react this way. He is sorry. I can tell. You don't know him the way I do."

I bring my fingertips to my forehead and throw my hands out in front of me. "How did you expect me to react? Listen to yourself, Pera. Do you actually believe the words that are coming out of your mouth?"

"People make mistakes, Pili. Nobody's perfect. They can be thoughtless and selfish. That doesn't mean you stop loving them. Love isn't a faucet you can turn off and on whenever you want. You have to keep it on and let it flow. *Si no*, it's not love. It's nothing but a . . . a stopped up sink!" She folds her arms in front of her. "You expect too much. You always have."

"And you don't expect enough. But this isn't about me or you anymore. It's about someone else. Someone who's watching you, learning from you, molding her character in your shadow. Your daughter. Everything you say and do will determine the person she becomes."

Pera stands up and stares into the piles of magazines and phonebooks stacked in the unused fireplace. *"¡¿Qué más quieres?!* What do you want from me?" she yells.

I glance down the hallway and turn on the stereo. Blondie's voice fills the room, singing "The Tide is High".

"I want you to stand up for yourself. Why are you putting up with this? Why? You deserve so much more."

"No," she says, running her finger slowly across the empty mantel and gathering a small mound of dust. "I don't."

Pilar

It's the space between that's the hardest. The gaps, nooks and crannies in our blocks of scheduled time, when we torture ourselves and others. Those brief interims between classes, when the hallways become raging rivers and everyone flails about trying to stay afloat while navigating from room to room. Then we drop anchor for forty-five minutes at a time and focus our attention on a teacher or a piece of lab equipment, a book or blackboard, and not on each other.

It's why I've come to dread that raucous trill of the bell ringing, when I have to leave the relative safety of the classroom.

I'm still waiting for the ax to drop. The entire school must've heard about me and Devin by now. Surprisingly, no one's said anything. Not even Becca has sought me out. After being supplied with this nuclear ammo, I fully expected her to make a beeline for me first thing this morning. Besides calling me a loser on my way to gym class, she's left me alone. I haven't run into Devin either, thank God.

It's not like I've been giving people any opportunity to approach me, though. I keep to myself and think of my name on that casting list, while I look firmly at the floor as I make my way to class. So far, all's quiet. But this could merely be the calm before the storm. It can't be trusted.

Sonny is waiting for me at my locker before lunch. "What's up, Meryl?"

"Hey, Sonny," I grab my brown bag from the top shelf and slam the door shut, "you seen Gabe? Maybe we should wait for him."

"No, haven't seen him since this morning. He wasn't in third period either."

"That's strange. Where could he be?"

Sonny bites her lip uneasily. "I think he's trying to avoid everyone because of what happened Friday night at that party."

Someone rolls a slide projector into a nearby classroom, and the wheels rattling over the metal threshold sound like thunder cracking. I grip my lunch bag with both hands and bang it against my thighs. "I guess you heard about what happened too, huh? Figured you would."

Sonny frowns. "Yeah, I heard some seniors talking about it this morning. Everyone is."

My skin prickles with humiliation. Each cell of my body screams. Each strand of hair tingles. It's like the universe has aimed a magnifying glass at me, and the sunlight is searing into me: "Gabe's embarrassed to be seen with me."

Sonny wrinkles her forehead. "What makes you say that? Why would he be? He's probably just feeling bad." She tugs on the straps of her backpack. "It sucks."

"It's all my fault. I'm such an idiot. I should've never gone upstairs with Devin. I am so phenomenally stupid."

"What're you talking about? How is it your fault, and what does Devin have to do with it?"

"Me and Devin? At the party. He kissed me. I thought he liked me, but . . . "

Sonny is stunned into silence and stares at me wide-eyed.

"It was all a joke between him and his friends. I'm a joke."

"You are not. He's the joke. Don't worry about it, Pi. Really. No one cares what that bottom feeder has to say. Cara Yarbrough hooked up with him last summer. She said he's hung like a garden gnome in a snow storm." Her lips twitch in anger on my behalf, and that's even more comforting than her kind words. "What a douchebag. Anyway, that's not what I'm talking about. I'm talking about what happened with Gabe."

"What happened with Gabe? Nothing happened."

"Yeah, it did. It's all over school. Connor wants to kick his ass. He's pissed because of him and Becca. Apparently, Gabe was all over her."

"He was not! It was the other way around. She was all over him."

Sonny nods her head slowly. "That does make more sense. Becca doesn't seem like Gabe's type at all."

"What exactly are people saying?"

"All I heard was . . . someone walked in on them in an upstairs bedroom, and Gabe's pants were unbuttoned, and Becca's shirt was off."

My first instinct is to defend Gabe. To grab a megaphone and run through the school proclaiming his innocence. But I can't. Because I don't know what happened. I wasn't there. I didn't see.

Pili

Pera's house has shrunk around me. I hardly fit inside its laminate-wood-paneled walls anymore. They've always reminded me of Carlos. All show and no substance. I've never felt at ease in this squat bungalow with its cracked square of a concrete patio attached in back like an afterthought. I've never closed the front door behind me and put my feet up and my guard down. The warped clapboards feel even tighter around me now. I yearn to bolt out the door, jump behind the wheel of my Impala and zoom down the highway with the wind whipping my hair like a sail.

But I stay put; my arms and legs shoot out through the windows, and my head presses against the low popcorn ceiling, threatening to poke through the roof. Like Alice after she bites the cake in the White Rabbit's house. There's a crushing sensation in my chest, and it's getting harder and harder to breathe. Pera must feel this way every single day. Stuck. Trapped. Immobile. There may as well be concertina wire hemming the scraggly lawn and metal bars on all the windows. I imagine Carlos in the gray uniform of a warden swinging a baton in his hand as he patrols the perimeter.

I always believed he was the one keeping her here—a distorted sense of duty or loyalty to him—but it turns out it's not him after all. Not God either. No, this prison is self-imposed. Pera has sentenced herself. She is held captive by her own guilt and regret. They hang like the sloshing buckets of a water carrier draped across her shoulders as she paces from one end of the mantel to the other.

I turn down the stereo and crane my neck to listen down the hall. The robotic voice of the electronic Speak & Spell I gave Miri last Christmas spells out a word, pausing between each letter as she pushes the corresponding button. "E-C-H-O. That is correct. Now spell, ENOUGH."

I take a step closer to Pera. "How long are you going to go on punishing yourself? It wasn't your fault. It was an accident. You didn't do anything wrong."

She turns away from the fireplace and holds her hand up like a crossing guard with a stop sign. "Don't, Pili. *Por favor . . .* I can't."

She drops her hand again, and every part of her sags with it; the corners of her eyes and mouth, her shoulders, the small pockets of flesh above her knees.

"Miri knows about him, you know." I have to pry my lips apart with my tongue. For once, the words don't want out. "She's heard you and Carlos arguing at night."

She looks up at me with a mixture of fear and surprise, and her hand presses against her mouth as though my words are coming from her.

"Why haven't you told her about Carlitos? She deserves to know." I wait for her to say something, but she remains silent. "It's okay to talk about him. To remember."

Her eyes jolt up from her feet to my face. They're wide enough to see the white around each iris. "You think I don't remember? That I don't think of him every single minute of every day? He's all I think about."

"No, Pera. You don't. You think of how he died, and that's not the same thing. I'm talking about remembering the good things, the things you loved: how the top of his head smelled when he laid it in your lap, how he laughed when he ran through the sprinkler, how his eyes squinted downward when he smiled, how he'd lie in bed with his hands behind his head listening to his favorite story, how his lips puffed out whenever he was angry or how he made that *vroom-vroom* sound when he pushed his truck around the floor. His perfectly rounded little toes. Remember how we stared at them completely mesmerized when he was a baby? The way they'd stick out from under his bed when he hid under there at bath time? Those are the things to hold on to, Pera. He deserves it. Miri does too. Those memories are her birthright. They're a part of her. He was her big brother. Still is. I can't pretend to understand it all, but some parts of us do go on. I know that much now. They have to. They mean too much."

Pera's eyes brim over, and the tears spill down her cheeks like water flowing onto dry land. I clutch her hands and resist the urge to wipe them. Let them drip down her face in long steady streams, splashing our ankles as they hit the floor.

Pilar

Gabe's become a ghost, a shadow in the background again. A wisp of a person drifting through the school like mist. I'll catch a glimpse of him floating around a corner. By the time I make my way through the throng of people, he's already slipped away. He doesn't meet me and Sonny in the cafeteria at lunchtime anymore either. He always has somewhere else he needs to be: "I promised Mrs. Miles I'd clean out her beakers." "I have to print out my English paper in the computer lab." Or today's excuse: "I have to work on my Trail of Tears project in the library." We both know his excuses are just that, but I play my part and pretend to believe him. That's what I'd want him to do for me.

The only time I do see him is at home, where he's more like himself, only quieter and a little withdrawn. Lately, he spends most of his time in Luz's room with a paintbrush in his hand. Her room is beginning to look like a bipolar art gallery, his somber paintings hanging next to her brightly colored animals and fairies.

It's been weeks since Jordan's party, but I still haven't asked him about what happened with Becca. I feel bad bringing it up. I figure, he'll tell me when he's ready. The rumors are still buzzing around school, though. Now, they've grown crazier and more convoluted, from the funny—Gabe was trying on Becca's bra—to the absurd—Gabe and Becca were performing a demonic ritual involving shaving cream and urine—to the disturbing—Gabe got Becca drunk and tried to rape her.

No one's been talking about me. Devin walked by me in the hallway on Tuesday and didn't even look my way. I feel relieved—and guilty for feeling it. It's like Gabe's offered himself as a sacrifice in my place.

Connor still wants to kick Gabe's butt, but he must be having a hard time catching up with him, too. I'm doing whatever I can to keep Gabe out of his way, like convincing him to watch rehearsals after school. I told him I could use some constructive criticism, which isn't exactly true. Mr. Leal gives us plenty. He said the main thing is to embrace vulnerability and relinquish control. I'm used to feeling out of control, but it's hard to let my guard down and be vulnerable. Once I get into the swing of things, though, and immerse myself in the words, it's smoother sailing.

I walk over to my mark and wait for my cue. A small group of people paints a trellis offstage left. Another group experiments with the sound board, moving levers up and down. In the wing to my right, Tara Simonton and Jessica Holley pull long dresses with poofy sleeves up over their jeans. And downstage in front of me, Mr. Leal discusses lighting with a few crew members.

I let the fact that I'm really a part of it sink in, that it's not a dream and my alarm clock isn't going to go off at any second. A feeling of intense gratitude washes over me again. It happens at every rehearsal.

Mr. Leal hops down from the stage and takes a seat several rows back. He crosses an ankle over his knee and nods for me to begin.

A pipe dangles from my lips, one of the few props in the entire play. I peek out from beneath the brim of my fedora. "'Right here's a big butternut tree.'" I rub my hand down the trunk of an imaginary tree and walk downstage right. Gabe sits a few rows from the front with his knees propped up on the seat in front of him, tightening the strings of his gray hoodie around his face. His nose and mouth peek out from the small opening. "'Nice town, y'know what I mean? Nobody very remarkable ever come out of it, s'far as we know. The earliest tombstones in the cemetery up there on the mountain say 1670-1680. They're Grovers and Cartwrights and Gibbses and Herseys—same names as are around here now.'" I take a few steps closer to the audience. "'Well, as I said: it's about dawn. The only lights on in town are in a cottage over by the tracks, where a Polish mother's just had twins. And in the Joe Crowell house, where Joe Junior's getting up so as to deliver the paper. And in the depot, where Shorty Hawkins is gettin' ready to flag the 5:45 for Boston.'" I pause for the sound of a train whistle, but a cock crows instead.

Mr. Leal rolls his eyes and cups his hand around the side of his mouth. "Does that sound like a train to you?" he yells. "Is poor Shorty supposed to ride a rooster to Beantown? Fix it, Sound. Let's get it right."

I remove an imaginary watch from my right pocket and pretend to look at it. "'Naturally, out in the country—all around—there've been lights on for some time, what with milkin's and so on. But town people sleep late.'" I tuck the watch back inside my pocket and cross center stage to Jake Hughes. "'So—another day's begun. There's Doc Gibbs comin' down Main Street now, comin' back from that baby case. And here's his wife comin' downstairs to get breakfast.'" Cassie Stern, a junior, enters from the right and pretends to pull up a window shade. "'Doc Gibbs died in 1930. The new hospital's named after him. Mrs. Gibbs died first—long time ago, in fact. She went out to visit her daughter, Rebecca, who married an insurance man in Canton, Ohio, and died there—pneumonia—but her body was brought back here. She's up in the cemetery there now—in with a whole mess of Gibbses and Herseys—she was Julia Hersey 'fore she married Doc Gibbs in the Congregational Church over there. In our town we like to know the facts about everybody. There's Mrs. Webb, coming downstairs to get her breakfast, too.'" Jessica Holley walks to my left side and places an imaginary frying pan on an imaginary stove. '"That's Doc Gibbs. Got that call at half past one this morning. And there comes Joe Crowell, Jr., delivering Mr. Webb's *Sentinel*.'"

Mr. Leal leans forward in his seat. "Logan, when she says, 'Sentinel,' that's your cue to cross stage right." Logan Ward, a freshman with freckles and flaming red hair, pretends to hurl newspapers into doorways. I step aside as he and Jake exchange lines and steal another look at Gabe, who's lowered his hood from his head and sits up with his fingers laced across his chest.

"Jake, stop messing with your bow tie. It's distracting. And spit out that gum. You're supposed to be a doctor, not a pop star. Logan, use more inflection. You sound like a hypnotist." Gabe nods in agreement. "Pilar, good blocking and gestures, but you're still not loud enough. Make your voice bigger." He pats his stomach. "Breathe from your diaphragm and project. Also, make eye contact with the audience. They should feel like you're really talking to them. Like you're in the play and not in the play. In the world of Grover's Corners and in the real world. Omnipresent. Like God."

I jab my thumb toward where Logan's walked offstage and stick my hand in my pocket. "'Want to tell you something about that boy Joe Crowell there.'"

Mr. Leal leans forward again and cups a hand around his ear.

I take a deep breath and start over even louder. "'Want to tell you something about that boy Joe Crowell there.'" Mr. Leal gives me a thumbs up. "'Joe was awful bright—graduated from high school here, head of his class. So he got a scholarship to Massachusetts Tech. Graduated head of his class there, too. It was all wrote up in the Boston paper at the time. Goin' to be a great engineer, Joe was. But the war broke out and he died in France. All that education for nothing.'"

A cellphone rings backstage.

Mr. Leal whips his tie over his left shoulder and throws his hands up. "Will someone shut that off! It's 1901, people. There're milkmen and paperboys, doctors making house calls and horse drawn wagons. There are no cellphones."

~~~

It's well after six o'clock when Mr. Leal dismisses us, but I take my time gathering my things, wishing rehearsals ran longer. Then there'd be even less of a chance of Connor and his friends hanging around.

Gabe and I head down the junior hallway to retrieve a book from his locker. The walls are covered in posters, anti-drug and anti-bullying announcements. I stop to read each one.

"Bully-free Zone."

"Choose math. Not meth."

"Be prompt. Be polite. Be positive."

"Bill does drugs. Bill is dumb. Don't be like Bill." (The word Don't is crossed out in pencil.)

"Buddies not Bullies."

I lean against the locker across from Gabe's and blow a strand of hair away from my face as he slides out a book with-
~~~

out looking at it and tosses it into his backpack. His movements are slow and sluggish, like he's got weights strapped to his wrists and ankles, but I'm glad he's taking his time. For once, I'm in no hurry to leave school.

"We should call Shane to pick us up. My feet are killing me after standing on stage the last three hours."

The setting sun pours through the strip of windows above the row of lockers, warming his eyes to the amber of melted caramel. He shuts his locker and stoops to zip his backpack. His uneven hairline dips down between the fragile bones at the back of his neck. I finally acknowledge the topic we've been avoiding. "What if Connor's waiting outside? He's no joke. Please let me call Shane, okay? We don't have to tell him anything."

"Then what? Are we going to call him every day, like a couple of scared little kids?" He frowns and hefts his backpack onto his shoulders. "You know, I used to tell myself it wasn't me. That it was those assholes at my other school who were the problem. But here I am, in the same shit again. No matter where I go or what I do, this keeps happening. So it turns out it's not them after all. It is me. It's always been me."

His voice is loud. I'm grateful for the empty hallway.

"It's different for you. You're fat, but so what?"

I flinch inside.

"You could lose weight. But what am I supposed to do? Crawl out of my skin? I can't do that. I can't change who I am."

I bite my lip and steel myself for more, but he doesn't say anything else, only looks at me with that expression I can't stand, the same one Mom wears when she catches me sneaking food.

He laces his fingers behind his head and closes his eyes. "I'm sorry. I didn't mean that."

"It's okay," I mutter.

"No, it's not. You're only trying to help. You care more than my own parents do. They just send me away. Make me someone else's problem."

"That's not true. It was Mom's idea for you to come. We all wanted you to, and I'm glad you did."

I want to tell him more. How it was for me before he arrived, all those lunches I ate in that cramped restroom stall, asking the librarian for help locating a book I'd already found just to have someone to talk to.

"Connor doesn't know you. None of them do. You're talented and kind and amazing." The words come rushing out of me unchecked, and my eyes scurry to the floor as the blood rushes to my face.

It doesn't matter what I've said. None of it is sinking in. He's not hearing me. He can't see what I see.

"I was stupid for thinking things would be different here. There's nowhere else to go."

He looks lost. Like a kid abandoned in a shopping mall. And I did abandon him, left him to talk to stupid Devin, then I left him at the party with Connor, Becca and the rest of them.

"What happened at the party with Becca, Gabe?"

"Nothing happened."

"Then why is Connor so mad at you?"

He looks at me incredulously and laughs dryly. "Come on, Pi. You've heard the rumors. I tried to rape his girlfriend. I'm a rapist. And a devil worshipper."

"That's ridiculous. Just because people box you up in their tiny brains and stick labels on you doesn't make those labels true. But why were you alone with her?"

"I went upstairs looking for you, and she followed me. She started kissing me and messing with my belt buckle right there in the hallway. I tried to be nice at first, but she wasn't getting the hint, so I finally had to push her off me and tell her flat out that I wasn't interested."

I'm eagerly soaking up his words. They don't make me happy exactly, but something close to it. "But how did you end up with her in a bedroom?"

"Bathroom. She started feeling sick. She was pretty sloshed. Could barely stand up. So I got her to a toilet and held her hair out of her face while she puked. That's where I was when I got your text. She got some on her shirt, so she took it off. I was standing at the sink trying to clean it when her friend came barging in."

"Hailey?"

He nods. "So I tossed it to her and took off."

"And the rumors started," I mutter under my breath.

"What's wrong with me? It's like I'm bad luck or something. Like there's a dark cloud following me. You should stay away from me."

His eyes glisten as he turns and heads down the hallway. I know that feeling well, of trying to hold it all in, so I let him go and lag behind as he makes his way to the front entrance. The metal chain looped through the door's handle-bar bangs against it as he pushes it open.

The parking lot in front of the school is deserted. I send up a silent thank you and walk slowly, widening the gap between us. He steps off the curb and across the grid of white lines marking the asphalt. I bring my thumb and index finger up to my eye and squeeze them toward each other until the narrow space between is just wide enough to fit his receding body. When he reaches the sidewalk at the other end, he turns around and waves for me to catch up. I quicken my pace and continue watching him through the frame of my fingers, then my hands, my arms—spreading them wider and wider the closer I get until he's too big for any of the confining spaces of my body, until he's boundless.

~~~

Luz takes a card from the top of the deck and flips it over. "The bottle," she announces.

"*La botella*. Bo-tey-ya," Buela enunciates, scrutinizing the *lotería* card on the table in front of her.

Luz points at my card excitedly. "You have it, Pipi! Put a bean on it. Now, you only need two more to win."

"*Ándale*, Luz. Flip the next one. I'm on a roll," Mom says, rolling a dried pinto bean between her thumb and index finger.

Luz turns over the next card on the pile. "The dancing man," she says loudly.

We stop inspecting our Mexican bingo cards and look up at her.

"*Qué* dancing man? There's no dancing man. Let me see that," Buela says, taking the card from her hand. "Oh, El borracho. The drunk man. See the liquor bottle in his hand?"

"No, Buela. That's water. He's thirsty from all that dancing."

"He's not dancing, Luz. His legs are wobbly from drinking too much," Mom says.

Luz sighs in exasperation. "No, Mommy. He's doing the hat dance. See it on the ground next to him? Someone made a mistake and named the card wrong."

Mom rolls her eyes. "*Bueno*, he's dancing. Next card."

"The lady in the nutshell," Luz says formally, scanning my card. "Pipi, you won!"

I place the last bean on the picture of the woman sitting in the narrow boat. *La chalupa*.

Luz hops out of her chair and pours herself a glass of milk. "When are Daddy and Gabe coming home?"
~~~

"As soon as the movie's over," Mom says, collecting the cards and stacking them into a neat pile.

Luz drains her glass and snatches a dish towel draped over the handle of the oven door. She lays it on her head and orbits the table in wide measured steps, humming that Beyoncé song about putting a ring on it.

Buela's eyes slide to the side as she gathers beans and sweeps them into her hand.

"Mommy, you want a veil like this? Or a longer one? I think you should get a purple one, but Buela says it's supposed to be white to match your dress."

Buela's eyes dart to the side again, and she mutters to herself. "It's a little late for white. That ship's already left the dock, *como dicen*."

Mom folds her arms across her chest and shoots a look at Buela, who is riveted by a small gouge in the wooden table. "What are you talking about, Luz? I'm not getting married."

Luz pulls the towel from her head. "Why not? Don't you want to marry Daddy and have a party with presents and a cake this big?" She holds her arm high above her head and stands on tip toes. "It'll be fun. And the best part is, I'll get to be the flower girl."

Mom closes her eyes, presses her palms together and brings her fingertips to her lips. "Girls, go play in your room. I need to talk to Buela alone."

I don't know why she bothers sending us out of the room. She could send us to the moon, and we'd still be able to hear them. It's like I said, Mom and Buela get louder and louder the more heated they get, and this conversation promises to be a doozy. I take Luz's hand anyway and lead her to my bedroom.

"Mamá, you need to stop. *¡Basta ya!* I don't want you filling Luz's head with any more wedding stuff. That's fighting dirty. Leave her out of it. You're only getting her all excited about something that's not going to happen."

"I'm not filling her head with anything. She wants you to get married. She wants to see you walk down the aisle in a beautiful dress and say, 'I do.'"

Their voices penetrate the closed door. Luz flops down on the bed on her belly and dangles both arms over the side. "Why are Buela and Mommy fighting?"

"They're not fighting. They're clearing the air."

I grab my headphones from around the bedpost, put them on her ears and play some music. She bounces her legs to the rhythm.

"No, that's what you want. She's following your lead. She never talked about Shane and me getting married until you got here. Now, it's all she talks about it."

"*Pues*, so what if she does? She wants her parents to get married. What's wrong with that? That's the way it should be."

"Mamá, I've told you a million times. Marriage changes things. I don't want to get married again. Why would I? So I can be at a man's beck and call night and day for the rest of my life? In the kitchen cooking and cleaning while he's out God-knows-where doing God-knows-what. That might've been fine for you, but I don't want that life."

"And what's wrong with the kitchen? *¡Dígame!* The kitchen is the best part of the house. The heart. *El alma*. Where should I have been all day? In the bathroom?"

"You're missing the point, Mamá. Shane and I are already in a loving, committed relationship. I feel more married to him than I ever felt to Julio. That's what matters, not whether or not we stand in a church and say some words. I did that once already, and you know how that turned out."

"Stand in a church? You say it like it's nothing but a pile of bricks. Well, it's not. *Es la casa de Dios.* And they're not some words, they're a sacred vow. To your husband and to God. Not something that blows away at the first sign of trouble. You should say them carefully. *Con gravedad*. Or not at all. They should land with a thud on the altar and shake the walls like thunder. Because that's what they sound like to the ear of God. That's what they're supposed to be anyway. That's what they were to me."

"No, Mamá. Not at the first sign of trouble. At lots of signs. Signs you chose to ignore."

"I didn't ignore anything. What are you talking about? *Estás confundida*."

"I was there, Mamá. I wasn't blind. You think I didn't see you sniff Papá's shirts for traces of perfume? Search his pockets for receipts for flowers you'd never received or dinners you'd never eaten? And when you found them, you'd get mad and still serve him dinner, anyway, scooping extra onions onto his pork chops with your eyes all red and swollen from crying. You cried in your room a lot. You thought I was asleep, but I wasn't. I heard you. I remember. And I promised myself I'd never let anyone treat me that way, especially not the person who's supposed to love me the most in the world. I promised I'd never be like you."

I wince.

There's a long pause, then Buela's voice again. "It's so easy to point fingers, isn't it? *Muy fácil.* But this isn't about me. It's about your daughters. Think of them. What kind of example are you setting for them? It isn't right living with a man who's not your husband. You're throwing your pearls to the swine!"

"Shane isn't swine. And I am thinking of my daughters. Teaching them to be strong and independent. To stand on their own two feet."

"Well, you're acting more like a woman who's never on her feet. *Una mujer de la calle. ¿M'entiendes? Tú sabes.* You're doing everything out of order. You're supposed to get married first, then have the baby."

"La Virgen was pregnant before she got married."

"That's completely different. And we're not talking about La Virgen. We're talking about you. Why buy the milk when you can get the cow for free? *Como dicen*."

"Am I the cow in this scenario? Well moo, Mamá. Moo!" Another lengthy pause. "And for your information, Shane wants to get married. He wants to buy the milk."

The front door closes, and I can barely make out Shane's even baritone. "We out of milk already? I just bought some yesterday."

"No, there's still plenty." Mom's voice is lower and calmer. "How was the movie?"

Gabe mumbles something.

"Buy more milk. Keep buying it and buying it. No matter how stubborn it is!" Buela says.

I hear footsteps in the hallway followed by the sound of two doors closing. Shane and Gabe have removed themselves from the line of fire. Smart.

"I don't want to argue anymore, Mamá. I know you feel bad that things didn't work out between you and my father. I'm sorry. But I'm not getting married to ease your guilt."

"Is that what you think?" Silence. "*Es verdad.* I wish things would've turned out differently. But that's not what this is about." Silence again. "I still believe in love and marriage, in promises made in good faith. So, *por favor*, don't give up on it, Mireya. That's all I ask."

Pili

Carlos whirls in like a vortex, sucking the last wisps of air from the room and making the roof compress even lower. He rolls his eyes when he sees me standing there. “Now what’d you do? Seems like every time you set foot in this house, my wife ends up in tears.”

My hands shake with rage. I clasp them tightly to keep them steady. “You’re kidding me, right? You could fill the ocean ten times over with all the tears you’ve made her cry.” Pera stands between us, but I step around her. “And I’ve stood by silently and watched you do it. But no more. I’m done holding my tongue. I’m finally going to say what I’ve been dying to say for the past seven years.”

Carlos shoves his hands in his pockets and his unshaven chin juts out defiantly. “We gonna have us a man-to-man chat now?”

“I’d say, yes, but we’re short two men.” I glower at him and make my voice an arrow. “And we don’t need to chat. It’s simple. You don’t deserve my sister. You never have, and you never will. She’s caring and strong, compassionate and courageous—things you can’t recognize because you know nothing about them. You try to make her blind to them, too. Make her feel small. But she's not small." I spread my arms out wide. "She's huge. Compared to you, she's a giant."

Pera folds her hands behind her neck, and her elbows hang down in front of her chest.

Carlos tosses his keys onto the scratched round table at the end of the couch and nudges past me. "I don't have to stand here and listen to this."

I turn to face him and throw the words at him like a lasso. "Yes, you do. All you do is drag her down and make her feel bad about herself. Lie to her. Betray her."

He whips around to face me. "What happens between me and Pera is none of your goddamn business. Things happen in a marriage. I wouldn't expect you to understand. Pera gets it. She's going to try to pay a little more attention to me. "

"Pay more attention to you? I suppose it's her fault you can't keep your pecker in your pants?"

He waves a hand in the air and sinks back into the sofa. "Why am I explaining this to you, anyway? I don't give a shit what you think. I'm sick of you butting your nose where it doesn't belong. Get the hell out of my house. Tell her, Pera."

Pera's eyes glaze over, and her fingers knead her throat in an upward motion. The door to Miri's room opens down the hall, and the synthesized voice of the Speak & Spell grows louder as she draws closer to the living room. "That is correct. Now spell: FEATHER."

She stands in the doorway with the electronic toy in her hands and a doll tucked in the crook of her arm. "Papi, guess what! I spelled all the words right, even the hard ones, like Rhythm. And that one has an extra h in it too. You can't hear it, but it's there."

She sits down next to Carlos and blinks up at him expectantly, but he only props his feet up on the table and closes his eyes.

Pera watches them intently, her hands still at her throat as Miri sets the Speak & Spell aside and holds the doll in her lap, brushing the yellow loops of yarn away from its round plastic face.

"You like my new doll, Papi? I adopted her. Isn't she pretty? Her name's Veronica, but I call her Roni for short."

Carlos sneaks a look at the doll through half-closed lids and runs his finger over a Wonder Woman Band-Aid stuck to one of the fabric arms.

Miri scoots closer to him. "She fell off the bed and cut herself, so I stitched her up. I'm the doctor, and she's my patient."

Carlos peels off the starry blue bandage and rolls it into a ball between his thumb and forefinger. "These cost money. They're not for playing." He tosses it into the brimming ashtray on the coffee table and fishes a cigarette out of a pack in his shirt pocket. "Besides, girls aren't doctors." His fingers stroke the sides of a chrome lighter, rotating it in his hand. A woman in a red bikini and fishnet stockings looks over her shoulder at me from beneath a row of shiny black bangs. Carlos flicks it open, separating her head from her body, and rolls his thumb over the metal spark wheel. "It's boys. Boys are the doctors," he says, staring into the ignited flame.

Miri's face takes on a hollow expression, the same one I've seen on Pera countless times before. The light has gone out of her eyes.

I open my mouth to speak, but Pera lays her hand on my forearm to stop me. My head hangs down in defeat.

She stares straight ahead with her face set like stone. "Get out."

Carlos smirks at me. "About damn time. And don't let the door hit you in the ass on . . . "

"Not Pili. You. I'm talking to you." She looks down at him, the doll's bright yellow hair reflecting in her pupils. "Get out."

Pilar

"Who's the girl who plays Mrs. Gibbs?"

"Cassie Stern. Why?"

Gabe extends his arms and puts one foot in front of the other on the curb like an acrobat balancing high above the ground. "She's too stiff and robotic. She needs to loosen up."

"Think so?"

"Yeah, she should try throwing in a few small gestures to humanize her character. That'll make it more realistic and believable."

"Thanks for the tip."

He smiles. "Seriously, though . . . when she says her lines, she should clear her throat or cough or something."

I swing around the stop sign at the end of our street. "I'll pass that along. Tell her to pick her nose or pull out her wedgie."

"Now you're getting it. It'd be better if she could let one rip, though. Farting is the ultimate reminder of mortality. The stinkier, the better." He skips over the narrow patch of grass to join me on the sidewalk and pats his stomach. "Wonder what Buela's cooking for dinner. I'm starving."

"Only you could jump from flatulence to food."

We're four houses away from home, when a gray truck without a muffler rumbles up from behind us and slows to a crawl. There's a dent in the front fender and a decal on the back window: the silhouette of a curvy woman next to a pair of deer antlers and the words, "Rifles and Racks," scrawled beneath her huge knockers.

It's like I've been jabbed with a cattle prod, jolts of electricity coursing through the layers of my body down to my fingers and toes. Connor sits behind the steering wheel, hanging his arm out the window. The truck rolls to a stop next to us, and he throws his other arm around Becca, who's sandwiched between him and a guy I recognize from the party, the one playing beer pong. Connor's eyes narrow as he takes a drag from his cigarette and flicks the butt to remove the rising column of ash before holding it between Becca's lips. She takes a drag too and immediately starts coughing, her hands flapping in front of her face. Connor and Beer Pong double over with laughter.

She flips her hair from one side of her flushed face to the other. "I'm used to menthol. They're like cough drops. Better for your throat and organs and stuff. You know, organic."

The guys laugh even harder, and Beer Pong slaps the dashboard. When they've regained their composure, they turn their attention to Gabe.

Connor pokes his head out of the window and sneers, "Hey faggot, where you off to in such a hurry?"

Gabe tenses up next to me. His eyes whip from the truck to our house to me as though he's doing the math in his head. I'm making the same calculations myself. Should we make a run for it? We might be able to reach our front door by the time they climb out of the cab. Well, I wouldn't, but Gabe could. A part of me is tempted to yell at him to run and save himself, but a bigger part is scared to be left behind.

Gabe won't run away. He'll stay and face them, even if it means getting hurt. I'm not sure if it's guts or a mere acceptance of his fate, like that of a drowning man who stops flailing and lets himself sink to the bottom. Whichever it is, I admire him for it. It's courage either way you look at it. I could never be that brave.

Gabe stares straight ahead and takes even steps on the uneven sidewalk. I concentrate on my breathing and try to match my pace to his steady one. It's hard. My legs want to move faster, a feeling they're not accustomed to, and I have to make a conscious effort to slow down. But it's too late to get away. Connor and Beer Pong are already out of the truck and heading our way.

Gabe stops beneath the massive oak in Ms. Eastbrook's yard and turns to face them. I pray that Shane will come outside to check the mail or turn on the sprinkler. Anything to bring him out of the house.

Then it occurs to me. Gabe doesn't want him to. He stopped short of our house on purpose. He doesn't want Shane to see what's happening, doesn't want him to know. That's the crazy part: he's the one who feels like he has something to hide, even though he hasn't done anything wrong.

Becca slides over to the driver's seat and swings her legs out of the open door. She's eating from a small bag of popcorn, popping the puffed kernels into her mouth with a remote expression on her face.

"Hey, you didn't think we forgot about you, did you? Heard you were messing with my girl. Trying to take advantage of her inebriated state," Connor says.

Gabe looks at the ground, his jaw twitching.

"He probably wanted to see what it's like to be with a girl for a change."

"That true?" Connor says, jabbing Gabe in the shoulder. "I think you might be right, Cody." He pokes him again. "You lookin' to catch some snatch, fruit fluffer?"

Gabe's cheeks redden, and his nostrils flare. Sweat trickles over his cheekbones and down the sides of his beautiful face, and his mouth quivers like it can't decide whether to open or stay closed. Then it does. His eyes fly from the ground to Connor's face.

"Fruit. Fluffer. That's almost poetic. Nice alliteration," he says.

Connor puffs his chest out into Gabe's like an enraged gorilla. "What'd you say, pole smoker? You saying I can't read? You calling me stupid?"

Gabe stumbles back but regains his balance, and his eyes drop to the ground again.

The sun sinks behind the sloped roof of Jude and Sadie's house, and the street lamps lining the sidewalk turn on, radiating small circles of light onto the pavement. A few neighbors drive by, and a small kernel of hope pops in my chest that one of them will pull over and stop what's happening. But no one does. They're all too eager to get home after battling traffic.

Beer Pong, whose name is apparently Cody steps up to Gabe's side, his shaggy blonde hair swaying like a hula skirt. "Hey jizz bucket, he's talking to you."

"Trying to take advantage of a defenseless girl," Connor says, shaking his head. "We should call the cops, but you'd probably enjoy prison. Love tossing all those salads, you sicko."

He shoves Gabe hard in the chest with both hands, and this time he falls back onto his elbows, the small of his back landing on the sharp corners of the books inside his backpack. Connor's eyes zero in on the leather band around Gabe's left foot.

He laughs and points it out to Cody. "Holy shit! He's wearing jewelry."

"I knew it!" Cody says, slapping his thigh. "Man, that is gay as shit."

I stand there helplessly, a big, useless, trembling mountain of nothing, and watch everything unfold before me.

Connor reaches down and gives the leather strap a hard tug, but it's sturdy and won't budge. He finally gives up and kicks Gabe in the ankle with his pointy boot, his face flushed with rage.

Gabe lets out a whimper, and his eyes well up.

"That a gift from your boyfriend? You're disgusting." Connor coughs up a wad of phlegm and spits it on Gabe.

The wind rushes through the thick, leafy branches like a hundred whispers, and a sprinkling of acorns rain down.

It would be the worst thing possible for Gabe to cry in front of them. It cannot happen. I can't let it.

He lies beneath the canopy of twisted limbs, a web of roots protruding from the ground around him, an anguished look in his honey eyes and the glob of spit soaking into his T-shirt. A slideshow of images flashes through my mind. Gabe sitting on a stool next to Buela, trying to make sense of her *telenovela,* Gabe and Shane nodding along to Led Zeppelin as they dice tomatoes at the kitchen counter; Gabe laughing with Mom, the living room rug rolled up and the coffee table pushed aside, as she teaches him how to dance the *cumbia*; Gabe at the kitchen table showing Luz how to mix red and blue paint to make purple; and Gabe standing next to me in the crowded cafeteria on his first day as Becca slinks away. Every beautifully ordinary moment.

I move in front of Gabe and stand between him and his tormentors like a force field. For the first time in my life, I'm grateful for my body, for the length and breadth of it, grateful that it's big enough to shield him completely.

"Leave him alone," I hear myself say.

Connor and Cody exchange looks of amusement. But I've woken a sleeping giant.

Becca jumps down from her perch and slithers over to us. "What the hell do you care? We all know Devin's the one you're pining for. He told everyone how you were all over him at the party. You actually believed he liked you. God, that is so sad. I almost feel sorry for you."

It hurts. Really hurts. I flinch but force myself not to look away, to keep my eyes locked on hers.

"He said it was so disgusting, he almost threw up. Said feeling you up was like sticking his hand inside a bag of marsh-mallows. Oh yeah, and he said his fingers got covered in pow-der like you'd been eating donuts or something. I heard that can happen to fat people. Food can get lodged between their folds. You really should be more careful about that. It hap-pened to this one lady in Waco. I saw it on my newsfeed. She thought she had a tumor. Turned out it was a sandwich that had gotten stuck between the layers of her stomach. It'd been there for months and was all rotten and moldy when the doc-tor pulled it out."

Cody laughs and covers his mouth with his hand. "Damn, Becks, that's gross."

Becca shrugs. "Fat people are gross. I mean, look at her."

Gabe leans up onto his elbows and tries to crab crawl around me. "That's enough. Shut the hell up!"

He tries to get up, but Connor pushes him down again with his foot.

"Uh-uh. You stay put. I'm not done with you yet."

The front door of our house slams behind me, and every-one looks up. I spin around expecting to see Shane, but it's not him. Buela stomps toward us in her housecoat and slippers, charging across the yard with a crazed look in her eyes, like a bull seeing red.

Becca and Cody take a few steps back, but Connor stays put. "Oh no," he says, his hands up in mock surrender. "Here comes Grandma. What're you gonna do? Throw your dentures at me? Stab me with your knitting needle?"

Buela is at least two feet shorter than him, but she marches right up and sticks a finger in his face. "*¡Eso!* I do have knitting needles. Two thick, long ones that fit in all kinds of places. And I'm not afraid to use them."

She jabbers away at all of them, her tongue lashing like the whip of a lion tamer. I help Gabe to his feet while an avalanche of words tumbles from her mouth like coins from a winning slot machine, flowing freely and profusely.

My Spanish isn't so great, but I catch a few phrases. (To Connor) Like a palm tree short too many coconuts. (To Cody) Head like an empty ice cream cone. (To Becca) Face like a rotting watermelon kicked in by an elephant.

Buela's eyes narrow to slits, and she zeroes in on Connor. "You and these other *idiotas* better get the hell out of here before I give you all the biggest *nalgazos* of your lives."

Buela's never threatened to kick anyone's butt before. Not to my knowledge, anyway. I should be embarrassed, but I'm not. I'm more awestruck than anything else. It looks like I'm not the only one. I can tell Connor and the others don't understand exactly what she's said, but they know it's not anything good. They gawk at each other uneasily.

Finally, Cody turns back toward the truck. "Whatever, old lady. Don't you have some houses to clean?" he calls over his shoulder.

Becca turns away too. "Yeah, you're lucky we don't report you to ICE. Get you sent back to Mexico." She places her foot on a front tire and heaves herself into the cab.

"*¡Lee un libro, grosera!* This is Texas. My family's been here forever! My ancestors were defending the Alamo while yours were still across the ocean drawing on cave walls with their own *caca!*"

Connor runs a hand over his short, spiky hair and stumbles on a bulging root as he steps back. Moving quicker than I thought possible for a woman her age, Buela whips her slipper off her foot and holds it high above her head like Yoda wielding a lightsaber.

"This lady is freaking nuts." Connor laughs and looks at Gabe, who looks right back at him.

"You are so not worth the hassle." He hops into his truck and shoves Becca across the seat. "Stay away from my stuff and stick to your own kind, fudge packer," he yells at Gabe.

Buela keeps her eyes aimed at the truck as it barrels down the street and disappears around the corner. Only then does she lower her arm. I hand Gabe his backpack, and he limps between us across the yard.

"Uncle Shane's not home, is he?" he asks Buela.

"No, he went to a meeting *para los* wounded warriors."

"Please don't tell him what happened. I don't want him to worry."

Luz is waiting for us by the front door. "Are you okay, Gabe? Why are you limping?" Gabe gives her a weak smile and nods his head.

"He fell," I say. "He'll be okay."

"What's a fudge packer?" she asks me.

"Someone who works in a candy factory," I say.

"Like Willy Wonka?"

"Just like that."

"Oh," she says and skips off to the kitchen.

Gabe drops his backpack on the coffee table and collapses on the couch. He lies back on the cushions and stares up at the ceiling.

Buela looks at me, the sagging skin beneath her brows shading her dark brown eyes. She looks tired.

"They go to your school?"

I nod. "They've been giving Gabe a hard time for a while now."

Buela lays her hands on my cheeks. "And you, too?"

I nod again.

Luz comes back from the kitchen holding up a drawing under her chin. It's a picture of Gabe standing on the moon between two green aliens with large football shaped eyes and stubby antennas sticking out of their heads. She drew his leather band around his ankle. Seeing it makes my chest ache.

"Look what I made you," she says, offering it to him.

He doesn't seem to hear her. His eyes stay glued to the ceiling.

"What's wrong with Gabe?"

"Nothing's wrong with him. Not a thing," Buela says. "He's had a shock, that's all." She eyes him closely, biting her lower lip. "Don't worry. I know what to do. Pilar, stay with him. Luz, bring me a bowl filled halfway with water and an egg from the refrigerator. Be careful not to drop it," she calls over her shoulder before disappearing down the hallway toward her room.

Buela's back a minute later lugging a large statue of La Virgen and a candle in a tall glass jar labeled with a picture of a red, flaming heart encircled in a crown of thorns and dripping bright red drops of blood.

"That looks heavy. Let me help you." I take the statue from her arms and set it on the table next to Gabe's backpack.

"I like carrying her. She feels good in my arms. The perfect weight. Like a newborn baby," Buela says, lighting the candle.

La Virgen's dark hair and eyes remind me of Mom, except unlike Mom's disapproving arches, her eyebrows are benign and slight, like the smooth curve of the moon beneath her feet. I run my finger over the prominent gold stars dotting her blue cloak and along the ridged fan of sun rays surrounding her.

Buela orders Gabe to lie down. He protests weakly, then does as he's told, and she places a round pillow under his head. I tug off his shoes.

"He's had too much negative energy. Those *pendejos* have gotten his mind, body and spirit all out of whack. I'm going to balance them out again."

Luz walks slowly across the living room rug and hands Buela the bowl of water, careful not to spill any, then runs back to the kitchen for the egg. Gabe's arms lay limply at his sides, and he continues to stare at the ceiling with a vacant expression. Buela removes a small vial of holy water from her pocket and pours a few drops into the bowl.

Luz returns with the egg, holding it gingerly in her cupped hands. "Are you gonna make him drink it? Like Rocky?"

"No, I'm going to give him a *limpia*."

"What's a *limpia?*"

"It's a cleaning."

"Like a bath?"

"Sort of."

Luz scratches her nose. "Why don't you put him in the bathtub and use soap?"

"It's not that kind of a cleaning. It's for your insides, not your outside," Buela explains.

"An egg?" I ask skeptically. "Does it really work?"

"Of course, it does," Buela says. "The *huevo* will absorb all of the bad energy."

Luz nods her head firmly and bolts out of the room and down the hallway. She's back a few seconds later, clutching her wicker Easter basket in both hands.

Buela dips the egg into the bowl and shakes off the excess water. Luz digs through the bed of green plastic grass in her basket and chooses a chocolate egg wrapped in purple foil, one of those with the yellow and white cream filling. She mimics Buela's movements, dipping it into the bowl as well and peeling off the dampened wrapper.

Buela rubs the egg on the crown of Gabe's head and prays an Our Father before sweeping it across his forehead and down his cheekbones to his lips. Luz shadows her with her own egg, leaving a light smear of chocolate above Gabe's left eyebrow. He relaxes his shoulders and closes his eyes, surrendering to Buela's ministrations. She continues to pray as she makes her way from one end of the couch to the other, with Luz following closely behind, sweeping the egg across his chest and stomach in a circular motion, and down his arms and legs, paying particular attention to the palms of his hands and the soles of his feet. She finishes with a final sign of the cross over Gabe's chest and holds the egg over the bowl of water. Her thumbs dig into its center, breaking it open.

Luz's fingertips are covered in chocolate as she breaks her egg over the bowl too, dropping in the chocolate shell as well. The sugary cream filling gushes out and she peers down into the water watching it mingle with the real yolk.

Buela bows her head before La Virgen once more, then carries the bowl to the kitchen, holding it out at arm's length like a dirty diaper.

Luz licks the chocolate from her fingers. "Did it work?" she whispers, leaning over to scrutinize Gabe's face.

"I don't know. I guess we wait and see," I whisper back.

Gabe's eyes fly open, and he sits up and lowers his legs over the side of the couch.

Luz sits down next to him and holds his hand. "Do you feel cleaner?" She brings her nose to his shoulder and sniffs. "You smell good."

"I'm not sure what all that was about, but I think I do." He breathes out a laugh. "Weird."

Buela walks over to Gabe and cups his face in her hands, turning it from side to side as she inspects it. "You'll be okay. Your color is almost back to normal."

Gabe thanks her.

"*De nada*," she says, waving her hand and gathering La Virgen in her arms.

Luz springs up from the couch and follows Buela down the hallway.

"What came first, Buela? The chicken or the egg?"

"*Ninguno*. God came first. That's who."

Pili

"She put you up to this, didn't she?"

Carlos' gruff voice scrapes across the shoddy walls and bores through Miri's closed bedroom door. I dig the Simon memory game from out of the toy bin, eager to fill the room with noise so Miri can't hear her parents through the thin walls. The red button lights up first, sounding an A note. I push it, and it lights up again followed by the green button. I press one after the other, then button after button following the random pattern of red, green, blue and yellow lights, creating a melody. I'm too distracted to follow the order, but I keep playing so the harmonic tones will continue to flood Miri's ears.

She kneels on the floor in front of me and reaches under the bed, her small legs flailing as she crawls in further. She finally emerges clutching a pink, plastic case full of toy medical supplies.

"Time for your checkup. Lie down, please," she says, laying it open on the mattress next to me.

I swing my legs onto the bed and lay my head on her pillow. The tree I painted looms above me from behind the headboard. The leaves are dotted with glitter, and Miri has drawn a smiley face on the trunk in white crayon.

She removes the thermometer from its slot and holds it under my tongue for a few seconds. “Uh-oh. You have a fever,” she says, shaking it out and placing it back in the box. “Two hundred degrees. You need medicine.” She yanks open the drawer of her bedside table and rummages inside for a roll of Lifesavers, then lays a red one in my palm. “Here. Eat it all or else you’ll need a shot.”

I suck on the candy while she wraps a plastic cuff around my arm. It’s too small to circle my bicep, so she slides it down to my wrist instead. “Is it true what Papi said? Girls can’t be doctors?”

Absolutely, irrefutably, unequivocally, one hundred percent not true. Don’t listen to what your Neanderthal of a father says. “What do you think?”

She looks up and to the side, contemplating. “I don’t see why not. Girls can grow people right inside their own bodies. They should be able to fix them.”

“That makes perfect sense. Good answer.” She squeezes the small plastic pump repeatedly, taking my blood pressure. “Well, Doc? Am I gonna make it?”

“It’s pretty high. Over five hundred. We better ask Papa Smurf for a second opinion.”

Miri puckers her lips in thought, then asks, “But why would Papi say that?”

Because he’s an ignorant, narrow-minded buffoon. “I don’t know, *gordita*. Maybe no one taught him any better. But that’s okay. You can teach him.”

“How?”

“By not believing it when someone tells you that you can’t do something. By following your dreams no matter what.”

She leaves the cuff on my wrist and throws herself into my arms, squeezing me tight. Her heart beats against my chest as Carlos’ voice resonates from down the short hallway, growing louder and louder. "It was your job, Pera! Why didn't you protect him? You sat up on that porch knitting a goddamn sweater and watched him die. You destroyed our family, our home. If you'd been a better mother, he'd be here now. You killed him. As sure as if you'd been the one plowing onto that sidewalk. You killed our son. And there's no getting away from that. Not ever!"

I wince at his words and wait to hear Pera's voice, but there is only silence. It takes all of my strength and resolve not to bolt from the bed and into the living room to shield her. But I know this needs to happen. Pera has to face his words, and she has to do it on her own. I stay rooted to my spot and hug Miri tight, covering her ears with my arm. I close my eyes and picture Pera in my mind's eye, willing her to finally stand up for herself. "Say something, say something," I whisper as I gently rock Miri. I imagine the words coursing through my body, emitting pulses of sound as they flow through each limb back to my heart. They radiate from my skin and travel through the house, around the doorway to the other side of the wall. I sit motionless listening for their echoes, waiting for them to come back to me.

"It's not about him anymore. It's about *m'ija,"* Pera says. "You want to know the truth? Who really put me up to this? Because it wasn't my sister. *¡Eras tú!* Yes, you! The way you treat our daughter. You don't see her. *Pues*, I do. And you can go on punishing me all you want, but I won't let you punish her. I won't let her grow up believing she's not enough." I hug Miri more tightly and brace myself for Carlos' barrage of words, which I'm certain is to follow, but he must be as stunned as I am because it's Pera's voice again. "She is enough. More than enough. She's everything!" I lower my arm from Miri's ears and let her hear her mother's voice. "And so am I. Because I'm her mother."

Pilar

Luz dances around the kitchen table in a sparkly blue dress covered in sequins and tulle. She flings a pink feather boa draped around her neck from side to side as she sings, "Five little turkeys standing in a row. One sat down and said, "I don't wanna go.'"

"*Por favor*, Luz. You're giving me a headache." Mom rubs her temple and sinks into her chair. "That better not be my good lipstick on your face."

Luz stops singing and gives Mom a pouty look. "But Mommy, I always sing the turkey song. It's a tradition."

Mom nods toward the empty chair next to Gabe. "Take off my high heels and sit before you fall down and hurt yourself."

Luz crosses her arms and flops down in the chair.

Gabe runs a hand over the pink feathers hanging from her shoulder. "Love the feathers. Very stylish."

"Yeah, nice outfit. But what's the occasion?" I say.

"Thanksgiving, silly," Luz says.

We all exchange confused looks around the table.

Shane passes Gabe a bowl of diced carrots. “Honey, Thanksgiving was months ago. In November.”

“That’s when we eat turkey, and Buela cooked one. A big one.”

Sure enough, Buela carries an enormous turkey sitting in a pool of its own juices to the table.

“Wow, Mamá. I didn’t know you knew how to cook a turkey.”

“I’ve done it before. You just don’t remember. The man at the meat counter recommended it. He said it’s low in fat and full of vitamins.”

Shane scoots a few water glasses to the side to make room, and Buela sets down the large platter at the center of the table.

“Besides, it’s always good to give thanks. Not just once a year.”

Shane rubs his hands together. “It looks great, Esperanza. I can’t wait to dig in.” He glances at Gabe. “How’d it go today? Not too rough, I hope.”

My eyes meet Gabe’s, and Buela stops pouring milk into Luz’s glass.

“Um, how did what go?” Gabe asks nervously.

Shane takes the roasted potatoes from Mom’s hand. “Your test. Algebra, right?”

I realize I’m holding my breath and let it out again. Buela resumes filling Luz’s glass.

Gabe’s shoulders relax. “Oh, right. Pretty good, I think. We find out our grades next week.”

“Knew you’d crush it. My man.” Shane reaches across Luz to give Gabe a fist bump. “And hey, I’m around if you need any help. With math or, you know, whatever.”

"I know. *Gracias*, Tío Shane."

"*¿Gracias*? ¿Tío?"

"Buela's teaching me Spanish. Even the bad words. The woman curses like a sailor." He winks at her.

Buela laughs in spite of herself and tosses her napkin at him. *"¡Ay, Gabriel, qué mentiroso!"*

Gabe laughs too. "I know. I am lying. Just messin' with you, Buela."

"Well, you're lucky your test is over with. I wish mine were. I've been studying until I'm blue in the face," Mom says. "My head's so full of enzymes and phagocytes and lymphocytes, it feels like it's going to explode." She presses her hands to the sides of her head. "There's so much to remember."

Shane reaches over to rub her shoulder. "You got this, Rey. You can do it. I know it's not easy, but you're doing great. Kicking butt and taking names."

Luz pulls a feather from her boa and reaches across the table to give it to Buela.

Buela sticks it in her stiff hair and mutters under her breath. "*Pues*, I wish she'd take someone else's last name."

Mom frowns at her but doesn't say anything.

"I mean it. I'm proud of you," Shane says. "Working and going to school. And taking care of us, too. There's nothing you can't do. You're amazing, and you're going to be an amazing nurse."

It's sweet, the sappy way they gaze at each other. Buela watches them, too, with a faraway look in her eyes. She only looks away when she realizes Luz has been calling her name and tugging on her arm.

"Is it time to cut the turkey, Buela?"

We say grace, and Buela stands up to slice the turkey. She brings the carving knife down to the crispy, golden skin then raises it again. Her eyes wander up to the ceiling, and her lips jerk this way and that like she wants to say something. We watch and wait as her eyes drop from the ceiling and flitter about the room, finally settling on Shane. Her mouth stops twitching, and she slowly lifts her hand to offer him the knife handle.

Mom's mouth falls open, and Shane leaps up from his chair so quickly, it almost tips over.

An unspoken something passes between him and Buela as he takes it from her hand.

"Thank you, Esperanza."

Buela looks down for a moment, and it might just be the light from the chandelier reflecting on her glasses, but when she looks up again, her eyes are shiny. She sits down next to me and grabs the pitcher of tea, the ice cracking loudly as she fills her glass. "Call me Pera," she says.

"Daddy, can I do the wishbone? Please?"

Shane hands Luz the y-shaped bone. "Okay, but you have to pick someone to pull it with you."

Luz circles the table, eyeing each of us carefully. "I choose . . . " she pauses for dramatic effect. "Gabe!"

Gabe bows his head and grabs hold of the other end of the forked bone. "I am deeply humbled by this honor."

"Now, close your eyes and make a wish. But don't say it out loud, or it won't come true. Pipi, you be the counter. When you get to three, we pull. Ready?"

"Ready," Gabe says, closing his eyes.

The rest of us watch in silence as they hold the bone between them. Gabe's eyelids flutter lightly, his thick lashes barely grazing his cheeks, while Luz shuts hers tight like she's wishing with all of her might. My eyes swing from one to the other. I'm torn. Like Meryl in *Sophie's Choice.* Then I realize, there's no losing this game. I'm rooting for both of them, for both of their wishes to come true.

"One, two, three!"

Their eyes fly open and the bone snaps in half, and Gabe is left holding the larger piece. We all clap, and Luz smiles and offers him her hand for a congratulatory shake.

"Good job, mister. You won fair and square."

Gabe smiles. "Thanks. I've never done that before. Beginner's luck, I guess." He gets up from the table, stacks up our empty plates and carries them to the sink. I get up to rinse them under the hot water and hand them to Luz, who loads them into the dishwasher.

When Gabe goes to clear more dishes from the table, she looks around to make sure no one's listening and motions me toward her. "You wanna know a secret, Pipi?"

I hand her a dripping plate and whisper back. "Sure."

"Okay, but you can't tell anybody. Promise?"

"Cross my heart." I mark an X on my chest with my finger.

She pulls me down closer to her and cups both hands around my ear. "I'm glad Gabe got the bigger piece."

"You are? Why?"

"He looked happy. I think it made him feel better."

"That's sweet, Luz. And I think you're right. I think it did make him feel better."

"It still would've been good if I'd gotten it, though."

I smile. "Yeah, that would've been good, too. And I bet I know what you wished for. It was that sparkly pencil case we saw at Target yesterday, wasn't it?"

She giggles. "No, silly. What I mean is, Gabe's wish would've still come true even if I'd ended up with the bigger piece."

"It would've? How?"

"Because that was my wish. For Gabe's wish to come true. So, see? It would've come out all right in the end either way."

Pili

I know he's gone even before I open Miri's bedroom door and peek into the living room. The whole house feels lighter. I listen for the sound of his truck peeling out of the driveway, but there's only the buzz of cicadas in the trees outside and an intermittent beeping and talking coming from Miri's room as she plays with her toys.

Pera stands facing the front door. She turns around when she hears me come into the room.

"I heard the door. You okay?" I say.

She doesn't bother pretending and shakes her head slowly from side to side. Her face looks swollen and feverish, like the men in those boxing movies Carlos likes so much. I walk toward her with my arms open wide. She collapses into them and rests her chin on my shoulder. When we finally pull apart, my fingers sweep her cheeks like windshield wipers.

"Miri?" she asks.

"She's fine. She's playing Operation."

"Do you think she heard us?"

"No, I made sure she didn't."

I walk to the front window and push aside the ugly damask curtain, the color of guacamole left out too long, a housewarming gift from Pera's mother-in-law. The driveway's empty. Nothing there but a shiny puddle of oil.

"Is he coming back?" I ask.

"Probably. But we won't be here when he does. My mind's made up. There's no going back now," she says. I turn to face her. "*¿Cómo es?* It's better to have loved and lost than never to have lost at all?" she says, giving me a weak smile.

I squeeze her hand. "I'm proud of you."

"Do you think he will forgive me, Pili?"

"Of course, he will. You've said it a million times. God is all about mercy and compassion. Don't lose faith now when you need it the most."

"That's not who I mean."

"Carlitos? . . . There's nothing for him to forgive . . . would you have forgiven Mamá?"

"*Sí,*" she says.

"Yes," I echo. "That's what families do. You'd want Mamá to go on with her life and be happy, wouldn't you? Carlitos would want the same for you. So you have to let this go now, Pera. You have to forgive yourself. For your sake and for Miri's."

"I know," she starts to say, but her words are blocked out by the blare of a siren. Its wailing fills the air, drowning out the cicadas and Miri's noisy toys. It sends a chill up my spine. I throw open the screen door and hurry outside with Pera right behind me. We hop down from the porch into the yard and turn toward the sound. A dark cloud of smoke billows up above Rosario Street, rising from the trees and rooftops. I envision the pin-up girl from Carlos' Zippo lighter. His words to Pera echo in my head as a sick feeling grows in the pit of my stomach. *You destroyed our family, our home. Our home.*

Pilar

The door to Buela's room is ajar, but I knock anyway before poking my head in. She sits at the foot of the bed with her eyes closed, a string of onyx rosary beads laced between her fingers. Gabe's iris and eyelashes painting leans against the window above the headboard behind her. Buela says it looks like shoots of grass sprouting up from the earth.

I've always loved the sound of her praying, the soft murmurs issuing from her fluttering lips. It's the most soothing soundtrack. They should sell it on iTunes as a cure for insomnia. It'd be a best seller, for sure. Better than thunderstorms, rainforests or ocean waves. It lulled me to sleep on many a summer night in Laredo. I'd lay in the cool sheets of Buela's bed, my damp hair soaking the scent of VO5 into the pillow while the faint shuffle of her slippers wore a path on the thick carpet.

I lay my head in her lap, curling my knees up to my stomach, and stare into the flitting flames of the candles on the dresser. One is labeled with a picture of a sad-looking woman with auburn hair looking heavenward, and the other is the one with the picture of the crowned heart that Buela used during Gabe's *limpia*.

La Virgen stands between them, my right eye level with the black sash tied above the slight bulge of her belly. Buela says she was pregnant when she appeared to Juan Diego, but I like to think she overindulged on a few too many loaves of unleavened bread. A teenaged fatty, like me, unaware of the extraordinary path before her, drawing water from the village well while skinny girls in snug woolen tunics with monogrammed pockets and bedazzled sandals on their dusty feet called her names and threatened to throw rocks at her.

Photographs dot the polished dresser top around her. More are tucked inside the frame of the mirror above it. They're mostly of Mom, Luz and me. My eyes start at the bottom right corner and make their way up and around to the other side. There's me in a high chair, a candle shaped like the number one stuck in the large, yellow cake in front of me. Then, Luz hula-hooping in our backyard. Me again, in the bathtub this time, surrounded by empty Tupperware containers. Mom in a Gremlins T-shirt hugging a Cabbage Patch doll. And Tía Pili wearing a hot pink boa and a tiara with the number fifty on it. It must've been taken before they found the lump in her breast. Another of me sitting on the front porch of our old house in Laredo, my face painted blue and streams of red juice dripping from the melting snow cone in my hand. Luz and I standing in front of the Christmas tree in velvety red dresses. And up in the left corner, this year's total flop of a school picture.

I'd googled the best pose for diminishing the appearance of a double chin the night before and positioned myself accordingly. I sat up straight as an arrow in front of the green screen backdrop and tilted my head at a forty-five degree angle to the right, lifting my chin ever so slightly. But it didn't turn out right. I look like an inquisitive giraffe.

My eyes wander down to my favorite picture directly above La Virgen's right shoulder. Mom lies in a hospital bed and gazes down at me, asleep in her arms. It's hard to believe I was ever that small, that there was a time when my body could fit inside such a narrow space. Below it is another photo of me and Luz. We're standing in front of the statue of the Mexican general in San Agustín Square in downtown Laredo. I remember how hot it was that day. After Buela snapped the photo, we ran to the hotel across the street and buried our arms in the ice machine at the end of the hallway.

The last photo on the left side is one of Mom in her wedding dress. She leans against the hood of Tía Pili's gold convertible with that impatient look on her face I know so well. And curled over the bottom edge of the mirror is a picture of a swarthy-looking man with dark eyes under thick brows. He wears a red shirt and leans against a doorframe, grinning. Mom's father, my grandfather. I never knew him. He died a long time ago. He was found stabbed to death in the parking lot of some bar in Laredo. It's not there anymore. They tore it down and put up a Popeye's Chicken in its place.

People said it was someone's jealous husband who did it, but no one was ever arrested. He and Buela weren't together anymore when it happened. Tía Pili heard about it from one of her regular customers, and she's the one who broke the news to Buela.

The candles cast shadows across my neck as I stand up from the bed to get a better look at the photographs arranged on the dresser. So that's the secret: have your picture taken by candlelight. Note to self: google ways to cause a power outage in a public building.

A black and white photo with scalloped edges sits in an oversized gold frame to the left of the statue. A smiling couple embraces in front of a square building with the words,

"Dolores Goods," hand-painted above the doorway. Buela's mom and dad, my great-grandparents, standing in front of their small grocery store. Buela sold it after Tía Pili died. Said she didn't have the energy to keep up with it. Mom and I used to drive by it sometimes, but it got to be too depressing. It looked different each time, more and more run down, the minty green paint fading to a sad yellow. Buela says it's a pawn shop now. There are thick bars on all the windows, and the words above the door have been painted over, replaced by a buxom cartoon mermaid with a chunky gold necklace spilling into her cleavage.

A smaller picture sits in an oval frame to the right of La Virgen. Tía Pili and Mom smile at each other with their foreheads pressed together, Mom's plump little hand splayed across Tía Pili's cheek. The picture was taken in the yard of the house on Rosario. We used to drive by there, too. Mom would pull over beside the curb across the street, and we'd sit in the car trying to catch a glimpse of it through the jagged slats of bamboo covering the chain-link fence and the overgrown yard full of broken-down cars and rusty appliances. Mom said it looked a lot different when Tía Pili lived there. The closed-in porches were once open with wrought iron railings and neat lines of roses leading up to them. She'd close her eyes, picturing it the way it used to be, leading me through the hallways from room to room as she described it.

A boy with a shy smile hugs a teddy bear to his chest beneath the sliver of moon under La Virgen's feet. Mom's brother. He died when he was four. He was riding his tricycle on the sidewalk in front of their house when a car swerved onto the sidewalk and barreled right into him. The driver had lost consciousness. Buela saw the whole thing from where she was sitting on the porch. She flew across the yard, her knitting needles clanking down the steps behind her, and cradled his lifeless body until the paramedics arrived and took him from her arms.

I pick up the polished silver frame to read the inscription etched across the bottom. *"Nunca Lejos."* Never far away. My fingers touch something soft taped to the backboard, and I turn it over to see what's there. It's a lock of dark curls sealed inside a small plastic bag. The frame grows leaden in my hand, and I return it to its spot on the dresser.

Buela slips her rosary into its leather pouch and joins me in front of the mirror. I lean my head toward hers and gaze over La Virgen to study our reflections inside the frame of pictures. My eyes bounce from my face to Buela's in search of similarities. We share the same heart-shaped hairline, the same slight curve on the bridges of our noses and our upper lips pucker out in the same way. Buela's cheekbones are high and pronounced like Mom's, but mine are too covered in fat to tell whether or not they're alike.

I spot an old photograph in a plain, wooden frame half-hidden behind the sun rays on La Virgen's right side. "Who's that?"

Buela leans forward and studies it through her glasses. "That's my great-great-grandmother. Elvira Rosa."

"Oh! The one who scared the Indians away, right?"

"*Sí*, that's how the story goes. They say she was something else. She ate too much and drank too much and used bad words, *pero su corazón era grande*. Elvira would give anyone the shirt off her back. And she was smart and loyal. She was born in 1836, the same day Sam Houston defeated Santa Anna at San Jacinto."

"Could you tell me the story again, Buela? Please?"

"*Ay,* Pili told it a lot better than me, but I'll try. Let me see. . . . It was a long, long time ago. Texas had just become a part of the United States. *Pero,* it was a dangerous time. Most of *los indios* had been wiped out by cholera, their bodies all blue *de deshidratación*."

"What's that?"

"*Ay,¿cómo se dice . . . ?* It's like when *no tienes* enough water in your body."

"Oh, dehydration?"

"*Sí, eso.* Anyway, a lot of *indios* died, but not all. Some survived and kept on raiding. They were mad because people were coming and invading their land, *entiendes*? I would be mad too.

"Elvira was eleven years old and traveling by stagecoach *con su madre y sus* five brothers. *Porque* that's how they traveled back then, you see. *No había carros* or buses or planes. Or Uber." Buela laughs.

"Everybody had fallen asleep except Elvira. She was drawing by the light of the moon. *Pues,* they were almost to San Antonio, when suddenly, the coach moved real fast to the side, *así*." Buela jerks her arm in a perpendicular motion in front of her. "Everyone sat up all scared, wiping drool from their mouths. Elvira peeked behind the leather curtain on the other side to see what had made the horses move like that. And that's when she saw them. Four Comanches riding horses right next to them. *Con* buckskin leggings and beaded shirts *y todo. Sus caras* were all painted white and their hair was long and braided.

"Her mother and brothers threw themselves to the floor, but Elvira stayed calm. She thought for a moment, then got a blue crayon from her drawing case . . . *bueno, no* crayon *pero* you know what I mean . . . *un pastel de pintura*. She rubbed it all over her face *así."* She sweeps both hands all over her face as if she's smearing it with paint. "*Entonces,* she sucked in her chubby cheeks, threw back the curtain and pressed her nose against the window. 'The Blue Death!' she yelled. 'Help us!'

And it scared *los indios* away, and they never came back. The End."

"Wow. I wish I could've met her."

Buela moves the frame closer to the front of the dresser. "Someday," she says.

Her hand glides over to the picture of her son.

I hug her tighter as her fingers close around it. "I'm sorry, Buela."

She squeezes me back. "It's okay, gordita. *Está bien*."

She backs up to the bed and pats the mattress next to her. "The people we love are never far from us. Not really. The past meets the present every day. Butts right up to it. Every minute. Every second. There's no separating the two." She runs her fingertips across the glass and brings them to her lips, her head slanting slightly like La Virgen's. "I'll see my Carlitos again. And Pili too. I know I will. Until then, I'm happy to be here with you and Luz. And your mother too, as crazy as she makes me. I worry about her. I don't want her to be alone."

"She won't be, Buela. Shane loves Mom. He's not going anywhere. And she's got you and me and Luz." My eyes scan the cluster of photographs. I lean forward and grab one of the three of us huddled together on the couch watching *The Sound of Music*. "She's got all of us."

Buela takes the photo from my hand and brings the two frames together, side by side.

"All of us."

Pili

"Something's burning, Mommy." Miri hugs her plush doll to her chest and buries her nose in its braided hair. "I saw the smoke from my window."

Pera sweeps her off the porch and runs to the car. I'm already turning the key in the ignition by the time they scoot in next to me.

The way home has never seemed so long. I drive by memory, the tires skimming the asphalt. My eyes stay fixed on the dark, cloudy spire billowing up ahead of us. Miri slides from me to her mother across the ribbed vinyl seat as the Impala swings this way and that, zigzagging through the streets. I peer up through the windshield with my chin grazing my knuckles and grip the steering wheel even tighter as we swerve onto Rosario Street. A part of me is tempted to turn back the way we came, past Pera's run-down bungalow to the edge of town and across the bridge into Nuevo Laredo.

Four houses away.

Neighbors watch from their shaded porches, fanning themselves in lawn chairs. I envy their detachment. My foot eases off the accelerator as we draw closer to home, and Pera locks her arms against the dashboard, trying to keep the future at bay.

Two houses.

We don't want to see. Don't want to know. But the smoky tower will continue to rise, even if we close our eyes. So we keep them open. We will have to bear witness to this. All of us.

My foot slams hard on the brake, and the car jerks to a stop, pitching us forward. My arm flies instinctively across Miri's chest, but Pera's is already there. We grab hold of each other and stare up at the house.

The depth and ferocity of Carlos' pain and resentment rage before us, their fury unleashed on all of us. Abuelito, Abuelita, Monina and Debi; Mamá, Papá, Pera and me. A fire truck idles beside the curb on Palmas Lane like a disconnected heart. A tangle of veiny hoses branches out from its side, spurting blood all over Mamá's roses. Dense, gray smoke pours out from the shattered glass of the transom window above the front door and curls up over the eaves of the roof. We watch in horror as tongues of fire lash out of the living room windows and dart across the porch. Our history eaten up by the gluttonous flames. Miri's too.

I glance down at her. Her face has gone an ashy white, and her almond eyes have widened to globes. Pera grips my forearm tighter, locking Miri securely between us and spurring me into action. I hit the gas, swerve around the truck and head up the driveway to the detached carport on the east side of the house. It appears untouched by smoke and fire.

There's still time.

I hop out of the car and sprint across the yard to the back entrance. Pera yells after me, but I keep running. There's not a minute to lose.

My palms lay flat against the kitchen door. It doesn't feel any hotter than usual, so I step to the side and throw it open. The smell hits me first. A toxic mixture of charred wood and melting rubber. A stark contrast to the perfumed scent of the grapefruit trees in the yard. A thick band of murky smoke rolls across the ceiling. The swishing tip of tail is the only visible part of the Kit Kat clock hanging above the stove.

Night has fallen inside the house, the outside world encroaching on our sanctuary. It's hard to believe there's a sun blazing outside. But it must be. I can feel its heat through the roof, scorching my back and the top of my head. I lift the collar of my shirt up over my nose and drop to my hands and knees, crawl across the tiled floor into the hallway, swinging my head to peek into the dining room. Bright orange tendrils hook around the door frame on the far wall, lapping at Abuelita's credenza. But there's no time to mourn the loss of it. The house hisses and snaps as I scramble past the room Pera and I shared. There's a loud pop, then the sound of breaking glass on the other side of the door. I imagine the large paper flowers peeling and crinkling down the walls, devoured by the indiscriminate blaze.

I keep moving.

A deep yet indistinct voice calls out from somewhere behind me. A fireman's perhaps. I ignore it and crouch lower, creeping faster into Mamá and Papá's room and kicking the door shut behind me. I run to the window with my head and shoulders bowed and hoist up the sash. A breeze sends the lace curtain floating up like the veil of a runaway bride. A sliver of smoke seeps through the edges of the door and swirls across the crown molding. I scurry over to the wall of pictures and snatch them two at a time, flinging them onto the tufted yarn flowers of the bedspread. An unbidden rush of recollection rallies and swells from every corner of the house, hushed whispers issuing from deep within. Every inch of floor space is stamped with our memories. Abuelita leaning against the curvy headboard with a tray of food across her lap as Abuelito reads to her, Mamá rubbing Papá's shoulders as he hunches over the side of the bed with his head in his hands, Pera and I stretched across it watching Mamá slip on her dangly earrings before church, Pera and I huddled on each side of her as she lies motionless between us in her silky dress with her hands folded across her stomach, and Pera bearing down on the mattress with me behind her. I turn away from the empty wall of faint shadowy outlines and gather up the corners of the bedcover.

The crackling has grown louder. My eyes tear up, and shards of glass cut my throat as the smoky ceiling lowers. I reach for the picture of Mamá and Papá on the dresser but knock it over in my haste. It falls through the crack between the dresser and the wall, and I sink to my knees to retrieve it, stretching my arm as far as it will go, my fingers groping blindly. The scalloped edge of the dresser's wooden skirt cuts into my shoulder, but I keep searching until my fingertips touch the smooth glass. They press down on it firmly and guide it out. Something else rolls out with it. Something round and hard and covered in cobwebs. A flashlight, the one Xochi used the night Miri was born. I switch it on but of course, the batteries are dead. I tuck it into my back pocket and heave the bundle from the bed, the bony, angular frames poking my arms and chest through the soft fabric as I make my way through the haze to the window.

Pilar

Gabe arches his neck to gaze up at the sixty-foot-high wall of water gushing down in front of us. "This is badass. It's like a waterfall in the middle of the city." He has to talk loud over the roaring rush.

I yell back at him, the soft mist spraying my face. "Right? I've always loved this fountain. It's one of my favorite places in Houston. We used to have picnics here all the time before Mom started taking classes. You should see it at night all lit up. It's even better."

Luz steps closer to the band of black granite at the base of the wall and peers down into the narrow crevasse where the water drains before recirculating back up through the pump. "It's shaped like a horseshoe so it's good luck. And it's magic, too. It never runs out of water."

She backs up and twirls around on the wet pavement. "Look, Pipi! I'm on stage like you!"

It does look like a stage. One from ancient times, maybe. The wall of water acts as the backdrop to a broad half circle of floor space fronted by a lower proscenium arch consisting of three separate archways.

She stands in the center arch and points to the wide expanse of vibrant green lawn before her. It's flanked on both sides by tree-lined paths stretching all the way to the far end of the park, where an exceptionally tall building mirrors the cloudy blue sky.

"Out there's the audience," she says, curtsying and blowing kisses to an invisible crowd, the sun reflecting off the towering sweep of windows and hitting her like a spotlight. "Thank you. Thank you."

Gabe tosses her an imaginary bouquet and claps his hands. "Bravo! Encore!"

"This would drive Mr. Leal crazy. The water's too loud. The audience wouldn't be able to hear the actors. No matter how much they projected," I grumble.

Luz shrugs. "That's okay. The water can say the lines for you, and you can do the motions. Like one of those people with the white make-up and striped shirts."

"Mimes," I say.

"Yeah, mines."

Luz takes long, exaggerated licks from an invisible ice cream cone in her hand, then rubs her belly in a circular motion and runs down the few steps into the lawn. Gabe and I step down after her and watch her cartwheel across it.

There's a sprinkling of people here and there enjoying the last breezes of spring before the stifling heat of summer sets in. A girl Luz's age in a T-shirt that says: "World's Best Big Sister," sits on a picnic blanket with her parents and baby brother. Her shiny, black pony tail swishes from side to side as she jumps to her feet and runs over to Luz.

"Not too far, Luz. Stay where we can see you!"

Gabe walks beside me with his hands shoved inside his pockets. "Thanks for showing me this."

"I thought you'd like it."

Luz skips over to the row of live oak trees with the girl at her heels. Gabe and I follow behind on the paved walkway beneath the leafy awning. I imagine us strolling arm in arm, me in a petticoat and a poofy dress and Gabe in a waistcoat and top hat.

"So, you psyched for next week?"

I twist my hair up into a bun. "I guess. I'm more nervous than anything."

"Don't be. Go out there and do your thing. You've worked hard for it. Now it's time to share your talent with the world. To bask in your glory."

My cheeks feel hot, and it's not just the eighty degree temperature. I change the subject.

"I can't believe the year's almost over."

We sit down on a slatted metal bench, the setting sun throwing beams of light around our feet.

Gabe watches the stream of cars drive by on their way to the Galleria mall. "Yup, looks like you'll be getting rid of me soon."

"You spending the summer in California with your dad again?"

"That's the plan. Then it's back to Dallas for another year of teenage angst." He's trying to sound lighthearted, but there's sadness in his eyes.

"Maybe it won't be so bad. It's like you said, high school isn't forever. One day it'll be a distant memory, a dusty yearbook on the shelf. You'll be a senior next year. One more year to get through, and you can get on with the rest of your life. Go to art school and hang out in coffeehouses with girls named Gretchen who read Kerouac and write poetry. Share an apartment with some friendly hipster type who also swims against the current. Get a job at a graphic design firm whose offices are in an old, haunted warehouse, with a boss who always comes in late 'cause he's in a band. Wear vintage sneakers and T-shirts with ironic sayings under your blazer and eat your noodle fusion lunch out of a mason jar. Sip pomegranate cocktails at happy hour. And paint and paint . . . until you've got enough inventory for a showing, which you'll have in a small but reputable gallery in midtown. Become a hit as this generation's Warhol, but better. Spend the rest of your life traveling the world for inspiration. It'll be wonderful."

Gabe smiles and looks at me with renewed hope. "You think?"

"I know."

He pushes himself up to sit on the backrest of the bench, his feet resting on the seat. "How do you know?"

"I just do."

Luz and her new friend wander around the trees collecting acorns and gathering them into the makeshift hammocks of their shirts.

"But promise me something."

He tucks his long bangs behind his ear, where they stay put. "Okay. What?"

"Remember that not all words are created equal. Some should definitely carry more weight than others. Be choosy about which ones you let in."

"I will if you will."

I picture a tiny, buff guy in a black muscle shirt and dark sunglasses standing on my earlobe like a bouncer outside of a nightclub checking words like IDs, turning some away and unlatching the minute velvet rope across my ear canal to let others through. Someone like the trainer I met the first time I went to the gym.

"It's a deal."

My eyes roam across the park, watching families kick soccer balls and couples lying on the grass. A few yards to our left a boy tosses a Frisbee with his dad. I look beyond them to the sheet of water cascading over the massive brick wall and feel the words I've been holding back the past few months rise up my throat, finally threatening to break free. This time I let them. Because of all the harsh ones Gabe's heard this year, he deserves to hear these too.

I turn to face him. "I'm going to miss you."

"Me too. Miss you, I mean."

"You don't know . . . "

He waits for me to continue, but there's a huge lump in my throat. I have to swallow hard to squeeze the words out around it. " . . . what you've done." I swallow again. "How it was before you got here." I yank off a loose thread hanging from my T-shirt and twirl it around my fingertip. "You saved me."

Gabe rests his elbows on his knees. "No, you've got it backwards. . . . I never told anyone this but . . . before Uncle Shane came to get me, I was actually thinking of . . . "

"Of what?"

"Never mind. It doesn't matter."

"It does matter."

I look down the path at the row of sturdy trees, their pruned limbs full of leaves. It's hard to believe something so massive could grow from one small seed.

"You're not still . . . are you?"

"No."

"Good. Because you're the best friend I've ever had." I press my fingertips over my eyes and lower them again. "And that's enough of a reason to . . . hang around. It's got to be."

Luz waves goodbye and hurries over to me and Gabe as her new friend runs back to join her family. She drops the hem of her shirt, and acorns rain down on our feet.

Gabe stoops to pick one up and runs his finger over the rough wood capping the smooth, brown nut.

"It is enough, Pi. More than."

Pili

A stream of water shoots up over the house, soaking me as I stumble off the wide porch clutching the bundle of pictures wrapped in the quilt. Pera and Miri wait in the shade of one of the trees bordering the far side of the yard with their fingernails between their teeth and their eyes cemented to the door. As soon as Pera sees me, she rushes over and throws her arms around me.

"Ay, Diosito, gracias, gracias," she whispers, backing away to give me air. She wipes my face with her sleeve. "Are you okay?"

Before I can answer, she pulls me close again. "Oh, thank God," she breathes into my sooty hair. "Thank you. Thank you. Thank you."

I slump against her and relax my arms. The blanket falls open, and an avalanche of pictures tumbles to the ground.

I look over her shoulder at the house. Smoke continues to billow out of the kitchen windows. The wind chimes have gone silent, the coppery pipes and colored glass fragments eclipsed by wafts of smoke.

Firemen in heavy, gray coats and clunky boots circle the house talking into two-way radios. One hurries over to us and places an oxygen mask over my face, his black hair glistening at his temples. He orders me to take long, deep breaths, and Pera echoes his words. "Breathe, Pili. Breathe."

Through the corner of my eye I spy Miri lean her doll against the tree trunk and run over to us. I pull off the rubber tube and wave the man away. "I'm okay," I sputter. "I'm okay."

He strides purposefully toward the other side of the house, talking into his radio.

Pera sinks down next to me in the grass, her relief now giving way to anger. "*¿Por qué, Pili?* Why? That's the stupidest thing you've ever done. You could've been killed."

"I had to get them out of there. They're all we have left to remember, to show they were here," I say.

Tears flood my eyes and spill down my cheeks. Pera looks taken aback. I can't remember the last time she saw me cry.

"The boxes . . . all of their things . . . gone. . . . I was too late," I sob.

Water sprays over both sides of the house now, from Palmas and Rosario, the two arcs overlapping. But the smoke continues to spiral up like a burnt offering. Miri wraps her body around my back, clinging to me from behind. The faces of our family lie scattered around us, each photo embodying a single moment of their lives, not the long stretches of before and after, beyond the camera's flash.

I lean forward on my hands and knees and gather the frames, frantically darting across the blanket to pluck them up from the grass. Miri stoops to help me.

"If there's nothing left, then it's like they were never even here," I say.

"Pili." Pera rests her hand on my shoulder, and I sink back on my heels and close my eyes. She takes the pictures from my trembling hands. "We don't need a bunch of old photos to remember them. Or dusty boxes or cars or houses. *No las necesitamos.* These things can't hold them."

She wipes the tears from my face and clutches my hands. "But it's okay. We don't need them. Because we're here. Miri is too. And when we're gone, her children will be here."

I open my eyes and look down at the array of photographs. Miri spreads the blanket out beneath us and arranges them neatly. I imagine what the collage must look like from above, how God sees it, how he views a life. Does He see it like we do? An orderly row of separate, isolated instances extending neatly from the cradle to the grave? I bet He doesn't. I bet He sees it differently. I bet He sees the whole thing all at once. The span of a lifetime in each fleeting moment, the end in the beginning and vice versa, the complete weight of it borne in every instant.

Smoke continues to rise and blend with the clouds. It's impossible to tell where one ends and the other begins.

Pilar

"You sure you really want to? I mean, seriously, I wouldn't wish it on my worst enemy."

Shane peels the skin off of a sweet potato in long, thin strips. "Absolutely. It'll be fun."

I shred a brick of Monterrey Jack into a glass bowl, shaking my head from side to side. "Shane, Shane, Shane. We have got to get you out more. Roller coasters are fun. Trampolines are fun. Drive-in movies. Catching fireflies. Building sandcastles. Fun, fun and fun. Going to the gym? Not fun."

"It could be. It's a matter of attitude. It's something we can do together. Help keep each other motivated."

"I don't think you realize how tall of an order you're asking to fill." I rest my hand on his arm. "You may not be aware of this, but exercising is not exactly my favorite thing in the world."

Shane laughs. "You don't say. Well, no matter. I'm up for the challenge." He hands the naked potato to Buela, who eases it into a pot of boiling water on the stove. "I'll sign up this weekend."

Gabe piggybacks Luz into the kitchen and sets her down on a chair.

"Can I help?" he asks.

Buela presses a spatula on the puffed up tortilla in the skillet and gestures toward a cutting board on the counter. "You can cut the onion, *si quieres*."

Gabe slices it up into thin pieces. "Did I hear that right? You joining the gym too, Tío?"

Shane pours vinegar and half a cup of sugar into a saucepan and stirs it up with a wooden spoon. "Yup. I figure it won't hurt to get a little more exercise." He pinches the skin at his slim waist. "Chisel up this work in progress I have here. It'll be good for my knee. You should join too. We could get a family membership."

"Nah. I'll be leaving in a few weeks. It wouldn't be worth it."

"Sure it will. You can start going when you get back from California."

Gabe sets down the knife and wipes his eyes. "I'll be in Dallas."

"Oh . . . right. Sorry. I just assumed you'd come back here. It's your decision. You must miss your mom. And having your own space. All of your things. I get it."

A window of possibility creaks open, and hope buds in my chest.

Gabe must feel it too, because he gets all flustered, and his words spill from his mouth like Styrofoam beads from a ripped bean bag. "No, I don't. I mean, yeah I do miss Mom and stuff. Sure I do. I can still visit her on breaks and for long weekends. At Thanksgiving and Christmas. Spring Break. And she can come here, too. There're tons of flights, and it's not that far of a drive." He stops to catch his breath. "I'd rather stay here for senior year. Would it be okay? I mean if I stayed?" His eyes leap to each of our faces like he's asking all of us.

Luz hops down from the chair and tugs Shane's arm. "Can he, Daddy? Pretty please with whipped cream and a gazillion cherries on top?"

"Yeah," I chime in. "He might as well stay. Otherwise, he'll have to re-enroll in his old school, transfer grades. Who wants to deal with all that nonsense?"

"Of course, he can." Shane strokes Luz's hair and looks at Gabe. "You'll have to talk to your parents and make sure it's okay with them. But you never have to ask us. This is your home. It always will be."

Luz runs over to Gabe and throws her arms around his waist with her eyes shut tight, and he hugs her back and clears his throat.

Shane places a colander full of spinach leaves inside the sink and sets a stool in front of it. "Come on, Luz. You can help too. Rinse these out. And make sure to shake out all the water. We don't want to be eating soggy quesadillas for dinner."

I'm so happy, I feel like I might float up to the ceiling like Uncle Albert in *Mary Poppins*. I have to focus on something else to keep me grounded. I clutch the cheese grater tightly over the bowl and hit the side of it with my palm to dislodge any clingy bits of Monterrey Jack before rinsing it at the sink.

"We're having quesadillas? With spinach and sweet potato?" I ask, totally confused.

"It's a new recipe Buela and I are trying out. I got it from one of the moms at the park yesterday. She said her kids love it."

"Spinach and *camote* are good for you. *Lleno de fibra y vitaminas*. So we're killing the bird with two stones." Buela adds another sweet potato to the pot. "You kids need to eat right so you can be healthy and strong. The spoon is mightier than the sword, *como dicen*." She shrugs her shoulders. "Besides, it's good to try new things."

Luz sets the colander on the counter and wipes her hands on her pants. "Are we eating before or after?"

"After. I'll warm them up in the oven when we get home. That way *tu mamá* can eat with us too. She's meeting us at the school after work."

"Fine by me. I'm so nervous, if I eat anything now, I'll end up blowing chunks all over the stage."

"Copy that. Stay away from the front row," Shane says.

~~~

Shane pulls up to the set of double doors at the front of the school. But it's hard to exit this car. Seems like I'm always torn between going and staying. Like Meryl Streep sitting at the stoplight in *The Bridges of Madison County*, her trembling hand gripping the door handle of her husband's truck as the love of her life drives away in the rain.

I look out at the dry, patchy lawn and the rectangular sign framed in the low brick wall.

WELCH HIGH SCHOOL
Home of The Wolves
Established in 1976

It's like I'm reading it for the first time.

Home of the wolves.

Home.

It's hard to imagine anyone could feel that way about this place. The word doesn't fit. It's a misnomer. Like the *lotería* card of the drunk man. Or dancing man, according to Luz.

Shane shifts into park and turns to look at me. "You sure you don't want us to go in with you?"
~~~

"Thanks, but I'll be okay. It'll give me a chance to calm myself down. If I see all those people walking into the auditorium, it'll make me even more nervous." I glance at the time on my phone. "See you inside."

"Okay, if you're sure. And hey, I'm proud of you no matter what. You're already that girl."

"What girl?"

"The one who decided to go for it." He nudges my shoulder. "Now, go in there and getcha some."

Gabe, Luz and Buela lean forward from the backseat.

Gabe squeezes my shoulder. "We're proud of you too. You're gonna kill it, Pi."

Buela makes the sign of the cross on my forehead. *"Qué Dios te bendiga, gordita."*

The twisted plastic whiskers of Luz's ratty kangaroo tickle my face as she brushes it against my cheek. "It's a good luck kiss." Her eyes widen, and she throws a hand over her mouth. "Oops, I mean a break-a-leg kiss."

I step out of the passenger seat onto the pavement and watch them disappear around the building to the parking lot in back, take a deep breath and sling my backpack over my shoulder. The pungent smell of disinfectant, canned ravioli and fear rises up to greet me the moment I step inside the dimly lit lobby. I tug my fedora more securely on my head and walk slowly past the front office and the nurse's station, my heart beating faster with every step. Before I had Sonny and Gabe to eat with, I spent more than a few lunch periods lying in there, staring at the dull burlap curtain pulled around the stiff cot. That is, until Mrs. Casey caught on and noticed a pattern in my menstrual cramps, how they always seemed to hit me right at 11:30.

A low murmur resonates from the far end of the hallway as more and more people arrive. Surprisingly, the sound doesn't fill me with dread. It's not fear I feel. It's hunger. Not for food, but for something else. For the feel of those scuffed yet solid beams beneath my feet and the warm glare of the floodlights on my face.

My eyes automatically veer toward the vending machines as I pass the cafeteria. For once, I don't want to climb inside them. I want to keep walking, to stand on that stage in front of my family. To show them what I can do and make them proud. My feet move faster as I pass the entrance to the serving lines and continue on to where the drama hallway crosses the main one, the exact spot Gabe caught up with me when I ran out of my audition. I lower my backpack and look up through the plexiglass dome of the skylight.

A faint crescent moon is already visible in the fading daylight. It reminds me of La Virgen. I imagine her looking down at me from her perch above it, the hem of her long dress draped over its center like on Buela's statue. Buela said the flowery designs on the rose-colored fabric matched the mountains and rivers of the Mexican landscape and that the stars studding her mantle coincided with the constellations that were in the sky the morning she appeared to Juan Diego. Heaven and earth united on her clothing. Talk about high fashion.

I unzip my backpack and double-check that I have my props.

And that's when I hear it. Coming from around the corner. The last voice in the world I want to hear. Beads of sweat pop up on my upper lip, and the small hairs on my arm stand on end. This cannot be happening. It must be some sick, cosmic joke. I'm beginning to think there's no such thing as coincidence.

"She's such a slut, I'm not surprised. But just wait. I'm going to make her life a living hell," Becca says.

"I can't believe she'd do that to you. I mean, you guys have been friends since, like, third grade," Lynn says. "I always knew she had a thing for Connor. She's always chatting him up and sticking her boobs in his face. And he's nothing but a. . . ." Her voice trails off as they come into view and see me standing there.

A wicked sneer crosses Becca's lips. I recognize the insatiable look in her eyes. It's the same one I've caught in my own on the refrigerator door. It dawns on me. I'm her rice pudding. Her temptation. Her binge. What she feeds on. She rolls her eyes.

"Could this day get any worse? My best friend is boinking my boyfriend. I have to sit through this stupid play because my dorky stepbrother is on the crew. And now, I have to watch your ugly fat ass, too."

"At least now, we won't be bored. We can watch her suck ass up there and make a fool of herself. We'll post a video. It'll be hilarious. Wow. Gonna have to zoom way out. Would you look at the size of those legs? They're like freaking sequoias," Lynn says. "And FYI, you look ridiculous in that hat. You so cannot pull off that look." Her eyes sidle over to Becca again. "Let's go get some seats. We do not want to miss this."

But Becca's not done feeding. "Save me one. I'll be there in a minute," she says as Lynn stalks off toward the auditorium.

She glares at me, her narrowed eyes snaking up and down my body. I imagine myself inside a massive Tupperware bowl on a refrigerator shelf. My legs tremble as she grabs my backpack from the floor and turns it upside down, shaking out the contents. Gabe's hoodie falls to the floor. I borrowed it to tie around my waist last week after I sat on a mustard packet at lunch. My props tumble out behind it: a pair of suspenders and a wooden pipe, followed by the worn pages of my script and a pencil with a broken tip. I stand there rooted to the spot as she gives it one last jiggle.

A crumpled piece of paper drifts slowly to the floor and lands on the carpet between our feet. It's the picture Luz gave me. The one of us in the field of flowers beneath the blue sky, the top-hatted sun smiling down on us as she hands me a bunch of rainbow-colored daisies. I'd forgotten all about it.

Becca grabs it and studies it with a grimace on her face as if possessed by a demon. I half-expect her head to do a three-sixty on her neck, á la *The Exorcist.*

"Who is Luz?" She mispronounces it in a way that rhymes with buzz. "What kind of stupid name is that? And what kind of horse has purple spots? Is she retarded? Probably, if she's related to you. Probably a whale-ass like you, too. She should go smoke a tailpipe now before she grows even bigger and has to be buried in a shipping container."

My eyes sink to the floor. I try to keep my promise to Gabe, not to let the words in, but the small bouncer checking ID's is nowhere to be found and the velvet rope hangs down over my earlobe.

I think of Luz and her unwavering faith in people, her innate ability for seeing the goodness in everyone. I imagine her there listening to Becca's words, and my cheeks burn with mounting rage as another realization hits me. She is here. Becca's not only doing this to me. She's doing it to Luz, hurting her too. As if she were saying these things right to her. Because Luz loves me. Because in a way I don't fully understand, Luz is a part of me. Connected by more than DNA, by something deeper than blood.

I snatch the picture from her unworthy hands and look at it. Really look at it, focusing on how Luz drew me. I sit on the purple-spotted giraffe, my denim-covered legs straddling its back and my hair a jumble of dark curls spilling over the shoulders of my pink shirt. My eyes zero in on the wand held high in my hand, and I realize something I hadn't before. It's like finding the hidden 3D image in a Magic Eye picture. It's not a wand after all. It's a sword, the thick crossbar of the hilt above my fingers. And what I thought were yellow sparks of magic are really beams of sunlight gleaming off of the metal. It's so obvious. How did I not notice it before?

This is how Luz sees me. And if she does, there must be at least a little of it in me. There must be some truth to it.

I pretend I'm the version of myself in the picture. My eyes travel from Becca's sandaled feet up to her limp, lifeless hair, and it's like I'm seeing her for the first time too, each separate, fallible piece. The middle toe of her left foot sticks out above the rest and hangs over the front of her sandal like a boiled shrimp over the edge of a cocktail glass, and her legs bow below the knee. There's a stain near the frayed hem of her tank top and a safety pin holding the cup of her bra to its strap. Her make-up is too light for her skin tone. A demarcation line of foundation runs across her jaw, separating her pale face from her darker neck. Clumps of black mascara stick to her wispy lashes, and her lip liner extends far outside the contours of her lips, making her mouth appear bigger than it is.

This is my tormentor. My bully.

An unexpected feeling of pity comes over me as I size her down. I feel sorry for her. Because whatever hole she's attempting to fill must be even more immeasurable than mine. Because she's mean, and a heart like hers will never find the beauty in others, will never even look for it. But most of all, because she'll never have Luz's picture in her backpack. She doesn't get to be her big sister, doesn't get to know her at all. And even though, life is full of Beccas, there are also people like my sister, the kind who use their wish on someone else, and I shouldn't worry about her living in this world but be grateful, for its sake, that she is.

I crouch down to restore everything into my backpack except Luz's picture. That I keep securely in my hand as I listen to the mounting rumble coming from the end of the hallway. Everything I love is waiting for me there, and I can't get to it fast enough. There's not a minute to lose. I've wasted too many already. I fling my backpack over my shoulder and look Becca in the eye. "Your time is up."

I step around her and walk away. She turns to hurl more insults at me, but her words grow less and less discernible the farther I get, until I can't hear them at all.

~~~

A large, round moon hangs above the painted trees and houses on the backdrop behind me. I stand beneath the trellis outside the Webb's kitchen.

This is it. I'm doing it.

I'm here.

Emily walks over to her mother, who serves strips of bacon from the skillet in her hand onto someone's plate. I can hear it sizzling and smell the grease. "'Oh, Mama, just look at me one minute as though you really saw me. Mama, fourteen years have gone by. I'm dead. You're a grandmother, Mama. I married George Gibbs, Mama. Wally's dead, too. Mama, his appendix burst on a camping trip to North Conway. We felt just terrible about it—don't you remember? But, just for a moment now we're all together. Mama, just for a moment we're happy. Let's look at one another.'"

Mrs. Webb continues doling out bacon and gestures toward the center of the table. "'That in the yellow paper is something I found in the attic among your grandmother's
~~~

things. You're old enough to wear it now, and I thought you'd like it.'"

They continue their dialogue, and I sneak a look at the lumpy silhouette of the audience backlit by the spotlight like the rising sun behind a sea of mountains. Most of the faces are shrouded in darkness, but the ones closest to the stage are bright and distinguishable.

I no longer have to wish for the sanctuary of home. It's here sitting in the front row. Turns out the sign in front of the school is right, after all, and every home is mobile.

Emily turns away from her mother and crosses center stage to stand beside me. The lights dim around us as she sobs into her hands. "'I can't. I can't go on. It goes so fast. We don't have time to look at one another. I didn't realize. So all that was going on and we never noticed. Take me back—up the hill—to my grave. But first: Wait! One more look. Good-by, Good-by, world. Good-by, Grover's Corners . . . Mama and Papa. Good-by to clocks ticking . . . and Mama's sunflowers. And food and coffee. And new-ironed dresses and hot baths . . . and sleeping and waking up. Oh, earth, you're too wonderful for anybody to realize you. Do any human beings ever realize life while they live it?—every, every minute?'"

"'No.'" I say my line, but I don't mean it. Because I do realize it. For a moment, I slip out of my role and stop pretending. I'm not the stage manager anymore. I'm me. The make-believe food disappears from the make-believe dishes. The imaginary walls dissolve, and the stage grows barren. Emily and Mrs. Webb become Tara and Jessica once again.

I look down at the captivated faces of my family lined up before me, and it's like we've traded places. Like I'm the audience and they're the ones on stage. Shane sits near the right aisle with an ankle crossed over his knee and his arm stretched across the armrest between him and Mom. She sits next to Buela with his sports coat draped around her shoulders, clutching his hand in both of hers. On Buela's other side, Luz unfurls the long ears of her stuffed kangaroo into a Y shape, a bouquet of peachy roses wrapped in cellophane on the floor at her feet. Buela whispers something to her, and she smiles and nods. Gabe and Sonny lean forward in their seats next to her. I can make out the blue tips of Sonny's hair and the dimple in Gabe's cheek even with the bright light shining in my face.

I stand there, completely present in the moment, wishing I could freeze time and have them here like this always. I start to think about how I'll grow up and leave our house one day. How Luz will too. How Mom's hair will turn gray and the lines around Shane's eyes will deepen, how Buela will be gone, and we'll all come back to stand by her grave with our hearts raw with memories. And I'll think, this is what remains of a person, words etched in stone and bones laying beneath, but also of the eternal things, the things about her that touched the deepest part of me and made me who I am, like how she fed us more than food, how she made us laugh, how she was brave for those she loved even when she couldn't be brave for herself. Those are the things that will last, the things I'll pass on to my children and they to theirs, and so on and so on down the line. Even if my great-great-grandchildren never hear about them, even if they do but forget, those things will still be a part of them because they were a part of me.

Miri

Pilar and I walk side by side on the carpet of dry, yellow grass between the perfectly spaced rows, our eyes swinging from stone to stone in search of their names. The sprinklers spray our calves with warm water, but we don't bother moving out of the way.

It's been a while since I was here. I used to come with Mamá every Saturday after Tía Pili died, but life got busier after *m'ija* was born, and my visits tapered off to Christmases and birthdays.

To be honest, I don't like coming here. I never have. It's too quiet. I prefer noise and hustle and bustle. I've always had a hard time keeping still, ever since I was a little girl. It used to drive Mamá crazy. I'd sit beside her in church trying to make time go by faster, inching my rear off the seat and slowly stretching out a leg to poke the feet of the people in front of us with my toe. I'd make a game of it and try to do it without them noticing. Mamá would narrow her eyes at me and threaten to pinch me hard, but I couldn't help myself. I've always felt a fierce restlessness, a sense of urgency. Like there's a big timer winding down somewhere. Maybe it's because my brother died so young or because of what happened to my father. Whatever the reason, Tía Pili understood.

She'd take my hand and lead me outside to the playground across the street, sit with me on the seesaw or let me run around until I came back to her all sweaty and worn out.

I miss her. I can't believe it's been nine years already. My eyes gaze longingly at the Impala sitting beside the curb like a golden nugget. Mamá insisted we take it, said Tía Pili would've wanted us to have it. She said her amiga, Horti, could give her a ride wherever she needs to go.

Besides, she wouldn't drive it anyway, and it'd sit in the carport behind her building growing rusty. That's what happens when you stay in the same spot for too long. You get stuck. And I hate feeling stuck. That's why I'm getting us out of here now, before it's too late and the dirt turns to cement around our feet. We're shaking off the dust of this town and starting fresh. You can't make a new start without turning to a clean page, and this one's already riddled with too many scratch outs. An hour ago, I dragged our suitcases across the plastic blades of our turf-covered porch and down the concrete steps to the driveway, where the Impala sat idling, and flung them into the trunk. Julio watched from the front door, his arms crossed in front of him.

"You're crazy, Boti. Overreacting, as usual," he called out to me.

I told *m'ija* to get in the car and slammed the trunk shut. "It's Mireya!" I yelled.

Mamá'll be okay. She has plenty of friends to keep her company. There're so many widows in her apartment complex, it seems like there's a shuttle leaving to the cemetery every ten minutes. And Tío Beto lives just a few blocks from her. Even those knuckleheaded cousins of mine, Checho and Rodi, have proven useful. They finally settled down to raise families of their own. Checho married Cristina Ortega, one of my best friends from high school. She came to the store to tell me the news. I shook my head and turned away to stack cans of corn on a shelf. I didn't say anything. Not even, congratulations. It's not that I wanted to make her feel bad, but I don't believe in saying things just because people want to hear them. You should tell it like it is, especially to your friends and family. If you can't count on them to tell you the truth, who can you count on?

But I can admit when I'm wrong, even if Mamá says I can't. It turns out I was wrong about Checho. He's a devoted husband and father. The complete opposite of my Julio. Not mine anymore. I'm shaking off the dust of him, too. He doesn't really believe we're leaving. He thinks we'll be back. I've threatened it too many times with no follow-through. But things are different now. Everyone has a breaking point. Mine's my daughter. She's growing up so fast. Sometimes I'll look at her out of the corner of my eye and catch a glimpse of the woman she'll become. She's not like everybody else. She's special. Passionate and strong. There's a fire in her. Not that Julio's noticed. He barely looks her way. He's on the road for days at a time. And when he is home, he's usually at some hole-in-the-wall bar with his friends. Some of those friends are other women. I've known about that for a long time, too. It used to really bother me. I got so mad at him once, I gathered all of his clothes into a big pile in the front yard and set them on fire. He had to go buy more clothes at the mall, wearing nothing but pajama bottoms. But Pilar's where I draw the line. All he does is let the wind out of her sails. Any time she shows interest in anything, he clips her wings. Like that Halloween a few years ago, when she wanted to be the man from that movie about Scotland. Julio tried to convince her to be something else, a witch or a princess. Said he'd buy her a pretty dress and a sparkly crown. But my baby stood her ground. Told him, no thank you. I was so proud of her. After dinner, I went out to the garage, pulled the plaid tree skirt out of the box of Christmas decorations and laid it on her dresser.

I used to think a bad father was better than no father at all. Not anymore. I've learned. An absent father who's there is even worse. Being a father's too important a role. You should do it right or not at all.

Julio doesn't get it. He looks at her with lackluster eyes. Seeing your reflection in that kind of mirror is sure to wear anyone down. You'll start to believe what you see. But I won't let that happen. So it's on to new faces and new places. We're hitting the road and fanning the embers.

"I found them, Mommy!" *m'ija* calls out, pointing to a massive headstone beneath the sparse shade of a mesquite tree. She traces her finger on the big block letters etched into the gray marble. MONTEMAYOR. The names of my great-grandparents are inscribed below on the left and right sides, Roberto Manuel and Elena Rosa. She pulls two roses from the bunch in her hand and props them on the thick lip at the bottom. Five smaller markers dot the ground in front of it, forming a lattice of grassy crosses. I follow along as she reads the names out loud, starting with my grandfather's. Jorge S. Montemayor, Amparo R. Montemayor, Deborah Montemayor, Armandina M. González, Pilar A. Montemayor, Carlos Ricardo Vásquez.

Somehow, it doesn't feel right. Something's missing. My eyes veer back up to the first marker and make their way over each smooth stone as I say their names again. "Buelo, Buelita, Debi, Monina, Pili, Carlitos."

Pilar kneels beside the last gravestone. It's made of pink granite and has a picture of a sleeping cherub carved into the corner. She lays the remaining flowers beside it and reaches up to take my hand. We link arms and walk back to the car in silence. It's loaded with all of our things. Our whole world inside Tía Pili's car.

Pilar straps on her seat belt. "What was he like, your brother?"

I adjust the rearview mirror and tell her every single thing about him that I can remember Mamá and Tía Pili telling me. People say it's not good to look back, to stay focused on what's before you, not behind. But I'm not so sure that's right. I think it's important to look back too.

Pipi

"Did you hear me clapping, Pipi? I was the loudest. Wasn't I, Buela?"

Buela arranges the roses Luz gave me in a vase and sets it in the middle of the table. "Eh? I can't hear you. You were so loud, you bursted my eardrums."

Luz smiles proudly. "The girl in the black clothes and black lipstick sitting behind us was loud too, but she was using her fingers to whistle, so it doesn't count."

Mom reaches over to squeeze my arm. "I'm so proud of you, *m'ija*. You were amazing! Standing up there in front of all those people. You're so brave. And talented."

"My favorite part was when they were up on top of the ladders," Luz says. "And the wedding part too. That was good. I thought the groom was going to run away, though. It seemed like it at first."

"He got cold feet. It happens sometimes. People can get nervous and start to doubt themselves," Shane says.

"Well, they should put on some thick socks and get on with it," Luz says, her eyes darting toward Mom. "What's so scary about getting married, anyway? It's just standing up. It's not like riding a roller coaster that goes upside down or looking under the bed at night."

"*¿Quién quiere más?* There's still plenty left," Buela says, her hand hovering above the platter of quesadillas, spatula at the ready.

Sonny holds out her plate. "I'll have one more, please."

Shane leans back in his chair and rubs his flat stomach. "I'm stuffed. I can't take another bite. They turned out delicious, Pera."

Buela flings another one onto his plate, anyway, and two more onto Sonny's. "We're a good team. Tomorrow, I'll show you how to make *menudo*." Buela sets the platter down next to the roses and leans in to smell them. "These are beautiful. They look exactly like the ones in front of the big statue of Fatima at church. Same color *y todo*."

"Who's Fatima?" Luz asks.

"Our Lady of Fatima. She's *Diosito*'s mother."

"I thought Mary was his mother."

"She is. She goes by lots of names."

"Daddy let me pick them out all by myself. I'm good at picking flowers." Luz shoots another look at Mom. "And at throwing them, too."

Mom picks up a loose petal from the tabletop and rubs it with her thumb. "You wouldn't be a flower girl, Luz. You and your sister would be my bridesmaids." We all stare at her, wide-eyed. "Why do you all look so surprised? I can keep an open mind."

"Okay," Luz says with a pout. "But can I still throw petals after I do the cleaning?"

We all laugh.

"We won't have to clean, Luz. Bridesmaids help the bride get ready for the ceremony. You know, help her into her wedding dress and hold up her veil. Things like that."

Sonny swipes a dollop of sweet potato from her plate and licks it off her finger. “Yeah, and they get to plan the bridal shower too. That would be fun.”

“A real shower or one with eggs?”

“Neither. One with games and presents,” I say.

Gabe walks in from the living room, poker-faced, and shoves his phone into the front pocket of his jeans. We all wait on pins and needles as he joins us at the table and takes a bite of food, chewing slowly.

The seconds drag on until I can’t take the suspense a second longer. “Well?”

“They said, yes!” he shouts, breaking into a grin.

Shane gives him a high-five, and Luz throws her arms around him.

“Mom said she’d call you guys later to hash out the details. And that’s not all,” he says, looking at me. “My dad said it’d be cool if you came too this summer. He’s working on a show, so. . . . ”

My heart starts beating so loudly, the rest of his words are drowned out. I can feel it swelling in my chest cavity like the Grinch’s on Christmas morning, pressing against my rib cage and stretching my skin. “Are you serious? You mean it? Really?”

“Really. But don’t get too stoked. It’s not as exciting as it sounds. I mostly lug equipment and sit around, but sometimes I get to help set up the blondes and redheads.”

Sonny and I exchange looks of confusion.

Gabe laughs. “They’re types of lighting. Not people.”

I jump up from my chair and fall to my knees in front of Mom with my hands clasped tightly like Juan Diego kneeling before La Virgen.

“Can I, Mom? Please? I’ll never ask for anything else as long as I live. I’ll go to the gym every single day for a year. I’ll wash your car, clean out the gutters, wipe the baseboards and the mini blinds, iron the bedsheets, vacuum the air vents. I'll do anything."

"I don't know, Pilar . . . "

"Please? Gabe's dad'll be there, and it'll only be for a week or two."

"Plane tickets are expensive."

I lean forward and lay my hands on her lap. "I can help pay for it. I have some babysitting money saved up."

"What if something bad happens? California's so far away."

"Nothing's going to happen. And even if it does, I can take care of myself. Have some faith in me."

Mom looks at Buela for backup. "She's still too young, isn't she?"

Buela shrugs. "She's almost sixteen. My grandmother was already married with a baby at her age. And another on the way, too."

Mom rolls her eyes. "You're not helping, Mamá."

"Well, *es la verdad*. Besides, she's a smart girl. She can take care of herself," Buela says, winking at me. "Miri, sometimes you have to leap before you look, learn to let go and let God take care of it."

The rough edges of the tiles dig into my knees, but I stay put. Finally, Mom nods her head slightly.

"Is that a yes?" I say, rising to my feet.

"You better call me every day. Every hour."

I throw myself into her arms and hug her tight.

"Okay, fine. Every two hours," she says, laughing.

My heart leaps in my chest like a bird taking flight. I pull away from her and look at the smiling faces around me. Friends and family.

Something happens when you take a moment to say thank you—for all you have, for who you are, for the ones standing next to you—to put the words out there, to really feel them. Even when things are at their bleakest, even when it feels all wrong. Especially then. Something happens. It comes back to you somehow.

Buela gets up from the table and grabs a mixing bowl from a bottom cabinet. "This calls for a celebration. I'm making flan."

"*Ay*, Mamá. We just ate a delicious, healthy meal, and now you're going to ruin it by making something fattening and full of sugar."

"You can't be healthy all the time, Miri. You have to have your cake and eat it too, *como dicen*. The nutritious and the delicious. The salty and the sweet."

"Yeah, Mom. There has to be a balance. You have to have both."

"*Es cierto, gordita*. You have to have both."